# Tracy Corbett

# SOMEONE TO LOVE

 CANELO

First published in the United Kingdom in 2022 by

Canelo
Unit 9, 5th Floor
Cargo Works, 1–2 Hatfields
London, SE1 9PG
United Kingdom

A CIP catalogue record for this book is available from the British Library.

Print ISBN 978 1 80032 335 3
Ebook ISBN 978 1 80032 334 6

This book is a work of fiction. Names, characters, businesses, organizations, places and events are either the product of the author's imagination or are used fictitiously. Any resemblance to actual persons, living or dead, events or locales is entirely coincidental.

Look for more great books at www.canelo.co

Printed and bound in Great Britain by Clays Ltd, Elcograf S.p.A.

1

# Someone to Love

Tracy Corbett started writing in her late twenties. As well as writing novels, she's written several short stories, pantomime sketches and magazine articles. Tracy describes her writing style as modern tales of romance, with engaging quirky characters, who overcome adversity, grow as people and conclude in satisfying optimistic endings. When she's not writing, she enjoys amateur dramatics, gardening and music. She works part-time for a local charity.

# Also by Tracy Crobett

*Someone Like You*
*Someone to Love*
*A Winter's Wish*

*For my funny, loving, and wonderful daddy,*

*Love and miss you every day x*

*George Frederick Corbett 22.06.1934 – 09.10.2021*

# Chapter One

Beth Lawrence had always prided herself in being the ultimate professional. She often stayed up late into the night, studying the latest family law legislation or reading numerous legal publications detailing complex case law. Nothing less would suffice. After all, her services didn't come cheap. Her hourly fee made her wince, adding pressure to an already stressful job. Her clients came with high expectations. And as such, she needed to earn their trust so they wouldn't feel 'fleeced' by her final invoice. They needed to feel special. Valued. Important. Like they were her only focus and they were receiving the best advice possible.

Of course, that was when they were actually paying for her services.

'He can't treat me this way!' the woman yelled, banging the desk, making Beth's cold mug of tea vibrate. 'I deserve better. Thirty-nine years I've looked after that man. Borne his children, supported his career, cleaned his house, and what thanks do I get?'

Beth already knew the answer.

'Tossed onto the scrapheap like I'm nothing!' The woman stood up, her hands flying into the air with indignant rage. 'Traded in for a younger woman, a woman half his age. A woman who fawns after him like he's God's gift. Well, he isn't,' she said, banging the desk again to make her point.

Beth moved her mug of tea to the window ledge. It was safer that way.

'*I'm* the one who supported his career. Raised his kids. Kept his house. *Me!* Not her. And this is how he repays me?' She waved the divorce petition at Beth. Anger coloured her cheeks, making her watery blue eyes appear venomous, like those of a provoked python, spitting and writhing.

Beth knew better than to interrupt. *Hell hath no fury like a woman scorned* wasn't said without good reason. She'd also learnt that hell has no fury like a scorned woman interrupted 'mid-rant' about her husband's infidelity.

'Why? That's what I want to know. What's she got that I haven't?' The woman opened her arms, inviting comment regarding her age-defying appearance. 'It's not like I've let myself go. Look at me. Not many women my age have a figure like this.'

Which was true. At sixty-two she could still turn heads. Her prominent cheekbones were enhanced by subtle make-up, and her pale grey-blonde hair was youthfully styled, softening the angular contours of her slender face. The woman oozed money, class and elegance. It was indeed a puzzle as to why she'd been rejected in such an unceremonious manner.

But such was life. Or rather, such were relationships. They rarely made sense.

As a family law solicitor, Beth had encountered all manner of betrayals over the years. Relationships that were once loving and faithful, now reduced to disputes over kitchen appliances and who got the dog. Deceit. Fraud. Adultery. Or those who'd simply fallen out of love. She'd seen it all.

She'd even had a case where a man had led two separate lives. Two wives, two sets of kids and two different homes. He'd somehow managed to juggle both existences for years, before the truth inadvertently came to light, courtesy of a misdirected tax bill.

Nothing shocked her any more. Little upset her, and she'd learnt never to become emotionally invested in any of her cases… which was why today's meeting was so tricky.

Beth took the opportunity of a lull in the woman's rant to raise her hand. 'I understand why you're upset—'

'Upset? I'm bloody furious!'

'But it wouldn't be appropriate for me to impart legal advice—'

'Why not?'

Beth sighed. 'Because you're my mother.'

'So?'

'So, you're divorcing my father. My judgement is hardly impartial.'

'Good, I need you on my side.' Connie Lawrence dropped into a chair and folded her arms, defiant in her outrage.

Not that Beth could blame her. She'd feel the same way if a divorce petition had unceremoniously landed on her doormat with no prior warning. It wasn't exactly considerate. In fact, it bordered on cowardice. Her father had a lot to answer for.

Beth picked up the discarded document from the floor. 'You're forgetting that Dad is also my employer.'

'I don't see why that's relevant. He's hardly going to fire you, is he?' her mother said, dismissively. 'Anyway, he can't. You're a partner now.'

'It's his firm. He can do what he likes.'

'And don't I know it. He's probably off bonking his floozy right now.'

Beth flinched. She really had no desire to invite images of her dad 'bonking' into her head. She'd been subjected to too many details of her parents' acrimonious split as it was – she didn't want to hear about their sex lives, too.

Her mother slapped her hand on the desk. 'You can't tell me he cares two hoots about this firm now he's with *Tiffany*.' She almost spat the word. 'When was the last time he put in a day's work and didn't leave you to run the business alone, eh? Tell me that!'

It was true that her dad had lost focus of late. He was rarely in the office, he didn't take on many cases, and instead he enjoyed long lunches, frequent golf afternoons and would often disappear at short notice in a flustered manner when his phone pinged.

The idea of her dad receiving a 'booty call' from his new lover was another horror she was fighting to ignore.

Taking a deep breath, she removed her glasses and wiped the lenses clean with the cloth she always carried in her suit pocket. Sometimes she wished she'd chosen a different career. Perhaps if she'd taken up acting, like her sister, or lazed about smoking weed like her brother, then she wouldn't be expected to act as family referee. Her siblings never seemed to experience the same level of grief she did. The curse of being the oldest child, she supposed.

Replacing her glasses, Beth fixed her mother with a look. 'It still wouldn't be professional or ethical of me to offer you legal advice, Mum. You need to trust that any solicitor acting on your behalf would remain impartial—'

'I don't want impartial. I want blood!'

Beth clenched her jaw.

'You know what he's done to me, how he's treated me. You witnessed it first-hand. I need you in my corner.'

'But it's not appropriate.' Beth raised her hand when her mother attempted to interrupt. 'The Solicitors Regulation Authority discourages any solicitor from acting for or against a family member. And they certainly wouldn't be happy about me taking action against my business partner. I have access to financial information I wouldn't normally be privy to.'

Her mother frowned. 'You're using legal jargon.'

Beth sighed. 'The bottom line is, I'm not able to act as your solicitor, Mum.'

But her mother didn't let up. 'You could give me informal advice, though? You know, off the record, so to speak.'

'It wouldn't be fair on Dad.'

'Fair! You want to talk about fair?' Another thump on the desk. 'After all that man has done to me? And you're taking his side?'

4

'I'm not taking his side.'

'But you won't take mine.' Connie fanned her face. 'Oh, the betrayal.'

Ouch.

Beth rubbed her temples. A headache was brewing.

What had she done to deserve this? She led a quiet life. She baked, she liked nature and long walks. She worked hard. All she wanted was a stress-free peaceful existence and not to be drawn into numerous family disputes. But fate, it seemed, had other ideas.

She took a deep breath. 'Morally, I'm on your side, Mum. Please don't think otherwise. I'm not happy that Dad's having an affair, or that he's instigated divorce proceedings without talking to you first. I don't condone his actions, but that's not the same thing as representing you in the divorce case.'

'So you agree he's in the wrong?'

'Absolutely, but he's also my dad. I love him. However appallingly he's behaved, it would be impossible for me to cause him pain.'

'So what am I supposed to do? Lie down and let him walk all over me?'

'No, you need a solicitor who won't be swayed by emotion or attachment and who will ensure a fair outcome. I can recommend several who would be ideal.'

'And how am I supposed to afford them? I no longer have your father's income, remember? I'm working as a flipping doctor's receptionist. Reduced to begging for scraps so your father can indulge in his midlife crisis.'

'Things are not that bad, Mum. You're exaggerating. Dad hasn't left you destitute.'

'But he hasn't left me with enough means to fight him in the divorce, has he? He's a lawyer. He specialises in defending wealthy husbands. He knows all the tricks, all the arguments, all the ways to avoid paying a huge settlement. You don't think he's going to use all that experience to save himself?'

Her mother had a point.

'All I want is an even playing field. Someone in my corner to ensure I don't get cheated. Is that too much to ask?'

Beth felt guilty. 'No, Mum. It's not. Leave it with me. I'll find someone willing to take you on. I'll pay their retainer, so don't worry about that. You can settle the invoice once the final settlement comes through. Okay?'

A sulky smile tugged at her mother's glossy lips. 'I don't have much choice, do I?'

Beth went over to the door. 'I need to get back to work now, Mum. I'll make some enquiries and pop over tonight to discuss them. How does that sound? Maybe we could have a bite to eat? That'd be nice, wouldn't it?'

Her mother reluctantly got up. 'It would be nicer if my daughter showed her mother some loyalty.' Connie Lawrence sure knew how to land a blow.

'I'm sorry, Mum.' Beth opened the door and kissed her. 'Try not to worry. I'll find someone suitable.'

'Good.' She patted Beth's cheek. 'Because I intend to take that bastard for everything he's got!' she shouted, ensuring that if her dad was in his office he'd hear.

Beth rubbed her ringing ear. 'Bye, Mum. See you later.'

Connie Lawrence walked off, her shoulders dropping, weighed down by the grief of her marriage imploding. It was tragic to watch such a formidable woman rendered so fragile.

'*Arsehole!*' her mum yelled at the portrait of her father in reception, giving him the finger. Not so fragile, then.

The front door slammed, followed by a ringing silence. Her mum disappeared down the steps onto the High Street, no doubt still calling her dad a few names and smouldering at the unfairness of it all.

Her father's office door opened a crack. 'Has she gone?'

Beth leant against the doorframe. 'She's gone. It's safe to come out.'

'I thought she might have calmed down by now,' he said, peering out, not quite convinced his estranged wife wasn't

6

about to return and dismember him. 'It's been months. It's not reasonable for her to still be so angry.'

Beth shot him a look. 'Don't play the victim with me, Dad. Mum has every right to be angry. You cheated on her. You left her for a woman younger than your kids, and now you're divorcing her. You can't possibly be shocked that she's pissed off with you.'

'We'd been unhappy for a while,' he said, defensively. 'It takes two people to end a marriage.'

'Yeah, but Mum wasn't one of the two people, was she, Dad?' She pointed a finger. 'And don't give me all that crap about "we'd been unhappy for a while". That's what every disgruntled husband says when he's trying to justify leaving his wife.'

'Well, on this occasion it's true.'

'Really?' She raised an eyebrow. 'So you told Mum you were unhappy, did you? You sat her down and confessed your feelings and made a concerted effort to resolve the problems in your marriage before you ran off with Tiffany?'

Her dad fiddled with his cufflinks.

Just as she thought.

'She knew I was unhappy.'

'Bullshit. She had no idea. And neither did us kids.'

Her father's expression turned belligerent. 'You're taking her side then?'

Beth held up her hands. 'I'm remaining neutral. As neutral as I can be, anyway. But if you think I approve of your behaviour, then think again. You're acting like a jerk, Dad.'

Whatever he was about to say was interrupted by his phone pinging. His cheeks coloured as he read the message, his brown eyes widening with schoolboy delight.

Kenneth Lawrence had also aged well. He was fit for his sixty-five years, and with his dimpled smile and silver wavy hair swept off his tanned face, he resembled a suave Don Johnson. Unfortunately, a younger woman telling him as much had rather inflated his ego. Hence the current mayhem.

'I need to go out. Er… an urgent client meeting,' he said, running a finger around his shirt collar, no doubt relieving the sudden heat he felt at receiving such a message.

Client, her arse.

'I'll be back later,' he called out. He grabbed his keys and disappeared from the building, leaving his office door wide open. 'Take any messages, will you?'

'I'm not your secretary!' she called after him, aggrieved at being left holding the fort again, but her complaint fell on deaf ears.

Infuriated, Beth watched him leave, his smitten-schoolboy behaviour at odds with his cut-throat business persona. He was a tyrant when it came to negotiating a settlement, with a reputation for 'hiding assets' and securing much lower alimonies for his clients than was fair. In contrast, Beth liked to fight for the underdog. Her clients tended to be the injured party, belittled individuals who'd been shafted by their supposed loved ones and deserved more than the meagre pittance they were being offered. It was hugely rewarding when she won, but the work didn't do a lot to improve her opinions regarding love.

Heading over to the tall sash windows at the back of her office, she twisted the blinds, taking a moment to enjoy the sight of a bustling Godalming High Street. The late spring sunshine blazed through the glass, heating the room.

The picturesque town below sported the usual familiar brand names, such as FatFace and WH Smith, but with the addition of several designer boutiques, antique dealers, picture framing shops and a fancy high-end jewellers. There was even a shop sporting fancy-dress outfits for pets. This was not your typical high street. This was how every high street aspired to be, but often couldn't afford.

Beth noticed a woman standing by the water fountain was waving at her. A woman she recognised. Her beautiful face was upturned towards the window, drawing attention from several workmen affixing scaffolding to the neighbouring building.

Beth smiled. The men's reaction was perfectly normal. Megan Lawrence was the kind of stunning beauty who constantly drew attention. Attention she was completely oblivious to – or that's how it appeared. Her sister was quite the actress, so maybe feigning surprise was all part of the pretence.

Megan lifted a paper bag from Cafe Mila and pointed to an empty wrought-iron bench in the pedestrian-only area of the High Street.

Beth was torn. She really needed to get back to work. She had court papers to prepare, a final letter before action to write and a child custody application to submit before the close of play. Her mother's visit had already delayed her. Time was of the essence.

But she needed to eat, and Cafe Mila's food was a lot more appealing than the cheese-and-pickle roll she'd stuffed in the fridge. Decision made. She could spare twenty minutes.

Buttoning her jacket, she locked the office and headed into the street.

'For a moment, I thought you were going to snub me,' her sister said, rising from the bench like the Greek goddess Aphrodite and kissing Beth's cheeks. She smelt of roses and looked like she'd spent the morning being polished. Her skin glowed, highlighted by deep red lips, smokey grey eye make-up and long glossy black hair.

For the most part, Beth shared her sister's features. The heart-shaped face, long legs, eye colouring and her hair a lighter shade than her sister's. But there the similarities ended. Megan was the high-end version of the Lawrence gene pool. A real 'showstopper', as their mother referred to her, adored by all who gazed upon her. Beth was referred to as the 'academic' one. Hair always up, thick glasses masking the appeal of her hazel eyes and legs never on display. Her looks were less striking than her sister's – softer, and usually hidden behind muted tones and sombre business suits. Beth didn't mind. She was happy to live in her sister's shadow.

'I got you a falafel pitta and a berry smoothie,' Megan said, opening the paper bag. 'Well, sit down. Don't leave me hanging.'

Beth joined her sister on the bench. 'To what do I owe the pleasure?' she said, accepting the offer of the smoothie. 'Being treated to lunch isn't a usual occurrence.'

'Can't I spoil my sister without a motive?' Megan fluttered her long eyelashes, her smile revealing pearl-white teeth and dimpled cheeks, inherited from their father.

Beth unwrapped the pitta. 'I guess not.'

'Although, I do have news,' her sister said, looking excited. 'Two bits of good news, actually.' She unearthed her vegan burger, teasing out small pieces of lettuce and tomato. The archetypal actress – always on a diet. Why her sister never just ordered a salad, she didn't know.

Beth took a bite of pitta. It was delicious. Unlike her sister, she was wholly averse to diets. She liked her food too much.

'I landed that acting job.'

Beth swallowed. 'The one in Greece?'

'That's the one. I fly out in a couple of weeks. Can you imagine? Two months filming on a Greek island.' She sipped at her iced tea. 'Heaven.'

Beth pulled the lid off her smoothie. 'Congratulations.'

'And the pay is fabulous.' Megan flicked her long dark hair over her shoulder. 'To be honest, it's the only reason I accepted the part. They needed someone at short notice and they were prepared to pay through the nose to secure me. My agent negotiated three times what I normally earn. How cool is that?'

'Very cool.' A dollop of falafel escaped the pitta and landed on Beth's grey skirt.

Damn it.

She unearthed a napkin from the takeaway bag and wiped at the mess. 'Why wouldn't you have taken the part otherwise? I thought you liked working abroad?'

'I do, but that leads me onto my second piece of good news.' Megan's smile radiated excitement. 'You'll never guess?'

Beth wiped her hands with the napkin. 'You won the lottery?'

'Nope.'

'You're going to be a contestant on *Love Island*?'

'Even better.' Megan shook her head, her expression dreamy. 'Think romance… love… and rings.'

Romance and love were two things Beth tried very hard *not* to think about. Besides having had two disastrous relationships herself, she'd spent the last decade dealing with messy divorces, not to mention watching her own parents' marriage disintegrating. Romance and love were a minefield she was happy to avoid. Life as a singleton was so much easier.

And then her brain caught up with her ears. 'Rings?'

She spotted the oval-shaped diamond ring glittering on her sister's finger – large, expensive and foreboding, like Aladdin's lamp about to unleash its genie.

'I'm engaged!' Megan thrust her hand under Beth's nose for closer inspection.

Beth was too shocked to admire the ring. She recoiled in shock, sending her smoothie flying. It landed straight down her front. And to think she'd been worried about the falafel staining.

She grabbed a handful of napkins, trying to absorb the worst of the spill. 'Engaged? Engaged to be married?'

'Well, of course engaged to be married.' Megan rolled her eyes, sliding away from the spilt smoothie. None had landed on her, Beth noticed. Typical.

Beth binned the napkins. 'Who to?'

Megan looked affronted. 'What do you mean, who to? Who do you think? Zac, of course.'

'*Zac?*' Thankfully, Beth had no smoothie left to spill.

Megan tutted, disappointed. 'Who else would I be getting married to?'

Beth refrained from comment.

'Lovely, funny, talented, gorgeous Zac.' Megan swooned a little, her acting attributes on full display. 'Darling Zac, who's kind… and adoring… and—'

'Twenty-three.'

Megan sloshed her. 'Don't you start. I'm only ten years older. That's hardly anything these days.'

'Right.'

'He's very mature for his age and knows his own mind, and he's clearly ready for commitment. Why else would he propose?'

But Beth was still trying to process the news.

'And he's as keen as I am.' Megan's smile returned. 'The wedding's this year.'

Time slowed.

'This year?' Beth tried not to panic. 'When exactly this year?'

Megan glanced away. 'June.'

'June?'

'The ninth.'

'As in… just over two months' time?'

'That's right.' Megan admired her ring, glistening in the sunshine. 'Isn't it romantic?'

That was one word for it.

'That's very soon, Megan. Why the rush?'

Megan turned to her. 'It's the only gap we have in our schedules until next spring. I'm filming in Ireland from August for six months on that Netflix series, and Zac's working on a film in Canada. We're hardly going to see each other. It's going to be hard enough being apart all that time as it is, we don't want to wait another year before marrying… or coming off the pill.'

Beth nearly fell off the bench. 'You want a baby?'

Megan looked coy. 'Maybe… at some point. Fertility decreases in your thirties, so the sooner we start trying, the more chance we'll have of success.'

Beth rubbed her temples. This was a lot to get her head around. An engagement, a wedding and baby talk all in one day. Then the penny dropped. 'But you've just accepted a job abroad. Didn't you say you'll be gone for two months?'

Megan nodded. 'That's right.'

'How on earth are you going to plan a wedding in two months' time, when you're not going to be in the country?'

Her sister unleashed one of her kilowatt smiles. 'That's where you come in.'

Alarm bells began to ring. 'Me?'

Her sister sidled closer. 'I thought maybe you could help Zac plan it. You know, like in *Don't Tell the Bride*, where the groom is tasked with arranging a surprise wedding for his fiancée.' Megan squeezed Beth's hand. 'It'll be so much fun.'

Fun was not a word that sprang to mind.

'Exciting, too!'

For her sister, maybe. As for her, she was experiencing a rush of pure terror. 'But don't you want to plan your own wedding? I thought most brides relished the prospect of organising their big day?'

Megan shrugged. 'Ordinarily, yes, but it's not possible with the timings. And besides, why shouldn't the groom do all the planning? It's the twenty-first century, equal rights, and all that.'

Beth tried to stem the building panic. 'And Zac's on board with this?'

Megan glanced away. 'Well, the thing is… I haven't actually told him yet.'

'About the job? Or the wedding?'

'Both.'

Oh, hell.

Megan grabbed Beth's hand. 'But he'll definitely be okay with it, especially if he knows you'll help him.'

Beth's head was reeling.

'Oh, say you'll do it. Say you'll help. Pleeeaase, pretty pleeeaase.' She made kissing sounds and nuzzled into Beth. 'I'll love you forever. You'll be my hero. My absolute favourite sister.'

'I'm your only sister.'

'And how lucky am I?' Megan was buzzing with excitement. 'What a sister you are.'

Sure. The best. The sister that mediated family arguments. The sister who got called out at two in the morning to deal with their druggie brother. The sister who searched for Grandma when she disappeared on a dementia walkabout. The sister who was lumbered with refereeing parental fights. And now, it seemed, the sister who was expected to arrange her sibling's wedding.

'Megan, I really don't think—'

'Besides, we only want a small wedding.' Megan cut her off. 'Close family and friends only.' She turned her wide hazel eyes on Beth and blinked innocently. 'I mean, how hard can it be?'

Beth stared at her sister.

Was she for real?

## Chapter Two

There had been a time in the not-too-distant past, when Connie Lawrence would have relished the idea of having her family over for Sunday lunch. All of them, chatting animatedly away, eating her out of house and home, and generally getting under her feet as she tried to cook.

But that was before Kenneth had absconded. Before the rug had been swiped so cruelly from underneath her and she'd been unceremoniously dumped for a woman more than thirty years her junior.

There was no getting away from it. It still smarted.

Life was now split into two distinctive sections: Before and After. Pre and Post that fateful Friday night when her husband had returned home late from work and announced he'd 'met someone else' and was leaving her. From that moment on, life had been severed in two. As though an axe had hurtled down from above and sliced through her heart, casting her adrift from the reality she'd once known.

Life beforehand had been pretty near perfect. A beautiful home, three great kids, disposable income, and the freedom to shop, socialise and enjoy the rewards of nearing retirement with no major concerns or worries. It hadn't been entirely plain sailing. They'd scrimped and saved like most young couples starting out. Motherhood had delivered both blessings and curses, testing her resolve and patience on a daily basis. But she wouldn't have swapped it for the world. She had one creative child, one academic and one she'd yet to fathom out.

But they'd coped. They'd worked together to make a happy and stable home. Over the years, Kenneth's career had soared, as had his income, easing their stresses and adding holidays abroad and material trappings into their world.

By the time they'd both hit sixty, they were living a life of luxury. Two of their three children had flown the nest and were forging successful careers, and despite their son showing no signs of financial independence, or leaving home, life was good. A long, happy, activity-filled retirement lay ahead, when they could reclaim some of the intimacy they'd lost over the years, rediscover their passion for life and see out their years in comfort.

But that was before the axe had cut off any chance of a happy ending.

Happiness and security now eluded her. They dangled out of arm's reach, tormenting her, reminding her of what she'd once had.

The timer on the oven beeped.

She glanced down and realised she'd annihilated the red cabbage. Her knuckles were white from gripping the knife, and the chopping board was stained red, like a crime scene, drenched in remnants of evil thoughts about her traitorous husband.

It might be safer to avoid using knives when dwelling over Kenneth.

She wiped her hands on her apron. 'Alex, love. Can you check the potatoes for me?'

No response.

He was lazing on the sofa in the corner of the large modern kitchen, his feet resting on the cushions, earplugs hanging from his ears.

'Alex!'

He glanced up. 'What?'

'The potatoes.' She nodded towards the beeping oven. 'Check them for me?'

He frowned, like the question was too challenging for him.

Anyone would think he was fifteen, not thirty. He was hardly the most dynamic of beings. At least he was good-looking, that was something. He had strong features like his sisters, but his mop of unwashed brown hair did him no favours.

'What am I checking for?' he said, gormlessly.

She supressed a sigh. 'To see if they're done.' She tried not to 'nag', as he regularly accused her of doing, but why should she have to do everything all the time? She was on her own now. She could do with the help.

'Can't you do it?' His gaze returned to his phone. 'I'm in the middle of something.'

Connie's agitation levels hiked up another notch. 'No, I can't do it. As you can see, my hands are full.' She stirred the gravy, spraying the liquid over the sides of the saucepan, unable to contain her annoyance.

'Can't you ask Beth or Megan?'

She slammed her hand on the countertop. 'I'm asking you! Now get off the sofa and check the bloody potatoes.'

'All right, keep your hair on.' He dragged his long limbs off the sofa, his gait sullen and laboured. To say her son lacked motivation was like saying David Attenborough had a passing interest in wildlife. Quite how he'd ended up so lazy, she had no idea. His sisters were the polar opposite. Energised, independent and driven. Attributes that Alex severely lacked.

Her youngest daughter appeared in the kitchen – as if she'd somehow sensed she was the subject of her mother's thoughts. 'What do you think about this one?' she said, padding over in her bare feet and shoving a magazine under Connie's nose. 'Beth thinks it's too much, but can a wedding dress ever be too much?'

'I've no idea, darling.' Her daughter's excitement over her forthcoming wedding irked. Why, she wasn't sure. Did that make her a bad person?

17

But Megan didn't pick up on her mother's tetchiness – or if she did, she carried on regardless. 'What do you think? Do you like it?'

'I can't see it, darling. I haven't got my reading glasses on.' Which was only a partial lie. The tears threatening to spill over were a warning sign. If she saw the dress in all its glory, modelled by a happy, youthful woman playing the part of the 'blushing bride', she might lose it completely.

That, or she'd start slashing the magazine in a deranged rage. She glanced at the knife. It balanced on the side, glinting in the sunlight. Taunting her. Reminding her how easy it would be to drive over to Tiffany's house and stab Kenneth. Or maybe both of them. Maybe just Tiffany? Yes, definitely just Tiffany. After all, she didn't want to leave her children without a father.

Eradicating Tiffany would solve all her problems. The floozy would be gone, out of their lives forever... but then she'd spend the rest of her days incarcerated, and that would be worse. At least, she was pretty sure it would be. Some days she wasn't so sure.

'Show me later,' she said, mustering a smile. 'After lunch.'

'It comes in white, ivory or champagne,' Megan said, unable to take a hint. 'I'm thinking champagne. Yes?'

'Whatever you think, darling. Have you set the table?'

'Beth's doing it.' Megan sauntered out of the kitchen, her eyes glued to the dress in the magazine.

'Don't leave empty-handed!' she called after her. 'Take the plates with you!'

No response.

Typical.

The water on the carrots boiled over. The oven continued to beep.

She swung around to find Alex leaning against the centre island, still staring at his phone. 'Alex! Potatoes!'

He looked startled. 'I don't know where the oven gloves are.'

Heaven give her strength. 'Then look for them. Or ask. Don't just stand there doing nothing.'

'Okay, stop stressing.' He pushed away from the island, his worn T-shirt and jeans hanging loose from his lithe frame. 'I can't see them.'

Connie drummed her fingers on the countertop. 'Hanging next to the oven. Now can you please check the ruddy potatoes and see if they're done?'

She switched off the gas, resisting the urge to inhale the fumes and end her suffering there and then.

She drained the carrots and shoved the Brussels in the microwave.

Alex opened the oven door, recoiling when the steam hit him straight in the face. Not the sharpest tool in the shed, was he?

Picking up the plates, she marched into the dining room.

Beth was laying the table. Megan was snapping at her sister's heels, trying to show her various wedding dress designs as Beth moved around the table, positioning cutlery.

Her eldest daughter looked about as enthused picking out a wedding dress as Alex had been about checking the potatoes. 'I have no idea why you're asking me, Megan. I have no taste in clothes, remember?'

'That's not what I said. I said, you have no taste in fashion,' Megan replied, undeterred. 'That's an entirely different thing. Wedding dresses aren't about fashion – they need to be timeless. I don't want the photos to date. I need something that isn't fashionable. That's why I'm asking you.'

Beth pinned her sister with a look. 'Well, thanks. Flattered, I'm sure.'

'You know what I mean. You're all…' Megan waved her hand, gesturing to her sister's conservative appearance. Hair up. Discreet make-up. No jewellery.

'All… what?' Beth's hand went to her hip.

Megan turned to her mother. 'Help me out here! You know what I mean.'

Connie shook her head. 'You can dig yourself out of this one.' She wasn't about to get drawn into a debate about her daughters' differing fashion sense.

It wasn't just that they dressed differently, they were polar opposites in character, too. Beth was studious, cautious and serious by nature. Megan was a firecracker. Funny, lively and hyper. Their opinions had always differed. Thankfully, it never seemed to stop them getting on.

'What about this one?' The magazine was once again shoved under Beth's nose for her to admire. 'You have to like this one.'

Beth ducked away from the magazine. 'I thought your friend Lily was making your dress?'

'She is, but I need to give her some ideas to work from – the wedding's only two months away.'

Beth rolled her eyes. 'Something I'm painfully aware of.'

Connie decided to rescue her eldest daughter and handed Megan the plates. 'Help your sister set the table.'

'Fine.' Megan sagged under the weight of the crockery. 'I can take a hint.'

Beth laughed. 'Chance would be a fine thing.'

Connie left them to it.

She passed by the lounge door and noticed her mother crouching on the floor, with the contents of her handbag emptied out in front of her. Her mother was frantically searching through the items.

Connie went over and knelt beside her. 'What are you looking for, Mum?'

'The thingamajigs,' she said, sounding confused.

Despite being eighty-four, Doris Emerick could roll around on the floor like a five-year-old. She'd been blessed with a body unravaged by age. It was remarkable. Shame her mind hadn't fared so well.

'Can you be more specific, Mum? What is it you need?'

'You know... the thingamajigs.' Her mum's cheeks were red and she was getting flustered. Being unable to recall basic words you'd once used so effortlessly was a cruel twist of the mind. Made worse because her mum was with-it enough to know what was happening.

'Purse? Hanky? Lipstick?'

'No. The thingamajigs. You know, for opening the whatchamacallit.'

'Corkscrew?' Although why her mum would be carrying a corkscrew in her handbag, she didn't know.

'No, the… the…' Her mum's upset was increasing.

'Keys?'

'That's it! Keys.' Relief flooded her face. 'I can't find my keys.'

Connie picked up the keys, which were right in front of her. 'Here they are, Mum.'

'Oh, bless you. You found them. What would I do without you?'

Good question.

She kissed her mum's powdery cheek. 'Put everything back in your handbag now. Dinner's ready.'

A loud bang reverberated from the kitchen.

Oh, hell. What now?

'*Mum!*' Alex came rushing into the lounge. 'I've had a bit of an accident with the potatoes.'

And this was her life post-Kenneth. The shitty 'after' version. A stress-filled, mournful existence, whereby she'd reverted to being everyone's slave. Running around after them, worrying about money and feeling aggrieved. Cheated. Power-less. Abandoned.

Yep, her 'after' life was a steaming pile of crap.

Fifteen minutes later, having rescued the potatoes from the kitchen floor and burnt her hand on hot fat, they were seated at the dining table eating lunch. Not that she had much of an appetite. The gaping hole ahead of her, where her husband used to sit, was another painful reminder that their once tight-knit family unit had been blown apart. A husband who up until six months ago had been her everything, but who now wanted a divorce.

The knot in her stomach contracted. It sat there, heavy and solid, an indication that all was not okay. Outwardly, she looked the same. Inwardly, she was in torment.

She pushed her plate away. The dark grey walls accented by white woodwork seemed to close in on her. The expensive marble fireplace no longer filled her with pride, and the large silver mirror hanging above the mantelpiece merely reflected the image of a sour-looking, depressed woman. Even the large double window that bathed the room in light offered no comfort. The room felt cold. Lacking. Like everything else in her life.

Not that anyone else seemed to notice.

Her family – what was left of them – were tucking into their food. Oblivious to her suffering.

Her elderly mum was staring at her plate, frowning at the carrots, like they'd committed some awful sin. She looked small and frail these days, like a doll. A well-kept doll, mind you. Her white hair was always set, her cheeks were rouged and her lips were pink. The emerald-green blouse she wore was pristinely ironed and she appeared to the outside world to be in 'good nick'. Yet her mind kept short-circuiting, dulled by age. Some days it was worse than others, but it was becoming more noticeable as the months passed.

Alex was hunched over his plate, refusing to engage with his siblings, bored by his sister's wedding chatter and burdened by the weight of the world. Not that he had much to worry about – or, at least, not that she could fathom. He had no job, no love interest and no ailments. What was there to be so morose about? She struggled to understand him.

Her gaze switched to her eldest daughter.

Even on a Sunday, Beth's attire was formal. Her white cotton shirt was paired with dark jeans, not a crease in sight.

But she was happy. Well, as happy as Beth ever was, and she was enjoying her food, making a valiant attempt to ignore her sister's constant wedding chatter.

Beth had been her rock since Kenneth had left. The one who'd contacted banks and utility suppliers. The one who'd set up an email account, and fended off nosey neighbours and intrusive extended family. Her very own Rottweiler. Effortlessly practical and fiercely protective – even if she did refuse to represent her in the divorce.

And then there was Megan. Beautiful, enchanting and captivating Megan, who could light up a room by simply walking into it. Connie had been like that once. In her heyday. The woman who could attract attention without even trying. When was it that she'd become so... invisible? So undesirable? So unwanted?

She dabbed at her eyes with a napkin.

Megan was still talking about the wedding, juggling eating with consulting her iPad, her attention focused on her upcoming nuptials. 'So that's the date confirmed. I'll contact Lily directly about making my dress,' she said, smiling at her sister. 'I wouldn't expect you to deal with that.'

Beth raised an eyebrow. 'Big of you.'

'Especially as you seem so disinterested in helping me choose a design.' She swiped the screen. 'And I've drawn up a guest list. I'll email you and Zac the names, so you can arrange invites.'

'Don't you want to pick out the design yourself?' Beth looked hopeful.

Megan didn't pick up on her sister's hint. 'That's okay, I trust you both. As long as it's white, tasteful, simple and yet striking, I don't mind what you choose.'

'No pressure, then.' Beth didn't look any more enthused about the wedding than Connie did.

Why was that, she wondered? Even just a year ago, she'd have been thrilled to think of her daughter getting married. Weddings were such joyous occasions. Filled with promise...

love… and the hope of a 'Happy Ever After'. She would have loved nothing more than to shop for dresses, pick out invites and taste cake samples.

Now the idea filled her with dread.

How was she supposed to muster any enthusiasm when her own marriage was disintegrating? Weddings were currently a very sore subject. The vows she'd shared with her husband had been discarded, like they meant nothing. All the promises to stand by her in sickness and in health, for richer or poorer, had been tossed aside. And forget love, honour and cherish. Loathed, dishonoured and rejected were now more fitting adjectives.

She realised Megan had asked her a question.

'Sorry, darling. I was miles away. What was that?'

Everyone was looking at her – even Alex.

Megan took a gulp of wine. 'Er… I said, we'll have to invite Tiffany.'

Silence followed.

Connie's insides clenched at the mention of her nemesis. 'Excuse me?'

Megan exchanged a look with her sister. 'Tiffany. We'll have to invite her to the wedding. You know… as Dad's plus-one.'

The blood drained from Connie's face. 'Are you serious?'

Megan nodded. 'I know it's not ideal—'

'*Ideal?*' Her raised voice startled everyone.

'Whether we like it or not, they're together.' Megan avoided eye contact. 'She's his partner.'

'Partner? *Partner?*' Connie stood up. 'That woman is not his partner! She's a money-grabbing… hussy. A husband-stealer who's only after his money.'

'You don't know that.'

She banged the table. 'Of course, I bloody well do! I've seen her Instagram posts, I'm not blind.' She glared at each of her kids in turn. 'Why else would she be with him? She's half his age!'

Beth raised a hand. 'Mum, calm down.'

'Don't tell me to calm down!' Connie paced the room, enraged beyond belief. 'Nobody in the history of calming down has ever calmed down because someone has told them to calm down!'

'I just meant—'

'How dare you suggest inviting that... that... *woman* to the wedding. Are you deliberately trying to wound me?'

Megan blinked back tears. 'Of course not.'

Connie grabbed hold of the mantle, needing the support. 'Isn't it bad enough that your father's caused me such pain, ruined my life and discarded me like a bag of rubbish.'

'Yes, Mum, but—'

'But nothing!' Connie stamped her foot. She wasn't having it. She wouldn't be persuaded to be rational, or calm, or tolerant. This was the final straw, this was not happening, not while she still breathed. 'She is not... I repeat *not*... coming to the wedding! Do you hear me?'

Megan's face crumpled. 'But Dad wants her there.'

'I don't care what your dad wants.' And then she stilled. They'd already spoken about this? She turned to her daughter. 'What did you say?'

Megan swallowed awkwardly. 'When I told Dad about the wedding, he asked if Tiffany could come. What was I supposed to say?'

'NO! That's what you were supposed to say. NOT BLOODY LIKELY!'

Her three children cowered.

'But...' Megan wavered. Her super-confident daughter was now floundering.

'But what? What else does that son-of-a-bitch want now? My kidneys? Come on, tell me. Spit it out. What does perfect bloody Kenneth want that he doesn't already have, eh?'

Megan's voice was barely a whisper. 'He wants her on the top table.'

Oh, that did it.

That was the final indignation that tipped Connie over the edge.

Any noise was blocked out by a hissing sound filling her head, like expanding foam. An explosion of hot pain rendering her unable to form coherent words.

He wanted that... floozy... that *tart* on the top table at their daughter's wedding? Over her dead body.

It was too much. Too torturous to contemplate. Not only had she endured the humiliation of being left for another woman – but that *woman* was now about to replace her as her husband's 'significant other' at their daughter's wedding. And what was more, her children didn't think it was such a big deal.

Well, it flipping well was.

No way was she about to stand by and watch them play the happy couple, canoodling throughout the ceremony, raising their glasses in a toast, usurping her starring role as mother of the bride. She wasn't having it.

She returned to the table and faced her children head-on.

They looked downcast. Guilty. Uncomfortable.

Good. So they should.

'Then I won't be there,' she said, aiming for an air of calmness, even though her insides were vibrating with rage.

'Mum, no—'

'I'm sorry, Megan.' She raised her hand, stopping her daughter in mid-flow. 'If that woman is going to be there, then I won't be. It's her... or me.'

A hush descended.

Connie half-expected the end credits of *Eastenders* to start rolling. *Duff... duff...*

But then her mum jumped up and yelled, 'I've found them!'

All eyes turned to Doris.

'My keys! I found my keys. They were here all along!' She waved her handbag about and then sat back down, seemingly relieved.

And this was Connie's life post-Kenneth.

# Chapter Three

When Matt Hardy had applied for his regular monthly visiting order, he hadn't clocked the date. It was only as he exited the 77 bus onto the Earlsfield Road that he realised he was visiting his dad in prison on April Fool's Day. How ironic was that?

Not that his dad being in jail was a joke, far from it. But that was the consequence of committing manslaughter – the state frowned upon such behaviour and locked you up. They were funny like that.

Matt reached the visitors' centre and queued along with everyone else waiting to visit inmates. Some people he recognised, some he didn't. It wasn't the kind of place where you made friends. People kept to themselves. He'd learnt the hard way that not everyone who visited the prison was a fan of the justice system. He'd once become embroiled in an unpleasant conversation with an outraged father, whose son had been banged up 'unfairly'. It didn't matter that the boy had robbed a post office and was caught driving with no licence, he was a 'good son' and the government were 'corrupt bastards' who'd used him as a 'scapegoat'. An attitude that didn't bode well for the kid's future once he was released, Matt felt.

Matt believed strongly that people should be held accountable for their actions, his dad included. People had to learn from their mistakes and pay the price, and with any luck, be rehabilitated back into society. A view he'd struggled to hold on to when confronted by the realities of prison life.

It wasn't exactly a nurturing place. More like survival of the fittest. By the time you left, you were either a quivering wreck or a hardened thug. Neither of which was overly conducive to rehabilitation back into the community.

He reached the front of the queue and held his arms open, ready to endure the indignation of being frisked, scanned with a metal detector and having a springer spaniel sniff around his crotch.

Having passed the security check, he showed the guard his visiting order, produced ID and was waved through to the lockers. No phones were allowed inside the prison, so his personal items were locked away for the duration of the visit.

It was a short walk to the main gate. A familiar sight, as depicted in the opening credits of the TV show *Porridge*. Sadly, his dad was no Ronnie Barker. More Ronnie Biggs.

HMP Wandsworth was a large, depressing grey-brick Victorian building with an imposing gated entrance. He remembered his first visit and how shit-scared he'd been, but he'd only been twenty-two at the time. Was it any wonder he'd freaked out?

That was ten years ago. A decade of monthly visits had dulled his fear, along with the humiliation of having a father in prison. What hadn't abated was the sadness of the situation – such an utter waste of a life – and the devastating impact it had had on his entire family.

But he was no longer angry. It was impossible to stay mad at someone for ten years. Not that he'd ever be okay with it, especially as his dad had never seemed that remorseful. In his dad's eyes, it had been 'bad luck'. An argument with another taxi driver that had escalated, resulting in a fight, and ending with the other taxi driver's accidental death and his dad being charged with manslaughter.

In Matt's view, it was an inevitable consequence of having a short temper and a thirst for alcohol. Nothing to do with 'bad luck'. Just bad behaviour.

Matt reached the large visiting room and waited to be escorted to his allocated seat.

The space was filled with low tables and plastic blue-and-yellow chairs. A balcony ran the circumference of the room, allowing the guards a bird's-eye view of the people below.

Finally, he was taken to the table where his dad was seated.

Pete Hardy stood up and opened his arms, waiting for his permitted hug. 'My boy!'

Matt hugged his dad, who smelt of tobacco and washing detergent. His pale blue sweatshirt was worn and soft to the touch. He could feel his dad's protruding belly and the scratch of his beard against his cheek. 'Hi, Dad.'

'Good to see you!' His dad slapped him manfully on the back, before sitting down.

Matt sat opposite. No further contact was allowed until the end of the visit – prison rules.

Happy that correct protocols had been followed, the guard stepped away and left them to it.

His dad was smiling, his teeth stained from smoking. 'So, how have you been?'

At fifty-seven, his dad looked older than his years. His hair was snow-white, collar-length and brushed away from his face. His chin sported an equally white bushy beard. He looked like Father Christmas… or rather, the wayward younger brother of Father Christmas. The one who'd shunned the family business and turned to a life of crime – breaking into houses to steal the kids' presents rather than leaving them under the tree.

Matt shrugged. 'Good, thanks. Busy.'

'Any major fires to put out?' His dad rested his arms on the table. 'Or just rescuing more cats stuck up trees?' He chuckled, as though he hadn't made the same joke a hundred times before.

Matt forced a smile.

His dad had an annoyingly antiquated view of his son's job, treating him like he was flipping Fireman Sam or something – someone who spent his days helping old ladies cross the road and putting out chip-pan fires.

Easy as it would be to react, he didn't. It wasn't like he needed his dad's approval – he'd moved past wanting that a long time ago. 'A few nasty road traffic accidents,' he said, lacking the energy to correct his dad's misguided views.

He'd tried numerous times to explain his role as Lead Officer for the Surrey Fire and Rescue Service, but the information never seemed to stick, so he'd stopped trying.

'We had the fire brigade here last week,' his dad said. 'One of the inmates tried to climb the fence. Got himself stuck and had to be lifted off by one of your lot.'

It hadn't been called the fire brigade for years. But Matt supposed his dad wouldn't be aware of that, as he hadn't exactly been out-and-about of late. 'Did he get down safely?'

'I think so. We were all herded inside, not allowed to watch and enjoy the show. Shame. It's not like there's much else to do in here.'

It was sad that someone stuck up a fence was considered entertainment. Matt searched for another topic. 'Are you still volunteering at the library?'

'Yep. Not exactly exciting stuff, but it kills a few hours each day.' His dad scratched his beard, his nails dirty and uncut. 'How's your mum?'

'Mum's fine.' As fine as a woman with a husband banged up could be.

Susan Hardy worked three jobs, rarely socialised and still had to endure endless 'curtain twitching' whenever someone new moved into the street. It didn't take much for the neighbour-hood gossip to start up. It wasn't fun for her.

'She's booked a visit for next week,' he told his dad, whose face lit up on hearing the news.

'Great. I was wondering when she'd be in. I miss her. I wish she'd visit more.'

And there was the problem.

His mum didn't want to visit – neither did his sister – which is why Matt made the effort to come each month, compensating for their lack of enthusiasm. Not that he could blame them. There was nothing enjoyable about a prison visit.

His mum had been widowed from her first husband in her early thirties, leaving her with a young son – Matt's half-brother, Chris. When she had met Pete Hardy – a man ten years her junior – he'd swept her off her feet, promised to look after her and enticed her into a whirlwind marriage. She hadn't stood a chance.

In the twenty years that followed, they had two kids together and set up home in one of the ex-army properties in Aldershot. They never had much money growing up, but that wasn't an issue. His dad's temper and excessive drinking were. Turned out, his dad was a bit of tearaway. Fighting, stealing, numerous misdemeanours – all things he'd kept hidden from his mum. He'd then joined the army and later worked as a bouncer at a nightclub. His last job, as a taxi driver, abruptly ended when he got into a brawl with another driver and bashed the guy's head against the pavement.

Even before that, the marriage had been riddled with arguments and broken promises. The final straw had been his dad's incarceration. And although his mum had vowed to 'stand by her man', was it any wonder that she didn't want to visit him that often?

'Leah's still refusing to visit me then?' his dad asked, looking disgruntled. 'You can't change her mind?'

'Leah's twenty-nine, Dad. She's an adult. She makes her own choices. I can't make her come if she doesn't want to.'

His dad sat back and folded his arms. 'I don't understand why she doesn't want to see me. Other blokes in here have done worse than me, and their kids still visit. I don't see what the issue is.'

And he never would, that was the problem.

His dad failed to understand how hard it had been on them, and the sacrifices they'd had to make. The bullying Leah had suffered from the local kids, being called 'the killer's daughter' and having stones thrown at her every time she left the house.

Matt had been older, he'd already left home and avoided such cruelty. But Leah had taken the brunt, and she held her dad entirely responsible.

Maybe if his dad had shown some remorse then it would have made a difference. Yet he never had, and it was too late now – the damage was done.

'Anyway, I'm here,' Matt said, changing tack. 'It's good to see you looking so well,' which was a lie, but nobody wanted to hear they looked like hell. 'Are you doing okay?'

'Top notch.' His dad glanced around the room, and then leant forwards. 'I've applied for early release.'

This was a surprise, given his dad only had a year left on his sentence. 'Is that something you're eligible for?'

He shrugged. 'I'm due for parole later this year anyway, and we all know how crowded prisons are. They need the space. I've behaved myself, toed the line, done my time. They offer early release for extenuating circumstances, so I figured I'd apply. I've got grounds.'

'You have?' And then a horrible thought struck. 'Are you ill?'

His dad shook his head. 'Nothing like that.'

That was a relief. His dad needed to be punished for his crime, but Matt didn't want him dead.

'I told them I wanted to attend my grandson's wedding.' He held his arms open, as if to say, 'How clever is that?'

Matt stilled. 'You know about the wedding?'

'Sure. Your mum wrote and told me the good news.'

'But… you barely know Zac. You've only met him a handful of times.'

'Through no fault of mine,' he said, indignantly. 'That stuck-up father of his stopped me seeing him.'

Matt wasn't a huge fan of his half-brother, but he fully understood why Chris hadn't wanted an impressionable young kid visiting 'Grandpa' in prison.

Matt rubbed his neck. 'Are you even invited to the wedding?' He couldn't imagine he would be. He wasn't even sure invites had been sent out yet.

'Why wouldn't I be? I'm the kid's grandpa. Zac's a man now. He can make up his own mind who comes to the wedding, and I've no doubt he'll invite me. You wait and see.'

'Right.' Technically, he was the kid's step-granddad, but he didn't feel pointing that out would be useful.

'Just think, all of us together again, like a proper family.' His dad sounded wistful.

A proper family? Was the man for real?

Matt felt he had to manage his dad's expectations. It wouldn't be fair to let him think everything would be okay once he left prison. 'You do know Leah and I have moved out, Dad? We don't live at home with Mum any more.'

His dad frowned. 'But we can have family dinners together? Arrange card nights and trips to the zoo. That'd be fun, wouldn't it?' His dad looked so hopeful, Matt didn't have the heart to point out that his kids were twenty-nine and thirty-two, respectively, and a little old for trips to the zoo.

But it wouldn't be fair to string him along, either. 'Things might not return to how they were, Dad. You do realise that, don't you?'

His dad frowned. 'How do you mean?'

'You've been away for ten years. Life has moved on, we're all different people now. Grown up. There might need to be some adjustment, it's not a case of slotting straight back into your old routine.'

His dad shrugged. 'Ten years banged up gives a man time to think. I've had enough of being shut away with a bunch of criminals. I want my freedom. I want my family, and I want my life back. That's what keeps me going. You'll see – once I'm out of here, things will be as if I never went away.'

Never went away? His dad made it sound like he'd been on an extended vacation, not served a decade in prison for manslaughter. And besides, it might be what his dad wanted, but was it what everyone else wanted? He doubted it. But he never got the chance to voice his concerns because the buzzer sounded, indicating that their time was up.

His dad stood up and opened his arms, a repeat gesture from earlier. 'Thanks for coming, son. You take care now.'

Matt hugged his dad. 'You too, Dad.'

'See you next month?'

'Sure.' It wasn't like he had much of a choice.

'We can chat more about the wedding,' he said, patting his belly. 'You might have to fix me up with a suit. I'm not as fit as I was. I have to make my family proud. Can't let the side down.'

Except he already had. Big time.

Matt walked away, nodding a goodbye.

Visits to the prison always left him feeling morose. It wasn't just the depressing building, or the sight of sad families trying to make the most of their restricted time together. It was the sense of loss, like leaving a puppy in kennels when you went on holiday. Not that his dad was cute and cuddly. Hell, no. But prison wasn't a kind place. Fights regularly broke out, misdemeanours happened daily. His dad had survived his stretch so far, but it was an unnerving experience walking away each time.

There was also the sadness of missing out on having a proper relationship with him, as one half-hour visit per month wasn't enough to keep them bonded. His dad was stuck in a time warp, his life paused, whereas the rest of them had moved on.

It was another forty minutes before he'd collected his phone and wallet, left the prison, and caught the bus into Wandsworth, where he'd arranged to meet his sister for coffee.

The Brew Cafe was situated on the Old York Road. It was modern and cosy, and considered to be one of the 'cool' places to hang out. According to his sister, anyway. Matt didn't care. As long as they served decent coffee, he was happy.

Leah was seated by the window. She glanced up when he approached and her face broke into a grin. She waved from behind the glass, beckoning him in.

He loved the way he never had to second-guess what his sister was feeling. If she was happy, she smiled. If she was sad, she cried. And if she was angry, she'd throw a saucer at his head – he still had the scar to prove it.

It meant their relationship was uncomplicated. Easy. No games or miscommunications. Something he couldn't say about any of the women he'd had romantic relationships with. His track record wasn't great. Three back-to-back bad experiences had dented his self-esteem and left him reluctant to try again, which was a shame, as he'd love to meet someone, but he wasn't sure his heart could cope with another battering.

The bell above the door tinkled as he entered.

Leah rushed over and threw her arms around him. See? Happy to see him. He had no problems understanding that.

His sister was a lot shorter than him and had to stretch up on tiptoe. 'I swear you get taller every time I see you.' She kissed his cheek and patted his chest, before returning to the table. 'I ordered for you.'

'Maybe you're shrinking,' he said, shrugging off his jacket and slinging it over the back of the chair. 'What did you get me?'

'Americano. Half-fat milk. No sugar.' She sat down, curling one leg under her. One of the benefits of being a PE teacher – flexibility. 'Did I do well?'

'You did.' Unlike his sister, he kept his feet rooted to the floor. His physique wouldn't accommodate bending a leg under him. His sister might be compact and small-framed, but he was all bulk. Well built, as his mother referred to him. Hagrid, as Leah called him.

He didn't mind being thickset, but it was a constant battle to keep his weight down. Thankfully, an active job and playing rugby at the weekends kept the belly in check. For now.

Leah sipped her cappuccino. 'So, how is he?' She grimaced and added another sugar to her coffee.

By 'he' Matt knew she was referring to their dad. 'Delusional, as usual.'

'Still playing the victim?' She stirred her coffee. 'The system is against me, and all that crap?'

He sighed. 'Not so much these days. He's less belligerent than he used to be. He doesn't moan quite as much about the unfairness of his sentence.'

Leah rolled her eyes. 'Because jailing a man for killing a bloke is so unreasonable. What were the courts thinking? They should've let him off with a slapped wrist.'

His sister shared his views on the punishment fitting the crime. She had strong morals, an unwavering sense of fairness and annoyingly straight teeth. Her only flaw was the inability to forgive. Once lost, there was no regaining her trust. It didn't take a rocket scientist to work out why.

'So why the change in stance?' she said, sipping her coffee. 'Has he found God? Taken up yoga? Been medicated?' She wiped a smudge of foam from her top lip. 'Please don't tell me he's finally accepted some responsibility for his crime? Anything else I could cope with. Not that.' She added another sugar to her coffee.

'He's applied for early release. He envisages he'll be out soon.'

Leah frowned. 'Is that likely? Why would they release him early?'

Matt sipped his coffee. 'So he can attend his grandson's wedding.'

A beat passed before Leah burst out laughing. 'No way! Are you serious? You're kidding me?'

'I wish I was.'

She stopped laughing. 'He thinks he's coming to the wedding?'

Matt nodded. 'He said… and I quote: "Why wouldn't I be invited?"'

Leah snorted, attracting a few strange looks from the other patrons. She waved an apology. 'Wow, he is delusional. Did you put him straight?'

'I tried to. I mean, I warned him there was a chance he might not be invited, but he dismissed the idea. He can't fathom why everyone wouldn't want him there.'

'Unbelievable.' Leah ran her hands through her wavy brown hair, shaking her head. 'You have to hand it to the man. I mean, that is one whole new level of narcissism.'

'The fact is, I have no idea whether Zac would want him there, or not.'

'More to the point, whether Chris would want him there.' She added another sugar to her coffee. 'I can't see that happening. Chris hates him.'

'I know.'

Their half-brother hadn't been a fan of his stepdad even before he'd been sent to prison. Chris's own father had died young, so up until the age of fourteen it had been just him and their mum. Chris hadn't reacted well to his mum meeting a much younger bloke. A bloke who drank, yelled at her and made Chris's teenage life hell. He'd liked it even less when they married and two snotty-nosed kids came along. He was forced to share, and he'd hated it. Understandably, Chris wasn't a fan of Pete Hardy, and he certainly wouldn't want him showing up at a family event.

Matt's phoned pinged. It was work. 'Shit.'

Leah emptied the bowl of sweeteners on the table, searching for more sugar. 'What is it? Bad news?'

'Someone's called in sick. I'm on standby, I need to go into work. Sorry.' He got up.

She looked up at him, forlorn. 'You're leaving so soon? Was it something I said?'

'I'm really sorry, Sis.' He bent down and kissed her forehead. 'I thought I had the rest of the day off.'

'And to think I skipped class for this.'

'I'll make it up to you. Dinner later this week?'

'I'll hold you to that. Somewhere horribly expensive, where I can embarrass you by slurping my wine and using the wrong fork.'

He laughed. 'Pizza Express it is, then.'

'Idiot.' She laughed and sloshed him. 'Bugger off, then. Leave me to drink alone. Don't worry, I'll be fine... if I could just find more sugar,' she said, heading off in search of a member of staff.

How on earth his sister wasn't diabetic, he didn't know.

# Chapter Four

There were days when Beth felt like the world was conspiring against her. When every effort to lead a calm, organised and composed existence was challenged by factors out of her control. Today was one of those days – and it wasn't even lunchtime.

'If you insist on bringing Tiffany to the wedding, Dad, then Mum's refusing to come.' Beth checked the clock on the dashboard. She was late. She hated being late.

The court hearing had overrun this morning. Her client had ignored her instructions to remain calm and had yelled at the judge instead, calling him a moron and completely undermining all the arguments she'd painstakingly prepared to overturn a custody agreement. Add to that her mother getting drunk last night and phoning her in the early hours to moan about her father, and Megan having a last-minute panic attack about what to pack for Greece, and was it any wonder that Beth was feeling a little fragile this morning? Now it seemed it was her dad's turn to annoy her.

'That's not my problem,' he replied, refusing to accept he *was* the problem. 'Your mother's being unreasonable.'

Beth swung her car into the small car park behind their offices, only to discover a delivery truck blocking her space. 'Is it really so unreasonable, Dad?' Beth leant on her horn, trying to attract the driver's attention.

'Tiffany's my girlfriend, and I want her at my daughter's wedding.'

Beth flinched at the word 'girlfriend'. It never got any easier to accept.

She leant on her horn again, using it as a vent for her frustrations. Why was the driver ignoring her? She wound down the window. 'Excuse me! Can you move your truck?' She doubted he could hear her above the engine noise.

Winding up the window, she refocused on persuading her dad to see reason. 'You've only been with Tiffany a few months, Dad. It's not like you've been together for years. Not like you and Mum.'

'What difference does that make? We're together now.' He'd never reacted well to being challenged.

'If you'd met Tiffany after the break-up maybe it wouldn't be so raw. But she's the woman you ran off with, Dad. She's the reason Mum's hurting.' Not to mention the reason behind her mum's late-night drinking.

Last night's phone call had involved a lot of slurring, swearing and something about needing to lock away the kitchen knives so she wouldn't be tempted to drive over to Tiffany's place and stab her. Her mum was not in a good place.

The truck driver appeared at the rear of the truck and opened the doors, lowering the loading platform and revealing numerous pallets waiting to be unloaded. This was not going to be a quick delivery.

Beth glanced at the dashboard. She was now twelve minutes late for her meeting with her future brother-in-law. A meeting she wasn't exactly enthusiastic about, but had been coerced into by her sister. Nonetheless, a promise was a promise. It would be rude to cancel, especially as Zac had travelled down from London to see her.

Crunching the car into reverse, she moved a few feet back. 'It's not like Tiffany and Megan are close, are they?' She pulled forwards, using all her effort to turn the wheel, before slamming on her brakes and narrowly missing colliding with the wall. She felt like Austin Powers in the film *International Man of Mystery*, when he was trying to negotiate a three-point turn in his golf cart.

'That's hardly my fault,' her dad said, sounding aggrieved. 'It's not like I haven't tried to get you girls together.'

Beth had absolutely no interest in 'getting together' with Tiffany. She might not be as angry as her mum about the situation, but the idea that Beth and Megan would welcome Tiffany into their lives and become friends was laughable. Besides, her mother would kill her.

Beth finally managed to escape the parking bay and whizzed onto the High Street in search of another space. Godalming wasn't known for its multitude of car parks – the town was old and with narrow lanes, built way before people owned cars. As it was a busy shopping area, parking spaces were like gold dust.

She pulled into Mint Street car park and scanned the rows of vehicles squashed into the narrow bays. She spotted a solitary space on the adjacent row and made a beeline for it.

'My point is that whatever your feelings are for Tiffany, surely your loyalty to Megan supersedes them. She's your daughter, after all.' She swung the car to the right, yanked hard on the steering wheel and pulled a hard left, skidding into the narrow space like a highly trained getaway driver. 'And if there's a choice between having her mum at her wedding or her dad's new girlfriend, which one do you think she'd favour?'

'It shouldn't be a choice. They should both be there.'

Her father could be very naive at times.

Beth switched off the engine and opened the door, trying not to hit the neighbouring vehicle. 'I know that's what you want, Dad, but it can't happen.' She squeezed herself between the two cars, disconnecting the phone from hands-free as she juggled locking the door with balancing the handset to her ear. 'I have to go, Dad, I'm late for a meeting. We'll talk later when I'm back in the office. Can you at least think about what I've said? This is Megan's big day and we need to do what's best for her. Okay?' Ignoring her father's grumblings, she hooked her bag over her shoulder and hurried away, struggling to gain any speed in her tight suit and court shoes.

'Excuse me!' a man shouted behind her. 'That was my space.'

He couldn't be talking to her – it was a public car park, with no designated spaces.

She glanced over her shoulder to see an irate man running after her. He was very large and didn't look happy. Oh, hell. This wasn't good.

She tried to speed up, unwilling to engage in a debate with a man-mountain about parking spaces.

'Don't ignore me,' he said, catching up. 'I said, that was my space.'

Realising she couldn't outrun him, she stopped and faced him. 'What are you talking about? I haven't taken anyone's space.'

'Yes, you have.' He pointed to his abandoned SUV, its engine idling. 'I was about to reverse into that space when you nicked it.'

She recoiled. 'I didn't nick it.'

'Yes, you did. I was sitting there, indicator on, patiently waiting for the previous car to leave so I could have the space, when you came racing around the bend and swooped right in.'

'I wasn't racing.' Her hand went to her neck. 'I never race.'

'You left tyre marks.' He pointed to the tarmac.

Her eyes were drawn to a set of black skid marks. 'They could've been done by anyone.' But even she could see that the marks followed her trajectory, swerving straight into the space she was parked in. The lawyer in her couldn't argue with the evidence.

'You nearly hit my car,' he said, moving towards her.

His close proximity made her take a step back. 'I most certainly did not.'

He was a big guy. Intimidating.

'You don't believe me?' He looked incredulous. 'I have a dashboard camera fitted to my car. You're welcome to watch the footage.'

Oh, crap. 'That won't be necessary,' she said, tugging on the hem of her suit jacket, trying to regain the moral high ground. 'Even if I do dispute your claims.'

'Whatever. You're still in my parking space.'

'It's not your parking space. It belongs to the council.'

His eyebrows lifted. 'Seriously? That's how you want to play this?' He gave her a cursory once-over, his expression indicating he wasn't impressed by what he saw. Bloody cheek. 'You're one of those people, are you?'

She didn't like the way he was studying her. 'What do you mean by that?'

'Someone who thinks it's okay to take what they want. Someone who doesn't give a crap about anyone else, and someone who wouldn't think twice about shafting someone else to get ahead.'

Her skin burnt hot.

How dare he. He didn't know her. He knew nothing about her. 'I am not like that,' she said, standing her ground. She'd never hurt a fly, not intentionally, anyway.

'Seems that way to me.'

It was time to end this unwelcome exchange. She was in danger of losing her rag, or worse, dissolving into tears. 'Look, not that I owe you an explanation, but I simply didn't see you. Okay? It wasn't a deliberate act to *nick* your parking space, I just didn't realise you were waiting for it.'

He folded his arms across his wide chest. 'Well, now you do – what are you going to do about it? Are you going to move your car?'

'Of course not. I'm late for a meeting.'

'Right. So you are one of those people.' He turned and stormed off, waving a hand dismissively. 'Thanks for nothing.'

What a thoroughly unpleasant man.

Slinging her bag over her shoulder, she turned and marched away. How dare he accuse her of deliberately stealing his parking space, as if she'd do such a thing. She simply hadn't seen him.

43

She'd been too preoccupied, trying to persuade her father to see reason and not bring his girlfriend to her sister's wedding. Was it any wonder she hadn't been paying attention?

Anyway, it was his word against hers… if you ignored the skids marks… and the dashcam footage.

Okay, so maybe she had been driving a little erratically, but that still didn't warrant him shouting at her in the street. Accusing her. Intimidating her.

The man was well over six foot. Wide, too, with large hands and thighs the size of tree trunks. She was five-nine herself, but it still wasn't pleasant to be accosted in such a way, and over such a trivial thing like a blessed parking space.

She reached Caffè Nero, twenty minutes late, and joined the queue of people waiting to be served. She needed a tea to calm her nerves – her hands were still shaking from being shouted at.

Slipping off her suit jacket, she hooked it over her arm, fanning her face as she shuffled forwards in the queue.

She couldn't see Zac anywhere so, unearthing her phone, she sent him a WhatsApp message, telling him she'd arrived. He replied saying he was seated at the far end of the cafe. She looked over, but still couldn't see him.

Having placed her order, she moved to the collection point where several takeaway cartons sat on the countertop and people were barging past her to collect them. It was frantic, but then it was lunchtime.

Her tea arrived shortly afterwards, served as requested in a china cup. Picking up the tray, she turned to leave, but a man smacked into her, sending her tray flying and spilling the contents of the mug straight down her front.

Shock initially desensitised her from the heat hitting her chest.

She glanced down to see her white shirt stained brown, the material now see-through, her lace bra visible through the fabric. Oh, hell.

And then her gaze shot up when the man said, 'Shit! Sorry!'

Her eyes locked with the shouty man from the car park who'd accused her of stealing his parking space. 'Did you do that on purpose?' she said, not caring if anyone overheard.

He looked shocked. 'Why would I do that?'

'Revenge? Payback for earlier?'

His eyebrows lifted. 'Seriously?'

'Did you follow me here? Is this your way of settling the score?'

He flinched. 'Of course not. It was an accident. I didn't see you.'

'How could you not see me? I was standing right here.'

He gave her a loaded look. 'Oh, like you didn't see me in the car park?'

Touché. 'So this *is* revenge?'

'No, it's an accident. For which I apologise, because that's what decent people do when they're in the wrong. They apologise. They don't deny responsibility.'

He was lecturing her about morality and responsibility? Flaming cheek. 'Don't take the high moral ground with me, matey.' And then she realised her breasts were stinging. The heat of the tea had registered with her brain. It was hot. Really hot.

She needed to take action. 'Excuse me.'

'Can I do anything?'

She brushed past him. 'No.'

'Can I get you another tea?'

'No, thanks.'

'Can I pay for the dry cleaning?' he called after her, as she headed for the toilets.

'I don't need anything, thank you. You've done quite enough.'

She barged through the toilet door, already unbuttoning her shirt, her chest burning. It was also bright red, the colour creeping up her neck.

Shrugging off her shirt, she unclipped her bra, not caring if anyone came in and saw her splashing cold water against her chest. Her skin was throbbing, the stinging making her eyes water. Soaking her stained shirt in cold water, she held it to her chest. The pain finally subsided.

She glanced at her reflection in the mirror. Strands of dark hair had come loose and trailed down her neck, her cheeks were flushed and she had smudges of brown mascara above one eye. What a mess.

Ten minutes later, the stinging had stopped. Her skin was tinged pink, but she was satisfied there were no serious burns. She had some E45 cream in her handbag that would soothe her skin... except she didn't have her bag with her – she must have dropped it. If someone hadn't handed it in, she'd have to cancel her phone and credit cards. As if her day could get any worse.

Her shirt was too sodden to put back on. As was her bra.

Thankfully, she wasn't well-endowed in the breast department, so she could get away with just wearing her suit jacket... except she didn't have that with her either.

She was semi-naked, with no means of calling for help and no way of retaining her dignity.

She dropped her head against the cool sink. This was her worst nightmare.

She was just at the point of resigning herself to putting on her soaking wet see-through clothing and walking into a busy cafe in search of her bag and jacket, when the toilet door opened and one of the serving staff came in.

Beth immediately stood up and covered her breasts.

If the girl was shocked, she didn't show it. She offered Beth her bag and jacket. 'The big guy who knocked into you said you might need these.'

Beth nodded for the girl to drop them on the floor, so she didn't have to unclasp her arms and expose herself further. 'Thanks.'

The girl shrugged and left her to it. 'No drama.'

Grateful for small mercies, Beth slipped on her jacket and buttoned it up. There was a little more cleavage on display than she'd like, but nothing too scandalous.

She couldn't be bothered to tidy her hair, but she wiped away the smudged mascara and made herself as presentable as she could before leaving the sanctuary of the toilets.

With shaky legs and a throbbing chest, she returned to the cafe. A few people looked over, but nothing too alarming.

Much as she'd prefer to head straight back to the office, she couldn't leave without speaking to Zac, as it would be rude not to offer an explanation. But to her utter dismay, the first person she encountered as she left the toilets was the man who'd knocked into her.

'Oh, please. Give me a break. Haven't you done enough?'

'I wanted to check you were okay.' His expression was no longer angry. His eyes dipped briefly to her chest, a fleeting movement, but she spotted it nonetheless.

Her hand came up to cover her bare neck. 'I'm fine.'

'I got you another drink,' he said. His deep voice had a slight gravelly tone to it. 'Tea, right?'

She cleared her throat. 'You didn't need to do that.'

'It was the least I could do. It's at the table, waiting for you.'

She followed his eyeline to a table where two drinks awaited. Was he for real?

'Are you somehow expecting me to forget what's happened, succumb to your less-than-impressive charms and join you for a drink?' She scrunched her jacket lapels closer.

'Well, I—'

'Are you mad?' She fixed him with a steely glare. 'Do you think *I'm* mad?'

His mouth twitched. Was he trying not to laugh?

That did it. She hoisted up her bag. 'If you think for one moment I'm—'

'Oh, great. You've met.'

Beth stilled at the sound of Zac's voice.

47

She turned to him. 'I beg your pardon?'

'This is my uncle Matt.' Zac must have sensed the tension radiating off them, because his expression turned wary. 'Is everything okay?'

Beth couldn't quite compute what was happening. 'This… this man is your uncle?'

Zac's eyes flitted between them. 'Er… yes.'

'Your uncle? As in… your biological uncle?'

Zac's eyebrows lifted. 'He's my dad's half-brother. Have I missed something?'

You could say that.

Zac turned to his uncle. 'This is Megan's sister, Beth. The woman I was telling you about.'

'That much I'd gathered,' he said, supressing a smirk. 'Matt Hardy. Nice to meet you.'

Beth refused to let go of her lapels. 'I would say likewise, but we both know that'd be a lie.'

He lowered his hand.

Zac looked mortified. 'Er… shall we sit down?'

Beth was torn. The idea of sitting down with this man to engage in small talk about weddings filled her with dread. Especially since she was minus a shirt and bra. But it wasn't Zac's fault, and it seemed cruel to make him suffer for his uncle's shortcomings.

'I can't stay long,' she said, figuring a short stay was all she could cope with. She still had a tingling chest, after all.

Following Zac over to the table, she noticed a few admiring glances from a group of girls seated nearby. She couldn't blame them. Zac was extremely good-looking. Tall, slim, with his black hair groomed into a fashionable quiff. He wouldn't have looked out of place on a catwalk.

They arrived at the table and sat down – Zac on one side, his long legs taking up all the space, and Matt on the other, leaving her with the seat squashed against the wall.

Matt's thigh pressed against hers. She tried to shift away, but the wall blocked her escape. Her day sure wasn't getting any better.

'Thanks so much for coming,' Zac said, looking between them. 'I really appreciate it.'

'No problem.' Matt smiled. 'Happy to help. What is it you need?'

'So, the thing is… Megan's flying out to Greece this Sunday to start filming a new project.'

'Okay.' Matt took a mouthful of coffee. 'How long will she be in Greece for?'

Pause. 'Two months.'

'Two months?' This was obviously news to him and he lowered his mug to the table. 'But the wedding's planned for June?'

'Yeah, well, the thing is…' Zac's smile was a little forced. 'Megan's left me to arrange everything while she's gone.'

Matt looked incredulous. 'By yourself?'

Zac shrugged. 'Kind of, yes.'

'Jesus.' Matt sat back in his seat, making it squeak. He looked too big for the chair, like it might buckle under him, but maybe that was just wishful thinking on her part. 'That's a bit selfish, isn't it?'

Beth glared at him. 'That's my sister you're talking about.'

'Sorry.' He held his hands up. 'But don't you think it's strange for the bride to run off two months before her wedding?'

Absolutely, but no way was she admitting as much. Not to a man like him, who'd use it as ammunition. 'She hasn't run off – she's accepted a prestigious acting job abroad. That's hardly the same thing. It was too good an opportunity to pass up.' If you could call remaking a low-budget version of *Mamma Mia* prestigious.

Matt didn't look convinced. 'But still.'

His self-righteous attitude irked. 'She's a fan of *Don't Tell the Bride*,' Beth said defensively, even though she thought her sister's plan was bonkers. But her opinions were private. Her loyalty was to Megan, not this idiot.

Matt frowned. 'You've lost me.'

'The TV show,' Zac said, helpfully. 'Where the groom is tasked with arranging the wedding as a surprise for the bride.'

Matt raised an eyebrow. 'That's a thing?'

Zac nodded. 'It's a hit show.'

Matt still didn't look convinced. 'And you're okay with that? Arranging everything yourself?'

Zac looked so forlorn. Beth suspected the meeting wasn't going quite as well as he'd hoped. Not when the parties involved had nearly come to blows. It was hardly the ideal start.

She shifted her chair, trying to move away from the heat radiating off Matt's thigh. It wasn't helping to cool her burning skin. She felt flustered and jumpy, and she was never normally either of those things. Then again, she'd never before experienced socialising with a man she'd just had a run-in with. It was kind of an unusual situation.

While taking a sip of tea, Beth was careful to hold on to her jacket lapels with her free hand. She didn't want to flash any flesh. He was a man who would notice, she was sure of it.

'There's no way I can do it alone,' Zac continued, his expression woeful. 'That's why I've asked you here. I was hoping that, as my best man, you'd help me.'

Matt barked a laugh. 'What, plan the wedding?'

Zac nodded.

Matt stopped laughing. 'Not just the stag weekend?'

Zac shook his head.

'But the whole thing? The ceremony? The reception?'

Another tentative nod from Zac. 'Beth's already on board, but I was hoping you'd help me, too.'

Beth inwardly cringed. Zac hadn't mentioned the involvement of his bloody uncle. This was not a welcome development.

Matt nodded in Beth's direction. 'You mean, me... and her?'

Beth frowned. '*Her* has a name.'

'What I meant was, why us? I can't speak for… Ruth here—'

'Beth.'

'*Beth*… but I've never been married, mate. I'd have no idea how to plan a wedding. Can't you ask your other uncle? Will runs an events company and he'd be much better at this than me.'

The man obviously didn't want to be involved any more than she did. On that, at least, they agreed. Torturous as the idea of arranging someone else's wedding was, she'd rather cope solo than have this man's input. He wasn't what she'd call sophistic-ated. Rustic, more like. Earthy. Uncultured. If he backed out, it would be a blessing. If not, the wedding would probably end up as a hoedown.

Zac shook his head. 'Mum and Dad aren't happy about the wedding, and they're barely speaking to me. I asked Uncle Will, but Mum made him promise to keep out of it. He doesn't want to fall out with his sister. I get that. You know how close they are.'

Beth felt bad for Zac. 'They'll come around, I'm sure,' she said, hoping she was right. They had enough dramas with her own parents feuding over the wedding, they didn't need Zac's parents causing issues as well. Even if she could understand his family's reservations.

'I hope so.' Zac looked at his uncle, all doe-eyed and pleading. 'Will you help me? Please? I love Megan. I don't want to let her down, but I can't do this by myself.'

'Christ.' Matt rubbed his chin. His beard was close-cut, a contrast to his collar-length wavy brown hair. He suddenly turned to face Beth, forcing her back against the wall as she tried to escape his scrutiny. The intensity of his stare was startling. 'Are you on board with this?'

Not in the slightest, but somehow she felt that voicing this might tip Zac over the edge. 'I've agreed to help, yes.' Under duress. And before she'd known there might be another accomplice, one who got possessive over parking spaces and reacted by chucking tea.

Matt held her gaze. It was strange to be scrutinised in such a way. He was looking at her like she had a screw loose. Charming.

He turned back to Zac. 'What is it you want us to do?'

Beth didn't like the word 'us'.

'I'm not sure.' Zac pulled a face. 'I don't even know what needs doing.'

'Great.' Matt closed his eyes.

'But I'll learn,' Zac said, sounding desperate. 'I'll buy wedding magazines. Research stuff online. Whatever it takes. I just need some help.'

Matt turned to Beth again. 'Do you have any experience of weddings?'

She shook her head. 'Only ending them.'

He frowned. 'Excuse me?'

'Beth's a family law solicitor,' Zac said. 'She specialises in divorce cases.'

Matt looked appalled. 'Let me get this straight. You have two months to plan a wedding. You have no idea what you want. The bride is abroad. And the only people you have helping you are a firefighter and a divorce lawyer?'

Zac attempted a rather feeble smile. 'Yep.'

Matt dropped his head on the table. 'Shit.'

Her sentiments exactly.

## Chapter Five

Matt could think of a dozen things he'd rather be doing on a free Saturday. Playing rugby, going for a run, hanging out with his mates in the pub… poking his eyes out with a blunt stick. Anything would be preferable to being coerced into attending a Hamilton family gathering. A gathering where he wasn't wanted, except by his nephew. A gathering where he'd be forced to endure snide comments from his half-brother, and where the sizeable gap between their respective lives would be most evident.

But his nephew needed him – the poor lad didn't have anyone else in his corner, so as much as Matt didn't want to be there, he felt obligated. Not that he believed anything he said would make a difference. His brother had never listened to his advice before, and he wasn't going to start now. But that was beside the point, it was about showing a united front.

The Hamilton residence was a rural farmhouse set in one of the quiet lanes of Chobham, Surrey. It was centuries old, with a wide gravel driveway and covered in creeping wisteria. He'd left his car in the neighbouring lane – he wasn't sure why, as there was enough space for another vehicle, but he'd never felt welcome in this house. He was an interloper, the proverbial black sheep. Tolerated, but never accepted, and certainly never welcomed.

Not that he'd done anything wrong. His only crime was being the son of Pete Hardy, the man Chris held responsible for ruining his life. His mother's life, too. By default, Matt was the enemy.

As Matt approached the front door, he admired the white-painted brickwork and wooden supporting beams, adorned with hanging baskets. It was the quintessential country cottage. The kind of place advertised in *Country Living*, where couples aspired to retire to.

The place was owned by Zac's grandparents, Bobby and Diane Taylor, a nice couple. Bobby was a retired policeman and Diane a former schoolteacher. Attached to the house was a barn extension, where his half-brother, Chris, and his wife Gemma lived – Zac's parents.

Matt had never fallen out with Gemma, but they'd never bonded either. No doubt her loyalty to Chris was a factor. He could imagine that conversations about Chris's childhood growing up with Pete Hardy as a stepdad hadn't helped. It didn't matter that he was a victim, too, just as Leah and their mother were – they were the great unwashed in Gemma's eyes.

He pressed the doorbell. The sooner he got this over with, the sooner he could leave.

When the door swung open, he braced himself and forced a smile.

Despite it being a Saturday, his brother was dressed in a button-down shirt and crease-free tan chinos, held up by a shiny leather belt, which was a perfect match for his shiny leather shoes. His dark hair was cut short, without a single strand out of place, and his chiselled jaw was clean shaven. He looked like the IT manager he was. Staid. Serious. Devoid of emotion.

Far from welcoming Matt into the family home, Chris stared at him like he'd grown two heads. 'What are you doing here?'

Nice greeting. 'Zac invited me.'

Chris looked puzzled. 'Why?'

His brother obviously had no idea he was coming.

Apart from them both being tall, the two brothers shared no other features. No one would ever have guessed they were related, and he questioned it himself sometimes.

When nothing further was forthcoming, Matt raised an eyebrow. 'Are you going to invite me in?'

'Doesn't seem like I have a choice.'

Nice to see you, too.

No handshake followed. No manly hug or fist bump. Chris didn't even crack a smile. He just continued to regard Matt with suspicion. What did he think he was going to do? Steal the family silver?

Chris stood back from the doorway. 'You'd better come in.'

'Thanks. Is Zac here?'

'Not yet. Everyone else is in the garden – you've interrupted a family barbeque.'

Good to know he wasn't considered part of the family. Not that this was news.

He followed Chris through to the garden.

The outside space was large and well-tended, with an immaculate lawn surrounded by flower beds and patio planters overspilling with various foliage. Seated around a large wooden table were Zac's family. His grandparents, Bobby and Diane. Zac's mother, Gemma, and his uncle Will and new wife, Lily. Will's daughter from his first marriage played up by the pond, throwing a ball for the family dachshund.

It was a picture of family harmony. Smiling and happy.

Matt's heart twinged. It was a far cry from his mother's ex-army house in Aldershot. How the other half lived, eh? And yet somehow he was still the bad guy. Go figure.

Gemma did a double take when she saw him. 'Matt? I didn't know you were coming?'

'So I gather.' He tried for a conciliatory smile.

Chris and his wife shared a look, no doubt wondering how quickly they could get rid of him.

'Zac invited him,' Chris said, as though his son had invited the Grim Reaper for lunch. Zac would be in trouble for this later, bad son that he was.

Gemma shielded her eyes from the sun, her expression laced with mistrust, as though Matt was trying to outwit them in a cunning ruse.

Gemma wasn't what Matt would call a warm person. She wore the same style of clothing as her husband, perfecting the art of 'country chic', with her tan trousers, loose blouse, and sunglasses perched on top of her blonde hair. She radiated seriousness, self-containment and rigidity. She was also incredibly judgemental. Where Zac had inherited his edgy style from, Matt had no idea. Maybe it was a rebellion against such conservatism.

Zac's granddad stood up and offered Matt a handshake. 'Good to see you, Matt. Can I get you a beer?'

Finally, a friendly face. 'Cheers, Bobby. Sounds good.'

'Take a seat, back in a tick.' He patted Matt's hand, a simple gesture, but one Matt was grateful for.

The only spare seats were in full sun, away from the protection of the large oak tree.

He sat down, wishing he'd thought to check that Zac had arrived before turning up. He could kick himself.

An awkward silence followed.

The wooden chair beneath him creaked and he prayed it wouldn't collapse under him. He could imagine Chris sending him the bill.

His phone pinged with a message from an unknown number. For a fleeting moment, he welcomed the distraction… until he realised the message was from Beth Lawrence.

> Zac gave me your number. We need to finalise the wedding budget. Please respond ASAP.

At least, he assumed it was Beth Lawrence. Who else would be asking him about wedding budgets? It was hardly the friendliest of messages, but then, she hadn't struck him as the friendly type.

He typed in a response. *Hi to you too. Will talk to Zac about budget. How's it going?*

A few seconds later she replied. *Fine. Please ensure that you do.*

She hadn't defrosted then? It was fair to say they hadn't got off to the best of starts. Although he was the first to admit that his actions last week hadn't exactly helped matters, it wasn't reasonable to still hold a grudge. He'd got over the whole debacle the moment he'd realised who she was, but she clearly hadn't. She still imagined him to be a guy capable of deliberately inflicting revenge by knocking hot tea over a person. Like he'd ever do that. But she didn't seem interested in changing her opinion of him, and that annoyed him. He was not that type of bloke.

He looked up to discover all eyes fixed upon him. What had he done? Had he been frowning? Made a noise?

He glanced around the table, making eye contact with his so-called family. A set of blank faces stared back. He felt like he was at a really stressful job interview, under scrutiny from the board of directors for a funeral firm. That, or on trial for crimes against the family – the Hardy clan had sullied the good name of the Hamiltons, and he was here to pay.

He glanced at Will, who gave him an embarrassed shrug. Will Taylor was Gemma's brother. He ran a successful events-planning company and had all the necessary skills to organise a wedding. If life was fair, it would be Will helping Zac arrange his nuptials and not Matt, but who said life was fair?

His gaze switched to Will's wife, Lily. She smiled nervously, her eyes flicking to Gemma and Chris to check they weren't watching. She was a costume designer and the bride's best friend – which placed her firmly in the 'enemy camp', poor woman. He could empathise. Agreeing to make Megan's wedding dress hadn't gone down well, but Lily's loyalty to her friend overrode any objections from her in-laws. Good for her.

Zac's grandmother gestured to a bowl of nuts in the middle of the table. 'Can I get you anything to eat, Matt? The barbeque won't be ready for a while.'

Diane was the peacemaker of the family, the one who mediated and soothed. Her grey hair was cropped into a short style, and she looked healthy and happy, an advert for how to age well. How his own mother should look… but didn't.

He shook his head. 'I'm good thanks, Diane.'

Bobby returned with the drinks and Matt accepted his beer gratefully. He was in need of something to dull the torment and readily knocked back a large mouthful, followed by another, and another. All the while, ignoring Chris's tutting. He didn't care. Anaesthetic was needed.

His phone pinged again. Another message from Beth Lawrence.

> Can you also chase Zac for the guest list? I need it ASAP.

She was certainly organised, he'd give her that, something he should be grateful for. After all, the more she took control, the less he'd have to get involved with.

He replied. *Will do. Anything else you need me to do?*

> No.

Charming. He tried again. *Chatty, aren't you?*

> No time. Working.

> On a Saturday?

At that point, Zac arrived. Matt was relieved. There was only so much tense silence and furtive glances from his estranged family he could cope with, and it wasn't like exchanging WhatsApp messages with Beth Lawrence was cheering him up.

Zac looked flushed. 'Sorry I'm late. Megan called from Greece. I didn't want to cut short our call. We don't get much of a chance to catch up.' He was dressed in his usual black attire, complete with guyliner and black nails.

Chris flinched at the sight of his son's painted nails. He wasn't what you'd call a progressive, his half-brother.

Zac approached Matt. 'I was worried you wouldn't come.'

Matt gave him a wry look. 'And miss all the fun?'

Zac turned his head away so his parents wouldn't see his grin.

Poppy came rushing over to greet her cousin and threw her arms around him. 'I'm so excited to be a bridesmaid,' she said, jumping up and down. At thirteen, Poppy was completely oblivious to the strained atmosphere surrounding her. 'I've chosen my dress,' she said, her tall, skinny frame almost reaching Zac's shoulder. 'It's pale gold with lots of netting and a giant bow. Mummy-Lily is going to make it for me.'

Mummy-Lily was Poppy's name for her new stepmother, a way of embracing her new mum without forgetting her old one, who'd tragically died ten years ago in a skiing accident.

Zac kissed Poppy's forehead. 'Sounds cool, kiddo.'

'That's if the wedding goes ahead,' Gemma quipped.

Zac sighed heavily and sat down next to Matt, his only ally. 'I guess it's time for the conversation then.'

Will patted his daughter's hand. 'Take the dog for a run around the garden, sweetie. There's a good girl.'

Poppy looked dejected. 'But I want to stay and talk about the wedding.'

'There isn't going to be a wedding,' Chris snapped.

'No wedding?' Poppy's eyes grew wide. 'Why not?'

Will glared at Chris before turning to his daughter. 'The adults need to have a talk, sweetie. You go and play. We won't be long.'

'But I'm thirteen, almost an adult. Why can't I stay?'

Lily got up and took Poppy's hand. 'Come on, Poppy. Let's go and pat the ponies in the neighbouring field.'

Poppy allowed herself to be dragged off. 'Ohhhkaaay.'

Matt resisted the urge to follow them. Patting ponies sounded nice.

He took another swig of beer.

Zac waited until they were out of earshot. 'Thanks for coming, everyone,' he said, rubbing his hands on his jeans. 'I know it feels like an ambush, but I'm sick of everyone busting my balls every time I mention the wedding.'

'Language!' Gemma glared at her son.

Matt shifted on the wooden garden chair, making it creak again. This was a fun way to spend the day.

Chris folded his arms. 'Is there a reason you invited Uncle Matt to this discussion? This is a family matter.'

There it was again, the dig about him not being part of the family. Rub it in, why don't you.

'Uncle Matt's helping me plan the wedding,' Zac said, defiantly. 'That's why he's here. He's also my best man.'

'An irrelevance, because there's not going to be a wedding,' Gemma said irritably. 'We've already spoken about this, you're far too young.'

Zac ran a hand through his black quiff. 'We haven't spoken about it. You lay down the law and we end up arguing – you never listen to me or let me speak. I'm not backing down this time, you need to accept my decision and stop blocking me.'

Gemma wasn't used to her son answering back. 'We can't sit back and watch you make a mistake.'

'It's not a mistake.'

'It is in our eyes.' Chris crossed his legs, a match for his crossed arms, which made him look totally closed off – probably the intention. 'It's a disaster waiting to happen.'

'But it's not your decision, is it?' Zac's tone was rebellious, even if his hands were shaking. 'I'm an adult.'

'Then start behaving like one.'

Ironic, seeing as Chris was the only one acting childishly.

Zac rubbed his eyes. 'What have you got against Megan?'

Good question.

Matt had only met Megan a few times, but she seemed nice enough. A bit of a drama luvvie, slightly self-absorbed, but clearly smitten with Zac. Just as he was with her. Surely that was all that mattered?

His phone pinged with another message from Beth Lawrence. The intrusion evoked a tut from Gemma, as he discreetly checked his phone.

> Link below to gift list set up at The White Company.

Gemma batted a wasp away, still glaring at Matt for not giving her his full attention. 'Megan's too old for you,' she said to her son, swiping at the wasp and sending it plummeting to the floor where she squashed it under her sandal. Job done. No one messed with Gemma. 'Ten years is a substantial age gap.'

Matt replied to Beth. *Is everything on the list white?*

> Yes.

> Seriously?

61

> Yes. Why?

> You know Zac only wears black?

> Your point?

> He'll look like a negative in his own home.

Pause.

> Are you trying to be funny?

> Yes.

> It's not working.

Well, that told him.

'If it doesn't bother us, why should it bother anyone else?' Zac said, looking at his disgruntled parents.

Another good question.

'You might not see the problem, but we do,' Chris said, rather patronisingly. 'An age gap of that magnitude means you might want different things at different times.'

'Like?'

'Like children,' snapped Gemma.

'Grandma Susan is ten years older than Grandpa Pete, and they've never had a problem,' Zac said, making Matt flinch.

It wasn't the best example to use. After all, his dad was hardly a role model. He was banged up for manslaughter, and they'd certainly had their share of problems, but it wouldn't be helpful to point that out right now.

'Please refrain from mentioning that man's name in this house.' Chris looked irritated. 'He is *not* your grandfather.'

Zac looked confused. 'He's married to Grandma Susan, what else does that make him?'

'Don't get me started.' Chris uncrossed his legs and then crossed them again. 'That man has no place in this family.'

Join the club, Matt wanted to say. It wasn't like the rest of them were welcome either.

Zac tried again. 'Apart from the age gap, do you have any other objections to Megan?' He looked at his uncle Will, who raised his hands, and said, 'Don't ask me. I haven't got a problem with her.'

Gemma glared at her brother. 'Don't take his side.'

'I'm not taking anyone's side.' Will took a long swig of his wine. 'I'm just saying, I've always liked Megan.'

Gemma's glare intensified.

'Thanks, Uncle Will. It's nice to know someone approves.' Zac gave his parents a pointed look. 'Megan's an amazing woman. She's loyal, kind, talented—'

'You haven't even lived together,' Gemma said, cutting him off. 'You have a romanticised view of love. Cohabitation is about compromise and money issues and fixing a broken tap. It's not all hearts and roses. Once the honeymoon period is over, reality hits home. It's not a fairy-tale ending.'

Zac looked incredulous. 'Jesus, Mum. I'm twenty-three, not thirteen. You think I don't know that?'

'Lust can make men do crazy things.' Gemma fanned her face, looking uncharacteristically flustered.

Zac glared at his mum. 'What the hell?'

They were now onto the topic of sex? Matt took another swig of beer, wishing he'd caught the bus here because he had a feeling one drink wasn't going to be enough.

'Men sometimes get confused,' Gemma said, sounding like a 1950s marriage guidance counsellor. 'They interpret lust as love. It's easily done. Especially if you're inexperienced.'

Matt choked on his beer.

Everyone turned to stare at him.

He reached for a napkin. 'Pardon me. Went down the wrong hole.' He was pretty sure Zac was anything but inexperienced, and that became increasingly obvious when he saw the embarrassed look on his face.

'By the time you realise, it's too late,' Gemma continued, oblivious to her son's anguish. 'The damage is done and you're stuck with a mortgage and a kid, and regretting your life.'

Was that her own experience she was referring to?

'How naive d'you think I am?' Zac raked his hands through his hair.

'Extremely,' Chris said. 'Otherwise you wouldn't be considering marriage.'

'Wow, thanks, Dad.' Zac stood up, sending the garden chair toppling over behind him. 'I'm about to marry the woman of my dreams and this is the response I get? I'm a naive romantic fool, who's acting on impulse and who can't tell the difference between love and lust? Not to mention throwing away his career? Have I missed anything?' He looked at the group. 'Anything else you'd like to throw at me?'

No one replied – they knew better. Zac was at boiling point.

Every instinct that Matt had urged him to keep quiet, shut his mouth and avoid getting in the firing line. But he had to step in, he couldn't let the lad suffer any more than he was.

'Can I say something?'

All eyes turned to him.

Chris rolled his eyes. 'Oh, this I've got to hear. What pearls of wisdom is my half-brother about to unleash? A thirty-two-year-old man who's never been married, who's had numerous failed relationships and who doesn't have any kids. The ultimate oracle of marital knowledge. Do enlighten us...?'

Heat crept up Matt's neck. There'd been numerous times over the years when he'd been tempted to thump his half-brother, and now was another such occasion. But it wouldn't help his nephew.

He swallowed back his annoyance. 'You've pointed out why this marriage might not work and therefore isn't a good idea, but Zac and Megan have a lot going for them, too. There are as many reasons why this relationship will work, as won't.'

Chris lifted an eyebrow. 'Name one?'

Matt tried to remain calm. 'Well, for a start, they love each other.'

Chris laughed. 'Love?'

Sometimes Matt really despised his brother. 'Strangely enough, that's the driving force behind most marriages, Chris. Love.'

'Like you'd know anything about love.'

The accusation hit home. As it was intended.

Matt gripped the chair arms, making them creak. 'Which is why I've never married. Maybe if I'd felt the way Zac does about Megan, I might have.'

That shut his brother up.

'Also, they're adults. Whether you like it or not, they're capable of making their own decisions.'

'Not necessarily good decisions,' Gemma added, clearly not wanting to be left out.

Matt turned to her. 'Based on what? An age gap? Because as far as I can see, that's all you've got.' He looked at them all in turn. 'They've been together for two years, the honey-moon period is long over. You're worried about Zac developing his career? Statistically, married men have more stable careers than single blokes. You want Zac to act responsibly? Nothing requires more responsibility than marriage, just as it requires commitment and stability, all the things you want him to demonstrate. Well, he is.' He gave Zac a discreet wink. 'And if they're really lucky, they'll also have plenty of hot sweaty sex.'

Chris and Gemma gasped.

Bobby and Diane smothered a smile, and Will openly laughed… until his sister glared at him.

Matt released his grip on the chair arms – the furniture had suffered enough. 'Seems to me they've got it all. Plus, they're in love, they want to get married. What else is there? Sounds near pretty damn perfect to me.'

'But—'

'And the more you resist,' he cut Gemma off, 'the more you risk losing your son. Because if he's forced to choose between you lot and the love of his life, I don't like your chances.'

Their shocked faces said it all. They hadn't thought of that.

Gemma's hand went to her cheek. 'Our son would never cut us out of his life.'

Matt shrugged and reached for his beer. 'Push him hard enough and he might.'

Zac picked up the overturned chair and sat down, looking resolute. 'I'm doing this, whether you approve or not. I'd prefer it if you were on board, but it's happening either way.' His statement might have had more impact if his voice hadn't wobbled, but Matt admired the lad for standing his ground.

Matt knocked back the dregs of his beer and stood up. 'Time to head off. As nice as that barbeque smells, something tells me I'm not a welcome addition to the party.'

No one disagreed.

Diane nudged her daughter, forcing her to grumble under her breath. 'Er… right, yes… stay if you like.' She turned to her husband, looking for confirmation. 'Right, Chris?'

Chris nodded half-heartedly.

How sincere. 'Thanks, but I'd better head off.' Avoidance was the best tactic when dealing with Chris. 'See you all at the wedding.'

They collectively flinched. Sometimes it was more fun to land a blow with words. He walked off, leaving a sea of unhappy faces in his wake.

Zac ran after him. 'Thanks, Uncle Matt. I owe you big time.' He gave him a hug. 'Your support means everything.'

Matt patted his back. 'No worries, mate.'

'It'll be fun, right? Planning the wedding?' Zac looked hopeful.

'Sure. A blast.'

'And don't forget we have Megan's sister helping us.'

How could he forget.

On cue, his phone pinged. *Why haven't you replied with the information? I need the info pronto.*

Jesus, give him a chance, he'd been mediating family arguments all afternoon. He typed in a reply. *Will send ASAP. Busy at the moment.*

Don't forget.

Yep, his first impression of Beth Lawrence was that she was focused, driven and one of life's achievers. He doubted she ever lacked confidence, and she was probably a tyrannical boss in the workplace. She was also prickly, combative and scary as hell, and not the kind of woman you wanted to piss off.

The fact that she was gorgeous didn't help, as it only added to the torment. He imagined she was the kind of ball-busting female who didn't tolerate fools easily and probably viewed most men with disdain.

Luckily for him, he wasn't interested in winning her over. She was far too high-maintenance for his liking, and nothing dented a man's ego more than a woman who looked at him like he was something nasty attached to the bottom of her shoe.

He preferred a quiet life. No drama and no stress. And Beth Lawrence was not a restful person. Of that he was certain.

# Chapter Six

There was a lot Connie had given up since Kenneth had left her. Gousto home deliveries. Weekly Italian takeaways from Positano's. Two-hundred-quid bottles of Château La Fleur-Pétrus red wine. But the one thing she refused to relinquish was her spa membership. A woman could only be pushed so far.

Ducking under the cool water, she pushed her hands forwards, propelling her body through the grand ballroom pool. Soft lighting shimmered above, distorted by the ripple of water. She relished the sensation of weightlessness and quiet. Quiet that didn't dispel even when she broke the water's surface and took a deep breath. It was utter bliss.

Slowly and methodically, she glided across the pool, concentrating only on the rhythm of her breathing and the tension leaving her muscles.

She'd hadn't reacted well when Beth had confronted her about her excessive drinking. Denial had been her first response. Justification had been her second.

She was hurting. Drinking helped to ease the torment, giving her respite. It allowed her to forget her woes, leaving her mellow and relaxed… until the next morning, when she awoke with a raging hangover. Then the previous night's peaceful oblivion would shatter into a thousand pieces, as her thoughts tumbled back into her mind like a tsunami, reminding her that she'd been dumped, that she was alone and facing financial ruin.

Reluctantly, she'd decided that the nightly drinking had to stop.

Not because she agreed with her daughter's concerns that she was heading for alcoholism, but because she couldn't function with a hangover. She was a working woman now. Albeit as a doctor's receptionist, but she had to start somewhere. And for someone with no discernible qualifications or professional training behind them, starting at the bottom was inevitable. Painful, but inevitable.

She ducked under the water, completed her turn, and used the pool wall to propel herself forwards. Twenty-eight laps completed. No one could say she wasn't in good shape.

Swimming had always been enjoyable. She'd never taken to golf, like her husband, or tennis, like her girlfriends. But she could happily spend hours in the pool, completing length after length, and rewarding herself afterwards with a sauna and a dip in the jacuzzi.

After completing her thirty laps, she was satisfied that she'd burnt off the anxiety that plagued her body. It would be back tomorrow, disturbing her sleep and hampering her appetite, but for today it was gone.

Dragging herself from the pool, she dripped over to the sunbed and wrapped herself in one of the spa's fluffy towels that smelt faintly of citrus. It was warm and cosy, a comfort for her damp skin.

There was no one else in the pool so, for the moment, it was her own private slice of heaven. She loved coming here. It was a way of hanging on to the life she'd enjoyed for so many years, a life that had been cruelly ripped away from her.

But thinking about her situation would only ruin her equilibrium, so she took a deep breath and shook away her thoughts.

One day soon she would have to give up her membership. She wasn't naive enough to believe it could continue. Her part-time salary barely covered her weekly food shop, so there was no way it would extend to a six-thousand-pound annual spa membership.

She headed for the changing rooms, wishing she could turn back time. She'd tell her twenty-year-old self to focus on getting a career, instead of putting all her eggs into one giant motherhood-sized basket.

But having a family was all she'd ever wanted. Her dream was to have a husband, a home and several children. By the age of thirty-two her dream had come true and she had it all. Kenneth was starting to earn good money, and she was content to be a stay-at-home mum. That was what Kenneth had wanted, too.

Wrapping herself in one of the spa's guest robes, she headed for the Sensory Room, intending to indulge in a short nap before lunch.

There had been times over the years when she'd debated taking up a career. The idea of teaching had always appealed, but the motivation had never been that strong. She was busy running a home, supporting Kenneth's career and taxiing the kids to various extra-curricular activities – a job would have got in the way. So she'd busied herself with local charitable events, joined various social clubs and enjoyed weekly trips to the spa.

Of course, if she'd known that her husband of thirty-nine years would bugger off and leave her once she was past her prime, she might have devised a better plan. She would have forged a career and earned her own income, so she wouldn't be left at the mercy of a man who no longer had her best interests at heart.

Hindsight was a wonderful thing, but not something she'd been blessed with.

The sound of a giggle greeted her as she left the pool changing rooms. Someone was having a nice time. A very nice time, by the sounds of it.

Glancing over her shoulder, Connie wondered who the lucky woman was… only to discover it was her husband's floozy, Tiffany.

What the hell was she doing here?

The shock sent her off balance. So much so that her disposable slippers lost their grip on the damp surface and the next thing she knew, her body slid inelegantly to a heap on the floor, her forehead smacking against the marble pillar as she did so.

Mortified at the thought of Tiffany seeing her sprawled on the ground, she scrambled behind the pillar, where she hid, praying that nobody had witnessed her tumble.

Tiffany let out another giggle. This was followed by the sound of a man's mumbled voice and another peal of laughter.

Connie shifted slightly, so she could peer around the pillar.

The man with Tiffany was Kenneth. Of course it was. Why was she even surprised?

Her husband of nearly four decades. The father of her three children. The man who'd promised her the world and then buggered off when someone more enticing had come along.

And now, the cruellest act of all, he'd brought his new bit of fluff to their special place. The place where they'd drunk champagne and celebrated anniversaries. The place where they'd flirted in the hot tub and enjoyed couples massages. The place where they'd savoured adult alone time, away from the kids.

But instead of treasuring those memories and showing an ounce of respect for their time together, he was sullying it all by bringing his new girlfriend here.

She wanted to kill him.

Both of them.

Her newly manicured nails scratched the marble tiling beneath her, as she thumped her head rhythmically against the pillar. The muscles in her neck contracted, the skin on her arms tightening.

So much for a relaxing spa day. She was a coiled spring.

'Are you all right, madam?'

Startled, she looked up.

A member of staff was looking down at her, a puzzled expression on his face. 'Do you need medical assistance?'

'Shush! Keep your voice down.'

He looked alarmed. 'Is everything okay, madam?'

'No, everything's not okay. Have they gone?'

'Has who gone?'

Connie jerked her head back. 'The man and woman who were just standing there.'

He glanced to where she'd indicated. 'There is no one there now.'

'Are you sure?'

'I'm positive. Can I help madam up?' He offered her his hand.

She took it and let him pull her upright. 'Thank you.'

'You're entirely welcome. May I be of any further assistance?'

'No, thank you. I'm fine.' She kept her back to the pillar, glancing surreptitiously around it to check that the man wasn't lying.

'Does madam require me to call security?'

'Yes.' Tiffany should be arrested and thrown out. They both should. But then she realised she had no grounds to have them expelled from the premises. 'On second thoughts… no, that won't be necessary.'

'Is madam quite sure?' Which translated to: 'Is madam quite sane?'

She ignored the implication. 'I'm fine. Really. Just a dizzy spell, too long in the sauna.'

'Then may I suggest one of our relaxation rooms. I can recommend the Sensory Room, a tranquil place to recover. Do you need me to escort you there?'

'No, I can make my own way.' She moved away, fearful he was about to call for an assessment of her state of mind. 'Thank you again for your help.'

'Not at all. Have a very pleasant day.'

Connie rubbed her sore scalp, checking that the coast was clear before moving away from the pillar. She darted across to the next pillar and hid behind it, checking her surroundings. Satisfied she was safe, she moved to the next pillar. Kenneth and Tiffany were nowhere to be seen, but she couldn't be too careful.

Then she realised the member of staff was still watching her. His hand was resting on his walkie-talkie, as though he was about to call for backup.

Forcing a smile, she moved away nonchalantly and, more significantly, trying her hardest to appear sane. This was what Kenneth had done to her. She was losing her marbles.

She was also torn. Part of her wanted to run, flee to the changing rooms, pack up her things and escape. A smaller part of her wanted to say 'to hell with them' and continue with her visit, devour a nice lunch and take a long nap in the oxygen bubble. But the biggest part of her wanted more info. Why were they here? Was it a day trip? A one-off visit? Or had Kenneth taken out membership for Tiffany?

This last thought stung like no other.

It was bad enough that she'd been replaced in his bed, but taking away her spa membership was another crime entirely. A much bigger sin.

Connie went into the changing rooms and secured a towel around her head. She dug out her large dark sunglasses and put them on. Along with her generic robe and slippers, her disguise was complete, and she could carry out surveillance undetected.

Checking the corridor was empty, she exited the changing rooms and headed for the outdoor pool. She felt like an MI5 agent searching for Russian traitors as she scanned the area, her back to the wall, looking for potential assailants.

No sign of them.

She searched the hot tubs and jacuzzis. Nothing.

The Tepidarium next. Empty.

The spa had twenty-three individual treatment rooms. If they were inside one of those, she'd never track them down. But that wasn't enough to deter her – sauna and steam room next. No Kenneth or Tiffany. Where were they? Had they left?

And then she heard that giggle again.

Connie slid over to the door of the nail bar and peeked in. Tiffany was having a manicure. Her dyed dark red hair was bouncy and shiny, and her terracotta fake tan made her glow. She was heavily made-up and wearing a Lycra red dress that hugged every curve.

'Everything okay, madam?'

Jesus! She wished people would stop creeping up on her.

The member of staff she'd encountered earlier was looking at her, his expression no less critical.

She rubbed her chest, her heart racing. 'I'm fine.'

'Are you planning to have a manicure?'

'I am,' she said, even though she'd already had one that morning.

She realised he was waiting for her to go inside the salon.

Lifting the collar of her fluffy robe and lowering her chin, she snuck inside and almost ran to the workstation behind where Tiffany was sitting.

With her back to the woman, she could overhear her conversation and might glean some vital information that could prove useful in her mission. Not that she knew what her mission was. But still. Information was power.

One of the nail technicians approached. 'Hello, my name's Lucy.' She sat down opposite. 'What can I do for you today?'

Connie adopted a deep voice and whispered, 'Manicure.'

The girl looked alarmed. 'Didn't I do your manicure this morning, Mrs Law—'

'Wasn't me.' She was such a liar. 'I'm Betty… Betty… er…' She couldn't think of a surname. 'Betty… Boothroyd.' Not ideal, but better than nothing. Connie just prayed the girl was too young to know who Betty Boothroyd was.

The girl took Connie's hands and looked at her freshly applied manicure.

'Chipped,' Connie said, pointing to where she'd clawed at the flooring.

'Shall I touch it up?' Lucy had clearly recognised Connie, but was discreet enough not to say anything.

'Do the whole thing, I don't like the colour.' The effort of putting on a strange voice was playing havoc with her throat.

'Would you like to choose a different shade?'

'You choose, I don't mind.' She glanced behind, checking that Tiffany hadn't spotted her.

Lucy pointed to the colour chart. 'How about a nice pale coral?'

Connie nodded.

While Lucy fetched the nail polish, Connie leant back in her chair, tuning into the conversation behind.

'Fed up with dating losers,' Tiffany was saying. 'Most of the men in Essex have no prospects or ambition. A girl needs security, a proper man who'll take care of her.'

A man like Kenneth, you mean?

It made Connie's blood boil. Tiffany didn't want Kenneth for any other reason than his money. Plus, he was old. Well, compared to Tiffany, anyway. The woman probably imagined bleeding him dry, burying him, inheriting his money and moving on to the next poor bugger.

Lucy returned with the nail polish. 'Been anywhere nice on your holidays this year, Mrs Law... er... I mean, Betty?'

Connie pointed to her throat. 'Infection. Can't talk.'

Lucy looked alarmed. 'Is it contagious?'

Connie shook her head. 'Not if I keep my mouth shut.'

Lucy didn't look overly happy, but began removing Connie's old polish.

With an excuse not to talk, Connie could refocus on the conversation behind her.

'My parents ran a betting shop,' Tiffany was saying, 'Cash rich, asset poor, as they say. Don't get me wrong, we had a good upbringing – my parents done right by us. But I wanted more, you know what I mean?'

Connie didn't hear the technician's reply.

'I know, right?' Tiffany let out another giggle. 'My first husband was a bookie, Vince. He used to work down at the races, made a fortune. Blew the lot on the stock market, stupid git.'

Tiffany had been married before?

This was news to Connie. Not that she knew much about the woman who'd replaced her. But still. Was Kenneth aware of this?

'That weren't why I divorced him, though. He was a randy sod, chased anything in a skirt. I weren't having it. My man needs to keep it in his pants, I can't stand cheaters.'

What a hypocrite! Tiffany had happily adopted the role of the 'other woman' when she'd set her sights on Kenneth, hadn't she? So much for hating cheaters. She was the biggest cheat going.

'Betty?' Lucy was talking to her.

'Sorry, what…' Connie cleared her throat. She'd forgotten to lower her voice. 'Sorry, what?'

'Could you relax your hand?' She nodded to Connie's bunched fist.

Connie uncurled her fingers. 'Sorry.'

Behind her, Tiffany was still talking. 'My second husband owned a nightclub, Foxy's. Do you know it? Posh place in Dagenham. That's where I started my career as an exotic dancer. Until Brian got jealous of all the men paying me attention. It's me or them, babe, he'd say. Course at first, I chose him, before I realised how much cash I was losing. So it was bye-bye, Brian.' She let out another laugh.

Connie was reeling. Tiffany had two ex-husbands? Surely Kenneth didn't know about this? And was he aware she'd been an exotic dancer?

'Betty…? Er… Mrs Boothroyd?'

Connie startled. 'Sorry, what?'

'My hand. You're squeezing my hand.'

Connie looked down, she had poor Lucy in a death grip. 'Oh, I'm so sorry.'

Lucy extracted her hand and rubbed it.

What was she doing? This was crazy. Why was she torturing herself, listening to the ramblings of the woman who'd usurped her? It wasn't helping, it was driving her nuts.

It was time to go.

'Apologies, Lucy. I'm not in the right frame of mind for a manicure. Maybe another time.'

'Whatever you say, Mrs Law... er... Mrs Boothroyd. You take care now.'

Connie got up, managing to knock over the polish, bang into the table and draw unwanted attention to her flustered state. 'Sorry, not feeling so good. Need to lie down.' She ran from the room, head down, tears descending... and smacked straight into Kenneth.

'Connie? What on earth are you doing here?' He tried to grab her, but she shoved him away. 'Hey, calm down. What's got into you?'

'What's got into me?' She shoved him again, hating the way his green shirt set off his brown eyes. 'I'll tell you what's got into me, you bastard!' She thumped his chest. 'Utter, utter, bastard!' How dare he stand there, looking all handsome and smelling divine, while she was a crumbling wreck.

Lucy appeared from the salon. 'Mrs Boothroyd? Betty? Are you okay?'

Kenneth looked confused. 'Who the hell is Betty?'

Connie screamed. Really screamed, like a proper banshee scream.

If she was faking a sore throat before, she wasn't now.

Aware of various staff appearing, and Tiffany saying, 'Why is that woman screaming, is she having a breakdown, or something?' – and knowing it was only a matter of time before security appeared and carted her off – she ran.

It was hardly an elegant exit. Her towel had slipped from her head, revealing damp matted hair. Her slippered feet slid on the marble flooring, threatening to send her flying. And the combination of crying and running made her breathing ragged and noisy.

77

When she finally reached the safety of the changing rooms, she barged into one of the toilet cubicles and locked the door behind her, dropping to her knees.

A wail escaped her.

She cried. Heaving, noisy, howling crying that wracked through her entire body.

So much for a nice relaxing morning.

# Chapter Seven

*Tuesday, 23rd April – 7 weeks till the wedding*

Beth loaded up the tea tray and headed upstairs to check on her mother. The Lawrence family home was eerily quiet, a far cry from years gone by when the place had been a bustle of noise and activity. Whether it was Megan acting out sketches, or Alex bashing out painful rhythms on his drum kit, there had always been chatter and noise.

Despite being the quiet one, Beth had enjoyed being part of an animated family. The background noise hadn't dented her ability to concentrate on reading or studying for an exam. In fact, it had helped prepare her for life as a solicitor, where she'd often had to fight for her share of the conversation or out-argue the opposing side. Battling with her siblings for peace and quiet had been a handy learning curve. So a silent family home was a strange anomaly, and one that unnerved her.

Still holding the tea tray, she kicked Alex's bedroom door. No response. She kicked harder, making the hinges rattle, until it eventually swung open.

Alex glared at her, headphones dangling from his ears. 'What?'

'Tea,' she said, recoiling as a waft of weed hit her senses.

'Oh, right. Cheers.' Alex took the mug, snatched up a few biscuits and slammed the door in her face. And she'd thought smoking pot was supposed to chill a person.

There was no way Alex would have been allowed to smoke in the house before the break-up – her parents would have hit the roof – but this was yet another effect of their split. Her dad was no longer around to lay down the law and her mum no longer cared enough to fight.

In an ideal world, Beth would try talking to her brother about his lack of ambition and slovenly lifestyle, but she had enough on her plate trying to contend with her mother's fragile emotional state and organising her sister's wedding. Not that her interference would have been welcomed anyway. Alex wasn't open to changing his ways, and Beth didn't have the energy for another battle.

Heading down the landing, she paused outside her mother's room. 'Mum, are you awake? I've made tea.'

A weak voice called out, 'Come in.'

Beth released the door handle with her elbow and entered the bedroom. 'Are you feeling any better?'

'Not really.' Her mother was lying on the bed, wearing a pair of her dad's old pyjamas. Her hair was unwashed and matted, and she had a sleep mask pushed onto her forehead. Despite it still being light outside, the curtains were drawn, and the air was tinged with a combination of stale perfume and musty breath.

Beth placed the tray on the bedside cabinet. 'Do I need to call the doctor?'

Her mother shook her head. 'I'm not ill, it's in here that I'm sick,' she said, rubbing her chest for dramatic effect.

Beth checked her mother's temperature. There were no signs of a fever, but nonetheless it wasn't normal for a person to spend four days in bed.

She'd become aware of her mum's meltdown at the spa last Friday when her dad had called her on Saturday morning and recounted a bizarre tale involving her mother running from security guards and calling herself Betty Boothroyd.

It was only when her dad had casually mentioned that Tiffany had also been at the spa that things had started to make sense. No wonder her mother had had a meltdown – what was her father thinking? Leaving her mother was cruel enough, but rubbing her face in it was a step too far. But he seemed oblivious to the hurt he continued to inflict.

'Can you sit up, Mum?' Beth flicked on the side lamp, making her mother blink from the sudden light. 'You need to have something to eat.'

'I can't face food.'

'You can manage a digestive, surely.'

Her mother rolled away. 'You have no idea how much it hurts.'

Beth rubbed her mum's back. 'It's not like I haven't had my heart broken, too. It's rubbish, but spending all day in bed isn't going to make you feel any better.'

'I'm different to you, I feel things. When Hughie left, you barely shed a tear.'

Beth flinched. That wasn't true at all, she just hadn't cried in public. In private, she'd bawled her eyes out.

She'd met Hughie at university, where they'd studied together, graduated together and ended up moving in together. It had all been very easy and companiable. No great dramas, lovers' spats or heightened make-up sessions, like some of her friends had experienced. Their relationship had been based on friendship, mutual respect and a desire to forge successful careers.

It was only when Hughie started working in London that everything changed. Quiet country living was no longer enough for him. He began partying, and meeting new and exciting people, and he became disenchanted with his safe and 'boring' little life.

When he'd finally left, Beth had been bereft. Partly because she genuinely hadn't wanted the relationship to end, but also because she'd felt aggrieved. She'd known the relationship wasn't the most dynamic of affairs. They hadn't enjoyed a wild sex life, or been overly slushy or romantic, but she'd accepted that. She'd compromised having a satisfying physical relationship for stability and security. She'd thought they both had. Turned out she was wrong.

She glanced at her watch. It was gone seven o'clock, and she was meeting Zac and Matt Hardy at half-past to discuss wedding plans. 'Come on, Mum. Please sit up and eat something. I can't leave until I know you've at least had some fluids.'

She wasn't sure which appealed the least, tending to her heartbroken mother or meeting up with a man she'd taken an instant disklike to. At least Zac would be there to soften the blow. Zac had tasked them with finding a suitable wedding venue, and she was excited to show him her presentation. With any luck, her dealings with Matt Hardy would be limited and fleeting.

Her mother shuffled up the bed and slumped against the headboard. 'Did I tell you that Tiffany is twice divorced?'

'You did, Mum.' Beth repositioned the pillow behind her mum's head.

'And that she was an exotic dancer at a nightclub?'

'That too.' Her mum's tear-streaked face had Beth reaching for the tissues.

'How am I supposed to compete with that?'

'You don't,' she said, dabbing her mum's wet cheeks with a tissue. 'And you shouldn't even try. You're far superior, Mum. Don't ever think otherwise.'

'Then why did your father leave me for her?'

Beth flinched. 'Because he's a fool. At some point he'll realise that.'

'You think he'll come back to me?'

Beth's heart sank. 'Is that what you really want, Mum? After all he's done?'

Her mum blew her nose. 'Some days it is, other days I want to cut off his balls with a bread knife.'

Beth didn't think either scenario would be in her mum's best interests, or her dad's, come to think of it. 'Whatever Dad does in the future is down to him. He's made his bed, as they say. The important thing is for you to focus on your life and what you want.'

'I don't know what I want.'

She stroked her mum's hair. 'But you will. Maybe not anytime soon, but at some point you'll want to move on and you'll realise there's another life out there waiting for you. Another man, even. Someone who'll appreciate you and make you happy again.' She handed her mum her tea. 'You're quite a catch, you know?'

'I don't feel like a catch. I feel old, and useless, and undesirable.'

'That's because your confidence has been knocked. It'll take a while to recover, but you'll bounce back.'

'You didn't.'

It took Beth a moment to find her voice. 'Choosing to be alone is a valid choice, Mum.'

'So you keep saying.' Her mum reached for the remote and switched on *The One Show*, a not-so-subtle hint that she was done talking.

Beth stood up, it was time to leave. 'I hope you have a better night, and don't forget you're meeting with the solicitor tomorrow.' When her mum didn't answer, Beth tried again. 'I said—'

'I heard you. I'll be there.'

'Good.' It was important her mum received solid professional legal advice to ensure a fair settlement. Beth picked up the empty tea tray. 'I'll call you tomorrow to see how you got on.' Again, no reply. 'Mum, I said—'

'I heard you. Now go, I'm watching the telly.'

With a sigh, Beth headed into the hallway and went downstairs, not entirely convinced that her mum was of sound mind, but satisfied she wasn't about to do anything stupid. At least, she hoped not.

Locking the front door behind her, she climbed into her car, needing a moment to process her thoughts before driving off. Why hadn't she bounced back from heartbreak, as her mother had so unhelpfully pointed out? She wasn't entirely sure she knew the answer.

It was a lovely spring evening, and as she drove through the village, she admired the huge rhododendrons lining the country lanes surrounding Godalming. The sight helped to cheer her a little, as she reflected on her situation.

Two years after splitting from Hughie, she'd met Owen. Funny, charming, flirtatious and fiery Owen, who'd captivated everyone, including her family, and had seemed like the perfect man. But underneath the polished façade were a few less attractive qualities. Vanity, deceit and selfishness beyond reason. Eighteen months into their relationship she'd discovered the existence of Sarah, his childhood sweetheart back in Wales, who he'd never actually broken up with, and who fully expected him to return to his home town at some point and marry her. Something which only came to light when one of Owen's school friends had visited London and drunkenly spilled the beans about his 'long-term fiancée'.

Beth had immediately broken things off. There was no way she was going to accept his pathetic explanation of Sarah being his 'backup' in case he never found anyone better. Talk about callous, not to mention the utter cruelty of stringing them both along for so long. But there was another factor lurking beneath, which had taken her a while to reconcile – the fact that she hadn't really liked Owen very much.

She'd fancied him and she'd had fun with him, but she'd never really *liked* him. Rather ashamedly, the lure of great sex had kept her interested – a trait she didn't find very appealing about herself. He might have used her, but she'd used him, too, and it wasn't a pleasant feeling.

Consequently, she no longer trusted herself to make logical decisions when it came to relationships. She deliberately steered clear of men she didn't fancy, as she had no desire to become embroiled with another Hughie, and actively avoided men she *did* fancy in case they turned out to be another Owen. Which really only left one option. Staying single.

Turning into the car park of The Stag on the River, she slowed her speed. The last thing she needed was another car park altercation with Matt Hardy.

His SUV was parked by the main gate, so she headed for the opposite side, just to be safe.

Exiting her car, she collected her laptop bag from the boot and smoothed down her suit skirt, checking her reflection in the car window. Not that she cared what Matt Hardy thought of her, but the last time she'd encountered him she'd been covered in spilt tea, and even though he'd been the cause of that, she didn't want to turn up dishevelled a second time.

With her hair secured, her jacket buttoned-up and her chin held high, she headed towards the pub, wobbling slightly as her court shoes sank into the gravel car park.

It took a while for her eyesight to adjust from the bright evening sunlight outside to the dark period building, with its low beams and dark wood panelling. Ordering herself a white wine at the bar, she scanned the area, but couldn't see either Zac or Matt. They must be in the garden.

Outside was a lot busier than inside, with an array of tables covering the expanse of lawn leading down to the Wey River, where large willow trees trailed seductively in the water. Shielding her eyes from the sun, her gaze settled on a man waving at her. Matt Hardy.

Ignoring the frisson of unease filling her belly, she made her way towards him, slaloming around the busy tables and wondering where Zac was.

As she neared him, Matt stood up, reaching for her as if he intended to kiss her.

She recoiled and extended a hand. 'Good evening, Mr Hardy. I hope you're well.'

He raised an eyebrow. 'That's how you want to play this?' He accepted the offer of her hand and gently squeezed, sending a jolt of something hot and liquid racing up her arm. And she'd thought shaking hands would be less intimate?

'It's not like we know each other,' she said, trying to regain her composure.

'Maybe not, but this isn't a business meeting,' he said, his eyes travelling over her grey suit. 'Even if you are dressed for one.'

'I've come straight from work,' she said, defensively. 'I work very long hours.'

'So you said.'

She narrowed her eyes. 'Meaning?'

'Meaning nothing. You just look like someone who's very work-focused.'

'There's nothing wrong with that.'

'Nothing at all.' He gestured to the bench seat. 'Shall we sit down?'

Beth placed her wine glass on the table, and then realised she was going to have to lift her leg over the seat while wearing a tight skirt.

Matt offered her his hand. 'Need help?'

'I'm fine, thanks.' She placed her laptop bag on the table, before discreetly easing her skirt up a few inches so she could straddle the bench seat. It wasn't the most elegant of manoeuvres, and she had to hold on to the table to stop herself from toppling backwards.

Matt Hardy watched her with a bemused expression on his face, his gaze occasionally drifting to her exposed knees. He waited until she was seated, before sidling in next to her. 'Did you receive the finalised guest list and budget okay?'

Why on earth hadn't he sat opposite? There wasn't enough room for them to sit side by side. And why did he have to be so large? But then she supposed Zac needed somewhere to sit, so she begrudgingly accepted his close proximity. 'I did receive the information, yes.'

'Thanks for setting up the gift list. It looks great.'

'Don't mention it.'

His smile made her instantly wary. 'Knowing how busy you are, I wouldn't want you to think I didn't appreciate it.'

'Er… thank you.' She allowed her gaze to linger a little on his blue eyes, just in case he wasn't being as sincere as he made out.

Unlike her, he was casually dressed. He was wearing dark blue jeans and a faded light blue denim short-sleeved shirt. The top three buttons were undone, revealing a glimpse of chest hair and a thin silver chain around his neck. As the breeze kicked up, it sent a waft of masculine scent in her direction and she experienced another jolt of unwelcome heat.

Clearing her throat, she averted her gaze and unzipped her laptop bag. 'Has Zac been delayed?'

'Zac's in Greece,' he replied, as nonchalantly as if he'd said, 'Zac's at the bar getting a drink.'

She turned to him. 'Greece? As in… the country Greece?'

He gave her a quizzical look. 'Is there another kind of Greece?'

'Well, no… but what's he doing in Greece?'

'Visiting Megan.'

Beth felt herself frown. 'She didn't tell me.'

'She didn't know.'

'How could she not know?'

'It was a surprise.' He picked up his beer and took a long sip, which drew Beth's eyes to his lips. 'Apparently, they had a tearful conversation on Sunday night about how much they missed each other, so he decided to surprise her by flying out there today.'

'Oh, right.' Beth booted up her laptop, rather alarmed by the news and struggling to drag her eyes away from Matt's mouth. 'How long does he intend to stay in Greece?'

He shrugged, making the bench seat wobble with his substantial bulk. His wide shoulders were quite distracting. 'Who knows?'

'But we're supposed to be planning the wedding? We have less than seven weeks before the big day, how can he just leave like that? Doesn't he realise how much needs organising?'

'I think he felt seeing Megan was more important.'

'More important than planning his own wedding?'

He gave a half-hearted shrug. 'Love makes people do foolish things. Haven't you ever done anything irrational in the name of love?'

'Certainly not.' Reaching for her wine, she took a large slug, wondering why she couldn't quite quench her thirst. Without Zac present to soften the effect of this man-mountain, the atmosphere between them was alarmingly different. She tried to regroup. 'I guess we could reschedule our meeting, but the venue needs to be confirmed – they won't hold the booking past this weekend. I don't think we can afford to wait.'

'I agree.' Matt took another sip of beer, and she averted her gaze so she wouldn't be distracted by the movement of his throat when he swallowed. 'Zac said he's happy for us to go ahead with any ideas we come up with.'

'So we're just supposed to go ahead and plan a wedding without either the bride or the groom being involved?'

'Looks that way.'

'It's absolutely ludicrous.' She fanned her face, warm from the glare of the early evening sun. At least, she was pretty sure it was the sun making her warm. 'I've a good mind to tell them to plan their own damn wedding. I mean, can you imagine the fallout if we get this wrong?'

He nodded. 'We'll never live it down.'

'We could cause a divorce before they've even got married.'

He grinned. 'At least they have a divorce lawyer on hand to deal with the split.'

She sighed. 'I'm glad you think this is funny.'

'I don't, but there's no point stressing,' he said, reaching for his beer again. 'It is what it is. They've left us to arrange their wedding, and they'll just have to accept whatever we come up with. What other choice do they have?'

She removed her steamed-up glasses and wiped them using her cleaning cloth. 'None, unfortunately.'

He nodded to her jacket. 'If you're hot, why don't you remove your jacket?'

'I'm perfectly capable of regulating my temperature, thank you.'

He lifted his hands in mock surrender. 'I was only trying to help.'

'Well, don't.' Shoving her glasses back on, she took another sip of wine, trying not to give in to his suggestion and remove her jacket, however much she wanted to. 'I suppose we might as well proceed with the presentations.'

He raised an eyebrow. 'Presentations?'

'You know, the presentations for our respective pitches?'

His gaze turned puzzled. 'We're not negotiating the purchase of an oil company.'

'No, but we've been asked to come up with ideas for the big day.'

'Ideas, yeah, not a flipping...' he gestured to her laptop, 'marketing presentation.'

'So you have nothing prepared?'

'Sure, I do.' He tapped the side of his head. 'In here.'

'How very informal of you.' Returning to her laptop, she typed in her password.

'Next you'll be telling me you've created a spreadsheet.' His teasing tone did nothing to ease her rattled state, especially as she *had* created a spreadsheet. The wedding planning website strongly recommended it.

Clicking on the wedding folder, her master checklist spreadsheet popped up on the screen.

His eyes grew wide. 'Oh, my, god. You have created a spreadsheet?'

She turned to glare at him. 'If you've quite finished.' Turning back to her laptop, she double-clicked on her PowerPoint presentation. The first slide showed a photo of a tiny church nestled in a small hamlet within Bodmin Moor. 'The Knights Templar,' she said, referring to her notes. 'Built in the twelfth century, a grade II listed building, secluded enough to be remote, but within a short drive from the A30.'

He squinted at the photo. 'Do they want a church wedding?'

She shrugged. 'I assume so.'

'Bodmin Moor? That's Cornwall, right? Why so far away?'

'That leads me on to my next slide.' She clicked the page. 'The main venue. The Jamaica Inn, also located in Bodmin Moor.'

A selection of images appeared in a slide show. First the large pirate-ship sign outside the building, followed by the sumptuous four-poster bed in the bridal suite, and finishing with the lavish period-designed banqueting area.

She waited for him to say something positive, or at least nod his approval, but instead he frowned and said, 'It's a bit... gothic, isn't it?'

'Gothic? Of course not. It's romantic.'

He raised an eyebrow. 'That's your idea of romantic?'

She sighed. Dealing with a Neanderthal was such exhausting work. 'It's a recreation of the inn in Daphne du Maurier's classic novel.'

'Still not getting the romance.'

'It was my sister's favourite novel when she was young. She studied it for A Level English literature.'

He didn't look convinced. 'And?'

'And, as she's now an actress, I thought it would be a nice nod to her favourite childhood story and her current profession.' She clicked on the next slide. 'Plus, it has a museum, a gift shop and the option to wear period dress from the era.'

'Fancy dress?' He looked appalled.

'Not fancy dress, period dress.'

'Same thing.'

'Not the same thing. Fancy dress is not classy.'

'Neither is dressing up as a pirate smuggler.'

She bit her tongue. 'They have walking tours across Bodmin Moor and organised games for evening entertainment.'

He shook his head. 'Why would we want that?'

'For the stag and hen dos.'

He looked incredulous. 'You think Zac wants a stag do involving organised games and visiting a stuffy museum?'

'I thought it would be fun.'

'For who?'

'Well, for everyone. Megan would love it. I would, too.'

'This is your idea of fun?'

She bristled. 'Yes.'

'Bloody hell.' He scratched his bearded chin.

She clicked on the next slide, her enthusiasm rapidly waning. 'The package includes a three-course meal, a string quartet and an evening buffet. I opted out of the disco.'

'Why?'

'Discos are tacky.'

'God forbid we chose anything tacky.' He took a slug of beer.

Was he being sarcastic?

Beth's blood began to boil. She'd spent hours on this presentation, she didn't need Matt Hardy criticising her every suggestion. 'What's your idea then?' She folded her arms, determined to be as derisive about his plans as he'd been about hers. 'I can't wait to hear what you deem to be *romantic*. I'm assuming it involves strippers?'

He gave her a loaded look. 'Do I look stupid?'

'Well—'

He lifted his hand. 'Okay, I walked into that one. No strippers, but also nothing so... theatrical,' he said, nodding at her laptop. 'I was thinking a small intimate venue, maybe in a barn or a marquee, with lantern lighting, displays of wild flowers and a swing band.'

Beth had wanted so much to laugh at his suggestions and dismiss his idea, but in truth, it sounded lovely. She wasn't about to admit as much, instead forcing a short laugh. 'And that's your idea of romantic, is it?'

'It is, yes.' He held her gaze, and once again she felt something shift beneath her.

Thankfully, her phone rang, preventing her from relinquishing her carefully thought-out plans for a period-themed wedding.

'It's Megan,' she said, lifting the phone to her ear.

Maybe she should ask her sister which option she'd prefer? But that would be telling the bride – something she wasn't supposed to do.

'Hi, Megan.' She angled herself away from the hulk next to her. 'How's Greece?'

A loud sob reverberated down the line. 'Poor Zac… I don't want to hurt him… I love him.' Hiccup. Was her sister drunk?

'Megan? What's wrong? Has something happened to Zac?'

Matt looked alarmed. 'What's wrong?'

Beth shushed him so she could hear her sister.

'It's me that's the problem,' her sister slurred. 'I'm evil.'

Oh, crikey, what had Megan done? 'What are you on about?'

'I love him.'

'I know you do.' Beth's pulse rate picked up. 'What's the problem?'

'It was a long time ago. I was young and foolish… but he needs to know.'

'What does he need to know?'

Her sister sobbed louder. 'Lovely… kind… sweet… loyal Zac.'

'What does Zac need to know, Megan?'

'It'll break his heart.'

'Megan, you're scaring me. What does Zac need to know?'

Pause. 'I'm already married.'

A stunned silence followed.

Megan burst into hysterical tears and ended the call.

Beth's mouth dropped opened. Her sister was already married? But who to? And when? And why was this the first she was hearing about it?

Matt was frowning at her. 'What's happened? What does Zac need to know?'

Oh, hell. Beth swallowed awkwardly. 'Er... that Megan... well, she's drunk.'

'Drunk?'

'Yes, drunk. Absolutely plastered. Completely inebriated.'

'And that's a problem because?'

'Because... Zac's never seen her drunk before and she didn't know he was coming. Like you said, it was a surprise... and now Zac's turned up unannounced... and she's... well, she's drunk.' Even to her own ears it sounded ridiculous.

He didn't look like he believed her. She could hardly blame him, she was babbling rubbish. She knocked back her wine and stood up.

He looked alarmed. 'You're leaving?'

'I have other plans. Sorry.' She shoved her laptop in its bag.

'But we haven't decided on whose idea we're going with.'

'We're going with mine, obviously.' Assuming there was actually going to be a wedding. What were the charges for bigamy? As a solicitor she should really know. 'It's the more developed plan, and we don't have time to source the kind of venue you're talking about.'

She yanked up her skirt so she could step over the bench seat, giving Matt an eyeful of her thighs. Unfortunately, she had to grab his shoulder to steady herself. His shoulder was warm and solid, which for some reason didn't help her balance issues.

'The Jamaica Inn is free on the weekend of the ninth of June,' she said, grabbing her laptop bag. 'I've made a temporary booking, so I'll phone tomorrow and confirm everything.'

'Can we at least chat about the other details? What about your checklist?'

'Another time. Sorry. Must go.' She almost fell over the table in her haste to escape. 'Bye. Chat soon. Good meeting!'

'I still don't think your idea is very romantic!' he called after her.

Sod romance. She had bigger things to worry about.

Like the bride already being married!

# Chapter Eight

*Saturday, 27th April – 6 weeks till the wedding*

Matt had always disliked clothes shopping. His bulk meant that he was too big for most places and kept knocking into people, forever apologising, and frequently banging his elbows on railings and knocking items of clothing off their hangers, incurring the wrath of the shop assistants. And that's before even trying the clothes on. With a forty-eight-inch chest, it was a job finding clothes that fitted, especially when everything these days was labelled 'slim fit'. Even as a kid, he'd never been a 'slim fit', wearing adult clothing from the age of eleven.

Suffice to say, he was less than enthused to be pounding the streets of Aldershot with his mother and sister, shopping for outfits for a wedding he wasn't even sure was going ahead.

The last discussion he'd had about the wedding was on Tuesday night, when Beth had gone from presenting her ideas to running off after receiving a call from Megan, leaving him confused and with no idea what the hell was going on.

He'd tried messaging her, but she'd been too busy to chat. He had no idea whether she'd even booked the venue. Zac had no idea, either. He was still sunning himself in Greece with his fiancée and seemingly perfectly happy to let Matt pick up the slack. Which was infuriating enough without Beth going quiet on him, too. How on earth was he supposed to plan the wedding on his own?

Susan Hardy emerged from the changing room wearing the lilac dress she'd selected from the 'pre-loved' rail, having nearly fainted at the prices of the new outfits in the large department store. Her shoulder-length brown hair had an inch of grey roots showing, and her face looked drawn and tired, but she managed a smile as she lifted her arms. 'What do you think?'

Leah nodded her appreciation. 'Pretty. And the length is good, it shows off your legs.'

'The lace is lovely,' his mum said, running her fingers over the material. 'What do you think, Matt?' She gave him an expectant look.

'It's a bit big, isn't it?' he answered honestly, incurring an evil glare from his sister. 'Well, it is.'

His mother had lost weight and her collarbones were visible beneath her pale skin. A symptom of working too many hours and stressing over money, no doubt.

'Only around the middle,' she replied, gathering in the excess material. 'I can always take it in.'

Matt hated the idea of his mum taking on another chore, she worked too many hours as it was. Even this morning she'd been at work, accepting the offer of an extra shift at the Co-op to fund today's shopping excursion. It broke his heart.

Unfortunately, along with a strong work ethic and determination to be self-reliant, his mum's inherent pride meant she refused any offers of financial help. Matt did his best to surreptitiously pay the odd bill or turn up at the house with a bag of shopping to boost supplies, but his efforts were rarely appreciated and usually resulted in causing offence, so he had to tread carefully.

He suspected his mum's resistance came from a misguided sense of shame, as though she was somehow responsible for her current situation. But there was only one person to blame and he was currently banged up inside. No amount of reiterating that fact had any impact on persuading his mother to accept 'charity', as she called it.

'It fits just fine everywhere else,' she said, running her hand over the intricate design. 'And it comes with a matching hat and jacket, and all for under two hundred pounds.'

'You didn't prefer the other one?' Matt pointed to the silver dress hanging on the rail, a dress that had actually fitted her and made her look a lot livelier.

His mum shook her head. 'I'm not paying four hundred pounds for an outfit I'll only wear once,' she said, dismissing his opinion.

'I've offered to pay for it,' he said, knowing it was an argument he wouldn't win, but feeling the need to try. 'I'd rather you wear something you feel confident and happy in, than settle for a dress that isn't quite right.'

He was given a reprimanding look. 'You're not paying for my outfit,' she said, pointing a finger. 'Besides, I prefer this dress.'

He didn't believe her, but he knew better than to argue. 'Will you at least let me pay for the alterations?' He moved out of the way when an assistant tried to get past him, causing him to knock into the hat stand behind and nearly send it flying.

'We can talk about it later.' Which meant she wasn't about to relent, but she wasn't about to argue with him either, and she disappeared into the changing room, decision made.

Matt checked his phone. Still no word from Beth.

He sent her another message. *Why have you gone quiet on me? Have you booked the venue? What about extra rooms for the wedding party? If you're busy, tell me what needs doing. Don't ignore me.*

'Who're you texting?' Leah retrieved a Twix from her pocket and took a bite.

He shoved his phone in his pocket. 'No one.'

His sister gave him a sceptical look, but didn't push the matter further. Good. He wasn't in the mood for an interrogation.

'I'm glad Mum's found a dress she likes,' she said, munching on her chocolate bar. 'It's our turn next. Are you ready to get suited and booted?'

'Not really. Are you sure you don't want to be a bridesmaid, like Zac wanted?'

Leah gave him a loaded look. 'I'm sure.'

'It could be fun, wearing a nice dress?' He knew trying to persuade her was likely to result in another glare.

'How about this,' she said, offering him a finger of chocolate, which he refused, even though the smell made him salivate. 'I'll agree to be bridesmaid, if you do, too.'

'Funny.'

'If I'm expected to wear a frilly meringue of a dress, why shouldn't you?'

'It's tradition.'

'It's also known as society pigeonholing people into stereotypes. I'm female, so by default I must like dresses and having my hair curled.' She rolled her eyes and took another bite of chocolate. 'It would be a lot more fun if everyone switched gender roles for the wedding. Zac would make a fabulous bride. He has great bone structure.'

'True. But could you imagine Chris dressed as a woman?'

Leah nearly choked on her Twix. 'Oh, god. No one needs to see that. Not that you could pull it off, either,' she said, patting his chest. 'You'd look like that woman from *Harry Potter*. You know, the giant headmistress who falls in love with Hagrid. Olympe Maxime.'

'Yeah, not happening.'

'Well, that's the only way you're getting me in a bridesmaid dress. I'd rather remove my own spleen with a blunt spoon,' she said, chewing on the Twix.

No one could say he hadn't tried, and it wasn't like Zac didn't know about his aunt's feelings concerning gender stereotyping.

But for all his sister's outward confidence, he suspected it masked an underlying fear of rejection. It was the reason behind her reluctance to visit their dad. Leah had always been a tomboy, favouring boys' clothes and outdoor activities, and avoiding anything frilly or pink. But the transition from sporty child to full-blown member of the LGBTQ+ community wasn't something their dad was aware of, and he suspected that Leah wanted to keep it that way. Matt had often wondered if Leah's elimination of their dad from her life was an act of self-preservation – a way of rejecting him before he had the chance to reject her.

His phone pinged with a message. It was Beth. About bloody time.

> Sorry for radio silence. Really crappy week.
> Venue booked, inc. guest rooms. Hotel ours for
> entire weekend.

Well, that was something.

His mum appeared from the changing room, having reverted to her previous outfit of tired jeans and faded sweatshirt. 'What time is our appointment at Jasper Martin?' she said, heading for the tills.

'Half-four.' Matt unearthed his wallet, only to have his mother slap his hand away.

'Don't even think of it,' she said, giving him the maternal eye. 'I can afford an outfit for my only grandson's wedding.'

Suitably chastised, he closed his wallet, but it was hard to stand back and watch his mum struggle. Especially when the situation wasn't about to improve any time soon, even if his dad was accepted for early release. What employer would offer a fifty-seven-year-old man with a criminal record a job? More likely, his dad would soon be back home sponging off his wife and adding to her money woes, not improving them.

They headed for The Wellington Centre and arrived with a few minutes to spare for their appointment. Zac had requested evening suits for the wedding, as opposed to formal morning dress, which was a relief, as Matt couldn't imagine himself in a tailcoat.

They were greeted by a short man wearing old-fashioned half-moon spectacles and a red paisley waistcoat. His white hair and squinty eyes made him look like an elf, especially next to Matt's large frame. 'Good afternoon and welcome to Jasper Martin,' he said, scuttling over. 'You must be the Hardy party?'

Matt gestured to his family. 'I'm Matt Hardy. This is my mother, Susan, and my sister, Leah.'

The man checked his notebook. 'I have a booking for two fittings. Will Mr Hardy senior be joining us today?'

'Not unless he's escaped from prison,' Leah said, lifting an eyebrow.

Their mum forced a laugh. 'Leah, please. The nice gentleman won't know you're joking.'

The assistant's alarmed expression cleared. 'You had me worried for a moment.'

'The second suit is for Leah,' Matt said, glaring at his sister and fighting to hang on to his smile, which was quite a feat.

The assistant frowned. 'This young lady here?'

'Leah's one of the grooms for the wedding,' Matt said, praying the assistant didn't have antiquated opinions. 'Hopefully, you can accommodate us.'

Shaking his head in bewilderment, the assistant turned away. 'Follow me, if you would. Our formal evening jackets come in two colours, black or cream, and two styles, single-breasted or double-breasted.' He led them into a secluded alcove at the back of the shop. 'Although we are limited on sizes,' he said, giving Matt's wide frame the once-over. 'Does the groom have an opinion on which option he would like to go for?'

Matt realised the man assumed he was the groom. 'I'm the best man,' he said, already feeling self-conscious about his size. 'The groom has requested black evening suits, with a single-breasted jacket. I'll email you his measurements, as he's currently abroad.'

The assistant's gaze travelled over Matt's large tall frame, down to Leah's slim short frame. 'We may struggle to accommodate your unique sizing requirements, but I'll see what we have in our storeroom. Excuse me a moment.'

When the assistant left, Leah sighed. 'We're not that unusual, are we?'

Matt shrugged. '*Unique* was the word he used.'

'I suppose we should be flattered.' She went over to a line of suits and selected a peacock-blue jacket with large lapels. 'Who wants to be an off-the-peg size anyway?'

Matt did. He'd give anything to be a regular size.

Leah tried on the jacket, which hung off her like a tent. 'How do I look?'

'Like a Butlin's entertainment officer.'

She did a twirl. 'Hi-de-hi, campers!'

Laughing, he shrugged off his Harrington jacket and threw it over a chair. 'Have a seat, Mum. We may be a while.'

His mum sat down, wincing as she did so.

Concern tightened Matt's insides. 'Is your back playing up again?'

'A bit,' she said, forcing a smile. 'Nothing a hot bath won't cure. Has Megan chosen the bridesmaid's dress yet?'

'Lily's making Poppy's dress. Megan has left her sister to choose her own maid of honour dress.'

Leah came over. 'Ah, yes, the mysterious sister.'

Matt raised an eyebrow. 'Why mysterious?'

Leah shrugged. 'You've hardly said anything about her.'

'That's because I don't know anything about her. Other than she's a divorce lawyer and she's been roped into planning the wedding, same as me.'

'That's it?'

'That's it.'

His phone pinged with another message from Beth.

> Have some free time today if you want to touch base on wedding plans?

He was about to reply saying he was busy at the moment, but he accidentally pressed the video-chat icon. The next thing he knew, Beth's face appeared on the screen. Shit.

'That was quick,' she said, her face zooming into focus. 'I wasn't expecting a call right away.' He could see a large sash window behind her and stark white walls. He assumed she was in her office. 'Sorry I haven't been in touch, it's been a crazy week.'

He moved away from his sister, chastising himself for his error and not wanting to be overheard. He noticed dark circles under Beth's eyes, almost hidden behind her glasses. 'Everything okay?'

'Sure,' she said, unconvincingly, but then paused and let out a deep sigh. 'Actually, not really.'

He moved into the secluded alcove. 'Anything I can help with?'

'No, but thanks for asking. Have you spoken to Zac?'

'I spoke to him last night, and he's fine with your ideas for the wedding. Even the dressing-up bit.' Something which still confounded him.

'You weren't expecting him to agree?' Beth tilted her head, allowing a tendril of hair to fall across her cheek.

'He's obviously more in love with your sister than I realised.'

A ghost of a smile passed across her lips. 'He's smitten.'

'Crazy, huh?' Then he noticed that Beth's concerned expression had returned. 'Are you sure you don't want to tell me what's wrong? Is it about the wedding? Is Megan having second thoughts?'

'It's not that,' she said, shaking her head. 'Megan's desperate to marry Zac, nothing's going to stop her.'

'You make it sound like that's a bad thing.'

'It's not... or rather, it wouldn't be...' She removed her glasses and rubbed her eyes. 'Ignore me, I'm just tired. It's been a horrible week.'

The shop assistant returned, tutting disapprovingly when he saw Leah wearing the blue jacket. 'These garments are expensive,' he said, gesturing for her to take it off. 'They're not playthings.'

Beth must have heard him, because she said, 'Where are you?'

'Shopping for wedding outfits with my mum and sister.' He moved behind a rail of coats in the alcove, discreetly watching what was going on in the fitting area. His mum was still resting in the chair, and his sister was hanging up the blue jacket, having been told off by the assistant.

'That's surprisingly nice of you.'

Beth's voice drew him back to the screen. 'It is? Why?'

'Most men wouldn't take their mum and sister clothes shopping.'

'They wouldn't? Why not?'

She seemed to consider this. 'In my experience men don't enjoy shopping, and they enjoy hanging around waiting rooms while women try stuff on even less.'

'It doesn't matter whether I enjoy it or not. We all need wedding outfits, and neither my mum nor sister drive – it would be selfish of me not to take them.'

Beth's eyebrows lifted. 'Fair enough.'

Matt glanced up to find his sister looking at him through a gap in the coats. 'Who're you talking to?'

He gave Beth an apologetic smile. 'Sorry, got to go. Time for my suit fitting.'

'Oh, okay, but—'

Matt ended the call.

Leah tried to peer at his phone. 'Was that her?'

He pocketed his phone. 'Who?'

'The sister, Beth.'

'I'm needed for measuring,' he said, heading towards the assistant, who was now tapping his foot impatiently.

Leah wasn't that easily dissuaded and followed him. 'It was, wasn't it? Why are you being so cagey?'

Matt positioned himself in front of the assistant and lifted his arms so the man could measure his chest. 'I'm not.'

'Yes, you are. Why don't you want to talk about her?'

'There's nothing to say. I hardly know her.'

Leah perched on the arm of a chair. 'But you've met her. What's she like? Is she beautiful like Megan?'

The assistant visibly shuddered when he checked the reading on the tape measure. A reaction that did nothing to ease Matt's self-consciousness about his size. 'A bit, I guess.'

Matt conjured up an image of Beth. Grey business suit. Thick-rimmed glasses and an uptight attitude. And then he remembered those wide full lips and found himself swallowing awkwardly. Who was he kidding? Conservative clothing aside, she was stunning.

The assistant held out a jacket for him to try on. 'This is our largest size in store.'

It was like squeezing into a wetsuit. The stitching around the shoulders audibly creaked as he tried to button up the jacket, but it refused to meet in the middle and his confidence took another hit.

Oblivious to his humiliation, Leah tapped her lip in contemplation. 'What does she look like?'

Matt tried to stand his ground while the assistant tugged the jacket from his arms. 'Christ, Leah. Do we have to do this?' Her determined expression told him that resisting was futile. 'Fine. She's tall… slim… long brown hair.' He had a flashback from their meeting in the pub garden, 'and shapely knees.'

'Shapely knees?' Leah laughed.

He shook away the image of Beth hoisting up her skirt to straddle the bench seat. It was oddly distracting.

Leah grinned. 'Is she sexy?'

The idea of calling Beth sexy almost made him laugh. He could think of a dozen other ways to describe her, but sexy? No way. At least, not in a conventional way. Not in any way, in fact. Bad-tempered, definitely. Prickly and annoying, most certainly. But sexy?

'Why are you blushing?'

He startled. 'I'm not.'

'Your cheeks have gone red. You like her, don't you?'

Matt glanced down in time to witness the assistant's wide-eyed expression when he measured the circumference of Matt's thighs. 'Beth Lawrence is the most irritating woman I've ever met.'

The assistant straightened and measured Matt's neck, adding to Matt's insecurities. 'I'll need to order in a larger dress shirt,' he said, jotting down the numbers in his notepad. 'The trousers we can accommodate from our High & Mighty range. The cummerbund and bow tie are no problem, but you'll need to have a jacket specially made.'

It was official. He was a lard-arse. 'How much will that set me back?'

'I'll obtain a quote and email it to you.' He waved Matt away like he was an errant schoolboy and beckoned Leah over. 'Your turn, young lady.'

Leah grimaced as she got up, no doubt offended at being labelled a 'lady'.

As she allowed the assistant to measure her slim chest, she glanced over, intrigued. 'How is Beth irritating?'

Matt plonked himself down next to his mum, making the chair creak. 'She's like an itch you can't get rid of. We've met twice and both times we've ended up arguing.'

'Promising.' Leah winked at their mum, who smiled. 'Getting under your skin might not be such a bad thing.'

He looked between them. 'Are you kidding me? It's a sign I should stay well clear.'

Leah was handed a jacket to try on, which hung off her. 'Too big, right?'

'Far too big.' The assistant tutted. 'Our jackets are cut for the male physique, there's not much demand for evening suits for women.'

'Well, that's just plain sexist.' Leah shrugged off the jacket and looked over at Matt. 'I was thinking about this the other day. You've had three significant relationships, but each one ended disastrously.'

'I wouldn't say disastrously,' he replied, defensively.

'Alison left you for one of your rugby mates.'

'Thanks for reminding me.' Matt glared at his sister. 'Do we have to have this conversation here?' He nodded at the assistant, who was doing a lousy job of pretending not to listen.

'Jenni buggered off with that bloke from work,' she added, slipping on another jacket.

'Like I need reminding.'

'And don't get me started on Petra.'

'Then I won't.'

'What a nutjob she turned out to be. How long was it before she wanted to move in with you? Six weeks? Talk about intense. Right, Mum?'

His mum jolted, woken from her semi-slumber. 'What? Oh, yes, she was rather unfortunate.'

Matt looked between his mum and sister. 'Is there a point to this?'

Leah buttoned up the jacket, which fitted perfectly. She looked like a female James Bond, licensed to annoy. 'They all had one thing in common.'

Matt frowned. 'Which was?'

'They were boring.'

'No, they weren't,' he said, stung by the accusation.

Leah gave him an incredulous look. 'Excuse me? They were dull and boring.'

He turned to his mum, expecting her to jump to his defence, but when nothing was forthcoming, he felt the need to defend his ex-girlfriends. Not just them, but himself, too. After all, he'd chosen to be with these women. What did that say about him? 'Just because they were easy-going and nice, it didn't make them dull.'

'Until they left you.'

He baulked. 'Thanks for that.'

Leah came over. 'But that wasn't your fault,' she said, hugging him.

'Miss, be careful with the jacket!' the assistant scuttled over, wiping his brow as if serving the Hardy family was akin to dealing with the Capones. He took the jacket from her. 'I think we're done here. I'll prepare the paperwork.'

Leah waited until he'd disappeared, before taking Matt's hand. 'For some inexplicable reason, you're drawn to unexciting women. It's probably something to do with you wanting a safe and quiet life, no dramas or scandal. Which let's face it, is understandable, considering where our father currently is. But it's never going to work.'

Matt frowned. 'How do you figure that?'

'Because you don't behave naturally with them. You put on this act, like you're this perfect polite gentleman who never wants to cause any fuss and who complies with whatever they want.'

He shifted in the chair. 'That's not true.'

'Yes, it is.' Leah's eyes narrowed. 'It was like you were always treading on eggshells around them.'

This was news to him. Why hadn't anyone pointed this out at the time? Would he have listened? Probably not.

'And we both know that's not the real you.' Leah glanced at their mum for confirmation. 'When you're with us, you behave very differently.'

He did? Again, something he hadn't been aware of. 'How so?'

'You argue back, for a start.' Leah nudged him in the ribs. 'You tease us, you're not afraid to disagree with us and you stand up for yourself. But you let Alison and Jenni walk all over you.'

This was an alarming insight into his past relationships, and something that was shocking to hear and difficult to compute. He rubbed his forehead, trying to recall how he'd behaved with Alison and Jenni. Perfectly normally, or so he'd thought. Maybe it had felt a little strained at times, like he was having to try all the time, but he'd assumed that was normal. Didn't everyone have to make an effort to get a relationship to work?

'There didn't appear to be any passion, either,' Leah said, making it sound almost as a question. 'Which meant that when someone else came along who offered them that, they...' She left the sentence hanging in the air.

'Buggered off,' he said, a wave of depression settling over him.

This really was turning out to be a crap Saturday. Shopping instead of rugby, too fat for clothes, and now an unwelcome insight into why he'd failed at every relationship he'd ever had. 'Well, thanks for the free psychoanalysis, guys. Good to know I'm so flawed.'

'You're not, love.' His mum grabbed his hand.

'God, no.' Leah hugged him harder. 'As men go, you're pretty damn near perfect. There's absolutely nothing wrong with you. Just the women you date.'

He gave her a disbelieving look, or he tried to – it was hard to move with both women clinging on to him. 'Is that supposed to make me feel better?'

'You need someone who sees the real you,' his mum said, her grip not letting up.

'Yeah, like this Beth woman.' Leah's lips twitched with mischief. 'You know it's tradition for the best man and maid of honour to hook up, right?'

Matt gave her a wide-eyed look. 'Not going to happen.'

'You said it yourself. She's hot and she gets on your nerves. It's a winning combination.'

Shrugging himself free from their collective clasp, he stood up, agitated beyond belief. 'I never said she was hot, and that's the most ridiculous thing I've ever heard. It's not a winning combination, it's a car crash waiting to happen. Why on earth would I be interested in a woman I have an uncontrollable urge to strangle?'

Leah clapped her hands. 'Oooo, even better.'

Matt shook his head. 'You're a very strange creature, Leah Hardy.'

'I know.' She stood up and kissed his cheek, leaning on his chest as she stretched up on tiptoe. 'Stop searching for easy and uncomplicated,' she said, her expression turning serious. 'You need a woman you can argue with, fall out with and enjoy making up with.' She patted his chest. 'Trust me on this. I know you better than you know yourself.'

And that was what worried him.

# Chapter Nine

### Friday, 3rd May

Who knew that confessing to your GP that you regularly fantasised about bludgeoning your estranged husband and his new floozy to death with a spade would result in an urgent referral for anger management classes. Other options included taking anti-depressants, enduring weekly counselling sessions or joining the local 'Stitch & Bitch' – where she could vent her frustrations along with a load of other menopausal women.

It was only after Connie had left her GP appointment that she'd registered the inappropriateness of confessing the true depths of her rage. Especially as the GP in question was also one of her bosses. It had never occurred to her to change doctors when she'd started working there. But then, she'd never envisaged a time when she'd be so consumed with anger that she'd lie in bed at night imagining ways to dispose of a body.

So, here she was, a week later, about to attend her first 'therapy' session and wondering whether she'd have been better off just agreeing to the medication.

Humiliation burnt in her cheeks as she pulled into the gym car park. Why was it that she'd been assessed as being mentally unstable, while her idiot husband could act like a hormone-driven adolescent and no one batted an eyelid. If anyone had lost the plot, it was him.

'Waitrose has changed,' her mum said, nodding at the building ahead.

'This isn't Waitrose,' Connie replied with a sigh, having explained a dozen times why they were here. 'It's a boxing gym.'

Her mother frowned. 'Who's Jim?'

On any other day, Connie might have laughed, but today she was feeling somewhat bruised and disgruntled. Not to mention agitated. As if enduring this torture wasn't bad enough, she was having to drag her eighty-four-year-old mother along for the ride. Most days Doris Emerick was safe to be left alone, but some days she wasn't. Like today, when she'd decided to dry her washing in the microwave.

It wasn't her mother's fault, Connie knew that. It was the disease. A disease that required careful handling, patience and resilience – all of which Connie lacked. Trained carers had the ability to remain detached and unaffected when their charge called them names and resisted eating or getting dressed, but it wasn't so easy when that person was your own mother.

'I'm having a boxing lesson,' Connie said, trying to sound upbeat and positive about the situation. 'Hopefully, there's a viewing gallery where you can sit and watch.'

'Why would I want to do that?'

'I thought a change of scenery night do us both good.'

'I'd rather go to Waitrose.'

'Me too, Mum.' Connie exited the car and retrieved her sports bag from the boot, heading around to the passenger side to help her mother out. 'Give me your hand, Mum.'

Doris reached into the door compartment and handed Connie the ice scraper.

'Not the ice scraper, your hand.'

'My bag?'

'Your hand.' She gestured to her mum's hand. 'So I can help you out of the car.'

'I can manage,' her mother said, lifting herself from the car with ease and reminding Connie that there was nothing wrong with her physical health.

As always, her mum looked pristine. Her ice-white hair was styled, her navy skirt and cornflower-blue blouse were neatly pressed, and she was wearing lipstick and powder. Her outward appearance was polished and smart, just as her home was – well, with a little help from the carers who now visited thrice daily.

Her mum's world was orderly and governed by routine. The dementia team looking after her said it gave the person structure and familiarity to their day, and it was often the last thing to be relinquished before the shift from occasional lapses in memory to full-blown confusion. Connie wasn't looking forward to that stage. She doubted her mother was either.

They headed for the building ahead and entered via an uninviting metal door. It was a rundown portacabin with limited light that no doubt attracted a very different type of clientele to the spa. There were no manicures or seaweed facials on offer, only a humid changing area and a poorly stocked vending machine. The inside smelt of sweaty feet and talcum powder, and once again Connie was struck by the depths to which she'd spectacularly descended.

How visiting a place such as this was supposed to improve her mental state, she wasn't sure. The sight of various perspiring bodies pummelling punchbags and sparring in the boxing ring would be enough to unhinge any sane person.

But she was here at the request of her GP, who'd assured her that providing a vent for her anger would help, so the least she could do was give it a go.

Looking around, she realised her expectations of finding a viewing gallery were somewhat ambitious. The best she could offer her mother was a plastic chair shoved along the side of the workout area.

'Waitrose has gone downhill,' Doris said, tutting her disapproval as Connie helped lower her onto a chair. 'They used to have a nice cafe, now look at it.' She nodded towards the boxing ring where two muscled men were beating the crap out of each other. 'The staff aren't even fully dressed.'

Connie removed her mum's knitting from her bag and handed Doris the intricate garment. Her mum's mind might be shot, but her dexterity skills were as sharp as ever.

'This should keep you occupied while I do my session, Mum. Can I get you a cup of tea?' Even though she had no idea whether the vending machine sold tea.

'No, thank you, dear. Are we meeting Jim here?'

Connie touched her mum's shoulder. 'Gym isn't a person, Mum. It's the name of the building.'

'Funny name for a building.' Doris began knitting.

'It's a gym, Mum. As in a gymnasium? You know, for sports.'

Doris subjected her daughter to a patronising look. 'I know what a gymnasium is, dear.'

'Silly me. Of course you do.' A stab of guilt reminded her it was wrong to underestimate her mother. Doris wasn't totally lost to the disease.

But then her mother said, 'It's where they make cheese,' and Connie felt like she was living in a parallel universe where she was the lunatic and everyone else was lucid.

Happy her mum was content to sit quietly and knit, Connie headed into the changing rooms and swapped her boots for trainers. She was already dressed in leggings and a sports top, which was just as well, as it wasn't a space she'd want to undress in.

Exiting the changing rooms, she was greeted by a muscular Black man with intricate tattoos and a shaved head. 'Mrs Lawrence?' he said, and Connie was surprised at his clipped Surrey accent, which felt at odds with his homeboy appearance. Not that she knew what a homeboy was – she'd just heard the phrase used in the film *Straight Outta Compton*… which disappointingly hadn't turned out to be a film about the small village of Compton in Surrey, but a rather alarming story of a group of hip-hoppers igniting a culture war in America. And she'd wondered why she was the only person over sixty in the local indie cinema?

'Call me Connie,' she said, accepting the offer of a handshake and nearly buckling under the strength of the man's grip.

'I'm Anthony, I'll be your coach. Have you done any boxing training before?'

'None.'

He jotted something down on a chart. 'Any strength training?'

'Only swimming.'

'Swimming is good, keeps the heart healthy.'

'My heart doesn't feel very healthy,' she said, rubbing an ache away when her chest twinged.

Anthony kept his eyes on the chart. 'The referral says you have anger management issues?'

His bluntness made her flinch. 'I've never actually acted on them, it's all in here,' she said, tapping the side of her head. 'This is where the rage storms.'

'Then let's try to address that for you. We'll start with some light skipping to get you warmed up.'

Following him over to a small side area, she noticed the suspiciously stained floor mat. 'How does this work? Do you ask questions, or do I just talk?'

'It's boxing,' he said, handing her a skipping rope. 'Not therapy.'

'But it's been prescribed by my GP, so there must be a process?'

He stepped away, indicating for her to start. 'It's more about enabling you to release your anger.'

'By skipping?'

'By releasing endorphins and expelling the tension you carry in your muscles.' He lifted the stopwatch hanging around his neck and clicked a button. 'Whenever you're ready.'

Untangling the rope, she began skipping – something she hadn't done since school. Her body felt cumbersome and heavy, like trying to lift a juggernaut off the ground. 'I'm not the one who needs anything expelling,' she said, struggling to coordinate her arms and legs. 'That would be my husband.'

'Try to keep a nice steady rhythm.'

Easy for him to say. 'He's destroyed my life.'

'Extend your arms, that way you won't keep hitting your head with the rope.'

On cue, she smacked herself in the face again. 'What kind of man abandons his marriage for a woman young enough to be his daughter?' She swung the rope higher, missing her head, but making her arms ache. 'He's embarrassed his kids and betrayed everything we had together.'

Why, was the question? What was lacking in their marriage that had made him leave? They'd been happy together – or so she'd thought. How had she got things so badly wrong? It was the lack of a decent explanation that hurt the most, as if announcing he was leaving her for Tiffany was sufficient, and no further reasoning was needed. But it wasn't enough – it'd left her with a host of unanswered questions and a sense of utter confusion.

'Okay, stop.' Anthony clicked the stopwatch. 'How do you feel?'

'Hurt. Angry. Stupid. Most of all, heartbroken. He was the love of my life.'

Anthony tilted his head. 'I meant how do you feel after skipping?'

'Oh, right. Fine.'

'Let's move on to the legs. Can you do twenty squats for me?' He demonstrated the move, his muscular thighs bobbing up and down with ease.

She attempted to copy him, bending her legs.

The sight of a few other gym users also struggling to keep up with their instructors helped to distract her. Aside from the toned patrons who made exercising look easy, there were a few people like her. Older people who didn't look happy about being encouraged to exercise and whose expressions reflected pure misery. Maybe she wasn't the only person struggling with a lack of self-esteem.

'Keep your back straight. Bend from the knees and lift your chin,' Anthony said, assessing her from all angles.

Her thighs were burning.

'Nineteen… twenty. Great, let's move on to the pads.' He headed over to a large punchbag hanging from the ceiling by a long chain. 'Nice soft knees for this one, centre your weight, and ensure you make contact with the top of your foot.' He kicked the bag so quickly and efficiently that she took a step back. 'Your turn. Nice and slow to begin with.'

Connie tried to replicate the move, but she lost her balance, stubbed her toes on the bag and crumpled to the floor.

'You didn't centre your weight.' He offered her his hand. 'Are you okay?'

'Fine,' she said, feeling anything but, as she clambered to her feet.

'Remember, top section of your foot. Tilt your body to make contact easier.'

Sucking in a breath, she tried again. The impact rattled up her body, sending her off balance, but she remained upright and didn't squish her toes.

'Much better. Try again. Put some weight behind it.' Anthony positioned himself behind the pad and held it steady.

Connie eyeballed the punchbag, visualising her husband's face on the front. She swung her leg up and made contact. Take that, Kenneth bloody Lawrence!

'Excellent. Again.'

Another strike, which landed perfectly. The impact stung, but she didn't care. Who did Kenneth think he was? Richard flipping Gere? Hardly. He was a pathetic sixty-five-year-old man. A pensioner, for crying out loud. Didn't he realise how stupid he looked, parading around with a big-titted, twenty-something, who was clearly only after his money!

'You're doing great, Connie. Keep going.'

She was getting the hang of it. Settling into position, bending her knees and kick! Each one landing on Kenneth's smug… annoying… imaginary face.

'Bastard!' she yelled, landing another kick. 'Lousy… lying… cheating bastard!' Another kick, this one harder, almost dislodging Anthony. 'How dare you leave me after all I've done for you! Supported your career… raised your kids… cleaned your dirty underpants… And for what? To be tossed aside for Tiffany Tart-Face!'

The alarmed look on Anthony's face dragged her back to the present.

Silence settled around her and she realised the whole place had stopped what they were doing and were looking at her. 'Sorry,' she mumbled, waving an apology at the other gym users. Embarrassing herself seemed to be her default setting these days.

Anthony cleared his throat. 'Time for the gloves, I think.' He led her away from the punchbag, and gradually everyone resumed their training.

'I'm sorry,' she said, genuinely mortified.

'It's not a problem.' He cocked an eyebrow. 'Did it help?'

'Actually… yes, it did.'

He smiled. 'Hold out your hands.'

A pair of padded gloves, which weighed a ton, were slid onto her hands. Her arms were definitely going to be feeling the effects of this workout later.

Anthony gestured to a smaller punchbag, this one attached to a heavy spring. 'Same centred stance, hands held high, we're aiming for small quick jabs. The idea is to get a rhythm going.' Once again, he demonstrated how it should be done and she watched in fascination as the punchbag rattled away as he hit it. 'Your turn.'

Her initial efforts were ungainly and it was hard not to topple off balance.

'Smaller jabs, don't follow through.'

Connie imagined Tiffany's face in front of her this time, and began to fantasise about ripping off her false eyelashes and tearing out her hair extensions, strand by strand. If that woman so much as attempted to attend her daughter's wedding then she'd burst her implants with her own stilettos! Jab… jab… jab…

'Good. Keep it going. Soften your knees.' Anthony circled her, watching her pummelling the punchbag, getting into a rhythm. 'Think about what you want, Connie.'

'I want revenge,' she said, increasing her speed.

He shook his head. 'You think that'll make you feel any better?'

'Hell, yes.' She punched harder, faster, imagining Tiffany's face pulped into a mash.

'A lot of people think that,' he said, raising his voice to be heard above the rattling. 'But when it comes to it, revenge can make things worse.'

'I don't see how.'

'How would your kids feel if you hurt their father? What about your mother over there, how do you think she'd cope with you charged for assault? All the while, your ex and this new woman are free to live their lives.'

She shot him a look. 'You're not helping.'

'This process isn't about inflicting physical pain.'

'You mean, I should focus on causing psychological pain instead?' She resumed punching, remembering stories about friends who'd subscribed their exes to embarrassing publications or inserted rotten fish into their curtain poles. Maybe she should try something along those lines. 'You're right, I need to be more devious in my approach.'

'That wasn't what I meant.'

'Please don't tell me I need to accept the situation and move on. I'm sick of people telling me that.' Her punches became a little wayward – he was distracting her.

'You're focusing a lot of energy on other people. People whose behaviour you can't control. In doing that you're neglecting your own needs.'

'I don't have any needs. I don't have a life.'

'Sure, you do. You've plenty of life left. Do you want to spend that time bitter and angry? Or fulfilled and happy?'

'Happy isn't possible.' She swung at the punchbag, hitting it with venom.

'Yes, it is. But you have to let go of your anger first.'

'Then what, eh? I'm a depressed woman in her sixties with a wobbly middle. I never used to wobble, but I've been drinking a lot of wine lately.'

'So stop. Regain control. In doing so, you'll regain some of that lost confidence. Use these sessions to get fitter, as well as expelling that anger. You'll be amazed at how much better you feel. Your husband will soon realise what he lost.'

Connie stopped punching.

That was it. She needed to make Kenneth realise what he'd lost. 'Anthony, you're a genius.'

He looked sceptical. 'I am?'

She pulled off the gloves. 'I'm going to make Kenneth pay by making him realise what he's lost. By the time I'm done, he's going to be rueing the day he left me and will be begging for me to come back.'

'That's not what I meant. It would be better for your mental health if you were able to accept the situation and rebuild your life.'

'I don't need a new life,' she said, handing him the gloves. 'I need my old one back. Thanks for the workout, I'll be back on Monday.' With a spring in her step, she headed over to her mother. 'Time to go, Mum. I have work to do.'

It was time to stop feeling sorry for herself and take back control of her life.

Starting right now.

# Chapter Ten

*Thursday, 9<sup>th</sup> May – one month till the wedding*

If there was one thing Beth hated more than being late, it was a disorganised start to the day. Her mornings were usually governed by an orderly routine, starting with a long hot shower, followed by consuming tea and toast at the breakfast bar while listening to Virgin Radio, and then taking her time selecting her suit for the day. Exactly one hour after rising, she'd be heading downstairs to her office on the ground floor of the building, ready for an eight a.m. start. It was all very regimented and quietly comforting. So when something disrupted that equilibrium, she became agitated and unsettled, and it didn't bode well for the rest of the day.

Today was one of those days.

'I hoped you'd have it sorted by now,' Megan complained, her voice faint amongst the background of noisy Greek music and a man shouting something about 'extras being needed on set'. 'You're a divorce lawyer, aren't you?'

Beth bit back her frustration and padded over to the tall sash window in her bare feet. She hadn't even had a chance to finish dressing this morning before her sister had phoned, demanding an update on the state of her pending bigamy.

Balancing the phone between her shoulder and ear, Beth gave the period window frame in her flat a hefty shove, desperate for some fresh air. Her mug of tea was sitting on the countertop, undrunk, and her toast was stone cold.

The expanse of trees in the communal space below created dappled sunlight that flickered rhythmically like old cinefilm.

She took a moment to breathe deeply, hoping to relax her stiff neck and calm her nerves. 'I deal with UK law, Megan. Not US. I've never been asked to annul a Las Vegas marriage before. This is a new one, even for me.'

Megan sighed. 'Isn't it the same process? Can't you just ask them for an annulment?'

'You could, yes, if you lived in Nevada and you knew the name of the chapel where the marriage took place, and you were able to provide details of the other party involved.'

'I've already told you I don't know the name of the chapel. All I can remember is that it had a white altar covered in flowers, and the officiant was dressed as Elvis.'

'Which pretty much describes every wedding venue in Las Vegas. Trust me, I've checked. You don't even know the exact date.'

'I was drunk. I don't remember much about that holiday.'

'Evidently.'

Beth retrieved a dislodged cushion from the floor and repositioned it on the padded window seat. She hated anything being out of place in her cosy little home. The flat was made up of three rooms, a bathroom, a bedroom and a lounge-diner with an open-plan kitchen. The generous Georgian sizing meant that apart from the small bathroom, the place was large and airy, with high ceilings, and felt a lot bigger than its 600 square foot.

'It was kind of a wild time,' Megan continued, sounding uncharacteristically morose. 'We'd all just finished our drama degrees and headed off to Vegas to celebrate.'

Unbeknown to Beth, eight years earlier, when her sister was supposedly attending auditions in London in an effort to further her acting career, she'd actually been partying in Las Vegas with a load of other post-grad drama students. A holiday that had resulted in several arrests, one drug bust, two drunken and disorderly charges, and her sister getting hitched to another drama student. Quite the holiday.

Beth caught sight of her reflection in the large gold mirror above the fireplace and groaned at the sight of her damp hair creating wet patches on her white shirt. She'd yet to put on a skirt and it was 8:20 a.m.

'Is there really nothing you can do? I'm desperate here.'

Beth searched for her glasses. 'I've ruled out applying to the US courts, for reasons already mentioned. Plus, the only ground we could realistically use in the application is insanity, and despite evidence to the contrary, you're not insane.'

'So that's it? I'm stuck married to some random guy I haven't seen in eight years for the rest of my life?'

'There's an option to apply to the UK courts, but there's no evidence of fraud, you're not related to each other and failing to obtain parental consent isn't applicable, as you were both over twenty-one at the time. Which leaves us with trying to get the marriage voided on the grounds that it was never consummated. It was never consummated... right?'

'Er, not after the ceremony, no. It was beforehand, in the back of the limo. Does that count?'

Beth rolled her eyes. 'Thankfully, no. You weren't actually married then.'

'So we go for getting it voided.'

'But I need the respondent's name, address and date of birth. All you've been able to tell me so far is his name. Do you know how many Freddie Woods there are on Facebook?'

'I'm guessing a lot?'

'Hundreds.' Beth lifted the cushions, searching for her glasses. 'I've filled in the petition form as far as I can, but you need to track down this Freddie bloke and get his details, and fast. The court needs up to thirty days to process the application and your wedding day is exactly one month today.'

'Maybe one of my old uni friends is still in touch with him?'

'Then ask around, because unless we can get hold of him, you can't get married to Zac.' Beth checked the kitchen, searching for her glasses. 'Have you told Zac yet?'

'I was hoping we could get it sorted and I wouldn't have to.'

'You don't think it would be kinder to warn him the wedding might be delayed?'

'But he's so happy, I can't ruin that for him.'

Of course he was happy, he was swanning about in Greece with his fiancée, while Beth was running around like a blue-arsed fly, trying to organise his wedding and simultaneously arranging his bride's divorce. 'Has he found his passport yet?'

Beth still wasn't entirely sure this wasn't an elaborate fib on Zac's part to delay returning to the UK and extend his holiday. Zac didn't seem like the devious type, but then, Megan didn't either, and she'd kept an eight-year marriage secret, so who knew what people were capable of.

'He's reported it to the police, and he's speaking with the embassy tomorrow about getting a replacement, so hopefully he'll be home soon. He feels really bad about landing you in it like this.'

Not bad enough to postpone the wedding, though, eh? Somehow she was still expected to perform miracles, and in less than a month.

The doorbell downstairs buzzed. Squinting at her phone, she tried to read the time, praying that her first appointment hadn't arrived an hour early. Maybe her father had a client booked in? Although these days her dad was rarely in the office before nine thirty a.m.

The buzzer sounded again and she silently cursed. She wasn't dressed, her hair was wet and she desperately needed a cup of tea. Whoever it was would have to wait.

Having failed to locate her glasses, she marched over to the door and yanked it open, intending to yell down the stairwell, but as she exited onto the landing, she smacked straight into a solid chest.

Her loud yelp was a reaction to the man treading on her foot, causing her to drop her phone, which bounced off the banister and proceeded to disappear down the stairwell. Her already agitated state hurtled straight into full-blown annoyance, especially as the cause of her grief was none other than Matt bloody Hardy.

'What the hell?' she yelled, torn between racing after her phone and stopping to rub her squashed foot. 'How did you get in here?'

'A man let me in.'

'What man?'

'I don't know.' He offered her a half-hearted shrug, standing on her landing looking all casual and relaxed in a V-neck T-shirt and jeans. 'The man who answered the intercom when I pressed the buzzer. I said I was here to see you, and he released the door lock. He told me to head up to the first floor.'

Her hands went to her hips. 'And you thought it was appropriate to come up to my flat uninvited?'

He tried to take a step back, but the landing wasn't big enough and he remained too close for comfort. The heat radiating off him was making her eyes mist over. 'It says Lawrence and Blandy on the door – I didn't know it was your flat. I had no idea you lived here as well as worked here.'

'Well, I do.'

'Evidently.' His eyes flitted briefly over her loose hair, partially buttoned-up shirt and exposed bare legs. 'Apologies for intruding. I'll leave.'

'Too bloody right.' She rubbed her sore foot on the back of her calf, not wanting to bend down in case she flashed her knickers. He'd seen far too much of her body already. But as he turned to leave, she felt obliged to ask, 'What was it you wanted?'

He glanced back. 'I figured we needed to talk about the wedding.'

'Couldn't you have phoned?'

'I was in the area, I thought I'd drop in,' he said with a shrug. 'It's hard doing everything remotely. I thought it would be easier in person and help speed things along.'

Her hands went to her hips. 'Are you criticising my efforts?'

'Of course not, but you don't always reply to my messages,' he said, carefully.

She was about to retaliate, when she realised he had a valid point. It seemed an unfair accusation when she was single-handedly trying to ensure the marriage actually went ahead, but he didn't know that. He was oblivious to the whole Megan debacle, and it needed to stay that way. Especially as Zac was still in the dark, too. For now, she had to carry on planning the wedding as though nothing was wrong.

'My office is on the ground floor. My name's on the door. Wait in there and I'll be down in a moment.'

'Are you sure? I don't want to inconvenience you.'

'I can spare a few minutes.'

'Thanks. I won't take up much of your time.'

Something she was grateful for. There was only so much Matt Hardy she could take.

Waiting until he'd fully disappeared down the stairwell, she limped inside her flat and slumped against the closed door. It hadn't been the greatest start to the morning. And now a man who irked her had seen her semi-naked and dishevelled, and had invaded her privacy.

Why was it each time she encountered Matt Hardy she ended up unravelling in some way? Was the universe punishing her for some crime she'd committed in a previous life? Whatever it was, her nerves couldn't take it.

Fifteen minutes later, having located her glasses in the bathroom, she was fully dressed in a navy trouser suit, with her hair tied up in a bun and her polished work demeanour firmly back in place. She was ready to face Matt Hardy.

Well, kind of. Something about the idea of finding him downstairs in her office unsettled her, like a sense of trepidation was making her hands clammy and her cheeks warm. She didn't like having a physical response to him, it gave cause for alarm. She preferred men who failed to evoke any kind of emotion, and left her feeling unaffected and disinterested. Those types of men were easier to ignore.

But maybe she should be grateful for the warning. She was on her guard, which meant she wouldn't be caught unawares.

She was ready to defend herself, like a lone wolf in the wild alerted to a lion on the prowl.

Well, she wasn't about to be anyone's lunch.

Armed and at the ready, Beth marched into her office, head high, shoulders pulled back. This was her hunting ground, not his. She had no reason to be intimidated. He was the one who should be wary.

'Good morning, Mr Hardy.' She left the door open, feeling safer that way.

He was standing by her desk, blocking out most of the natural light coming in from the sash window behind. 'We're still doing the whole Mr Hardy routine?' He had an eyebrow raised.

She straightened her jacket. 'Force of habit. What can I do for you?'

He handed over her phone. 'I hope it's not broken.'

'Oh… thank you.' She'd almost forgotten about her phone.

She took the device, flinching at the frisson of heat his touch evoked when his fingers brushed hers. The display lit up with a missed call from her sister. Megan was probably confused as to why their call had ended so abruptly when her phone had gone hurtling down the stairwell. She'd message her sister later.

'Sorry again for invading your personal space just now. It was an honest mistake.'

She glanced up and offered him a weak smile. 'No harm done.' Except that he'd seen her undressed, and that put her at a slight disadvantage. Although what disadvantage, she wasn't sure.

'How's your foot?'

'Fine.' She gestured for him to sit down. 'You wanted to discuss the wedding?'

He sat down, unnervingly close, despite the desk between them. 'Megan mentioned—'

Whatever he was about to say trailed off when her father appeared in the doorway. 'I need you to cover the office for a while,' he said, giving a cursory knock on the open door before waltzing in uninvited. 'Oh, sorry. I didn't realise you had a client with you.'

Beth stood up. 'This is Matt Hardy, Dad. Zac's uncle.'

'The chap who's been roped into organising the wedding?' He came over.

Matt stood up and extended his hand. 'Pleased to me you, Mr Lawrence.'

'Call me Kenneth.' Her dad shook Matt's hand. 'You're a brave man. You wouldn't catch me planning someone else's wedding. I didn't even get involved in planning my own.'

Although it was meant as a light-hearted joke, Beth wasn't sure it was something he should be overly proud of. She refrained from comment, nonetheless.

'Stark mad, the pair of you. Good luck with it.' He smiled at Beth. 'I'm heading out.'

'Before you go, sir.' Matt turned to him. 'You're actually the reason why I'm here. I wondered if we could have a chat about suits for the wedding.'

Beth felt her eyebrows raise. He'd called her dad, sir? The man-mountain had manners, she'd give him that.

'No need,' her father said, dismissively. 'I have my own Savile Row tailor – they've already measured me up for a set of tails.'

'That's just the thing, sir. Zac has requested evening suits.'

Her dad frowned. 'For a wedding?'

'Yes.'

Her dad looked perplexed. 'It should be top hat and tails.'

Matt glanced at Beth, as if unsure how to proceed. 'Maybe if it was a traditional church wedding, but they've opted for a ceremony within a hotel, so they feel tuxedos would be more fitting for the occasion.'

'No church?' Kenneth Lawrence reacted as if Matt had announced the wedding was to be held in Strangeways. 'My baby girl should be getting married in a church. It's only right and proper.'

Beth wasn't sure which hypocrisy to point out first. Her father's lack of religion. His non-existent church visits. His infidelity, or his 'baby girl' already being married. But as no one else in her family knew about this last one, she bit her tongue. 'We did look at a church option,' Beth added, trying to be helpful. 'However, Megan and Zac said they'd prefer a civil venue.'

Planning another couple's wedding was stressful enough when the people involved agreed, but as Beth and Matt hadn't, they'd been forced to ask Megan and Zac their preference on this matter. Matt had been proved right – the couple didn't want a church ceremony. Despite the opportunity to gloat over his victory, Matt hadn't. Beth still wasn't quite sure why.

'Still no excuse to abandon the whole traditional tails,' her dad said, puffing out his chest. Beth realised he was trying to appear taller, stretching up his torso, no doubt a little intimidated by Matt's imposing frame.

Matt's voice was surprisingly gentle as he addressed her father, as if used to putting insecure men at ease. 'The thing is, we've only a month to go before the day, and the groom's family have ordered evening suits.'

'Then they can reorder tailcoats.'

Matt glanced at Beth. 'That's not going to be possible.'

'I don't see why not? They're hiring them, aren't they? Why can't they just change the order?'

Matt looked uncomfortable. He flexed his hands and rubbed them on his T-shirt. 'Some of us aren't a regular size, sir.'

'Your point?'

A beat passed. 'I'm having my jacket specially made. It's too late to change the order.' His voice was low and hesitant, and far from his normal confident self – he actually appeared vulnerable.

Beth studied his face, trying to fathom the reason for his discomfort. Was money an issue? Or was he self-conscious about wearing formal clothing? It wasn't everyone's preference.

He certainly had no reason to worry about his appearance. Despite his character shortcomings, he was a striking man. Large, definitely, yet handsome. He reminded her of Russell Crowe in Gladiator… a thought she immediately quashed when an image of Matt dressed as a Roman warrior filled her head. That was one distraction she did not need.

'I'm sorry, but as the bride's father I'm insisting on wearing a formal tail suit,' her father said, waving his hand about. 'You younger lot can wear what you like.'

Matt looked conflicted. He clearly didn't want to get into an argument with this man, but the idea of the two families dressed in different outfits was ludicrous.

It was time for Beth to step in. Who'd have ever thought she'd take sides with Matt Hardy? 'Dad, we can't have half of the congregation wearing tails and the other half wearing tuxedos.'

'Why not?'

She lifted her hands. 'Because it would look ridiculous.'

'If they don't like it, they can change it.' Her dad was in one of his belligerent moods.

'Matt has explained why he can't do that. And besides, this is Zac's decision to make, and he's opted for evening suits. We have to respect that.'

A laugh startled them. Connie Lawrence stood in the doorway, leaning against the frame. 'Your father has a bit of an issue with showing respect,' she said, her voice cutting through the tension and taking an already awkward conversation up another notch.

Beth inwardly cringed at the sight of her mother. As if this morning wasn't bad enough. Refereeing arguments between her parents was challenging enough at the best of times, but doing it in front of Matt Hardy, of all people, was beyond excruciating. 'Mum, what are you doing here?'

It was too much to hope her mother would take the hint and leave. Instead, she sauntered into the room like she was on a catwalk, her gait slow and rhythmic, with a definite sway to her hips.

Beth's eyes grew wide, as did her father's.

'I thought I'd pop in and say hi,' her mother said, with an enigmatic smile.

Far from looking her usual miserable or angry self, Connie Lawrence looked fully back to her pre-split days. Bouncy silver-blonde hair enhancing her strong cheekbones, make-up immaculate, and filling the office with a strong waft of perfume. Her low-cut cream blouse gave a flash of nude bra, and her fitted designer jeans and heeled boots showed off her shapely figure.

'And who do we have here?' she said, stopping in front of Matt.

Matt extended his hand. 'Matt Hardy. Zac's uncle.'

'Ah, the elusive uncle.' Connie bypassed his hand and kissed both his cheeks, resting her hands on his chest. 'Goodness me, you're a big fella,' she said, allowing her gaze to roam appreciatively over his physique.

Beth's mortification skyrocketed. 'Mum, please.'

'Oh, calm down. Matt doesn't mind, do you? When a man's this good-looking, he's used to being admired.' She smiled up at him. 'Am I right?'

It was Matt's turn to adopt a wide-eyed expression. Poor bloke.

Beth wanted the ground to open up and swallow her whole.

In contrast, her dad made a scoffing sound. 'Leave the poor man alone, Connie,' he said, looking part-flustered, part-annoyed. 'The man's half your age.'

Beth closed her eyes. Oh, hell. Of all the things her dad could have said.

Connie swivelled to look at her estranged husband. 'Excuse me?'

Beth needed to intervene. If an almighty fight was about to ensue, there was no way she wanted Matt Hardy with a front row seat.

But her mother surprised her by laughing. 'That's a bit rich, coming from you, Kenneth. Remind me again how old Tiffany is?'

Her father lifted his chin. 'It's different for men.'

'Poppycock.' Her mother's expression turned flirtatious. 'This is the twenty-first century, Kenneth. Women are empowered. We cougars get to date whoever we want, age is just a number. Isn't that right, Matt?' She trailed her fingers down his arm. 'And let's face it, men are all the same age lying down.'

'Mum!' Beth's hands came up to her mouth. 'What the hell?'

To his credit, Matt merely smiled, and refrained from reacting to being used as a weapon in her parents' war.

Unlike Matt, her father had never mastered the art of restraint and decided to retaliate. 'You're making a fool of yourself, Connie.'

'You'd know all about that, darling.' She subjected her husband to a megawatt smile. 'Anyway, I'd love to stay and chat, but I have plans.' She turned to Matt. 'Unless of course I can persuade you to join me for an early tipple somewhere cosy?'

'Mum, please.' Beth's cheeks burnt with humiliation. She had no idea what had come over her mum, but this was not normal behaviour.

'Oh, sorry, am I encroaching?' Her mother glanced between Beth and Matt. 'I didn't realise you were interested, darling. Good for you. It's about time you got back out there and started having some fun. He's quite the hunk.'

Beth audibly groaned. For months she'd been urging her mother to snap out of her rollercoaster ride of angry tirades and morbid depression, but if she'd known the next phase involved turning into a predatory sex vixen, she'd have stuck with the endless crying and excessive drinking. That behaviour was way easier to deal with than this performance. What was her mother playing at?

'Bye-bye, Matt.' Connie kissed him again, lingering a little as she did so, her fingers grazing over his soft beard. 'You do smell good,' she said, turning to her husband with a sigh. 'Au revoir, Kenneth. Say hi to Tiffany for me.' She sashayed over to the door, pausing for effect before making her dramatic exit. 'Do let her know that she's welcome to attend the wedding. I look forward to waving at her from across the room, where I shall be firmly ensconced at the top table.' Connie smiled, her eyes narrowing in warning. 'I hope I've made myself clear?' And with that, she sauntered out.

Beth was left with her mouth hanging open.

Her dad looked equally stunned. 'What the hell was that all about?' he said, running his finger around his shirt collar, loosening the fit. 'It's like she's a changed woman.'

Changed, indeed. Her mother had had a personality transplant, and it didn't bode well. She was clearly up to something, and Beth could only imagine the dire consequences for her entire family when they discovered what that was. But victories were hard to come by, and if her mum had changed her mind about attending the wedding then that was to be celebrated, not questioned.

In the meantime, she had Matt Hardy to deal with. A man who no doubt wanted to run a mile from her outrageous family. If he'd disliked Beth before, heaven only knew what he thought of her now.

True enough, his alarmed expression indicated he'd rather be anywhere else than stuck in an office with her and her bonkers parents. 'I'd better be off,' he said, edging his way over to the door. 'You're clearly busy, and I don't want to take up any more of your precious time.' He turned to her dad. 'If you could have a think about the suit situation, I'd be very grateful, sir.'

But her father wasn't listening. He was lost in his own thoughts. No doubt wondering what substances his former wife had resorted to taking to make her act like a crazy person.

Beth followed Matt out of the office and caught up with him by the main exit onto the High Street. 'I'm so sorry about that,' she said, embarrassed at the way her father had ignored him. 'They're not normally so rude. They're going through a divorce and things are a little strained between them.'

Why she felt the need to give him more details, she had no idea. It wasn't like she owed him an explanation, but for some reason she didn't want him to judge them too harshly. They were her parents, after all.

'I guessed it must be something like that,' he said, his voice deep, but surprisingly soft. 'It must be tough for you, being caught in the middle. I imagine it's not easy.'

For some strange reason, this passing comment, delivered with such sincerity and kindness, threatened to undo her. Tears pricked at her eyes, as she considered the stress of Megan's secret marriage, a lack of caffeine and her parents' latest exchange. 'I'll speak to my dad about the suit,' she said, struggling to remain composed.

'Is there anything I can do to help?' His hand came out to touch her arm.

The sudden intimacy startled her, especially as she could feel the heat of him through the sleeve of her jacket. 'I'm fine, really.'

'Okay, but call me if you change your mind. I'm not as organised at planning things as you are, but task me with anything that needs doing, I don't mind.' His brow was furrowed with concern, his eyes locked on hers, and for a second all her troubles disappeared.

Until a car horn blasted and broke the moment.

He squeezed her arm. 'Take care, Beth.'

She watched him walk off down the Hight Street and experienced a sudden sense of longing. For what, she wasn't sure. It wasn't like she wanted Matt Hardy. She wasn't attracted to him or interested in him. So why was she fighting an inexplicable urge to run after him?

Clearly, her parents weren't the only ones losing their mind.

# Chapter Eleven

After a hard week at work and several miserable incidents to deal with, including a double fatality when a lorry had collided with a stationary car on the hard shoulder, Matt wasn't overly enthusiastic about spending another precious day off dealing with wedding stuff, especially when he had a prison visit booked for the afternoon. Conversations with his dad left him exhausted and slightly depressed, and he was feeling especially downcast on this occasion, as after the visit he would be heading over to his half-brother's house in a feeble effort to get Chris enthused about his son's wedding.

Three times Matt had booked an appointment for Chris to visit the suit hire shop, and three times Chris had failed to show up. His half-brother seemed to think his actions would result in Zac cancelling the wedding. A more realistic outcome would be Zac getting married anyway and Chris missing the event – or at the very least, not having a decent suit to wear.

To add insult to injury, Matt was now standing inside a bespoke cake shop, surrounded by samples of sugary decadence that he desperately wanted to eat, but couldn't, not if he wanted to avoid bloating into the size of an elephant. It was torment of the worst kind.

The owner had gone to great lengths to create a magical place where customers would be enticed by the confectionery on offer. The walls were covered in floral wallpaper, the woodwork was painted rose-pink and the small boutique was filled with decorative tables displaying multi-tiered cakes balancing precariously on top.

The odds of him knocking into something and bringing the whole display crashing down were giving him the shakes. He was not built for quaint boutiques.

Feeling conspicuous, he was about to head outside into the sunshine to wait for Beth, when the bell above the door tinkled and she appeared.

'Hi,' she said, coming over, the darkened lenses in her glasses clearing as they adjusted to the electric lighting. 'You found the place okay then?'

'There aren't many pink buildings in Chobham High Street,' he said, gesturing to the pastel decor. 'It wasn't exactly hard to miss.'

She smiled, and he was hit by two realisations. Firstly, she'd greeted him with a friendly tone and hadn't sarcastically referred to him as 'Mr Hardy'. Secondly, it was the first time he'd seen her properly smile. Not a forced grimace, or a placating stretch of the lips, but a genuine smile that brightened her whole face. For a moment he just stared, struck by how lovely her eyes were when she wasn't glaring at him. Was it a trick? Lulling him into a false sense of security? Whatever it was, he wasn't about to let his guard down just yet.

'You look a little out of place,' she said, casting a glance over the fragile displays.

'You think?' He quirked an eyebrow. 'I'm scared to move, in case I knock anything over.' It was only then that he noticed the shadows still visible beneath her eyes. Things obviously hadn't improved then.

'Let's head to the back,' she said, nodding to an area behind. 'There's more space there.'

Grateful, he followed her lead, tucking in his elbows as he slalomed his way past the numerous display stands. There was something very different about Beth today. Her usual assertive bluster was absent, and she seemed less agitated than she had been during their previous encounters. Not that he was complaining – he just wasn't sure whether it was safe to relax, or whether it was the calm before the storm.

It was the first time he'd seen her out of a suit, and he wondered if that was a contributory factor. Having said that, he wouldn't describe her outfit as casual. Her hair was tied up, her fitted jacket was buttoned-up and her dark jeans and low-heeled boots were pristine. Everything was neat, and neutral, and understated. A contrast to the fiery temper he knew lurked beneath the tranquil exterior.

She glanced back. 'Did you manage to speak to Zac?'

'I did. He has no opinion about wedding cakes.'

'Helpful.'

Matt gave her a wry look. 'I thought so, too.'

They reached a curved wall filled with blown-up images of various cake designs, everything from traditional white to shocking pink. Simple and elegant, to gaudy and elaborate. He had no idea so many designs existed.

Beth peered at the photos. 'Any idea when he's coming back from Greece?'

'No, and I can't say I'm happy about it.'

She turned to him. 'You're not?'

'I'm pissed off beyond belief. Aren't you?'

'Yes,' she said, seemingly surprised by his answer. 'But I've given up trying to talk to my sister about it, she just gets upset. She says he's stressed enough about losing his passport and doesn't need me putting pressure on him to come home.'

'Not exactly fair when we're left organising their wedding, is it?'

'My sentiments exactly.' She turned back to the photos.

They were actually agreeing? Wonders would never cease.

Matt glanced at her profile. She had a cute nose. 'On a positive note, they've bought the rings from a local jeweller, so that's another item you can tick off your list.'

She turned to him. 'Are you about to make another sarcastic comment about my spreadsheet?'

He grinned. 'Your spreadsheet has turned out to be very useful. I stand corrected. And I was impressed by the private website, too.' Any scepticism he'd felt about the need for a wedding website had disappeared when he'd taken a look at the content. Beth had added information about the venue, the itinerary for the day, travel arrangements and a comments section to add any dietary requirements. There were also links to local hotels, taxi firms and the gift list. 'Did you really create it all by yourself?'

She gave a little shrug. 'I used an existing template and then added the relevant info.'

'It must have taken you hours.'

'One of the few benefits of not sleeping,' she said, with a sigh. 'It's amazing how much you can get done in the middle of the night. Although setting up the password proved a bit tricky.'

She tried to make light of it, but she was clearly struggling with the amount of stress being loaded on her. 'Doesn't sound like a lot of fun.'

'It's not,' she said, turning back to the photos. 'But it's done now and hopefully it'll help the day run smoothly.'

'I'm sure it will, you've done a great job. Thank you.'

He couldn't be sure, but he thought he saw a faint blush in her cheeks.

'What about this one?' he said, pointing to a cake decorated with playing cards and dice. 'Marriage is a gamble, after all.'

Beth smiled. 'High stakes and huge losses. As I know only too well, doing my job.' She pointed to another design. 'Why would anyone want cricket stumps on their wedding cake?'

Matt shrugged. 'Maybe to show how bowled over they are?'

She surprised him by laughing.

He'd never heard her laugh before. It was a nice sound.

She pointed to another cake. 'A tiger?'

'To show that he's a pussycat in bed?'

She smothered a laugh. 'You can find the romance in anything.'

He wasn't sure whether that was a compliment or not.

'You don't find giant liquorice allsorts romantic?' he said, careful not to knock over a three-tier monstrosity balancing on a table, with a jelly baby perched on top.

'It doesn't do anything for me, but novelty weddings are all the rage.'

'Like recreating Daphne du Maurier's Jamaica Inn, you mean?'

'That's not a novelty, that's a concept. Different thing entirely.'

He laughed. 'Whatever you say.' They moved further down the display. 'Did I tell you I've been in touch with the officiant? He's emailed through a list of documents the couple need to supply before the day. Nothing too onerous, just copies of their birth certificates, passports and proof of address.'

Beth frowned. 'Zac doesn't have a passport.'

'I know, but as long as the documents arrive before the day, it's not a problem. Hopefully, he'll have a replacement sorted by then.'

Beth had a puzzled look on her face. 'I'm surprised there's so little to it. I'd have thought more checks would be needed before being allowed to marry.'

'Not for a first marriage. If you've been widowed then you have to supply a death certificate, and if you're divorced you need to include the decree absolute, but as neither Megan nor Zac have been married before, it's not an issue.'

Beth paled.

He reached out to touch her arm. 'Are you okay? What have I said?'

She swallowed. 'Nothing. I'm fine.'

For a moment he feared her good mood might disappear, but she shook away whatever thought she was having and pointed to another photo. 'What about this one?'

He dragged his gaze towards the photo of a pure white creation with lace icing cascading down the side. 'Maybe a bit plain? Mind you, I have no idea what Zac would like, and I don't think he knows either. Perhaps we should pick the tiger cake as payback for being dumped in it.'

'He certainly hasn't helped ease an already stressful situation.'

'I think there's more going on than a lost passport.'

She turned to him, her look inquisitive. 'Meaning?'

He had no idea whether Megan knew about her future in-laws' aversion to the marriage, but Beth was already aware of the situation. Zac had mentioned it when they'd met in the cafe. 'Don't get me wrong, I genuinely believe Zac has lost his passport – nobody could fake panic like that. But there's still the issue of his parents not being entirely on board with the wedding. They think he's too young, that he's rushing into it, and they're worried he's making a mistake.'

'I was hoping they might've come around by now,' Beth said, sounding disappointed. 'I don't think Megan knows they object to the wedding. If she does, she's never mentioned anything to me.'

'I wouldn't have said anything, but my half-brother's making life stupidly hard at the moment. I think Zac's almost relieved to be stuck in Greece for a while.'

'Making life hard how?'

'Criticising every decision we make. Refusing to get measured for his suit, even refusing to confirm he'll be at the wedding. Zac hoped they'd soften to the idea over time, but they haven't, so I can't really blame his reluctance to come home.'

'It's not very fair on you, though, is it? You're the one stuck dealing with the flack.'

Matt shrugged. 'I can take it. I don't give into Chris's bullying.' Slightly embarrassed by the look of sympathy in Beth's eyes, he cleared his throat and pointed to a three-tiered cake with drapes of icing cascading down each layer, decorated with deep golden roses. 'What do you think about this one?'

It was a few seconds before Beth broke eye contact and turned to the photo. 'It's beautiful,' she said, nodding her approval. 'Good choice.'

He wasn't used to Beth agreeing with him. Should he be worried? 'You like it?'

'It's elegant and classy. The gold roses add a touch of glamour.'

'That was easy, I thought we'd be here hours.'

'No need, you've picked the perfect cake. Besides, you don't look very relaxed in here.' She tipped her head towards the tasting counter. 'Shall we choose a flavour?'

'Guess we'd better.' As he watched her walk off, he felt the need to ask, 'Are you sure you're okay? You still seem a little subdued.'

She looked slightly thrown by the question, as though no one ever considered her welfare. 'I'm fine,' she said, removing her glasses and rubbing her eyes. 'I'm just struggling to resolve the same problem I had last week. I won't bore you with the details. I'm sure I'll sort it out, one way or another.'

'Anything I can help with?'

'It's confidential, so no, but thanks for asking.' Replacing her glasses, she offered him a half-smile and went over to the tasting counter. 'I went for a long walk this morning over Chobham Common, that helped.'

He joined her by the counter. 'You like walking?' He hadn't put her down as the outdoorsy type.

She nodded. 'Especially in the countryside. I like nature, I find it helps to reduce the strain of working a fifty-hour week.' She peered at the cake samples on display. 'Not to mention the stress of arranging a fast-track wedding, trying to motivate my lethargic brother into getting a job and refereeing my parents' arguments – as you witnessed the other day.' She turned to him. 'Sorry about that, by the way.'

'Don't worry about it. Seems like we both have challenging families.'

She lifted a menu and read through the various options available. 'Rich chocolate cake, red velvet, plain vanilla or lemon drizzle. Personally, I'd go for the coffee and walnut.'

Coffee and walnut was his favourite, too. Shame he had to abstain from eating it.

'I think my sister would prefer a Victoria sandwich,' she said, looking at the selection. 'Or maybe the chocolate. Not that she'll eat much, she's forever dieting.'

'Me too,' he said without thinking, and then inwardly cringed. The words were out before he could stop them. Sharing his weight issues wasn't something he usually did.

Beth looked surprised. 'You're on a diet?'

Instead of answering, he lifted two plates and offered her the samples. 'Raspberry jam and buttercream, or chocolate ganache?'

It was a feeble attempt to change the subject, but she took the hint and tasted the Victoria sponge. 'Oooo, that's nice.'

His hands were occupied holding the plates, so she broke off a small section of cake and lifted it to his mouth. He wasn't sure which distracted him the most, the sensation of her fingers brushing against his tongue or the crumb of cake balancing on her lower lip.

She tilted her head. 'Good?'

The sugary sponge connected with his taste buds. 'Very good.'

She took a bite of chocolate cake and her eyes fluttered shut. 'This is even better.'

He found himself transfixed by her mouth, unable to avert his gaze, but when her eyes reopened, he dragged his eyes away. 'You try it,' she said, offering him a small morsel of cake.

His endorphins went into overdrive, as the taste of chocolate hit his senses and created a buzz that started in his brain and shot down to his toes. He avoided chocolate like an alcoholic avoided drinking. One measly mouthful was never enough, and he instantly craved more.

'How come you don't get on with your brother?' she said, dragging his mind away from chocolate.

He swallowed awkwardly. 'It's a long story,' he said, breaking the moment by dumping the paper plates in the bin. Things were still too fragile between them to risk the whole 'my dad's in prison' conversation. 'Are we decided on the chocolate cake?'

She nodded. 'Gets my vote.'

He headed for the till, eager to escape the confines of the tiny shop.

Once outside in the quaint high street of rural Chobham, Matt checked his watch. He had an hour to kill before heading off to visit his dad. 'Do you want to grab a coffee, or something?' He wasn't quite sure why he felt the need to prolong their meet-up. The task was complete, the wedding cake was chosen and ordered, so why not escape?

'Thanks, but I have chores to run.'

'No problem. Just a thought.' He was stupid for even asking.

'I have a fitting for my maid of honour dress,' she said, pointing to the bridal boutique opposite.

'I'll leave you to get on with your day then.' He turned to leave.

'Unless... you know, you wanted to see it?'

He turned back. 'You want me to see your dress?'

'A second opinion would be useful. I would've asked my mum, but she hasn't been in the right headspace of late. Plus, she'd only criticise my choice and pick out a dress that would suit Megan instead.'

Matt frowned. 'She'd do that?'

Beth waved away his concern. 'It's fine, really. It's not a problem. It's just... well, my mum and Megan are very alike. You know, confident, happy to be the centre of attention.'

'That's not you?'

She gave a small shrug. 'Are you surprised?'

'That you lack confidence? Yes, you're one of the most assertive people I've ever met.'

She rolled her eyes in a self-deprecating manner. 'Annoyingly so, right?'

'It's certainly confronting.' He smiled so she'd know he was teasing.

She sighed. 'You're right. When it comes to work, I'm fine. Ask me to make a legal decision or fight for my client's rights and I have no problem. It's just away from work that I struggle.'

'In what way?'

She opened her mouth as if to say something, but seemed to change her mind. 'It doesn't matter. Forget I said anything.' She crossed the road towards the bridal shop.

Intrigued, he followed her. It seemed incredible that someone as ballsy as Beth might lack confidence. But then, it wasn't like he really knew her, was it? They weren't spending time together through choice, they'd been thrown together through coercion.

They entered the bridal shop, and once again Matt felt out of his comfort zone. The space was filled with racks of white frilly dresses exploding into the space, like the time he'd mistakenly added bubble bath to a hotel jacuzzi.

The shop was painted midnight blue, with fancy gold accents, making it seem more like a nightclub than a bridal boutique.

A stern-looking woman wearing huge glasses appeared from nowhere and smiled at Beth. 'Ah, Miss Lawrence, perfect timing. Your dress is hanging in the booth waiting for you.' She gestured for Beth to follow her. 'Do take a seat in our waiting area,' she said, glancing back at Matt. 'We won't be long.'

Matt sat down on the comfy gold sofa and looked around. Apart from the array of white chiffon frothing at him from every corner of the room, there was a section dedicated to bridesmaids. Hanging on the end was a dark bronze-coloured dress that caught his eye. He could imagine Beth wearing something like that – it would suit her tall frame and autumn colouring. He averted his gaze elsewhere. What the hell did he know about women's clothing? He struggled to shop for himself.

In front of the changing booths was a small platform surrounded by floor-length mirrors and overhead spotlights, casting the space in a warm glow. He guessed it was intended to show off the bridal dresses in their best light.

A few moments later, Beth appeared from the booth and stepped onto the platform, looking uncertain and self-conscious… and he could see why. The dress she had on was bloody awful. Oh, hell. This wasn't going to go well.

'What do you think?' she said turning, revealing the full horror of the garment.

It was a murky grey colour, floor-length, with a shapeless bodice and horrible drapey sleeves. The cut did absolutely nothing for her and the shade drained her face of any colour.

He had two choices. Be honest or lie. Voicing his true opinion wouldn't be conducive to improving their fragile relationship moving forwards. They were finally getting along and he wanted to keep it that way. One misjudged comment could be catastrophic – just ask his mother.

Then again, he'd been accused of being too compliant when it came to women. His sister said he was guilty of agreeing with everything they said, just to keep the peace. Leah had encouraged him to be more assertive and honest. Maybe it was time to test out her theory – although if this blew up in his face, he'd be having serious words with his sister.

He cleared his throat. 'What colour would you call that?' he said, trying for a neutral tone and not giving anything away too soon.

'Caviar,' the assistant replied. She was standing by the side of the platform like a security guard, arms folded, a serious expression on her face.

Beth looked over at him. 'Not a fan?'

He tried to look thoughtful. 'I'm just wondering if it's right for a wedding?' he said, praying she wouldn't take offence. 'It's quite… sombre.'

Beth looked down at the dress. 'I didn't want anything too bright or garish, in case it detracted from Megan's dress.'

'The bride needs to be centre of attention,' the assistant said, her stern expression not letting up. 'We can't have the maid of honour stealing the show, can we?'

Right, so that's why Beth was dressed in an unflattering boring dress, the assistant was running the show.

'Not that anyone could upstage Megan,' Beth added, looking dejected. 'She'd look amazing in a bin bag.' She inspected her reflection again, pursing her lips quizzically. 'The dress comes in other colours if you think a different one would be better?'

It wasn't just the colour, he wanted to tell her, it was the whole thing. But how was he supposed to voice that without upsetting her? Then again, it wasn't like she looked overly convinced by the dress.

He got up from the sofa and addressed the assistant. 'Could you give us a moment?'

The woman hesitated, but when Beth nodded, she disappeared.

Matt approached the platform. 'At the risk of sticking my neck out, can I make an observation?'

She sighed. 'It's okay, you can say it. I look awful, don't I?'

'It's not you, it's the dress.'

'There wasn't anything else I liked any better.'

He rubbed his chin. 'What was it about this dress that appealed to you?'

She looked down. 'Well, it covers my broad shoulders... and I feel kind of invisible in it.'

'Why would you want to feel invisible? You're maid of honour at your sister's wedding. It's a special occasion, don't you want to look nice?'

She shrugged, but didn't reply.

It was time to test out his sister's theory. 'While I was waiting, I saw this dress I thought you'd look amazing in. Can I get it?'

Her expression grew suspicious. 'You want to choose my dress?'

'If you don't like it, just say.' He went over to the rail and unhooked the bronze-coloured dress. 'What do you think?' he said, bringing it over and holding it up.

She studied the dress. 'It's lovely… but isn't it too short?'

'It's knee-length,' he said, holding it next to her. 'And you have great legs.'

Her expression grew wide-eyed. 'I do?'

He cleared his throat. 'Trust me, you do.' He handed her the dress. 'There's no harm in trying it on. Is it the right size?'

She checked the label. 'It is.'

'Then you've nothing to lose by giving it a go.'

'Okay.' She didn't sound convinced, but she disappeared into the changing room.

Five minutes later, she reappeared wearing the dress.

The sight left him breathless. 'Wow.'

She stepped gingerly onto the platform and turned slowly, viewing herself from all angles in the mirror. 'You don't think it's too bold?' she said, alarmed by the sight of her exposed back, where the material was cut away.

'You look incredible.'

The assistant returned, pausing mid-stride when she spotted her client in a different dress.

Matt wondered whether he was about to incur her wrath, but she surprised him by nodding her approval. 'Good choice,' she said, circling the platform. 'The halterneck flatters your broad shoulders, and the colour works wonders for your skin tone. Will the colour match the other bridesmaid's dress?'

Beth looked over at Matt and he tried desperately to remember what Lily had said about the design. 'Poppy's wearing a sparkly pale gold dress,' he said, hoping that was right. 'It's very swishy with lots of netting, according to her stepmum. So you really don't need to worry about upstaging anyone. You've got strong competition from a thirteen-year-old.'

Beth studied herself in the mirror again, and something like embarrassed joy flashed across her face. 'You've convinced me. I'll take this dress instead.'

'Come with me,' the assistant said, marching over to the changing cubicle. 'I'll check whether any alterations are needed, although it looks like a perfect fit.'

Matt couldn't agree more, it was a perfect fit indeed. And then the alarm on his phone sounded, reminding him where he was supposed to be. 'Sorry, but I need to leave.'

He wasn't certain, but he thought Beth looked disappointed.

'I'm heading up to London to visit my dad. I don't want to be late, or I might not be able to see him.'

'Oh?' Beth looked concerned. 'Is he in hospital or something?'

*Shit.* 'Sorry, by visit, I meant *meet*. I'm heading up to London to *meet* my dad,' he said, trying to backtrack and not have to admit that his dad was in prison. 'I don't want to leave him waiting and wondering where I am.'

Beth look relieved. 'That's okay. Thanks for your help with the dress.'

He held her gaze. 'No problem. You really do look great in it.' Then he ran off like an embarrassed schoolboy, feeling stupidly pleased that his efforts to be assertive had paid off.

Leah would be delighted. She'd also gloat about how she knew him better than he knew himself. Maybe it would be better to keep quiet. After all, he wouldn't want her to read anything into it. She was already convinced he had the hots for Beth, and telling Leah about today's shopping trip wouldn't convince her otherwise.

And he definitely wasn't interested in Beth Lawrence... was he?

# Chapter Twelve

When Beth's head dropped onto her chin for the umpteenth time, she sat up and looked out of the window, hoping she hadn't missed her stop. The late afternoon sunshine hitting the windows, combined with the gentle rhythm of the train rattling through the remote villages of Cornwall, had lulled her into sleep.

Checking the app on her phone, she discovered that Launceston was the next stop. Unearthing a bottle of water, she took a long sip, trying to shake the heaviness threatening to send her back to sleep. As she gazed out of the window, she admired the pretty countryside as it whizzed by, with its green fields, sheep grazing and endless blue sky – a welcome tonic to her shattered nerves.

It had been another horrible week, with long working days interspersed with family dramas, including her mother and brother having a blazing row over a stash of weed discovered in Alex's room, Grandma Doris locking herself out of her home, and Beth arguing with her sister over the precariousness of her marital status.

Thankfully, Freddie Wood had been tracked down via an old drama friend on Facebook, and Beth had subsequently been able to message him. The bad news was that he'd yet to reply and it was now two weeks before the wedding, and the courts needed thirty days to deal with the annulment application – something that Megan felt was 'semantics' but which Beth knew could result in criminal charges, and her sister's upcoming marriage being declared null and void before the couple had even uttered, 'I do'.

Unfortunately, Megan was determined to forge ahead with the wedding as planned. She was refusing to even consider a postponement and was continuing to keep her poor fiancé in the dark.

Consequently, Beth was exhausted. She wasn't sure whether a weekend away was a welcome break, or another issue to be overcome.

Removing her glasses, she rubbed her tired eyes. The knots in her shoulders were causing the onset of a headache. She rummaged in her bag for a packet of painkillers and swallowed a couple of tablets, hoping to dull the pain.

The train slowed and Beth spotted the Launceston sign as they approached the station. Gathering her belongings, she made her way to the exit, hoping she wouldn't have to wait too long for a taxi.

Once on the platform, she extended the handle on her suitcase and made her way to the front of the building, wondering how the next two days would pan out. It was an odd situation to find yourself in, planning a weekend away with a man she hardly knew. But their efforts to arrange the wedding remotely had hit a number of hurdles and a physical visit was required.

Beth hauled her suitcase over the bumpy pavement, wondering how she'd allowed herself to be dragged into this fiasco in the first place. Like she didn't have enough on her plate.

She was so lost in thought, it took a moment to register her name being called. Glancing around, she realised that Matt Hardy was leaning out of his car window, waving at her.

Squinting as her glasses adjusted to the sunlight, she headed over to where he was parked up. 'What are you doing here?'

'I thought I'd save you a taxi journey,' he said, exiting the car. For a moment, she feared he was about to kiss her, but realised he was bending forwards to pick up her suitcase. 'How was your train ride?'

'Long,' she said, inhaling a waft of masculine scent, which made her instinctively step back. She wasn't ready to deal with the impact of Matt Hardy. 'How did you know which train I'd be on?'

'Lucky guess.' He opened the boot and tucked her suitcase inside. 'You said you'd arrive late afternoon. I figured I could check out Launceston while I waited.'

'Have you been waiting long?'

'Not long.' He came around to open the passenger door for her.

She climbed in and waited until he'd settled in next to her. 'Is it a nice town?' she asked, noticing his large frame was too big even for an SUV.

'Idyllic,' he said, starting the engine and pulling onto the main road. 'You were right, it's the perfect setting for a wedding.'

Finally, she'd got something right. 'When did you arrive?'

'This morning. I was on a late shift last night, so rather than waste the day, I came straight down. I got here mid-morning.'

'You haven't slept? Aren't you tired?'

He gave a half-hearted shrug. 'I had a nap at the hotel. I'm okay for the moment. It'll hit me later. Hopefully, not during dinner,' he said, with a grin. 'Apologies in advance if I snore during dessert.'

He expected them to have dinner together? She wasn't sure whether this was grossly presumptuous or just an innocent assumption. Why shouldn't they dine together? It didn't mean anything. It wouldn't be at all romantic. Just two acquaintances enjoying a meal together.

'I met with the officiant this afternoon,' he said, driving away from the town with its grey buildings and narrow cobbled streets. 'He seemed nice enough, reminded me of Rowan Atkinson.'

'Let's hope he's not like his character in *Four Weddings and a Funeral*.'

Matt laughed. 'That's all I could think of while he was talking, especially when he got the names mixed up and kept referring to Zac as Matt.'

'That could prove rather awkward. How do you feel about marrying my sister?'

He glanced over and grinned. 'Not my type.'

What was his type, she wondered? And then immediately quashed the musing. It was none of her business. What did she care who Matt Hardy fancied?

'I told him you might want to meet him. He's available tomorrow, if you do.'

'I'm happy if you are. It's not like we'd find a replacement at this short notice.'

'True.' His arm brushed against hers as he reached for his phone. 'I also visited the florist,' he said, handing her the handset. 'They're not open tomorrow or Monday, as it's a Bank Holiday, so I took photos. The passcode is—'

'You can't give me your passcode.'

He looked genuinely puzzled. 'Why not?'

'You hardly know me.'

He gave her a wry smile. 'What are you going to do, send nude photos to my contact list? Go ahead, it'll make the lads at the station very happy.'

Her eyebrows raised. 'You have nude photos of yourself on your phone?'

'Of course not, I meant you.'

'Well, I'm hardly going to send nude photos of myself, am I?'

'I think we're safe then.' He grinned and gave her his passcode.

Beth wasn't quite sure how she felt about scrolling through someone else's phone; it seemed incredibly personal – especially when the screen flashed open with an unread message from

HMP Wandsworth. Alarmed, she chose to ignore it. None of her business.

She clicked on the photos and flicked through the pictures. 'These are lovely,' she said, admiring the abundance of cream roses, orange ranunculuses and white gardenias surrounded by dark waxy green leaves.

'I thought the colours would match the bridesmaid's dress.'

'You have good taste.'

'I do?'

'You chose the perfect cake, picked me out a much better maid of honour dress and now you've chosen the ideal flower arrangements. You should change career, you're a natural wedding planner.'

'God, no thanks,' he said with an eye-roll. 'I'm glad you like the flowers, though.'

'Have you always been good at picking out stuff?'

'No idea.' He approached a junction, pausing while he negotiated the traffic. 'Maybe it was living in a house with two women. Not that my sister ever liked anything particularly girlie, but my mum does.'

'You always dress very nicely.'

'Are you being sarcastic?'

'Not in the slightest.' She thought how nice he looked in his green T-shirt with a motorbike on the front. 'You always look… comfortable.'

'Is that a compliment?'

'As someone who's never comfortable, it's an enviable quality.' She turned to study the views outside, watching as the landscape switched from village to rural.

A few moments later, he said, 'Do you own anything comfortable?'

She thought about it. 'Pyjamas. A onesie my sister bought me for Christmas. Oh, and fluffy socks. I get cold feet in bed.'

He glanced at her. 'That's it?'

'I find shopping stressful. I become agitated and uptight, which equates to me buying more suits.'

He grinned. 'How many suits do you own?'

'My wardrobe looks like an M&S clothing rail.'

He laughed. 'I'll introduce you to my sister, maybe you can swap clothes. Her wardrobe is full of sportswear. Mind you, she's a PE teacher, so I guess it's inevitable.' He pointed ahead. 'We're here.'

Beth strained to see out of the window. The Jamaica Inn was situated on a grassy mound in the middle of Bodmin Moor. No built-up housing or shopping precincts to spoil the views, just a backdrop of rolling fields merging into the distant skyline.

'This is rather lovely,' she said, relieved that her choice of venue wasn't a total disaster.

'Wait until you see inside.' He parked up in the gravel car park.

Climbing out of the car, Beth inhaled deeply, enjoying the tickle in her nose. Her headache had eased, thankfully, and she was able to enjoy her surroundings.

The two-storey building ahead was made from grey stone and designed to look like a period inn from centuries past. The large Jamaica Inn sign swinging from a wooden post depicted a pirate, complete with eyepatch and tricorn hat.

Matt appeared with her suitcase. 'I thought we could have an early dinner and head over to the barn to watch The Smugglers afterwards.'

'The who?'

'A local acoustic band. They play covers, feel-good rock and pop, according to their flyer. They also happen to be available on the ninth of June. I know you weren't keen on a disco, so I thought this might add a bit of variety to the evening instead. What do you think?'

'I'm happy to check them out, assuming I stay awake that long.' She watched him stifle a yawn. 'You, too. Busy shift last night?' She didn't know much about his job, other than the fact he was a firefighter.

'It was a strange one,' he said, stretching out his back. 'Two hours trying to remove a terrier who'd got himself stuck in an iron gate, and then a horrible incident involving a kid trapped under a goalpost. The bar was lying across his neck, restricting his airway.'

'Oh my god, was he okay?'

'He wasn't badly injured, just very shaken.'

'Understandably.' Beth rubbed her neck, unnerved by the image of a child nearly choking.

'When the hospital gave him the all-clear, we took him for a ride in the fire truck to cheer him up.'

'Are you allowed to do that?' She couldn't imagine joyrides were normal protocol.

'It's not in the rule book, but where kids are involved, it sometimes helps to soften the trauma.'

'Did it work?'

'He certainly enjoyed letting off the siren.' Matt checked his watch. 'Five o'clock. How about we meet up at seven? That way we both have time for a nap. Do you want to check out the bridal suite first? The manager said it isn't booked tonight, so it's available if we want to take a look.'

'I suppose we should.' Beth wasn't quite sure how she felt about being in a bedroom with Matt Hardy, or finding out more about what his job entailed. Maybe he wasn't such a Neanderthal after all. Still, they wouldn't be in the bridal suite long. It's not like they were here together on a romantic getaway. This was a business trip.

In contrast to the bright sunshine outside, the inside of the inn was dark, with low-beamed ceilings and wooden panelling covering the walls. Large beer barrels sat on the stone flooring and the subdued lighting was suspended from old carriage wheels. It was charming, quaint and very atmospheric. Hopefully, Megan would approve.

After checking her in, the manager handed Beth her room key and directed them to the first floor.

Matt insisted on carrying her suitcase upstairs. Too tired to resist, she let him.

The corridor was dark and long, with a deep red carpet and a series of wooden doors. Beth found her room and headed inside. 'Oh, wow.'

Matt stood by the doorway. 'You like it?'

'It's amazing,' she said, heading further inside.

The room was large and airy, with a beamed ceiling, double doors leading to a balcony and a huge king-sized bed. The focal point was an old-fashioned stand-alone bathtub sitting on a raised slab of slate in the middle of the room.

'You'll be able to stargaze,' Matt said, depositing her suitcase by the bed.

She spotted the free-standing telescope positioned in front of the windows. 'Have you been in here already?'

'I was allocated this room, but I figured you'd like this one better.'

Why would he do that? 'What's the other room like?'

'Like this one, but no bathtub.'

She frowned. 'Didn't you want a bathtub?'

He laughed. 'Not one that small – there'd be no room for any water.' He headed for the door. 'Do you want to check out the bridal suite?'

'I guess.' She followed him across the corridor and into another large room, which was even more stunning than her own. 'Wow, look at that bed.'

'Finally, something built for my size,' he said, bouncing onto the huge four-poster, with its dark wooden structure and draping voile canopy. 'Maybe I should've booked this room instead.' He flopped back onto the mattress.

A strange sensation fluttered inside Beth's chest as she watched him stretch his arms above his head. The room was filled with sunlight, casting him in a warm glow, and she had a sudden inexplicable urge to join him… which was ridiculous, of course. What was she even thinking?

Rapidly coming to her senses, she backed away in a flustered manner and said, 'Dinner at seven then. See you in the restaurant.'

Safely back in her room, she stripped off her clothes and settled into the ornate bathtub, ready for a long soak and keen to eradicate images of Matt Hardy lying on a four-poster bed, looking big and solid and tantalisingly good. The lack of sleep was playing havoc with her common sense.

At seven p.m. sharp, having enjoyed a short nap, Beth headed down to the restaurant. She was wearing a cream linen dress that had looked nice on the hanger, but felt like cardboard to wear. Another disastrous purchase. Would she never learn?

Matt was already waiting at the bar.

He stood up when she neared. 'Nice dress,' he said, laughing. 'Comfy?'

'Not in the slightest,' she said, making him laugh harder.

For some strange reason she didn't mind him laughing at her, which was unusual, as self-deprecating humour wasn't one of her attributes. Maybe it was because there was no malice in his teasing. Or perhaps it was because she sensed he had body-image issues himself. Maybe it was simply that she didn't have the energy to argue with him any more.

'What can I get you to drink?' he said, beckoning the barman over.

'A large glass of Chardonnay, please.'

'Spritzer?'

'Not today, I'm in need of neat anaesthetic.'

He leant against the bar. 'Is my company that bad?'

'The jury's still out,' she said, averting her gaze when he glanced over.

His grin indicated he wasn't offended.

'Like you feel any differently?'

'You're growing on me,' he said, with a good-natured shrug.

'Charmed, I'm sure.'

He nodded to the restaurant. 'Shall we eat?'

The waitress led them to a small table near the open fireplace. It was an intimate setting, with candlelight and soft music playing in the background. Their knees touched under the table, and despite shifting position several times, she gave it up as a lost cause when it became clear there was no way of avoiding his close proximity.

They each picked a different starter and main course, sampling potential options for the wedding meal in two weeks' time. Customer reviews for the food were glowing, and the descriptions sounded fancy enough for a celebration, but hearty enough not to leave anyone hungry. Hopefully, they wouldn't be disappointed.

'Tell me about your parents,' Matt asked, as they waited for their starters to arrive. 'I sense things are tense. Any dramas likely to unfold at the wedding?'

Beth took a long swig of wine. 'Why else do you think I'm drinking?'

'Is it really that bad?'

'You saw it yourself. How much worse could it be?' Beth rested her arms on the table. 'My sixty-five-year-old father left my mother for a twenty-eight-year-old exotic dancer from Essex called Tiffany. Not that I have anything against Essex, exotic dancers or women called Tiffany – except when they cause my usually sane mother to turn into the she-devil possessed.'

'Your mother didn't take the break-up well?'

Beth removed her glasses and wiped the lenses with a napkin. The heat radiating from the fire and the man next to her had made them steam up. 'Calling it a break-up implies there was some level of involvement on both sides.'

'There wasn't?'

'Sadly, no.' Beth slid her glasses back on. 'My father came home from work one Friday evening, ate his dinner, packed a bag and announced that he was leaving my mother for... *the love of his life*... and walked out, leaving her with a string of unanswered questions, a broken heart and the washing-up.'

'Ouch.'

Beth took another swig of wine, hoping to ease the tightness in her chest. 'My mother has gone from endless crying to excessive drinking, followed by hell-hath-no-fury-scorn like you've never seen. And now we have her latest behaviour, which you saw the other day, and for which I apologise again.'

'It's hardly your fault.'

'And all the while, my dad's been strutting around like a teenager on heat, flaunting his new bit of stuff and failing to take any responsibility for his actions.'

'Parents, huh?' He gave her a sympathetic look.

'The real high point? My father announcing that he wanted Tiffany at the top table at Megan and Zac's wedding. I thought my mum was going to spontaneously combust – she threatened to boycott the wedding. She's now agreed to attend, but only on the proviso that Tiffany isn't on the top table. So we get the pleasure of watching the three of them sparring like something from of *The Witches of Eastwick*.'

Their starters arrived, much to Beth's relief, as the alcohol was loosening her tongue. She was divulging far more than she should be about her wayward family, but there was something calming about Matt that enabled her to open up. Maybe she was being naive, but he'd trusted her with his phone passcode, so it seemed only fair to share something personal, too.

Suddenly hungry, the conversation lulled into silence as she tucked into her Cornish Camembert, and Matt devoured his mushroom pâté.

The restaurant was busy, with all the tables filled, but it didn't feel claustrophobic or noisy. Beth found the low chatter of the other couples and the glow from the open fire strangely comforting. She was finally able to relax. No doubt the wine was helping. Matt had ordered a bottle, and she was on her second glass already.

Matt finished his starter and sat back in his chair, his eyes turning inquisitive as he reached for his beer. 'Can I ask you something?'

'You can ask me anything,' Beth replied, wiping her hands on the napkin. 'I can't promise to answer you.'

When he smiled, she felt a tingling in her toes. He had a great smile, damn him, his eyes crinkled and his cheeks plumped up like a couple of juicy plums. 'When I met your mum the other day, she made a comment about it being time you got back out there and had some fun.'

Something Beth recalled only too well. 'That's not a question, that's a statement.'

'Okay, what did she mean by that?'

Beth let out an exasperated sigh. 'I would have thought it was self-explanatory.'

'Bad break-up?'

Beth shrugged. 'Nothing that caused any permanent damage.'

'But enough to put you off relationships?'

The waitress returned and removed their empty plates. 'I hope everything was okay with your food?'

'The food was delicious, thanks.' Matt smiled at the girl, waiting until she was out of earshot before resuming his questioning. 'So, what happened?'

It was too much to hope he'd drop the subject.

Beth took another swig of wine. 'Like I said, nothing overly dramatic. I've had two long-term relationships. One was ended by him, and the other was ended by me. No regrets. No hangups. No residual emotions or feelings for either man, just a desire not to…'

'Not to…?' Matt leant closer.

She met his gaze. 'Not to not repeat the same mistakes again.'

'Which were?'

'Settling for a man who I know isn't right, but is a supposedly safe bet. And steering well clear of cheating charmers.'

'Sounds fair enough.' Matt topped up her wine glass. 'So why the reluctance to try again?'

'Who said I was reluctant?'

He raised an eyebrow.

Beth sighed. 'Because in both cases I failed to notice what was happening. Everyone else could see that neither man was right for me, but I didn't. No one was even surprised when the relationships ended, they knew it was inevitable. But dummy here couldn't see what was right under her nose.'

Whatever he was about to say was interrupted by their main courses arriving. The waitress served Matt his sticky grilled chicken and Beth her red wine risotto.

'And that bothers you?' Matt asked when the waitress had disappeared. 'That you didn't see what was happening?'

'Damn right it bothers me,' she said, placing a fresh napkin over her knees. 'I see broken relationships all the time. I can spot a pending divorce a mile off, but when it came to my own relationships, I was clueless.'

'So you're never going to try again?'

She picked up her fork. 'Not until I can be trusted to make a sensible choice.'

'Define sensible?'

She sighed. 'Trustworthy, safe, reliable.'

'Sounds like you're picking out a used car.' He tucked into his food, his expression indicating it tasted good.

She took a mouthful of risotto and felt sure her expression matched his. The taste was heavenly.

For the next few minutes, they concentrated on enjoying their meal, content to remain silent, until Matt said, 'What about attraction?'

More fool her for thinking they were done discussing her love life. 'Attraction is overrated,' she said, taking another swig of wine.

He frowned. 'How do you figure that?'

'It blindsides a person. It makes them act on physical impulse, rather than logical thinking. Look at my dad... His behaviour is hardly rational, is it?'

'No, but can you be truly happy with someone you're not attracted to?'

160

She had no idea, but if you weren't overly invested in a person, then you wouldn't be overly devastated when it all went tits-up, would you?

Unsurprisingly, Matt wasn't done. 'If there's no attraction then a relationship is doomed from the start. Trust me, I've been there. At least if there's attraction, the relationship stands a chance of going the distance. Without it, you might as well not bother.'

She wanted to ask him more, turn the tables and delve deeper, but the waitress returned and ruined the moment. 'The band have just come on stage in the barn, if you wanted to see them,' she said, collecting their plates. 'You were asking about them earlier.'

'I was, thanks.' He gave her a friendly smile. 'Can you add the bill for the meal to my room?'

'Of course.' The waitress smiled and disappeared.

Matt stood up and offered Beth his hand. 'Shall we head over? Unless you'd prefer to have dessert first?'

'I'm too full for pudding,' she said, standing without taking his hand. 'You didn't have to pay for dinner. I can afford my own meal.'

'I'm sure you can,' he said, gesturing for her to exit ahead of him, like the annoyingly perfect gentleman he was. 'Are you looking forward to seeing the band?'

'I suppose so.' Her legs felt slightly wobbly beneath her, as they made their way from the restaurant and headed outside. The cool evening air hit her like a slap, fuelling the effect of alcohol coursing through her veins. She was officially tipsy.

The barn was already filled with patrons dancing to The Cure's song, 'Friday I'm in Love'. The space was filled with hay bales, lanterns and farming instruments. Three young guys stood on stage, wearing granddad shirts and trouser braces with turned-up jeans, looking very cool and playing their guitars enthusiastically.

Beth was about to head for a bench seat, when Matt caught her elbow and swung her onto the dance floor, effortlessly capturing her in his arms and instantly swaying to the music.

Her initial instinct was to object, especially as the buzz in her blood was magnifying the feel of his warm body pressed against hers. But she hesitated long enough to make escaping impossible. Besides, the strength of his grip holding her steady and moving her to the music was making her shoulders relax another notch.

Having fought against the urge to escape, she went with her second instinct, and gave into the moment and enjoyed being held. It had been a long time since she'd danced with a man. But there was no need to panic. It was just Matt. Kind, courteous, gentle-giant Matt. No need to worry about her judgement letting her down on this occasion. He was the human equivalent of a used car. Trustworthy, reliable and safe.

As her guard lowered further, though, another feeling started creeping in. Slowly at first, like a snake winding its way through the undergrowth, so stealth-like and unobtrusive that it took a while to register the prickling sensation that was heightening her senses. She suddenly became aware of his wide chest pressing against hers, the way his beard was tickling her cheek and the feel of his hand splayed across her back.

Her belly began to clench, and like a lightning bolt, she realised too late what it was.

Attraction.

# Chapter Thirteen

*Sunday, 26th May*

Matt took in a deep breath as he admired the views ahead, savouring the chill of fresh morning air hitting his lungs. Wispy clouds moved at speed through the mottled blue sky, and the distant trees moved in unison as the breeze toyed with them, bending their branches and scattering the nesting birds. Three large flags flapped in the wind, each one attached to a pole, advertising the unique combination of rural countryside and commercial tourist attraction. The Cornish flag, a Union Jack, and a skull and crossbones. The Jamaica Inn had certainly lucked out in terms of location. There wasn't another building in sight, only the expanse of Bodmin Moor stretching ahead, green, wild and enticing.

Tempted as he was to head off exploring, he'd promised to meet Beth after breakfast and check out the hotel's remaining attractions, including the farm shop and the museum. Neither venue topped his list of appealing activities, but it was on their itinerary, and he knew better than to upset Beth's rigid scheduling.

As he left the sunshine behind and entered the stone outbuilding converted into a museum, he fully expected his good feeling to fade. It seemed criminal to waste such a sunny day being stuck inside. But then he remembered how it had felt last night, dancing with Beth, and the idea of spending another day with her kept his mood afloat. Especially when he entered the museum and saw her dressed in a black cape, eyepatch and huge tricorn hat.

Unaware of him standing there, she was threatening the rubber parrot attached to Blackbeard's shoulder. A warm sensation filled his gut as he discreetly watched her. She leant against the makeshift bar of an olde-worlde tavern and pretended to load the barrels of a huge pistol, blowing make-believe smoke away from the tip, as if it had just been fired. This was a side of Beth he hadn't seen before. Playful, daft, relaxed.

His mind drifted back to the previous night, when their eyes had locked on the dance floor and he'd felt something pass between them – until she'd run off in a fluster. The optimist in him wondered if she'd felt the connection, too, and simply panicked. The pessimist in him told him she was drunk and had probably run off to throw up.

'Hand over your silver, you bilge-sucking scallywag,' she said, aiming the pistol at the statue.

'I hope that thing's not loaded,' Matt said, making Beth startle and nearly drop the pistol.

She turned and aimed the gun at him. 'You'll pay for your treachery, you son of a biscuit eater.' Then she frowned and said, 'Apparently, that's an insult.'

He moved closer. 'I think it means bastard.'

'Oh, right.' She gave a small shrug.

'Nice outfit.'

'I was thinking of wearing it to the hen do. It's that or a barmaid wench, which I can't see me pulling off.' She tilted her head quizzically. 'My mother, maybe. Me, not so much.'

'You're still insisting on fancy dress?'

'It'll be fun,' she said defensively, her scowl returning.

'Most sane people would consider it torture.' Her relaxed demeanour from yesterday had vanished and her agitation was back. Why, he wasn't sure. 'Are you sure it's not just an avoidance tactic?'

She narrowed her eyes. 'Meaning?'

'It saves you picking out an outfit.' He removed her hat, admiring the way her long hair tumbled onto her shoulders. 'Do you ever wear your hair down?'

'God, no. Too unruly.' She stepped away from him.

'It suits you loose. You have very pretty hair.'

Anyone would think it was the first time she'd received a compliment. Her mouth dropped open and she looked lost for words. When her cheeks flushed, she looked away, fumbling with the clasp on the cloak, as she struggled to remove it.

He resisted the temptation to help her, knowing it would only annoy her. 'Did you sleep okay?'

'Terrible.'

'Shame, I slept like a log,' he said, realising a beat too late that wasn't helpful. 'Why couldn't you sleep?'

'No idea.' She turned away, and replaced the cloak and hat on the hanger, removing the eyepatch from over her glasses and rubbing the lens. 'I stargazed for a while, so that was nice. Shall we look at the exhibits?'

'Sure.'

He followed a step behind, studying her outfit of pristine jeans, sparkling white trainers and rigid cotton top. Her attempts to be casual were hilarious – like when his dad used prison jargon during their visits, spouting phrases picked up from the younger inmates, which just sounded ludicrous coming from a fifty-seven-year-old man.

Thoughts of his dad dampened his good mood, so he switched to watching Beth admiring the exhibits in Daphne du Maurier's writing room, complete with ancient typewriter, and feather quill and inkwell.

Beth was subdued today, and he could tell by her body language that she was agitated. Her shoulders were hunched and her hands kept balling into fists. Every now and again her fingers would stretch out, almost as if she was reminding herself to relax. Was he the cause of her anxiety? He hoped not.

'Why don't you have a girlfriend?' she suddenly asked, stepping around a barrel of gunpowder on the floor.

The question momentarily threw him. 'How do you know I haven't?'

'Have you?'

He viewed her suspiciously. 'Why do you want to know?'

She shrugged. 'Curiosity, I guess.'

'Ask me nicely, and I might tell you.'

She shot him a look. 'Forget I asked, it's none of my business.' Turning sharply, she walked off to look at a display of photos.

Okay, the situation was becoming very strange. Yesterday they'd been almost friendly, but today he was back to being enemy number one, and he had no idea why.

But then he remembered questioning her last night about her love life and realised she was probably feeling a bit exposed, having divulged personal information about herself, when he'd revealed nothing.

He went over and stood next to her, keeping his gaze focused on the display. 'I don't have a girlfriend. I haven't had much success in the past with relationships.'

She angled her body away, as if disinterested. 'How come?'

He deliberated how much to say. 'My parents' marriage was... complicated. I grew up in a house with a lot of shouting and arguments and drama. My dad drank too much, and my mum took the brunt. I was so determined not to become like them, I think maybe it influenced my choices when it came to dating.'

She frowned. 'In what way?'

'I avoided anything that had the potential to become difficult or challenging. I opted for safe instead.'

'Oh, you mean like a used car?' Her sarcasm wasn't lost on him.

Fair enough, he'd deserved that. 'Which is how I know that safe doesn't work,' he said, looking her straight in the eye.

She blinked a few times. 'How many women are we talking about? Hundreds? Thousands?'

'Three,' he said, turning and heading over to a display cabinet filled with swashbuckling swords.

She followed him. 'Three?'

'Two long-term, and one that lasted a few months.'

She seemed to mull this over, the cogs in her brain almost audible as she processed the information. 'Let me get this straight. You opted for safe, but when things became too boring and you realised you weren't attracted to them, you left, making them feel rejected and heartbroken. Right?'

'Wrong. They left me.'

A pause followed. 'All three of them?'

'All three.' He turned to her. 'So, you see, you're not the only one who doesn't trust their own judgement.'

A lengthy pause followed. They were staring at each other with a mixture of annoyance and something far more primal. He could almost feel the air crackling around them, sparking and threatening to combust. They were either about to start kick-boxing or kissing. And he wasn't sure which would cause the most damage.

The moment was broken by a group of kids racing through the museum, being chastised by their parents.

Both Matt and Beth simultaneously cleared their throats, backed away like they'd been caught in a compromising position, and swiftly transitioned from the museum into the gift shop.

The neighbouring room was filled with a range of paranormal memorabilia and publications about ghosts, as well as the usual offerings of books, toys and puzzles. The shop included a selection of clothing – nothing in his size, of course, but there were a couple of nice scarves he thought his mum might like.

With the silence remaining between them, they finished the tour and ended up in the farm shop. They were greeted by an array of delicious goods, ranging from cheeses to pastries to expensive liquors. As a man who used avoidance to manage his cravings, he didn't find the experience as enjoyable as intended. It was more like mental torture, testing him and luring him down the path of indulgence.

He knew his issues with food came from his own making. Aside from possessing a terrible sweet tooth, he worked long shifts and often missed meals. There were times when he was too tired to cook anything healthy, so he'd end up eating processed meals or takeaways. Then came the onset of guilt, which would result in him starving himself the next day to compensate. He didn't need a nutritionist to tell him this wasn't conducive to healthy living.

'Would you like to go on a picnic?' she suddenly asked, turning so quickly he almost bumped into her. Okay, not what he'd expected. But before he could even utter a response, she backed away. 'Sorry, stupid idea. Forget I said anything.'

He caught her arm. 'I'd love to.'

She chewed on her lip. 'Don't feel like you have to do me any favours.'

'I'm not. It's a beautiful day and we're in a beautiful part of the country.' He let go of her arm. 'Why wouldn't I want to get outdoors and enjoy the sights? It's a great idea.'

Her eyes darted about, landing everywhere except on him. 'I could put together a hamper and meet you outside the main entrance in twenty minutes. Maybe you could head back to the gift shop and buy one of those waterproof picnic blankets.'

Eager to escape the farm shop, he readily agreed. Partly because he was willing to do anything to improve the atmosphere between them, but mostly because if he stayed any longer, he was in danger of raiding the cake counter. 'Sounds like a plan. See you outside.'

Twenty minutes later, Matt was waiting outside the inn and wondering if his actions had caused her to bail on him. After leaving the farm shop, he'd made the spontaneous decision to buy Beth a gift and leave it outside her bedroom door with a note saying, *Even pirates get to be comfortable sometimes*.

As there was no sign of Beth emerging from the inn, he feared he'd been too presumptuous and ruined things between them. Maybe he'd scared her off with an inappropriate gesture. What had he been thinking?

Luckily, his panic turned out to be unfounded when Beth emerged from the inn carrying a rucksack. Her hair was down and she was wearing the sweatshirt he'd bought for her, and he breathed a sigh of relief.

She pointed to the *Keep Calm and Drink Rum* slogan on the front of the soft blue hoodie. 'Funny,' she said, looking less stressed than earlier.

'Comfy?'

'Very. Thank you for the gift.' Her weak smile switched to a frown when he unhooked the rucksack from her shoulder. 'I am capable of carrying my own bag,' she said, sounding exasperated.

'I'm sure you are,' he said, stuffing the picnic blanket inside and hoisting the rucksack onto his back. 'Shall we head onto the moor?'

After a few seconds spent glaring at him, she sighed and walked off. 'Fine.'

Matt had no idea what the etiquette was these days with regards to female empowerment, and although he'd lived with two strong women who'd demanded his respect and busted his balls when he'd inadvertently underestimated them, he also had his own sensibilities to consider. Sensibilities that wouldn't allow him to watch a woman half his size carrying a heavy rucksack over rural terrain when he was built like a carthorse. It just wasn't right.

His size didn't have many uses, but when it did, he was keen to capitalise. Like at work, where his strength proved an asset when lifting a motorbike off a fallen rider or retrieving someone from the window of a burning building. Being called upon to use his size for good helped to compensate for the jobs where his smaller colleagues were needed to squeeze through tight gaps and use their agility to navigate their way inside a crushed vehicle. Something he couldn't do, not unless it was an artic lorry. Of course, the downside of being built like a Sherman tank was that he was perpetually hungry.

'What did you get us for lunch?' he asked when his stomach rumbled. Even as he said it, he was dreading opening the rucksack and discovering Cornish pastries, crisps, sugary drinks, chocolate cake – all the delicious things on offer in the farm shop that he shouldn't have but desperately wanted.

'Smoked salmon salad, a selection of dips and crudités, and a fruit medley for pudding.'

He stopped walking.

'And fresh mango juice to drink,' she said, pausing when she saw his expression. 'What? Did I buy something you don't like?'

'No, it sounds great.'

'Good.' She gave a little shrug. 'We had a big dinner last night, and we're bound to indulge again tonight, so I figured I'd keep lunch light.' She said it like it was no big deal and continued walking.

Except it was a big deal. To him, anyway. He would have eaten whatever she'd bought, because it would have been rude to refuse, and because when presented with temptation, his resolve would have cracked, but she'd saved him from the inevitable guilt. Was it a fluke? Her own personal choice? Or was she being a kind and sensitive soul, saving him from his own weakness?

They crossed the lane and jumped over one of the ditches created to prevent the sheep from wandering onto the road. As they ventured onto the moor, he felt the tension leave his body. It was good to be outside.

'Look over there,' Beth said, pointing to a group of wild ponies in the distance, grazing on the long grass. The wind caught her hair and she pushed it away from her face, studying a nearby stack of boulders. 'You don't get that on Chobham Common.'

'Some of the stacks are thought to be prehistoric.'

She glanced at him. 'How do you know that?'

'Tour guide pamphlet in the hotel room.'

'And I was thinking you were cultured.'

He grinned. 'Nope, just curious.'

They continued walking.

Bodmin Moor proved to be more than just an attractive landscape. The outer area was filled with soft grasses, rambling heathers and low drystone walls made from local cobbles. It was only as they headed further away from the inn that walking became more challenging. Marshy soft ground created a deceptive cover for the soggy soil beneath, making progress slower and less stable. Random boulders stubbed your toes if you weren't paying attention, and large tree roots threatened to topple you without warning.

He was about to warn Beth about one such hazard, when she said, 'Mind, it's slippery,' and deftly hopped over the offending stream like a mountain goat. She was surprisingly more at home amongst nature than he'd expected. Not for the first time, he'd underestimated her.

Their approach to tackling the terrain differed as much as their personalities. Beth avoided the tricky areas, swerving around the wet marshes and switching paths to steer clear of the bogs. No wonder her trainers remained so pristine, she was clearly an expert in dirt-avoidance. In contrast, he marched through the mud, not even trying to avoid getting splattered. Partly because his bulk didn't allow for sharp changes in direction, but mostly because he didn't mind getting dirty. A rugby trait, no doubt. Outdoor winter sports were not suited to anyone averse to getting caked in mud.

'Shall we head up there?' Beth pointed to a mound with the ruins of an ancient crumbling church on top.

He caught up with her as she reached a thicket of brambles. 'Wait up,' he said, causing her to glower at him as he overtook her. 'I'm thinking of your white shoes.' He stamped on the brambles to create a flatter pathway.

'I don't need a man to help me.' She sounded put out as she followed him.

'I know you don't.' He carried on walking, amused by her indignation.

'I am more than capable of walking by myself.'

'Agreed.'

'I regularly walk in the countryside,' she said, a few feet behind him. 'I manage quite happily, and so far without incident or injury.'

'I'm sure you do.'

'I don't need a man with a Tarzan complex rescuing me like some helpless damsel in distress. I am no Jane.'

'Never thought you were.' He tried desperately not to laugh.

'Retrieving hapless females from burning buildings might be commonplace for you, but I don't need help, thank you very much. It's not necessary for you to mollycoddle me, or... *shit*.'

He turned at the sound of her expletive, not immediately sure what had happened. She was upright and appeared intact – if you discounted her hair being blown across her face by the wind. 'What's wrong?'

She pointed downwards.

His eyes dipped to her feet. Her once pristine white trainers were now buried ankle-deep in mud, and he began laughing, mostly at her disgruntled expression.

Her hands went to her hips. 'Yeah, not helpful.'

He turned away and continued walking up the mound.

'Hey, where are you going?'

'To set up the picnic,' he called, waving a hand. 'You don't need any help, remember? You're more than capable of...' He stopped and turned to face her. 'What was it you said again? You don't need a man with a Tarzan complex rescuing you like you're some kind of damsel in distress. Did I get that right?'

'Fine. I'll do it myself.' Another glare. 'Thanks for nothing,' she muttered, as she tried to lift a foot from the mud.

Matt allowed the torture to go on a while longer, as he continued up the mound to deposit the rucksack at the top, fully intending to head back down and help her, but not wanting her to know that just yet. He watched her balancing on one foot, trying to extricate herself from the mud. 'How's it going down there, Jane? Making any progress?'

'Quit with the sarcasm,' she yelled, using her arms to aid her balance. 'You've made your point.'

He jogged down the mound and came to a halt in front of her. 'Which is?'

She raised an eyebrow. 'Are you seriously going to make me do this?'

He grinned. 'It seems only fair.'

'And I thought I'd misjudged you, and that underneath the Neanderthal exterior was a gentleman.'

He folded his arms. 'That's your idea of apologising? To call me a Neanderthal?'

'You know what I mean.'

'Actually, I don't. Do you want my help or not?'

'No, I don't want your help.'

He turned to walk off. 'Fine.'

'But I accept that on this particular occasion I need it.'

He stopped. Wow, how it must have pained her to admit that.

Supressing a smirk, he turned and approached her. 'So, just to clarify, you would like my help?'

Biting her lip, she closed her eyes and nodded, angrily pushing her hair away from her face when the wind picked up. 'Could you please stop enjoying this so much, and just give me your hand. It's not like I need the bloody marines, I just need something to lean on so I can pull my foot out.'

'Some*thing*? Wow, you sure know how to objectify a bloke.' He bent forwards, wrapped his arms around her middle and lifted her into a fireman's lift. It was worth it to hear her squeal of indignation.

'What are you doing!?' she yelled, the noise sending a huddle of sheep scattering across the moor.

'Rescuing you, caveman-style.' Easing his way through the muddy terrain, he was careful not to drop her. 'This is how us Neanderthal types do it, Tarzan-style.'

'Put me down!' She pummelled his back with her fists.

'What, back in the mud? Trust me, you don't want that. Hang on, we're nearly there.'

He knew he was playing with fire, but it wasn't like he had anything to lose. In two weeks' time the wedding would be over and they'd never have to see each other again. A thought that didn't give him as much pleasure as he'd anticipated.

Ignoring her complaining and calling him a range of unflattering names, he reached the top of the mound and lowered her to the ground. 'There, that wasn't so bad, was it?'

His reward? A thump on the chest. 'Bastard!'

'I think you mean, son of a biscuit eater.'

She opened her mouth to continue yelling… blinked a few times… and then started laughing. Laughing so hard, she had to rest her hands on her knees to stop herself falling over. 'Idiot,' she said, straightening and thumping his chest again, this time with no force. 'I suppose you think you're funny?'

'You don't?' He nodded to her muddy trainers.

'Oh, for crying out loud,' she said, when the wind lifted her hair again and flapped it across her face. In her flustered attempts to control it, she sent her glasses flying. 'Bloody hell!'

Laughing, he reached out and caught her hair in his hands, smoothing it away from her face. Gently and slowly, he collected all the wayward strands and eased them into a ponytail, holding it behind her head. 'Better?'

Her gaze travelled slowly up to meet his. It was a good few seconds before she nodded, causing her head to tug against his grip. It was such a slight movement, but it sent a bolt of electricity racing through him.

Their faces were so close, their bodies almost touching. And then he became aware of her eyes, no longer hidden behind thick-rimmed glasses, watery from the wind and staring up at him with such questioning intensity that he was knocked sideways.

It wasn't just her eyes, but her flushed cheeks and her partially open mouth, all combining to draw him closer and undermine his resolve.

Forget chocolate cake. He'd been presented with something a lot more enticing.

The next thing he knew... he was kissing her.

## Chapter Fourteen

It had been a long time since Connie had gone to such lengths to impress a dinner guest. It had been even longer since she'd spent a whole day getting ready for the event and taking such care over her appearance – she'd even forked out for a new dress. The mint-green silk floral wrap-dress felt wonderfully soft against her newly buffed skin, and the low neckline did wonders for her cleavage. At nearly two hundred pounds it hadn't done wonders for her depleting bank balance, but when a woman was being forced into fighting to save thirty-nine years of marriage, she was entitled to splurge a little.

The timer on the oven beeped, reminding her to the check progress on the lemon meringue pie. The top was still pale, so she reset the timer for another ten minutes and headed into the dining room to check on her staging.

The drop-down pendant lights were dimmed low, casting the room in a romantic glow. A flourish of iridescent white lilies spilled from a vase set in the centre of the table, and cut-glass crystal flutes were positioned deliberately close together. The idea was to create intimacy, encourage romance and evoke cosiness, so they could reconnect and explore whether their marriage could be saved, or whether it was dead in the water.

On the table, a bottle of Château La Fleur-Pétrus had been decanted, Kenneth's favourite. Another two hundred quid she couldn't afford, but she hoped it would act as another reminder of the life they'd once shared. Somehow she couldn't imagine

Tiffany being a wine connoisseur, the girl was more likely into the weirdly flavoured gins all the youngsters raved about these days. Something she was certain Kenneth definitely wasn't a fan of – or not the Kenneth she knew. He might have gone off the rails of late, but she knew who he was deep down. No one could change that much in just a few short months, surely.

Connie knew his habits, his taste in music and food preferences. Could Tiffany say the same? Did she know about his hernia that niggled when he exercised? That he couldn't sleep without a glass of water on the bedside table? That he hated having his feet touched, but loved a back scratch?

A thump from upstairs reminded her that she wasn't alone in the house. It wasn't ideal having her son around when she was attempting to seduce her estranged husband, but Alex had promised to stay in his room for the evening and not disturb them, so she just hoped he'd stick to the agreement. If not, she'd be demanding her fifty quid back. It said something about the state of your life when your children resorted to bribing you.

The sound of her phone ringing prevented her from lighting the scented candles. Checking her reflection in the mirror above the fireplace to ensure that her carefully blow-dried hair hadn't flattened, she headed for the kitchen, pleased with the way her gait felt sturdier and leaner these days. Thrice-weekly boxing sessions and an increase in her trips to the swimming pool were paying off. Not just physically, but mentally, too. She felt stronger, more stable, with less of a desire to run Kenneth and Tiffany over with the garden mower.

Her rage hadn't diminished entirely. She still fantasised about publicly humiliating the pair of them, just as they had humiliated her, but the highs and lows didn't fluctuate as much as they once had. Days could pass now without her feeling the need to disembowel Tiffany with a serrated bread knife, and as far as she was concerned, that was definite progress.

Pressing the speaker button on her phone, she opened the fridge and removed the tray of marinating chicken. Conversations with her mother tended to be less infuriating if she had a distraction. 'Hi, Mum. Everything okay?'

'I've had a letter from the DVLA. They want my organs.'

Okay, slightly random. Connie poured herself a glass of cheap supermarket wine, a precursor to the expensive stuff later. 'Why are the DVLA writing to you?'

'No idea.'

Connie stirred the creamy garlic sauce bubbling away on the hob. 'Can you read me the letter?'

Various noises followed, as her mother tried to locate the piece of paper. 'It says... we have received your driving licence renewal form.'

'Why have you renewed your driving licence?' Connie stopped stirring the sauce. 'You're not allowed to drive any more, Mum.'

'Of course I am. Don't talk nonsense.'

Connie silently cursed. How did her mother even complete the form? She could barely operate the TV controls these days. A well-meaning neighbour probably helped her. It'd happened before, with various off-limit activities being reinstated that Connie subsequently had to cancel. 'Your driving licence was revoked when you were diagnosed with dementia, remember?' Although asking someone with memory problems if they remembered something was probably daft on her part. She carried the sauce over to the counter and poured it over the chicken.

'How am I supposed to do my shopping?' her mum asked, sounding annoyed.

'I take you.'

'No, you don't. I take Lucille for a spin.'

Lucille was the 1970s old-style VW Beetle that her mother had managed to keep on the road for over thirty years. 'Mum, you sold Lucille ten years ago.'

'Don't be daft, she's parked in the garage – I polished her only this morning. Next you'll be telling me I no longer have a garage.' Doris's incredulous laugh was caused no doubt by her daughter's ludicrous claims.

Tempting as it was to point out that her mother did not own a garage, as she now resided in a small retirement flat in a community village in Godalming, Connie knew the fallout wouldn't be worth it. Correcting a person whose reality no longer matched your own was exhausting. It was also confusing, often leaving Connie wondering which one of them was of sound mind.

She decided to change tack. 'You don't need to worry about the letter, Mum. I'll deal with it when I pop over tomorrow after work.'

'But they want my organs. I have to register them.'

Connie vaguely recalled seeing an article on the news about the DVLA taking over the organ registration system and realised what the letter was about. 'They're just asking if you want to sign up to be an organ donor, Mum.'

'Well, I don't. How dare they!'

'That's fine, Mum. You don't have to.' Connie grated Parmesan over the chicken and placed it in the oven.

'How on earth do they expect me to function without my organs?'

Connie stilled, unsure whether to laugh or cry. 'They don't take them until after you've died, Mum.'

'Oh… oh, well, in that case, they can have them.'

With that, her mother ended the call.

Sighing, Connie removed the lemon meringue pie and placed it on a heat mat. Dropping her head on the counter, she closed her eyes, counting to ten in an effort to combat the rising stress levels. She needed to stay calm and serene. Tonight was about making an impression, not resorting to having a screaming fit because her mother was losing the plot.

The doorbell rang.

Game time.

With a deep calming breath, Connie shook away her anxiety and took her time walking to the front door. It wouldn't do to appear too keen, she needed to retain the illusion of being slightly aloof and unobtainable. Kenneth had to want her, to desire her, and be unsure as to whether he could have her. He needed to prove that he was worthy, and with any luck, resort to begging. It was the least she deserved. Making Kenneth suffer and break a sweat might go some way to repairing her crushed self-esteem.

But she was getting ahead of herself. One thing at a time.

Fixing what she hoped was an alluring smile, she opened the door, only to be greeted by a strong waft of aftershave she didn't recognise. A gift from Tiffany, no doubt.

'You look nice,' Kenneth said, and offered her a bottle of wine and a bunch of flowers.

It was a promising start, and a glimmer of hope shimmered within her, until she realised the wine was a cheap bottle of Chardonnay and the flowers were a supermarket purchase. It was a far cry from days gone by, when she'd been showered with expensive jewellery and sexy lingerie, and whisked away on city breaks.

Still, it was better than a kick in the teeth… just.

'Thank you,' she said, mustering as much grace as she could. 'Come through to the dining room, dinner won't be long.'

He followed her down the hallway, his eyes scanning the ornaments and paintings, probably checking she hadn't sold any of their joint assets before the divorce had been finalised.

The solicitor she'd met with had been confident of securing her a decent settlement and arguing for sole ownership of the house. Hopefully, it wouldn't come to that and her marriage could be saved, but it was useful information to know nonetheless. It gave her a sense of power, which meant she could play hardball.

When Kenneth ran a finger over the sideboard and checked for dust, she bit the inside of her cheek to stop herself thumping his perfect nose. Let it go, she told herself, be calm and rise above such pettiness. The solicitor had told her not to give her husband any ammunition.

She focused on the positives instead, like the effort he'd made with his appearance. He looked good in his lightweight linen suit, with an open-neck shirt and casual boating loafers. But whereas Kenneth had always embraced the ageing process with dignity and never fought against the inevitability of old age, there was now an air of 'middle-age crisis' about him. The gelled hair, the silver chain around his neck, the lack of socks, and good heavens… was he wearing an earring?

'You've had your ear pierced?' she said in a slightly high-pitched voice, inspecting the gold hoop dangling from his ear.

'I had it done last week when we visited Brighton.' He walked around the table and sat down. 'It's good to add a spot of spontaneity to life, don't you think?'

It was hard to decipher whether this was a dig or an innocent remark. Either way, he sounded smug.

Fighting her annoyance, she poured two glasses of wine. 'I couldn't agree more,' she said, handing him one. 'I've recently taken up boxing.'

He almost spilled his drink. 'Boxing?'

His shock was all the tonic she needed and her annoyance immediately dissipated. She'd retained the upper hand. 'It's surprisingly empowering. Anthony – that's my trainer – he says I have quite the left hook.' She smiled and lifted her glass. 'Cheers.'

He clinked glasses with her, his brown eyes slightly wider than normal. He was starting to see her in a new light and her self-esteem improved another notch. 'Remind me not to get on your bad side.'

'Oh, it's too late for that,' she said, waiting a beat before laughing. It was good to make him squirm a little.

He joined in the laughter, albeit a little forced. 'You had me worried there.'

'That was my intention.' She allowed another lengthy pause before smiling to show she was teasing. 'Here's to our beautiful daughter, Megan.' She lifted her glass in a toast. 'May she live a long and happy life.'

'And be as happily married as we were.' He realised his mistake almost instantly, and the smile fell from his face. 'You know what I mean... as happy as we were... before, you know?'

'Before you buggered off and left me for another woman?' Her tone was light and cheery, as though she didn't have a vengeful care in the world. Her open and unwavering smile unnerved him further and she could tell he wasn't quite sure what was going on. That was her intention. Keep the bastard on his toes.

'It wasn't like that,' he said, taking a huge gulp of wine.

'No?' She gave him a questioning look, extending the moment to increase his suffering. 'It seemed that way to me. Anyway, it's ancient history now,' she said, leaning against the fire surround. 'Anthony has encouraged me to move on. He's been teaching me to expel my anger and find peace. It's quite liberating.' She adopted a dreamy expression, allowing her fingers to trail down her exposed neck.

Kenneth's eyes tracked her downward motion, causing him to visibly swallow and become transfixed, like a snake hypnotised by its master. Putty in her hands.

Connie allowed herself a small self-satisfied smile. 'Do you remember that holiday we took in Antibes when we were first married?'

Kenneth blinked, as if casting his mind back. 'The one when it rained solidly for days and we were stuck inside the hotel room?'

'That's the one.' She walked towards him, holding his gaze. 'We watched *The Sting* dubbed in French, and ate lobster and drank champagne in bed.'

'And the chambermaid ran from the room when she caught us mid-romp.'

Connie offered him an enticing smile. 'We didn't care.'

His eyes locked with hers. 'We carried on like she'd never been there.'

'Totally absorbed in what we were doing.' She was standing right by him now, gazing down at him in the chair, dominant and imposing.

His hand came up to settle on her waist.

She could feel the weight on her hip bone, the heat burning through the flimsy silk of her dress, heating her blood and creating a familiar buzz. It had been a long time since Kenneth had looked at her with such wanting, such intent, such heat... and then her ruddy phone rang.

Still, it was always a good idea to leave a man wanting more.

'Excuse me, I need to check on dinner,' she murmured, sashaying from the room with as much allure as she could muster. 'Help yourself to more wine.'

Connie's aroused state switched to sinking dismay when she saw it was her mother calling again. Talk about bad timing.

With a deep breath, she answered the phone, trying to sound like a supportive daughter and not a petulant teenager whose date had been interrupted. 'Yes, Mum, what is it?'

'The thingy's disappeared,' her mother said, sounding flustered.

Connie didn't have time to decipher another of her mother's incomprehensible ramblings. 'What is it you're trying to do, Mum?'

'On the iPad. One minute it was there, the next it had vanished.'

'You were trying to do something on your iPad? Can you be more specific? What were you looking at? Facebook? iPlayer?'

When Beth had suggested buying her grandma an iPad, Connie had been sceptical, not least because Doris found it extremely difficult to remember new instructions these days. But her daughter had convinced her it would stimulate her grandma's brain and enable the family to stay in touch more easily. Of course, Beth hadn't factored in that Connie would be the one expected to provide round the clock technical support and that her IT skills weren't exactly on a par with those of Bill Gates.

'It was there, then it wasn't.' Her mother was breathing heavily. 'Where has it gone?'

'I can't answer that, Mum.' She lit the hob, placing the pan of buttered asparagus on top. 'It'll have to wait until tomorrow, when I come over.'

'Can't you come over now?'

Connie closed her eyes and willed away her agitation. 'No, Mum. I'm just about to serve dinner.'

'But I wanted to look at the thingy on my iPad.'

Connie supressed a sigh. 'Can't you watch TV instead?'

'Have I broken the iPad?'

'You won't have broken it, Mum. Whatever it is, it will still be there. Leave it for now and I'll look at it tomorrow, okay? Please don't worry, we'll sort it out.' Connie checked the timer. Her carefully developed plan was in danger of going south if she didn't return to the dining room soon. She had to capitalise on the good progress she'd made. Kenneth was beginning to soften towards her, she just knew it. 'I need to go now, Mum. I'll call you in the morning.'

'Aren't you bringing over dinner?'

'The carer gave you dinner earlier.'

'No, they didn't. I haven't seen anyone all day.'

This wasn't true, but her mother was clearly in one of her belligerent moods. 'Yes, you have. Now, go and watch some TV, okay?'

'I'll call Beth. She'll make me dinner. She won't leave me to starve.'

Connie bit down on her lip, battling the urge to say something she'd regret and knowing darn well that her mother would remember it – even if she forgot everything else. That, it seemed, was the real cruelty of dementia. For the carer, anyway.

With great effort, Connie kept her temper and said through gritted teeth, 'You call Beth, if that's what you want.' Knowing full well that Beth would give her grandma the same answer. 'Night, Mum. See you tomorrow.'

Connie ended the call, the brief relief she felt instantly replaced by guilt. She tried so hard to be patient, yet it was just so difficult sometimes. But there was nothing that could be done tonight. Her estranged husband, however… well, that was a different matter.

Having checked the chicken and seasoned the hasselback potatoes, Connie returned to the dining room with a renewed determination to win over her ex-husband. A feeling that withered slightly when she realised he was on the phone to Tiffany.

'You know where I am,' he mumbled into the phone. 'I told you. Yes, I did… Don't be like that, honey. You know how I feel about you.'

Connie topped up her wine – she needed a stiffener.

Tiffany clearly wasn't happy about Kenneth meeting up with his ex. Good. Maybe it was time to make the little minx suffer a bit more.

'Kenneth, darling!' she trilled deliberately loudly, making her ex-husband flinch. 'Oh, sorry, I didn't realise you were on the phone.' She feigned mortification, waving her hand and pulling a distressed face – her daughter wasn't the only one who could act. 'Apologies. More wine, darling?'

Kenneth flushed an odd colour and turned away, mumbling into the phone, 'It's not what you think,' and 'of course, I still love you.'

Connie took another slug of wine, relishing trouble in paradise, before reminding herself that she was supposed to take it easy with the booze. Alcohol had a habit of fuelling her behaviour, both good and bad. Instead, she loosened her dress to enhance the gap at the front. Tiffany wasn't the only one who could play games.

By the time Kenneth came off the phone, he was red-faced and flustered.

'Anything wrong?' Connie adopted the lightest of tones.

'Everything's fine,' he replied, taking a mouthful of wine. 'But I may have to go.'

The hairs on Connie's arms sprang to attention. 'You can't. I mean, we haven't had dinner.'

'I know, I'm sorry.' He gave a half-shrug.

Connie wasn't giving in that easily. Rallying her deflated spirits, she moved over to him, keeping her voice and movements seductive, and was careful not to sound pleading. Pleading would come later, but only if push came to shove.

'I asked you here so we could talk about the wedding,' she said, smoothing down the front of Kenneth's jacket lapel, tilting her head to expose more of her neck. 'Our daughter is getting married next weekend and we've yet to discuss gifts, or speeches, or seating arrangements.'

He stepped away and cleared his throat. 'What's there to discuss? Beth has it all in hand. She'll tell us where to sit.'

The rejection stung. Connie couldn't believe he was bailing on her. But perseverance and an unwillingness to see her plan fail propelled her towards him, almost trapping him against the window seat. 'It's important that we present a united front, Kenneth. For Megan's sake, if nothing else.' She batted her eyelashes, something that used to work on him. Not any more, it seemed.

He ducked past her and headed for the door. 'It'll be fine. We got on okay tonight, didn't we?'

'You've barely been here half an hour.' She swung around to face him, her voice betraying her panic. 'That's hardly a test. And what about dinner? I've spent all day cooking. I've made your favourite dessert, lemon meringue pie.'

He rubbed the back of his neck. 'You shouldn't have gone to so much bother.'

'I wish I hadn't,' she muttered, glancing up at the ceiling.

'Really, Connie, you're making too much of this. It was just a casual visit. I had no idea you meant for it to be so... intimate.' His eyes dipped to her exposed cleavage.

'You seemed happy enough earlier,' she said, with an edge to her voice.

'That was before.'

'Before, what? Tiffany rang and told you to come home?' She wasn't going down without a fight. 'What are you? A grown man, or a naughty schoolboy?'

Kenneth's shoulders lifted in indignation. 'Don't speak about Tiffany like that.'

'Like what?' She opened her arms. 'I haven't said a word about *Tiffany*.'

He pointed a finger at her. 'No, but you implied I'm under the thumb.'

She took a step towards him. 'Aren't you?'

They were inches apart, staring each other down. The air crackled between them like Chernobyl about to erupt. Sirens blaring, warning lights flashing. It was just like the old days, in decades past, when they'd been young and in love and passionate for each other and had fought like the fiery beings they were.

Kenneth's gaze was fixated on her mouth. 'Not in the slightest,' he said, leaning closer.

She closed the gap and whispered in his ear, 'Then stay and have some dinner.'

She felt him shiver and knew he was on the brink of caving... until ruddy Alex barged into the room. 'Mum...? Grandma has no Wi-Fi. She keeps calling me. And she says she's had no dinner – can you go over there?'

Connie rarely swore. This was one of the few exceptions.

She turned sharply to face her son, who clearly hadn't clocked the charged atmosphere in the room, and glared at him, suppressing the urge to brain her youngest child.

Kenneth had recovered a beat quicker. 'Alex, is that weed I can smell?'

Oh, hell.

He turned to Connie. 'You let him smoke weed in our house?'

It was as if someone had lit a touchpaper. 'Of course, I don't! Not that he takes any notice of me these days. And this isn't *your* house any more.' How dare he come in here and start laying down the law.

'I paid for it. The equity will come to me.'

Did he seriously just say that? 'Not according to my solicitor, it won't.'

Kenneth looked shocked. 'You have a solicitor?'

'Of course, I do. What? Did you think I was just going to roll over without a fight?' She advanced on him. 'Think again, buster.'

'So that's how it is? You've turned into the scorned wife, determined to bleed her ex for all he's worth because he had the audacity to want a better life for himself.'

Connie felt like she'd been slapped. A better life? 'If I have turned into that woman, Kenneth, it's because you've turned into the kind of man who's so desperate to cling onto his fading youth and be adored and flattered, like some weak, pathetic saddo, that he'd leave his home and family for a tart with two brain cells!'

Alex appeared in her peripheral vision. 'Seriously guys, chill, will you?'

Kenneth waved Alex away. 'Stay out of this, Alex. It has nothing to do with you. Get back to your drug-taking, or whatever it is you do all day. It certainly isn't working, that's for sure.'

Connie saw red. No one talked to her son like that… well, no one other than her. Mother's prerogative, and all that. 'Hey, don't speak to him like that. Unlike you, he's done nothing wrong.' Other than buying and smoking illegal substances, but now wasn't the time for semantics. She stepped in front of her son, protecting him from further abuse. 'Leave him out of this. This is between you and me.'

'You're defending him?'

'Too bloody right, I am. Because that's what a good parent does. They stick around, no matter what the provocation, or how tough it gets. They don't abandon their kids for a new life just because they're vain and selfish and *bored*!'

Kenneth looked unnerved. 'You're being hysterical.'

Hysterical? He didn't know the half of it.

'Like an unhinged female. I can't talk to you when you're like this.'

If this was supposed to shame her into submission, it did the opposite. 'Fine. Put 'em up.' She adopted her boxing stance.

Kenneth's eyes grew wide. 'What are you doing?'

'Let's sort this out once and for all, like proper grown-ups.'

'By boxing?'

'Works for me. Come on, what are you afraid of?' She began shuffling, like a female middle-aged menopausal version of Muhammad Ali.

Alex tugged on her arm. 'Mum, please…'

'You're insane.' Kenneth darted for the door like a deer being chased by an irate bear.

'And you're a lousy, cheating coward! So I guess we both get to be disappointed!' she yelled after him.

The front door slammed, rattling the pictures in the hallway.

'Christ, Mum. What the fuck?' Alex ran his hands through his hair.

'Language.' She smacked her son's arm. 'Show some respect.'

His expression softened into concern. 'Are you okay?'

'I'm fine.' She smoothed down her dress. 'Hungry?'

Alex stared at her, wide-eyed. 'Er…'

'I take it that's a yes.' She patted his chest. 'Take a seat, I'll serve dinner. Seems a shame for it to go to waste.'

Ignoring the shake in her legs and the tremble in her hands, she marched into the kitchen, determined to enjoy the meal she'd spent all bloody day preparing.

One way or another, she wasn't going to give Kenneth the satisfaction of making her cry. No way.

'Not ever,' she said aloud… as the tears began to tumble.

## Chapter Fifteen

Beth sat in her car with the engine idling, staring at the red-brick building ahead emblazoned with the words 'Guildford Fire Station' and wondering whether she'd finally lost her marbles and was emulating her mother's recent unstable behaviour. Or worse, was she suffering from a cognitive impairment like her grandma? What other explanation could there be for 'stalking' a man?

Realisation made her drop her head onto the steering wheel, ashamed by her loss of rational thinking. She was supposed to be the sane one in the family. Well, not any more, that ship had sailed. And the cause of her meltdown? One measly kiss. Okay, maybe not measly. Phenomenal, in fact. Mind-blowingly amazing. But that was beside the point. It was an additional stress, and her life was already jammed full of issues to contend with – she didn't need another one. Certainly not one that had driven her to the point of 'stalking'.

Stalking was perhaps a bit of an extreme description for her behaviour, but she'd googled the man, hadn't she? She'd discovered where he worked, and instead of heading home after her client meeting this morning, she'd made a sudden detour and was now carrying out what could only be described as 'surveillance'.

If she'd hoped that learning more about him would dampen her physical attraction towards him, then her plan had woefully backfired. Matt Hardy was the Lead Officer for the Surrey Fire and Rescue Service, head of operations, and in charge of a large crew of firefighters. The station's Facebook page contained numerous glowing endorsements of his talents as a team leader, grateful comments from various people rescued over the years, and numerous images of him wearing his uniform – which far from curing her of her ridiculous 'crush', only served to fuel the growing sense of heat building within her.

He'd even set up a JustGiving page to raise money for a family who'd lost their home in a fire and weren't insured – was it any wonder she was falling for the man?

Switching off the engine, she took a few deep breaths and tried to ease the tightness gripping her chest. It wasn't just her unhelpful feelings towards Matt Hardy causing her grief. There was also the highly disturbing matter of not having submitted the annulment application yet. She'd yet to hear back from Freddie Wood and the wedding was only one week away.

Her sister seemed remarkably unperturbed by the whole situation. As far as Megan was concerned, it was a 'minor blip', and certainly not anything that should derail her entire wedding. Her plan was to address everything post-wedding, confess to Zac about her first marriage and plead ignorance to the courts when it came to the issue of resolving her marital status.

Despite Beth's protests that 'ignorance' was not a viable defence for breaking the law, Megan was determined to forge ahead and marry the 'love of her life' next Sunday as planned. Something which did nothing to ease Beth's levels of anxiety. Unlike her sister, she wasn't a rule breaker. She liked order, and structure. She lived a law-abiding existence, and knowingly committing bigamy did not sit comfortably with her.

She banged her head against the steering wheel, slowly and repeatedly, like a deranged patient in an asylum, trying to obliterate the myriad of conflicting thoughts tormenting her fatigued brain. She just wanted this damned wedding to be over with, so she could return to her safe and boring life, and not have to deal with any further family dramas, or Matt flaming Hardy.

Not that ridding herself of Matt made her feel any better. In fact, the idea of not seeing him again after next weekend only added to the sinking feeling in her stomach. At some point she'd gone from loathing the man to liking him, and she still wasn't quite sure how that had happened.

A rap on the window made her jump.

As if stalking Matt Hardy wasn't embarrassing enough, being sprung by the man himself was mortification at its worst.

She looked up to see him smiling down at her, his handsome face backlit by the glowing sunlight. He was wearing his uniform. Black trousers and a short-sleeved black shirt, adorned with various insignias and a large silver badge confirming his rank. How on earth was she supposed to resist that? Life really wasn't fair at times.

'I spotted your car from the window,' he shouted through the glass. 'You'll have to move it onto the forecourt if you want it washed.'

What on earth was he on about? Her face creased into a frown.

'Charity car wash,' he said, pointing to where a line of cars were waiting to be cleaned by a team of firefighters. 'Isn't that why you're here?'

Beth had two options. Admit the truth, and suffer the humiliation of being caught 'stalking', or blatantly lie. Lying won.

Cracking open the window an inch, she said, 'Er... I was going to have my car washed, but the line is too long. I have to get back to the office. Sorry. Another time maybe.'

Before she could start the engine, Matt opened the driver's door. 'At least come and have a look around.' He offered her his big hand. 'I'd like you to see where I work.'

And this was what bothered her. Even though she had run off last week after their kiss, he'd mistakenly taken their mad moment of intimacy to mean something.

Her coming here today had made it look like she was also interested in pursuing something, and she most definitely wasn't... at least, she didn't think she was. It was hard to decipher what she was thinking, while he was looking at her like that. All handsome and doe-eyed, and mouth-wateringly tempting. It wasn't like she didn't like him, she did. If she was honest, she *really* liked him. She trusted him, too. But could she trust herself? That was the real issue.

Having already bailed on him last weekend, she knew she couldn't do the same again now, or the wedding next week would be excruciating. She needed to rein in her attraction, get a grip of her sanity and bring things between them firmly back into the 'friend zone'.

'I can manage,' she said, exiting the car without his help.

'Of course you can. Silly me.' He gave her a wry smile, his amused gaze travelling over her work attire. 'Nice suit.'

'Quit with the sarcasm. I had a client meeting in Guildford this morning,' she said, buttoning up her jacket. 'Like you, I also have to work weekends sometimes.'

'Fair enough.' He checked the road was clear, like the good firefighter he was, and gestured for her to cross with him. 'Did you get home okay last Sunday?'

It didn't take him long to bring that up, did it? 'Fine. You?'

'No problem. I met with the photographer after you'd left. Nice woman. Impressive portfolio.'

'Right, yes... well, thanks for meeting with her. Sorry I had to rush off.' The memory of her stumbling across Bodmin Moor all red-cheeked and flustered – muddy and windswept, with Matt in hot pursuit, calling after her to check she was okay – sent a wave of humiliation rushing through her. It hadn't been the most elegant of exits. At one point, she'd slid into a ditch in her haste to get away.

'Headache, right?'

'That's right. A sudden headache.'

Ahead, she could see a large banner hanging from the fire station with the slogan 'Adventure Before Dementia' – something that did little to eradicate the niggling feeling that Matt was a kind-hearted and decent bloke who arranged fundraisers, and she was a fool for not believing that.

'A headache that only came on after I'd kissed you?' He glanced at her as they reached the busy forecourt. 'Was it that bad?'

A niggle of guilt kicked her in the ribs. Rejection stung, no matter what the reasons, and although she knew why she'd run off, she hadn't stopped to explain it to him.

'The two things weren't linked,' she said, offering him a weak smile. 'My headache had been building all morning. I shouldn't have suggested the picnic, it was foolish of me. I'm really sorry.'

His brow furrowed. 'No problem. Are you okay now?'

'Absolutely fine, thank you. Shall we head inside?' She walked off before he could reply. A few heads turned her way, the guys washing cars glanced over, their eyes darting between her and Matt, grinning and nudging each other.

Great, she was the subject of gossip. Just what she needed.

'All right, boss?' one of them shouted. 'Need a hand showing the nice lady around?'

Beth didn't see Matt's response, but whatever it was, it was met with laughter.

She sped up, eager to escape any unwanted teasing, which wasn't an easy task in heels and a tight skirt.

Matt caught her up by the entrance to the garage. 'Do we need to talk about it?' he said, catching her arm.

She kept walking, dislodging his hand. 'Not necessary, it was just a headache.'

'I meant the kiss.'

She kept walking. 'Nice fire engines. How many do you have?'

'Three.' He followed her over to one of the vehicles. 'And you're deliberately steering the conversation away.'

'Naturally.'

'Because you're embarrassed?'

She pointed to a contraption hooked onto the side of the truck. 'What's that?'

'A water carrier.' He lowered his voice, seemingly not wanting to be overheard by a few members of staff milling around. 'Because you regret it?'

'Do you have a fire pole like you see in the films?'

'Yes.' He darted in front of her, blocking her path. 'Didn't you enjoy it?'

She stopped and looked up at him. He seemed even bigger in his uniform, more imposing somehow. 'It was a mistake. It shouldn't have happened, okay? So if we could forget the whole thing ever happened and just move on, I'd be very grateful.' She spotted a door with his name on. 'What's in here?'

'My office,' he said, gesturing for her to enter. 'After you.'

She really didn't need to check inside his office, especially when she saw how small it was, but it seemed churlish to refuse.

It was simply kitted out with a desk and chair and a few wall cabinets. Practical, industrial and functional. No fuss, a bit like him, really. A few framed certificates hung on the walls, team commendations and awards for service.

When she heard the door shut behind her, she turned to see him looking at her with an earnest expression. 'In which case, I owe you an apology.'

She raised an eyebrow. 'What for?'

'I misread the situation.' He came towards her. 'I kissed you because I honestly thought what I was feeling was mutual and you felt the same.'

She swallowed awkwardly, aware of his size and his heat encroaching on her space. She wanted to back away, but the ruddy desk was behind her.

'Maybe it was the romance of the setting, I don't know.' He rubbed his close-cut beard, his expression tormented. 'We'd had such a nice weekend, and it felt like we were getting along, and you know… flirting a bit.' He seemed sheepish, his tentativeness a contrast to his imposing frame. 'I guess I got carried away. I'm sorry. It's just…' he trailed off.

'Just what?'

He held her gaze, his eyes firmly fixed on hers. 'You looked so pretty with your hair down, and you were smiling and laughing… you have a really infectious laugh.'

'I do?'

He nodded. 'It's addictive,' he said softly, making the hairs on her arms spring to attention.

*Addictive?* Was he being serious? She searched his expression for sarcasm, expecting him to admit he was joking, but he seemed genuine. 'I only remember being agitated and prickly with you.'

He smiled. 'You were that, too.' There was a hint of teasing in his voice. 'But I don't mind that, I'm not sure why. I guess it's part of what makes you… you. One minute you're irate, the next you're sweet and thoughtful. You're strong, yet vulnerable, combative, yet willing to let your hair down. Literally,' he said, glancing at the rigid bun wound so tightly on her head it was making her scalp ache. 'It feels… real. Like you're not trying to be anything other than who you are, and I like that.'

The air left her lungs with a whoosh. 'You do?'

'I do.' The room suddenly felt a lot smaller, his presence a lot larger. 'But it's clear I overstepped and misread the situation, and for that I'm truly sorry. It won't happen again.'

Right. Well, okay. Good.

His response was better than she could have hoped for. He wasn't pushing things, or arguing his case – he was apologising. Accepting defeat and promising to back off. She should feel relieved. Instead, she felt a crushing sense of disappointment like she'd never experienced before. 'It won't?'

He shook his head. 'Not if it isn't what you want.'

A heavy pause followed. Neither of them reacted, each one waiting for the other to make their next move. The ball was in her court. She was faced with two options. Back off or say, 'to hell with it', and jump in head first.

'What if it is what I want?' The words were out before she could sense-check them.

He stilled. Understandably so, as she was giving him mixed messages.

A beat passed, before he said quietly, 'Is it?'

Was it?

Oh, hell.

Her small nod coincided with her launching herself at him and banging her mouth abruptly against his. It was clumsy and inept, but he didn't seem to mind, and any awkwardness soon morphed into the kind of embrace she'd only ever witnessed in films and never experienced first-hand. It felt like she was being consumed. Eaten alive by this bear of a man, with his big hands and wide chest.

The closer he pulled her, the hotter she became. It was like he had several pairs of hands, all of them exploring her curves, squeezing her bum and sending her mind into a frenzy. Holy cow.

Her suit jacket strained at the seams as her arms reached up around his neck, deepening the kiss. A kiss that sent waves of lust crashing through her. She'd lost all semblance of control. She couldn't get enough of this man, he was intoxicating. She wanted more… craved more… needed more… until the door flew open and a male voice said, 'Whoa, shit. Sorry, boss.'

The heat vanished as though someone had turned the fire hose on her.

Matt sprung away, stepping in front of her like the true gentleman he was, shielding her behind him.

She was grateful, as there was no way she wanted his work colleague seeing her in this dishevelled state. Her glasses were at half mast, her shirt was untucked and her jacket had lost a button. She suspected this was nothing compared to the state of her face, which she imagined was smeared in lipstick.

Frantically shoving everything back into place and wiping her mouth, her embarrassment shot up another notch when the man said, 'Your mum and sister are here to see you, boss. Shall I show them in?'

'NO!' Matt sounded panicked. 'I mean, no, that's okay, Neil. I'll come out. Don't bring them in here.'

But Beth knew it was too late when she heard a woman say, 'We know where his office is, thanks,' and Matt let out a groan. This was followed by, 'Hey, there Matt... Jesus, why are you covered in lipstick?' Pause. 'Oh, shit! Have we caught you doing the dirty? Mum... Mum... come in here. You'll never believe this.'

It was Beth's turn to groan. She stayed ducked behind Matt, grateful for his size, holding onto to his trouser belt, her forehead leaning against his back and wishing the ground would open and swallow her whole so she wouldn't have to face his family. But she knew she could only stay hidden for so long.

'This is a nice surprise,' he said, sounding like it was anything but. Then again, nobody wanted to be caught smooching by their family, did they? 'What brings you down here?' His voice sounded a little strained.

'We wanted to support your charity event,' a different woman said, who Beth assumed was his mother. 'It's such a good cause, so we felt it was important to come down, even if we don't have a car. Maybe we could help make tea, or something?'

'Plus, we haven't seen you in over a week,' the younger woman said. 'So we thought we'd track you down and see what's been keeping you occupied. And now we know.' She sounded amused.

Beth knew it was time to reveal herself, however excruciating that might be.

With a final wipe of her mouth and forcing a smile, she stepped out from behind Matt, hoping she looked presentable enough. 'Hi, I'm Beth.'

She was confronted by two very different women. Matt's mother was pale and drawn, wearing ill-fitting clothes that looked too big for her. Whereas Matt's sister looked like the picture of health… apart from the KitKat she was munching on. Her wide smile accentuated her heart-shaped face and there was a definite twinkle in her eye. Her small frame was a complete contrast to her solid older brother.

'Oh, we know who you are,' the sister said, bounding over.

Beth was squashed into a hug, and hit by a waft of chocolate, mixed in with a sweet-scented perfume. 'Er… you do?'

'Of course. You're the woman Matt—'

'Has been helping to plan the wedding,' Matt cut in, clearly fearful of what his sister was about to say. 'Can you let go of her, please, Leah?'

'Ooops.' Leah released her hold and stepped away, leaving a smudge of chocolate on Beth's suit jacket. 'Bugger. Sorry.' She pulled the sleeve of her yellow top over her hand and began rubbing at the mark.

Beth stepped away. 'It's fine, really. Don't worry, it'll wash out.'

Matt shot Beth an apologetic look. He looked more uncom- fortable than she'd ever seen him and her heart melted a little. Poor bloke. 'Beth, this is my sister, Leah.'

Beth fixed Leah with a smile. 'Nice to meet you.'

'Not as nice as it is to finally meet you,' Leah said, with a wink. 'We've heard *so* much about you, but I'm eager to hear more.'

Matt made an odd noise.

What had they heard about her? It was unnerving not knowing how Matt had described her. Prickly and combative? Or sweet and thoughtful? Strangely, the latter description unsettled her more. No one had ever called her *sweet* before.

'And this is my mum, Susan.' He gestured to the older woman standing by the doorway, clearly a lot less demonstrative than her daughter. 'This is Beth Lawrence, Mum. She's Megan's sister and maid of honour at Zac's wedding.'

'And we all know what happens between the maid of honour and the best man at weddings, don't we?' Leah took a bite of KitKat, seemingly enjoying making her brother squirm. 'Seems to me like it's already started. Nice work, Bro.' She gave Matt a beaming smile. 'She's even more gorgeous than you described.'

Matt let out another groan. 'Please ignore my sister,' he said, turning to Beth. 'She has a habit of jumping to conclusions.'

'Oh? We didn't just walk in on you two chewing each other's face off, then?' Leah's grin didn't let up. 'Because if that ain't something happening, then I don't know what is.'

'*Isn't*, not ain't.' Susan Hardy glared at her daughter. 'You're a schoolteacher, for heaven's sake.'

'I teach sports, Mother. Not English.' Leah rolled her eyes. 'My students don't look to me for elocution lessons.'

'All the same.' Susan stepped forwards and held out her hand. 'It's lovely to meet you, Beth. How are the wedding plans coming along?'

Beth shook the woman's hand, noticing a slight tremor. 'A bit tricky, to be honest. Megan and Zac don't arrive back from Greece until Thursday night, so it's all a bit precarious and last minute.'

'It sounds like you and Matt have done a sterling job arranging everything in their absence. I hope Megan and Zac appreciate all you've done for them, as it can't have been easy.'

Beth felt a rush of warmth towards Matt's mother. She was the first person to acknowledge the burden that had been put upon them. 'Not easy, no. But we've done our best.'

'I'm sure you have. My son's never shied away from commitment or hard work, but he says he couldn't have done it without you.' Susan gave Matt a soft smile. 'Let's hope everything goes smoothly on the day.'

Leah snorted. 'Hardly likely when the two families can't even agree on what suits to wear.'

Beth felt a rush of heat hit her cheeks. 'I'm hoping my dad will see reason and change his mind,' she said, ashamed that her father was causing such grief.

'And I hope my dad gets refused early release and doesn't show up at the wedding.' Leah took another bite of KitKat. 'But we don't always get what we want, do we?'

Beth felt Matt stiffen next to her, his whole body tensing like he'd been tasered.

Beth was confused. 'Early release?'

'Let's head outside.' Matt ushered them from the room. 'It's daft to be stuck inside on such a nice day.'

Beth followed him over to the door. 'I didn't realise your dad might be coming to the wedding,' she whispered, aware of the sudden tension. 'He wasn't on Zac's list of invites.'

Matt shook his head, his brow furrowed. 'He won't be.'

'Are you sure we don't need to add him to the top table?' It suddenly occurred to her that he'd barely mentioned his dad during their conversations. He'd only ever talked about his mum and sister, and the awkward situation with his half-brother. Was this the cause of the tension, she wondered?

Matt rubbed his eyes, as if trying to block something out.

Then his mother appeared and placed a hand on Beth's arm. 'My husband's currently in prison,' she said, squaring her shoulders as if braced for the fallout. 'I'm sorry if you didn't realise that.'

*Prison?* Beth was too dumbfounded to react.

She looked at Leah, who shrugged as if to say, 'Whatever'.

Beth turned to Matt, whose eyes were forlorn and downcast. 'You never mentioned that.'

Matt shook his head. 'No, I didn't.'

A horrible silence followed.

'Apologies for keeping you in the dark, my dear.' Susan's assertive tone was a contrast to the shake in her hands. 'My husband's serving ten years for manslaughter.'

Bloody hell.

It was times like this when Beth wished she possessed her sister's acting talents. Deep inside, she knew the kindest response would be to act as though it wasn't a big deal. All families had their dramas, right? Hers included – although maybe nothing quite so dramatic as being banged up, the Megan issue aside. But unfortunately, her open-mouthed shocked expression ruined any attempts at nonchalance, and all she could manage was a feeble, 'Oh.'

Oh, indeed.

And then she was hit by a horrible sinking feeling.

It seemed she didn't know Matt quite as well as she'd thought.

# Chapter Sixteen

Matt sucked in a breath and reminded himself that in forty-eight hours' time this would all be over and he'd be back home in Surrey, beer in hand, watching a film, knowing he'd never have to suffer any of this crap again. It was the only thing keeping him going.

The breeze picked up, flapping the flags on their poles as the wind rolled in from Bodmin Moor. It was an overcast day, not the best weather to be outside trying to control bunches of golden balloons that tugged on their decorative strings, eager to escape and disappear into the Cornish sky.

'Bloody hell,' moaned Beth, as she frantically tried to flatten the roll of thin red carpet, laid down for the bride and groom's arrival at the Jamaica Inn. No sooner had she secured one end, than the other side lifted and rolled towards her. 'You could help,' she snapped, searching for stones large enough to weigh down the edges.

'You instructed me to hold these balloons. I can't do both,' he snapped back.

In truth, he was as grumpy as she was. The stress of planning the damned wedding, coupled with the strained atmosphere between them which had yet to thaw, had resulted in a frosty greeting this morning. It was hardly his fault his dad was in jail, was it?

The wind kicked up another notch, rattling the champagne flutes lined up on the trestle table decorated with flowers and confetti… which was currently blowing around the forecourt, making it look like it was snowing.

Beth glared at him. 'Don't just stand there, do something.'

'What is it you want me to do? I have no control over the weather,' he quipped, glaring at her. 'This was your idea, remember? I told you it was too windy to set up outside, but you wouldn't listen.'

'It wasn't this windy earlier.'

'Well, it is now!' The balloons fought to escape his grasp. 'The forecast warned of high winds.'

She turned away from him. 'No need to be so smug.'

'I'm not being smug, I'm simply pointing out that we can't control the weather, and we'd have been better off doing this inside.'

'Well, it's too late now, isn't it? Megan and Zac will be arriving any moment, so how about you stop rubbing it in that I misjudged the weather and help me.'

He gritted his teeth. 'Like I said before, what is it you want me to do?'

'I don't bloody know, do I!'

'Fine.' He stormed over to the hotel entrance and tied the bunches of balloons to the wooden porchway, ensuring they were firmly secured and wouldn't fly off.

Still grumbling, he went over to the trestle table, picked up the tray of champagne flutes and placed them on the floor. He then lifted the table and shuffled it nearer to the hotel, hoping that repositioning it in front of the brickwork might protect it from the wind. Replacing the tray of champagne flutes on top, he moved the flower displays in front, so they acted as a barrier.

Finally, he joined Beth on the red carpet and helped secure the edges with stones.

'Happy?' he said. All semblance of relaxation had disappeared, and she was back to being buttoned-up and starched to within an inch of her life.

'Oh, ecstatic,' she replied sarcastically.

He bit his tongue – he was a whisker away from saying something they'd both regret. 'This weekend is going to be painful enough without you bitching at me all the time.'

She straightened. 'I am not bitching.'

'You haven't stopped bitching since we arrived this morning, and it's totally unfair.' He went in search of another stone.

'Unfair?' She ran after him, darting in front of him so he'd get the full impact of her hands-on-hips stance. 'You mean like not telling me your father was in prison?'

'Keep your voice down,' he said, checking the forecourt was empty, but it appeared they were the only ones stupid enough to be outside on a day like that. 'I don't want the whole world to know. And why should I have told you? What business is it of yours?'

She visibly flinched. 'Oh, I don't know. Maybe the minor matter of him potentially being at the wedding?'

Matt stepped closer, stung by the unfairness. 'Which he isn't going to be, and never was going to be. It was wishful thinking on his part, so there was no need for me to bring it up.'

She held her ground. 'Maybe not, but what about what was happening between us?'

Was she serious? He threw his hands in the air. 'Are you for real? There wasn't anything happening between us. Something you'd made perfectly clear.' He took another step towards her. 'Or at least you did, before you changed your mind, and then changed it back again. Talk about giving mixed messages.'

Her face flushed pink with indignation. 'That's because I didn't know if I could trust you. Turns out I was right.'

'Why? Because I failed to mention one tiny detail?'

She looked incredulous. 'Hardly tiny – your father's in bloody jail!'

'And has been for the last ten years, so it's old news. It's also private and humiliating and painful. So, excuse me if I don't blurt it out to every person I meet. Like you, I also have to trust a person before I share private information, and that is not something I'm about to apologise for.'

What she would have said next, he'll never know.

A taxi pulled up and the rear door shot open.

'We're here!' Megan sprang from the taxi, looking all tanned and glamourous in a white dress and killer heels. She ran over and hugged Beth, leaving Zac to pay the driver. 'It's our wedding weekend! I'm so excited!'

Having squashed the air out of Beth, Megan switched her attentions to Matt and ran up to him like an overzealous puppy. 'Darling!' She threw her arms around his neck and he was hit by a strong waft of perfume, which immediately disappeared when the wind picked up. 'How are you?' She didn't wait for an answer and kissed his cheek, before returning to Beth. The whirlwind that was Megan Lawrence.

Zac emerged from the taxi, looking less assured than his wife-to-be, and shot Matt a tentative glance. And so he should be worried, after absconding to Greece for a month.

Matt went over and helped him unload the suitcases.

'It's good to see you, Uncle Matt.' Zac held out his hand, unsure of the greeting he was about to receive.

Matt pulled him into a hug. 'Come here, you daft thing. It's good to see you, too.'

Zac held on, his relief palpable. 'You're not mad at me?'

Hell, yes. But what was the point of yelling now? The damage was done. Besides, he'd had enough yelling for one day. 'Let's just say, I'm happy you're home.'

Behind them, Megan was chattering away, hugging her sister and enlightening Beth as to the wonders of Greek culture. Beth looked somewhat dumbfounded, as though struggling to keep up with all the twists and turns of Megan's chaotic life.

'We need to talk, Megan.' Beth lifted her hand, attempting to interrupt her sister.

'But I need to hear about the wedding preparations. What surprises do you have in store for us?'

'Nothing that can't wait. We need to talk *now*.'

Megan sensed that Beth wasn't joking and gave a little shrug, flashing them all with her 'aren't I adorable' smile, before linking her arm through her sister's. 'Whatever you say, darling. Let's head up to your room... Oooo, is that champagne?' Megan ran over to the tray of flutes and picked up a glass. 'A toast! To us!'

Beth stormed over and almost dragged her sister inside the hotel. 'Excuse us,' she shouted back to Matt and Zac. 'We need some sister time.' And with that they disappeared inside.

Clearly, he wasn't the only one in Beth's bad books, which should make him feel less aggrieved, but didn't.

Matt turned to Zac. 'I'll give you a hand inside with your luggage.'

But Zac was distracted by the sight of another two taxis pulling into the forecourt.

'Er... no need, I can manage,' he mumbled, wheeling the suitcases towards the hotel entrance. 'You stay here and greet the other guests.'

'Coward!' Matt called after him. 'You'll have to face them sometime!'

'Not until I have to!' Zac yelled back, disappearing inside the hotel lobby.

Matt was left to greet his extended family solo. His day was getting better by the minute.

Forcing a smile, he opened the door of the first taxi and offered his hand to Zac's grandmother, Diane. 'Welcome to the Jamaica Inn.' Christ, he sounded like a hotel doorman, rather than a member of the family. No doubt that's how they saw him. A glorified porter. 'How was your journey?'

'Good, thank you.' Diane kissed his cheek. 'How's everything going?'

'Great,' he lied. 'We're all set.'

Set for what, he wasn't sure. Armageddon, probably.

His sister-in-law and half-brother also exited the taxi, both simultaneously frowning as they inspected the building ahead.

'Is this where we're staying?' Gemma tutted when the wind dislodged her sunglasses.

Matt reined in his annoyance. 'I sent Chris the website link,' he said, fighting to hold on to his smile. 'I thought you'd check it out before coming down.'

'We were far too busy,' Chris replied, brushing loose confetti from his shirt. 'Where's the porter? Why isn't he here to greet us?'

Matt shrugged. 'Not sure there is one. It's a small hotel.' This was met with further raised eyebrows. God, he wanted this weekend to be over with. 'Can I get you some champagne?' He headed over to fetch the drinks tray and offered them a glass.

'Lovely,' Diane said, accepting. 'Thank you, Matt.'

At least someone had some manners, unlike his sister-in-law, who frowned and said, 'I hope it's chilled?'

'It was,' Matt replied, extending the tray. 'But I've been out here a while waiting.'

The dig was lost on her, and she walked off towards the hotel.

He turned to his half-brother. 'Chris? A glass of bubbly to celebrate your son's wedding?'

Chris shot him a look and followed his wife inside the hotel. 'Hardly.'

Charming.

Behind him, the passengers in the second taxi emerged and were stretching their legs.

Matt headed over to greet Zac's grandfather. 'Champagne, Bobby?'

'Don't mind if I do,' he said, accepting a glass. 'It's a special occasion, after all. Cheers!' From the red tinge to his cheeks, Matt suspected it wasn't the man's first today.

Matt's next stop was to greet Will and Lily, who were unloading the taxi. Their daughter, Poppy, danced over and met him halfway. 'Hello, Uncle Matt!' she said in her sing-song voice. 'I'm so excited about the wedding. Can I have some champagne?'

'No!' chorused Will and Lily in unison.

Matt shrugged. 'Sorry, kiddo.' He watched her skip off and join her grandparents.

When he offered Will and Lily the tray of drinks, Will shook his head. 'Maybe later, once we've settled in.' He turned and smiled at his wife. 'Unless you'd like some, darling?'

'Oooo, yes, please.' She accepted a glass and took a long swig.

Matt raised an eyebrow. 'Thirsty?'

She waited until Will was out of earshot. 'If you'd spent four hours stuck on a train with your family, you'd need a drink, too.'

Matt grinned. 'I hear you. Here, have another.'

She downed the contents and took another one. 'Our little secret,' she said, placing a finger over her lips.

'I won't breathe a word,' he whispered, counting down the hours until he could get obliterated, too.

Another taxi pulled into the forecourt. This time his mum and sister emerged, both smiling and seemingly a lot more excited about the upcoming event than the other half of his family.

He went over. 'You have no idea how good it is to see you.'

Leah grinned. 'That bad, eh?' She was wearing a top embossed with the slogan 'Grooms-woman Extraordinaire'.

'It's on a par with root canal surgery.'

Leah laughed. 'Fear not, brother. The cavalry have arrived. From now on, all will be well, and if not,' she said, accepting the offer of a champagne flute, 'then we'll get stinking drunk and drown our sorrows in alcohol.'

'You're not drinking already, Leah? It's barely five o'clock.' Susan Hardy shook her head disapprovingly.

Leah rolled her eyes. 'It's a wedding, Mum. Of course I'm drinking.' She turned to Matt. 'Have the bride and groom arrived?'

'Yes, thank god. Chris and the rest of the family are here, too. We're having pre-dinner drinks in the bar from six thirty.'

Leah looked disgusted. 'Dinner? Like a formal meal? What about strippers, and raucous drinking, and tying the groom to a lamp post?'

'Buffet and karaoke, I'm afraid. Unless you want to join the hens, and then it's a disco in the barn.'

Leah sighed. 'It'll have to do, I guess.' She turned to their mum, who was trying to wheel the suitcases across the gravel. 'Leave that, Mum. I'll do it.'

Matt went over to help. 'Let me.'

Leah shot him a glare. 'I can manage a couple of suitcases, Matt.' With an exaggerated eye-roll, she marched off, luggage in tow.

What was it with women taking offence at him offering to help?

His mother touched his arm. 'I'm sorry about the other day, with Beth. I didn't realise you hadn't told her about your dad. Was she very upset?'

'She was fine,' he said, dismissing her concern. 'It's not like we're that close.'

'No?' His mother tilted her head. 'I thought maybe you two were an item?'

'Nope, false alarm.'

A look of regret washed over her. 'I'm sorry, love. You must be disappointed.'

He feigned disinterest. 'Seriously, it's no big deal. Have you heard from Dad?'

'Not since Monday.'

'I'm assuming he was refused early release?'

'Seems that way. I'm sure he would've told us if it had been good news.'

Good news for who, though? It wasn't that Matt didn't want his dad released – just not this weekend.

'You head inside and get settled, Mum. I'm going to wait out here for the other guests – the couple's friends are still due to arrive. I'd better hang around for them.'

'See you later then.' Susan kissed his cheek and headed into the hotel, leaving him alone with the champagne, the howling wind and a sinking feeling in his gut.

A feeling that intensified when a car horn blasted.

He realised the driver of one of the taxis had yet to depart and was waiting expectantly. 'Is anyone going to pay me?' he shouted, unloading the suitcases from the boot.

Cursing, Matt disposed of the drinks tray, and went over to settle the bill and carry his bloody half-brother's luggage inside. And he'd tried to convince himself they didn't see him as a glorified porter. More fool him.

It was another fifty minutes before all the guests had arrived and been checked in. He'd greeted Megan and Zac's friends with a warm smile, served them champagne and welcomed them to the venue, all the while cursing Beth for having deserted him. So much for them being in this together.

The arrival of Beth's family had caused quite a stir, with Kenneth and Tiffany turning up at the same time as Connie, like a well-timed theatrical farce. Evil glares, followed by snide remarks, ending with them all dispersing into the hotel like spitting snakes. Grandma Doris appeared to be the only normal member of the family. Beth's brother Alex was clearly as disgruntled as his estranged parents, grunting about 'hating weddings' as he shuffled inside.

Matt had thought his family were going to provide the biggest problems this weekend. Turned out, they had stiff competition.

Consequently, his plan to have a relax in his room before the evening had to be abandoned. He barely had time for a shower, before heading back downstairs for the stag and hen dos.

The bar area was already packed full of people, mostly couples chatting and getting into the wedding vibe.

He found his family in the restaurant, sampling the delights of the buffet and seated around two tables pushed together. At least his mother and Leah were being included, that was something.

He ventured outside and was immediately hit by the swirling wind, which was getting worse. The disco was underway in the barn, and a few of Megan's friends were already dancing and looking slightly worse for wear. Poppy was also on the dancefloor with Lily, looking surprisingly grown-up in a blue jumpsuit. Her hair was curled, her lips were painted pink, and in her low heels she was nearly as tall as Lily. The kid was growing up fast. Will had his work cut out.

Far from being able to relax and enjoy himself, Matt spent the next two hours flitting from one venue to the other, checking that everything was okay and nothing was getting out of hand. He 'encouraged' some of Zac's mates to rein in their drinking and gave directions to the loos when one of Megan's friends threatened to be sick. And it was only nine p.m. He'd gone from hotel porter to security bouncer.

Zac had appeared early on in the evening and was enjoying himself with his mates, steering clear of his parents.

Megan hadn't arrived until much later, dressed up to the nines in a sparkly short dress, wearing bright red lipstick, and clearly ready to party. In contrast, Beth had appeared behind her looking like her sister's sombre shadow, her face like thunder and shrouded in a long black dress.

Despite being miffed with her, he still found himself heading over, sensing all was not well. 'Is there a problem?' he asked, trying not to sound grumpy.

She frowned. 'Why would you ask that?'

'You don't look happy.'

She shrugged. 'Neither do you.'

'I was stuck outside in the wind for two hours, waiting for the rest of the guests to arrive. What's your excuse?'

So much for not sounding grumpy.

He braced himself for the flurry of abuse he felt sure was coming his way, but instead of retaliating, her shoulders sagged. 'I'm sorry for leaving you to do that alone. It was unfair of me, but I really needed to speak to my sister, it couldn't wait.'

Her apology took some of the sting out of his annoyance. 'Is there a problem?'

Her hesitation indicated there was. Her eyes flitted about the room, as though she was searching for a way out. In the end, she sighed and shook her head. 'Everything's fine.' Her tone indicated that it wasn't, but she didn't want to add anything.

If she didn't want to talk, so be it. 'You know where I am if you change your mind.'

Someone tapped him on the shoulder.

He turned to see a concerned-looking Will. 'Have you seen Poppy?'

'She's in the barn, dancing with Lily.'

'Not any more. She went to the loo, but never came back. We can't find her. You know this place better than us – any idea where she might be?'

'She can't have gone far, we're in the middle of nowhere, surrounded by a remote moor.' He realised a beat too late that his attempts to reassure Will only made the man even more alarmed. 'What I mean is, she's a sensible girl, she wouldn't have wandered off.'

'I hope not,' Will said, looking dejected. 'But where is she?'

'I'll search the hotel. Stay here in case she comes back. Call me if she shows up.'

'I'll come with you.' Beth followed him into the lobby. 'Should we split up?'

'Good idea. You check upstairs, and I'll start down here.'

Matt knew logically that Poppy was okay and that they'd find her. Searching for a missing person was a common enough occurrence for his colleagues in the police, and the person was usually found safe and well. Panicking from the offset wouldn't help anyone. The trick was to keep calm and methodically search the hotel, hoping to discover her hidden away somewhere, oblivious to everyone's worry.

Poppy wasn't in the lobby, the restaurant or the bar. The gift shop and farm shop were closed, which just left the open-plan section of the museum.

With only a faint light shining in from the ornate lamps outside the venue, it was dark inside. He called her name, but got no response. He was about to leave, when he heard a faint noise. The space appeared empty at first glance, but then he heard a giggle. Further investigation revealed two people sitting on upturned gunpowder barrels behind the olde-worlde bar. And then the smell hit his senses.

Matt rubbed his forehead. Seriously? Someone was smoking weed at a family wedding?

He moved closer to investigate and realised there was one male and one female. The man he recognised as Beth's brother, Alex. The identity of the female made time slow. 'What the hell?'

His voice made them both jump.

Alex waved a hand. 'Hey, man.'

'Give me that.' Matt snatched the joint from Poppy's hand and dropped it to the floor, squashing it under his foot. 'Are you kidding me?'

'Hey, man! That's decent shit.' Alex tried to get up, but Matt pushed him back down.

'Stay there! And I don't care what it is, you shouldn't be smoking, and certainly not with a child. Have you lost your sanity?'

Alex frowned. 'Child? What child? There's no child here, just…' He waved a hand at Poppy. 'What was your name again?'

'Her name is Poppy,' Matt snapped. 'And she's thirteen years old.'

Alex swayed. 'Whoa, shit! You never said you were thirteen. You look older.'

'Well, she's not. Get up,' he said, grabbing Alex's T-shirt and pulling him upright.

Alex lifted his hands in surrender. 'I don't want no trouble.'

'You should've thought of that before you gave pot to a thirteen-year-old. Christ, if her father hears about this, he'll call the police and have you arrested.'

'Please don't, Uncle Matt.' Poppy jumped to her feet. 'I'm sorry! Please don't tell my dad.'

Matt was conflicted. The right thing to do was report Alex, but that would ruin the wedding. There was no coming back from the bride's brother getting the groom's teenage cousin stoned. He looked down at Poppy. 'How much did you smoke?'

'I didn't smoke any,' she said in a rush. 'I promise, I didn't have any. I was just holding it for him and pretending.'

'I saw you raise it to your mouth, Poppy.'

'I was smelling it, nothing else, I swear. It smelt awful. I didn't smoke it.' Tears pooled in her eyes.

Call him a mug, but he believed her. 'You'd better not be lying to me.'

'It's the truth, I promise. Please don't tell my daddy.' She clutched hold of him.

He had to think fast. 'Go to the ladies' room and wash your hands to get rid of the smell. Then go to the restaurant and apologise to your father for disappearing. He was worried sick when he couldn't find you. Tell him you were looking around the museum, or something. Do not run off again at any point this weekend, you hear me?'

'I promise.' She nodded frantically.

'You so much as sip any alcohol, go near this idiot again or do anything wrong, and I'm telling your father, okay?'

She nodded frantically. 'I'll behave, I promise.'

'You'd better. Now go.' Poppy ran off. 'Not you,' he said, stopping Alex when he went to follow. 'You're having an early night.'

'No way, man.'

Matt bunched Alex's T-shirt into a fist and drew him close. 'You have two options, mate. Go to your room and sleep it off. Or spend the night in a cell for giving drugs to a minor.'

Alex looked startled. 'I didn't know she was a minor.'

'You think that's a defence?'

Alex shook his head.

'Maybe you'd prefer me to drag you into the restaurant and announce to your family what you've done? How do you think they'd react?'

'Beth would kill me.'

'Too bloody right she would.' He looked at Alex's stricken face. 'So what's it to be?'

'I'll sleep it off.'

'Good choice. I'll escort you up there, in case you change your mind.'

Matt ushered an unhappy Alex out of the museum and up the stairs, almost dragging him and ignoring his grumblings about it being unfair. No wonder Beth was so stressed, if this was the kind of crap she had to deal with.

When they reached Alex's room on the first floor, Matt opened the door and shoved him inside. 'Don't get any funny ideas about leaving. My ultimatum stands. You so much as show your face downstairs before tomorrow morning and I'm calling the cops. You hear me?'

'I hear you,' Alex mumbled, flopping onto the bed.

'Good. Sleep tight.' Matt closed the bedroom door and leant against it.

Christ, what a night this was turning out to be.

He closed his eyes and let out a long breath. Had he done the right thing? He had no idea. He'd chosen not to sabotage the wedding, but it didn't sit comfortably with his conscience. He didn't like lawbreakers, and he certainly didn't like covering up for them.

The landing lights dimmed when the sensors failed to detect any movement, as he stood there motionless, guarding Alex's bedroom door.

His phone pinged with a message. It was Will, telling him that Poppy had reappeared and was fine. She'd lost track of time in the museum and all was good.

Poppy had managed to hoodwink her father into believing her story, had she? He probably should feel relieved. It was the better outcome in terms of maintaining family harmony, but it didn't make him feel any less guilty.

He let out another sigh. At least if he stayed hidden away up here, his evening couldn't get any worse. Then he remembered that Beth was also looking for Poppy.

Before he could call her, a woman's voice said, 'What are you doing up here?'

He looked over to see a swaying Connie Lawrence walking towards him, barefooted, her strappy shoes dangling from one hand. Her silver dress was low-cut, and she wore the look of a woman who'd had way too much to drink and had lost all semblance of propriety. Not a good combination.

'Is that your bedroom?' she said, zigzagging her way closer, her voice low and sultry.

'No idea whose room it is,' he lied. Her level of drunkenness must be bad if she'd forgotten which room her son was staying in.

'Then why are you standing there? You look like you're waiting.' She was in front of him now, leaning in, smelling of wine and perfume. 'Who are you waiting for?'

'Just enjoying a quiet moment.'

'You know what I enjoy?' she said, pressing herself firmly against his chest, trapping him against the door.

No, and he had no desire to find out. He was just trying to figure out how to extricate himself from her embrace without offending her, when she leant in and kissed him.

*Shit.*

Okay, this was not good. Not good at all.

With her mouth squashed against his, he gently took hold of her upper arms and was about to manoeuvre her away from him, when a voice said, 'Mum? What are you doing?'

It was Beth.

*Shit. Shit. Shit.*

'Matt?' Her voice went up an octave when she realised who her mother was kissing. 'Oh, my, god! Are you for real?'

And he'd stupidly thought his evening couldn't get any worse.

## Chapter Seventeen

Beth stifled a yawn. She was still suffering from a fitful night spent tossing and turning, battling to rid her mind of the image of Matt and her mother kissing. It was the climax to an already awful evening, spent pacifying the hotel staff, policing wayward hens, avoiding overly amorous stags and preventing her mother from chasing Tiffany onto the moors in the hope her nemesis would be eaten by the Baskerville's hound. As it turned out, it wasn't Tiffany who needed protecting, it was Matt. Not that he was a victim, far from it. He'd been on the other end of that kiss. He hadn't exactly been fighting her mother off, had he?

Beth checked herself in the ornate mirror and groaned. 'I look like a ghost,' she said, sniffing the grey lace material and getting a waft of mothballs.

'That's how you're supposed to look,' Megan replied, emerging from the changing room looking like Elizabeth Taylor's more attractive younger sister. Beth hadn't expected anything less. They were tucked away at the back of the museum, getting into their fancy dress costumes ahead of a day spent re-enacting thieving piracy and skulduggery. 'Aunt Patience is described as being ghost-like. A broken woman, bullied and beaten by her wretch of a husband.' Megan sidled up next to Beth. 'How do I look?'

'Bloody gorgeous, and you know it.' Beth tried not to sound aggrieved.

The image reflected back, of the sisters standing side by side, couldn't have highlighted their differences more starkly. Megan looked like the screen starlet she was, her dark hair tumbling onto her shoulders like liquid chocolate, her blood-red period gown flattering her slender figure and pale complexion. She looked both feisty and sexy. A contrast to Beth, dressed in an insipid grey ill-fitting itchy gown with unflattering ruffled neckline that made her look like the sad downtrodden abused creature she was supposed to be.

Megan kissed Beth's cheek. 'Thank you for organising this, it's such a fab idea. I love dressing up. And Zac looks so sexy in his Jem outfit, all manly and rugged,' she said, sounding like the smitten bride-to-be.

Beth raised an eyebrow. Zac was an absolute sweetheart, but rugged he wasn't. He looked more like Adam Ant in his dandy outfit, complete with guyliner and quaffed hair, than fictional brooding hero. But if he was Megan's leading man, then that was all that mattered.

'Talking of Zac—'

Megan pressed her finger against Beth's lips. 'Not now.'

Her sister could hardly expect to remain silent on the topic of her bigamy forever. The wedding was tomorrow. 'You can't keep changing the subject,' Beth said, dislodging Megan's finger.

'Of course I can.' Megan flashed her a wide smile. 'I'm the bride, it's my prerogative. And besides, we have more important things to talk about, like our mother kissing the best man last night.' Megan's laughter bounced off the stone walls.

Beth groaned. 'I'm regretting ever telling you.'

'Why? It's funny.'

'It's not funny, it's humiliating.' The shock of finding her mother glued to Matt's face was as raw this morning as it had been last night. It was like being punched in the gut – a hammer blow she was still recovering from.

Megan gave her a searching look. 'Humiliating for who?'

Beth went in search of a shawl. The wind was still swirling a gale outside, rattling the leaded windows and sweeping through the draughty museum. 'Well… everyone. I mean, what was she thinking?'

'That she'd like to kiss a hunky man? And why not? Good for her, I say.'

Beth yanked the lace shawl off the hanger. 'No, not good for her. Or anyone else, for that matter.'

'The poor woman has been dumped. Her self-esteem is at rock-bottom, why shouldn't she have a bit of fun with an inappropriate man?'

Beth struggled to untangle the shawl. 'So you admit he's inappropriate?'

Megan sighed. 'Well, I doubt she'll marry him, but I don't think that's the point.' She came over and took the shawl from Beth. 'Don't you want Mum to be happy? Isn't it a good thing for her to be getting over Dad and exploring other romantic options?'

'Not with Matt.'

Megan smiled. 'Ah, so it's not the principle you object to, it's the man himself.' She unravelled the shawl and draped it around Beth's shoulders. 'Why shouldn't Mum fool around with Matt Hardy? He's handsome, sexy. A firefighter, for Christ's sake. Why shouldn't she indulge?' Megan tied the shawl. 'Unless, of course, there's a reason why he's off limits? Say, for instance… if you had the hots for him yourself?'

Beth scoffed and avoided eye contact.

Megan's hands rested on Beth's shoulders, a mischievous glint in her eye. 'You like him, don't you?'

'So what if I do?' Beth gazed at the wooden flooring, embarrassed to admit her feelings. 'He kissed my mother. That kind of kills any attraction.'

Megan gently shook her shoulders. 'Oh, please, it was completely one-sided, and you know it. I love our mother, but she's a terrible drunk. He wouldn't have stood a chance.' Her sister tugged on the shawl, forcing Beth's attention away from the floor. 'Have you kissed? Been out on a date? Hooked up? Spill.'

'A couple of kisses, nothing else.'

'Oooo…' Megan jumped up and down like an excited child. 'And…?'

'And nothing. I came to my senses both times and put an end to it.'

Megan stopped jumping. 'Why?'

'You know my track record.' Breaking free from her sister, Beth went over to an upturned beer barrel and sat down, removing the dainty period shoes so she could rub her aching feet. 'I'm a disaster when it comes to men, I can't trust my instincts.'

Megan followed her. 'Nonsense. There's nothing wrong with your instincts.'

'My dating history would indicate otherwise.' She went in search of her trainers in the changing area.

'Things didn't work out with Hughie, because first loves rarely do,' Megan said, perching on the beer barrel. 'The relationship ran its course and fizzled out. It happens. That's life.'

Beth re-emerged from the changing area, carrying her white trainers, their colour dulled from her previous encounter with Bodmin Moor. 'What about Owen? You can't tell me that just fizzled out. The man lied to me.'

'Exactly, *he* lied, Beth. He pretended to be someone he wasn't and behaved like a complete jerk. That's on him, not you. You did nothing wrong.'

Beth slipped her feet into her trainers. 'Except for falling for his bullshit.'

'And as soon as you realised it was bullshit, you left. Quite rightly.'

Beth shook her head. 'It took me long enough, though, didn't it? Talk about clueless. I had no idea he had a fiancée back in Wales.'

'You're being too hard on yourself. Relationships are like recruiting for a job. You interview someone and they appear perfect for the position, but only time will tell if they'll work out. Sometimes they turn out to be a model employee, and other times, they turn out to be the worst employee on the planet and you wish you'd never hired them. There's no way of knowing which one they'll be at that first interview. You just have to go with your gut, take a chance and hope for the best.' Megan came over. 'Relationships are the same. All you can do is make a decision based on what you know in the beginning and see how things develop. If they turn out to be the real deal, then great. If not, kick their sorry arse into touch. What you mustn't do is beat yourself up about it if it doesn't work out. That's such a waste of a life and you're too special not to be happy.'

Beth stood up. 'I'm happy.'

'But you could be happier.' Megan took Beth's hands. 'Are you attracted to Matt?'

Beth shrugged. 'He's okay.'

'Just okay?'

Beth wasn't about to admit the extent of her attraction. Admitting that even the mention of his name made her insides contract wouldn't put an end to her sister's questioning – it would only prolong the interrogation.

'Well, he certainly likes you.'

Beth stilled. 'What makes you say that?'

Megan grinned. 'The man looks at you like you're a bowl of ice cream and he's the spoon.'

Beth's cheeks grew hot. The idea of Matt looking at her like she was ice cream did something strange to her insides. After all, she knew what a sweet tooth he had. She was glad of the howling wind outside, since it detracted from the tsunami raging inside her. 'Even if what you say is true, I'm not sure I can trust him.'

'Only one way to find out.' Megan let go of Beth's hands and danced away, getting into character as the whimsical heroine. 'Trust is a gradual thing that develops over time, until you feel safe and comfortable enough to open up about your hopes and dreams, and trust that the person will accept you, faults and all, and not judge your mistakes.'

'Oh, you mean like admitting to your fiancé the night before your wedding that you're already married? Mistakes like that, you mean?'

'You're already married?' The sound of Matt's deep voice made them both jolt.

He was standing in the doorway, dressed as the evil Joss, Aunt Patience's wicked tormentor of a husband and bullying innkeeper of the Jamaica Inn. Matt's usual relaxed demeanour was absent – his rugged appearance, messy hair and huge frame gave him quite an intimidating look. The shirt he was wearing was loose-fitting and open at the neck, revealing a smattering of chest hair that did nothing to ease Beth's unease.

His dark gaze switched between the sisters, settling on Megan. 'You're already married?'

Megan looked stricken. 'It's not what you think,' she said, glancing at Beth, no doubt hoping for moral support.

'So it's true?' His voice was low and unnervingly menacing.

'Technically, yes,' she said, swallowing awkwardly. 'But I can explain—'

'Does Zac know?' Matt stepped into the room, his bulk blocking out the light from the doorway.

They were interrupted by their mother appearing behind him, looking flustered and still in her dressing gown. 'Grandma Doris has gone missing,' she said in a rush. 'I can't find her anywhere. A member of staff thinks he saw her heading towards the moor. I don't know what to do – should I call the police?'

Beth ran for the door. 'Let me look for her, she won't have gone far. I'll find her.'

'I'll come with you.' Matt followed her.

'I can manage.' She sped up, eager to escape his presence.

'I don't want to end up searching for two lost people.'

She audibly growled. 'Could you be any more patronising? What makes you think I'd get lost, too?'

'It's treacherous terrain. Even an experienced explorer could get into trouble out there. And it's blowing a gale.'

'I can see that,' she said, reaching reception. 'I'm not stupid.'

'You don't have your phone on you.'

She stopped by the exit, turning to glare at him. How did he know that?

'Not unless it's hidden under that dress,' he said, scanning her flimsy gown.

Smart-arse. 'Do you have your phone on you?'

He unearthed it from his trouser pocket. 'I do.'

'Fine. But I'm taking the lead, okay? This is my grandma, my family, and my problem to resolve.' She pushed open the door.

'Believe me, I have no wish to involve myself in your family dramas.'

'Huh! Bit late for that, don't you think?'

'Meaning?'

'You kissed my mother.' She let the door slam in his face and marched across the forecourt, satisfied that she'd had the last word.

He appeared a moment later, catching her up as she half-ran, half-shuffled towards the road in her long dress, battling against the strong wind. 'Wait up!'

No way was she waiting for him. 'Do you often go around kissing daughters and mothers from the same household?' she said, crossing the road. 'Is it like your thing? Do you have a fetish, or something?'

'Of course not, and for the record, she kissed me.'

Beth yanked up her dress and hopped over the ditch. 'I didn't see you objecting.'

'I didn't have time. The second she kissed me, you showed up.' He jumped the ditch behind her, landing safely on the other side and not face down in the muddy water. Shame.

'Apologies for interrupting you. How inconvenient.' She marched across the moor, holding her skirt in one hand, searching for her grandma. There was no sign of her. The sky above was a mottled grey, the clouds moving at speed, creating shadows across the landscape. Even the weather was being theatrical this weekend.

'What is your problem? You've been busting my balls all weekend.' He caught her up again and they stopped to scan the area. 'Do you know what your grandmother is wearing?'

'You know damn well what the problem is.' She swung around to face him. 'And of course I don't know what my bloody grandma is wearing. Her nightgown, probably.' The idea of Grandma Doris being out here, alone, made Beth feel sick. A dollop of cold hit the back of her neck. She looked up. 'Great, it's started raining.' That was all they needed. 'Grandma Doris!' she yelled, scuttling away and hoping for a reply. But if her grandma had answered, it was lost in the wind.

Matt climbed onto a large boulder, shielding his eyes as he searched the area. The horizon was obscured by rolling mist. The poor light masked the rocky boulders, creating a blur between land and sky.

'Can you see anything?'

'Nothing.' He jumped down. 'And I still don't understand why you don't trust me.'

Beth resumed walking, noticing that her white trainers were once again caked in mud. 'I would've thought that was obvious. First you lie to me about your dad, and then you hook up with my mother. I'd call that untrustworthy, wouldn't you? Grandma Doris!'

'It sounds like an excuse to me. You're searching for reasons to reject me, because you don't have the courage to see if this thing between us means anything.' He cupped his hands around his mouth. 'Doris! Are you there?!'

'There is nothing between us.'

'Fine.' He turned to face her. 'Then stop busting my balls, because if you don't care about me, why are you so bothered about me kissing your mum?' He walked off before she could respond.

She had to run to catch him up, the shawl around her neck was now wet and irritating. Her hair was falling out of its clasp and her glasses were steaming up. 'You said she kissed you.'

'She did.'

'Like I'm going to believe anything you say. Grandma Doris!'

'I don't lie, unlike you.' He stopped so abruptly she almost smacked into his back.

She stumbled to avoid falling into him. 'What's that supposed to mean? I don't lie.'

He pinned her with a steely glare. 'So Megan isn't already married then?' He offered her his hand. 'Mind the ditch.'

However much she wanted to rebuff his offer of help, there was no way she was negotiating that ditch without help. Reluctantly, she took hold of his outstretched hand. 'It's complicated.' She leapt inelegantly, slipped and almost fell into the water face-first. Matt managed to catch her and she landed with a thud against his chest.

They were nose-to-nose. His face was wet, his jaw clenched, and she could see his breath misting in the air. 'You bang on about how you can't trust me, and how I lied about my dad, and all the while you're hiding the fact that Megan's already married. Talk about hypocritical.'

She flinched in his arms. 'It's not the same thing.'

'It sure seems that way to me. Is she even allowed to get married tomorrow?'

There was no point lying. 'Not legally, no.'

'Great.' He gently released his hold. 'My poor clueless nephew gets to be humiliated in front of his whole family. A family who've been against this marriage from the start. Do you have any idea how crushed he's going to be?'

Guilt kicked Beth hard in the ribs. 'That's what I've been trying to tell my sister.'

'And yet you're still protecting her.' He jumped onto another boulder. 'Doris!'

'I've been begging her for weeks to come clean, but she was adamant she could get an annulment before tomorrow.'

He jumped off the boulder. 'And has she?'

'No.'

'Then why did you agree to arrange this wedding when you knew she was already married?' He sounded so disappointed in her, and she wasn't sure whether her face was wet from the rain or from crying. Either way, she felt rotten. And complicit.

She wiped her face with her sleeve. 'I only found out after I'd agreed to plan the wedding.'

He frowned at her. 'You didn't know your sister was married?'

Beth shook her head, and then a faint sound made her turn. 'Did you hear that? Someone's calling. Grandma Doris!? Can you hear me?'

It took a few moments, but eventually they spotted her. Across the moor, a small figure was waving. Beth's relief was palpable.

'Wait here,' Matt said, sprinting over.

'Wait!' It was pointless, he was already gone.

Beth hoisted up her wet and now very muddy gown, and made her way over to her grandma. Please be okay, she prayed. This wasn't the weather to be outdoors, at any age, let alone eighty-four.

By the time Beth reached them, Grandma Doris had been lifted off the muddy ground and was lying in Matt's big arms, looking tiny and frightened and very frail.

'Are you okay?' Beth asked as she reached them. 'Are you hurt, Grandma?'

Her grandma shook her head. 'Just a bit shaken. Where am I?'

'You're on Bodmin Moor.'

Her grandma looked confused. 'How did I get here?'

'It's Megan and Zac's wedding tomorrow. We're all staying at the Jamaica Inn for the weekend. You must've gone for a walk and got a bit lost.'

'I need to get home – the carers will be waiting.'

'The carers didn't come with us to Cornwall, Grandma.' Beth stroked her damp brow.

'I'm very tired.' Her grandma yawned and dropped her head against Matt's chest, letting her eyes drift shut.

'Let's get you back to the hotel for a lie-down.' Beth looked up at Matt, grateful he was there – she couldn't have carried her grandma alone. 'Do you need a hand?'

'I've got her, but we'd better get a move on, the weather's getting worse. I can't see my feet, so can you lead the way?'

'Of course, no problem. Can I message my mum and let her know Grandma's safe?'

'My phone's in my pocket. You know the passcode,' he said, ruefully, but his voice had softened, all traces of anger and annoyance gone. He was back to being Matt. Kind, helpful and no longer looking at her like he wanted to throttle her.

It was an odd sensation, sliding a hand into his trouser pocket, especially when the trousers fitted so snugly, stretched against his big thighs.

Having entered the passcode, she messaged her mum, and then slid the phone back into his pocket. 'Thank you.'

'No problem, anything to help.' He offered her an almost smile and she felt some of the tension leave her. It was time to focus on getting back to the inn.

Beth lifted her dress so she could see the ground beneath her and began gingerly testing the terrain as she led the way. It was hard to see through the pelting rain and mist, but she knew Matt was relying on her. For all her bluster that she didn't need a man to help her, she now had to prove her worth and help to keep her grandma safe. Matt, too. One misstep and they could all end up stuck down a crevice.

Behind her, Matt carried her sleeping grandma in his big arms, protecting her like she was an injured bird. 'Did you really not know your sister was married?' he said, his voice a hushed whisper so as not to disturb her grandma.

'I honestly had no idea. It was something that happened eight years ago in Las Vegas. Drunk drama students misbehaving, a prank that got out of hand. She was so wasted, I think she almost forgot about it, too. She's never even seen the bloke since.'

'Is the marriage legal?'

'I haven't been able to get hold of any paperwork to find out. We managed to track down the man on Facebook. His name's Freddie Wood, but he's yet to reply to any of my messages, so I haven't been able to apply for an annulment. Mind, this bit's slippery.' Beth waited until they'd safely negotiated the treacherous bog. 'Believe me, I'm as mad about it as you are. It was bad enough being coerced into arranging this wedding in the first place, but knowing it's illegal and shouldn't be going ahead has been giving me sleepless nights. I'm a solicitor, for crying out loud. I could be disbarred if anyone found out I allowed the wedding to go ahead.'

Matt sighed. 'No wonder you've been so stressed.'

'I've tried reasoning with Megan, but she's determined to marry Zac tomorrow. She convinced me that we'd be able to track down Freddie and get everything sorted before the big day, and Zac would never need to know.'

Matt slowed as the mud became slippery. 'That's a big secret to keep from someone.'

'Tell me about it.' Beth waited for him to catch up, before resuming walking. 'I can only imagine how Zac's going to feel when he finds out. And how can he not find out? Megan has no choice but to confess – time's up, not that she sees it that way. She's convinced the whole thing will just go away if she ignores it. I don't know what to do.'

'Not much you can do.'

She glanced back. 'You don't think I should tell Zac?'

'It's not your secret to tell. This isn't your mess, Beth. Or your responsibility. You've done all you can, you've told her what the consequences will be. It's up to her now.'

Whatever she'd imagined his response would be, it wasn't that. 'I feel bad for Zac.'

'Me too, but what's worse? Him finding out in a few weeks' time, and dealing with it privately, or being humiliated in front of his whole family tomorrow?'

She paused. 'I hadn't thought of it like that.'

'It's a shitshow, either way.'

'A great big shitshow.' She stepped over an uneven mound. 'Be careful, it's softer than it looks here.'

Matt placed his feet carefully. 'You haven't done anything wrong, Beth.'

'Then why do I feel so guilty?'

'Because you're an honest person. You're not a rule breaker, you'd never behave like that yourself, and it doesn't sit comfortably with your conscience.'

He was right. 'I'm dull, you mean?'

'You're not dull. You're honourable, reliable and trustworthy.'

She sighed. 'Like a used car.'

He laughed. 'Like a used car.'

The sight of the Jamaica Inn in the distance was a welcome relief. They were nearly safe, just a few more obstacles to overcome. 'How's grandma doing?'

'Sleeping like a baby.'

She offered him a weak smile. 'I'd be sleeping, too, if I was tucked up in your arms. Lucky Grandma.' He met her gaze and a look passed between them, loaded with intensity. Suddenly, she wasn't quite so cold. 'I'm sorry I reacted badly about your dad – it was judgemental of me. It's hardly your fault he's in prison.'

'You don't need to apologise. You didn't react any differently to anyone else when they find out.'

'But I used it as an excuse to justify backing off, and that was unfair of me.' She waited until his eyes met hers. 'Is it the reason why you and Chris don't get on?'

He nodded. 'Chris is very protective of our mother. He hates what my dad has done to her.'

'It can't have been easy on you or your sister either.'

'It's not, but he's still my dad. Whatever he's done, I love him. I don't approve of his behaviour, but I can't cut him out of my life completely. Chris doesn't understand that.'

But Beth did – she felt the same way about her own father. 'Family, huh?'

'Family.' He rolled his eyes. 'Come on, we'd better get a move on.'

Having climbed over the final ditch, they reached the road and Beth could see a flurry of activity outside the inn. Her mother was hovering by the doorway, looking concerned, no doubt awaiting the safe arrival of Grandma Doris.

A taxi was parked on the forecourt and a white-haired man was unloading a bag from the boot. His hair was wavy and unkempt, a match for his bushy beard. He looked like a slightly dishevelled Father Christmas.

'I wonder who that is?' Beth said, straining to see. 'We're not expecting anyone else.' She turned back to Matt, who'd stopped dead in the road. 'Do you know that man?'

'I do,' he said, looking ashen. 'It's my dad.'

# Chapter Eighteen

It probably wasn't the best idea for Connie to be having her hair done in the middle of a storm. Sleeting rain pelted against the salon windows, making the glass rattle as the wind howled outside, and every time the door opened, the customers were subjected to a blast of cold wet air. So much for it being the height of summer – Cornwall was bleaker than a Dickens novel when the weather wasn't good.

Connie shivered as another gust circled her ankles. She glanced outside the window, watching the holidaymakers battling against the wind, as they headed in search of respite, their rain-sodden macs stuck to their bare legs. That was the thing about British families on holiday – if it was summer, then they wore shorts, no matter the weather.

Although Connie figured there was a decent chance her blow-dry wouldn't last the journey back to the hotel, she didn't regret her trip. In truth, she'd needed the escape – things had become a little intense of late.

She'd left her mother in the capable hands of Alex – or so she hoped. He wasn't the most reliable of minders, but he'd been on surprisingly good behaviour all day, something that was out of character and probably highly suspicious, but she was desperate, so she was willing to quell her maternal scepticism and pray for the best.

In true Alex style, her son had started drinking the moment they'd arrived at the hotel yesterday, and she'd resigned herself to managing his behaviour, apologising for his drunken misdemeanours and ignoring his feeble attempts to hide his weed addiction. Instead, he'd retired to bed early last night and emerged this morning in a sheepish mood – hangover-free – and hadn't downed his usual three pints with lunch. This was suspicious enough, but when he'd offered to look after his grandma this afternoon, so Connie could get her hair done, she'd nearly fainted from shock. Who was this imposter purporting to be her son? Still, she wasn't about to look a gift horse in the mouth and had escaped before Alex could change his mind.

Whatever had instigated her son's improved behaviour, at least it was one fewer member of the Lawrence family causing an upset or scandal. And, rather humiliatingly, she was forced to include herself in that group. After all, she'd propositioned the best man last night. It wasn't her finest moment – the memory made her squirm, and she noticed her already red cheeks deepening further in the stark salon mirror.

There seemed to be a fine line between a woman's behaviour being seen as 'empowering and liberating' as opposed to 'inappropriate and embarrassing'. Sadly, her ill-advised flirtations had been firmly rooted in the second category. Why was it that a man could date a woman several decades younger and be viewed as a 'lucky old goat', while a woman seducing a younger man was seen as 'slightly desperate'?

Either way, it wasn't like she particularly wanted a fling with a younger man – she just didn't want to be judged because of it. But kissing Matt Hardy hadn't been down to logic, passion or the desire to assert her right as a middle-aged woman to re-engage in a meaningful sex life, it had happened because she'd been drunk. And that was never a good enough reason for being the centre of gossip – at any age.

The stylist held up a hand mirror and showed Connie the back of her hairdo. It looked good, although how long it would last remained to be seen.

Connie collected her things and headed for the front desk to settle up.

Maybe she should feel guilty for needing a break from her family, but there was only so much drama she could take, and discovering that her mother had gone missing on Bodmin Moor this morning had left her nerves in tatters.

Connie tried to be a good daughter, she really did. She bit her tongue, she solved problems, she kept her mother safe and she'd managed to keep her in her own home. But it didn't stop the cycle of emotions from repeating. The resentment, the annoyance, the loss of patience, concluding with overwhelming guilt and the promise to do better next time. Except next time was never any different.

Paying for her blow-dry, she accepted the receptionist's offer of help in putting on her coat. She was going to need it in this weather.

Pulling up the hood, she scanned the street outside, hoping for a break in the weather. Her plan to shop and explore Launceston had been abandoned, but she wasn't quite ready to return to the wedding preparations at the hotel.

Across the street she saw the sign for a pub and decided to enjoy a quick glass of wine before calling for a taxi. After all, she still had one last conundrum to mentally unravel – Kenneth's unexpected gift, and what had caused such a turnaround.

Her solicitor had mentioned during recent discussions that men often changed their minds about divorce once they realised the financial implications and the detriment to their lavish lifestyles. Suddenly, they weren't quite so keen to be 'free' and often returned home, tail between their legs, begging forgiveness.

But as a family lawyer, wouldn't Kenneth have already been aware of the cost of divorcing? Or was he banking on the fact that his experience in the field would enable him to come out of any settlement quids in?

Making a run for it, Connie exited the salon and splashed across the road to the pub.

The Bell Inn was a traditional English pub with ornate brass fittings, a solid wooden bar and a low-beamed ceiling. The frosted stained-glass windows dimmed the light, casting the space in a flickering glow. It wasn't busy, just a few local patrons propping up the bar or playing pool. It was therefore unsurprising that the lone figure of a woman seated at one of the tables, sipping a pint of Guinness, caught Connie's eye.

She recognised her as Susan Hardy, grandmother of the groom and mother of Matt Hardy – the man Connie had attempted to seduce last night.

Shame almost made her turn tail and exit the pub in a flurry, sod the rain. But there was something about the woman's slumped demeanour that radiated misery. Why else would she be drinking alone in a pub on the eve of a family wedding?

Connie ordered a glass of Pinot Grigio and headed over. 'Would you like some company?' she asked, gesturing to an empty wooden chair.

Susan Hardy didn't immediately respond, almost as if she hadn't realised the question had been directed at her. When she eventually glanced up, she flinched, as though she'd been caught doing something illegal.

Connie offered the woman an appeasing smile. 'If you'd rather be alone, I can sit somewhere else. I won't be offended.'

Susan seemed hesitant. 'I'm not much company, I'm afraid.'

Connie shrugged off her wet coat and sat down. 'Me neither, I only came into town to escape my family.'

Susan raised an eyebrow.

'Don't get me wrong, I love them dearly, but it's not exactly relaxing back at the hotel. If I'm honest, I can only stand so much of watching my ex-husband canoodling with a younger woman.' It was the first time she'd used the phrase 'ex-husband', and she wondered if it was a significant development, or merely her subconscious trying it out to see how it sounded.

Susan stared down at her beer. 'I imagine that would be hard. You hide it very well.'

'Not really, although I am getting better with practice. You should've seen me a few months ago, I was a raving banshee.'

Susan smiled. 'I doubt that.'

'Trust me, I was positively unhinged. Anyway, my face was aching from faking a smile, so I used the excuse of visiting the hairdresser as a way of escaping. Not that this blow-dry will last in this weather. It's already wilting.'

Susan looked up. 'It looks gorgeous.'

'Thank you, let's hope it still looks that way tomorrow.'

Susan tentatively touched her own hair, lank and lifeless, seemingly self-conscious about her appearance.

Connie spotted a set of badly bitten fingernails, along with bruised eye sockets and sallow complexion. She imagined the woman was both devoid of sleep and burdened by stress. It was a look Connie recognised, she'd looked the exact same way just a few weeks ago. 'Is there any reason why you're drinking alone? It's none of my business, I know, but I'd be happy to listen if you need to unload.'

Susan looked apprehensive.

'Completely confidentially, of course. Us women need to stick together. It seems to me that we're expected to look good, raise our kids, keep our husbands happy and never complain about our lot. It's rather unfair, if you ask me.'

Susan gave her the ghost of a smile. 'It's certainly hard work pretending all the time.'

'Tell me about it.' Connie rolled her eyes. 'And if you dare criticise, or point out the unfairness of the situation, you're accused of nagging, or being too demanding. Well, sod that, I say.' Connie took a swig of wine. 'I'm done indulging my ex-husband's philandering ways. It's time he made a decision. Shit or get off the pan, as my old dad used to say.'

Susan laughed.

Connie leant closer. 'Do you know he left me a gift at the hotel this morning?'

Susan looked intrigued. 'What kind of gift?'

'Expensive French perfume. I had to google it — I'd never heard of it before. Maison Francis Kurkdjian. According to the Harrods website, it boasts a musky almond scent with a sweet jasmine top note. I wasn't sure whether I was dousing myself in perfume or ordering lunch. It retails at over two hundred quid a bottle.'

Susan's pale eyes grew wide. 'Goodness. I don't spend that much a month on food.'

'And this is from the man who a few weeks ago bought me cheap supermarket flowers. Some turnaround, huh?'

'You think he's up to something?'

Connie sat back in her chair. 'You bet, I do. The question is what?'

'Maybe he's trying to win you back?'

'In which case, he's got some cheek. Why bring Tiffany to the wedding if he wants a reconciliation? Tiffany is the other woman, by the way.'

'I'd gathered as much.'

Connie waved her hand about. 'Any decent man would finish his affair before returning to the wife. But no, Kenneth wants to have his cake and eat it. If I turn him down, he'll be back with her before the day is out, you mark my words.'

Susan took a sip of beer, using both hands to steady the pint glass. 'Are you going to turn him down?'

Connie mulled it over. 'I'm undecided.'

'Do you still love him?'

Connie shrugged. 'Yes, but I've come to realise that love might not be enough. You have to respect someone, too, trust them, and most importantly, like them. And I'm not sure I like Kenneth very much these days.'

Susan sighed. 'I know that feeling.'

'Don't you like your husband either?'

Susan sighed. 'I honestly don't know any more. I feel like I barely know him. We've hardly spent any time together these last ten years.'

Connie picked up her glass of wine. 'Does he work away a lot?'

'He's been in prison.'

Connie choked on her wine, spraying Pinot Grigio down her front. 'Goodness me.'

Susan patted Connie's back. 'Manslaughter, before you ask.'

Connie accepted the offer of a tissue and wiped her mouth. 'When did he get out of prison?'

'Yesterday.'

'Yesterday?' No wonder the woman was looking so tortured. 'Did you know he was coming to the wedding?'

Susan shook her head. 'Neither did anyone else, including my grandson.' She picked up her pint of beer. 'Hence the need for this.' She took a long slug.

Connie shook her head in bewilderment. 'And I thought my life was complicated.'

'The worst part is that he has no shame. He rocked up at the hotel like bloody Jesus returning from the desert, expecting a rapturous welcome and endless delight at his prodigal return. The fact that he wasn't invited to the wedding was totally lost on him, as was the mortification on his children's faces. Matt is utterly embarrassed, and Leah is furious as hell.'

'What about you?'

Susan seemed to consider this. 'I guess I'm depressed, mostly.'

'Can you ask him to leave?'

'Not without causing a scene. But the last thing I want is to have to pretend to play happy families all weekend.'

'I know that feeling.' Connie reached over and touched Susan's hand. 'Have you ever considered boxing?'

Susan looked startled. 'Boxing?'

Connie nodded. 'I can highly recommend it. Aside from the physical benefits, it's a great stress reliever, especially if you attach a photo of your husband to the punchbag.'

Susan started laughing.

'Trust me, it's great therapy. You can yell and scream at the bastard all you want, and no one cares… Well, apart from the other boxers, but they've got used to me now and don't take any notice. I urge you to try it.'

Susan smiled. 'Maybe I will.'

Connie raised her glass. 'In the meantime, here's to dealing with complicated families, being stuck in the middle of arguments and not letting the bastards in our life get us down.'

Susan clinked glasses with her. 'Hear, hear. Good luck for tomorrow.'

'You, too. I have a feeling we're going to need it.'

An hour later, Connie was arriving back at the hotel in a taxi, having decided that two glasses of wine were definitely enough. Sufficient to dull the pain of dealing with her family, but not so much as to cause an embarrassing repeat of last night.

Her plan to have a quick nap before the formal evening meal was interrupted by the sound of Kenneth's voice behind her, as she climbed the stairs to her room.

'Connie, darling, where have you been?' He appeared on the landing, looking his usual smart self in a tailored suit. He had refused to partake in any of the fancy dress activities scheduled for the day. 'I've been looking for you.'

She viewed him sceptically. 'Is everything okay?'

'Everything's fine.' His attempt to be charming increased her level of suspicion. 'I was hoping we could talk.'

'What about?'

'Well, us, silly.' He rolled his eyes like she was the one being unreasonable. It was a tactic he'd used many times in court to win over a judge, but she wasn't so easily duped. 'I've missed you.'

She raised her eyebrows. 'Have you been drinking?'

'Just a couple of whiskies.' He came closer, pinning her with a seductive gaze that had once reduced her to a quivering wreck.

'Where's Tiffany?'

'Let's not talk about Tiffany.' He took her hands and drew her close. 'Let's talk about us. We were so good together.'

Was he for real? 'We were, Kenneth. Until you left. Or have you forgotten that?'

'That's in the past. I want to focus on the future.'

It was odd, but instead of feeling elated by the prospect of them having a future together, she felt nothing other than distrust. Her solicitor's words rang loudly in her head, reminding her that Kenneth would do anything to avoid a big payout. 'Have you and Tiffany fallen out?'

He looked affronted. 'Why would you think that?'

She tried to withdraw her hands from his clasp, but he wasn't letting go. Besides, it was nice to feel his hands, warm and soft. But she'd been fooled before. 'Kenneth, only recently you were banging on about how in love you were with Tiffany, and how she'd given you a second lease of life. What happened?'

'Nothing happened.'

'I don't believe you.' She tugged her hands, but he still wasn't letting go.

'Tiffany is a wonderful woman, but she's not you.'

'Damned right she's not.'

He drew her closer, breathing in her scent. 'You're wearing the perfume I bought you. You smell divine.' His warm breath against her neck caused a shiver to ripple up her spine. 'What was it Paul Newman used to say? Why go out for hamburger, when you can have steak at home?' He kissed her neck.

She tried to quell the effects of another involuntary shiver. 'Except Paul Newman hadn't eaten the entire contents of McDonald's before saying that.' She tried to ignore the heat growing in her belly. 'You've been eating hamburger for months, Kenneth.'

'And now I want steak.' He tried for another charming smile. 'Forgive me, Connie.' When he tried to kiss her properly, she instinctively jerked away, which wasn't the reaction she'd expected. She'd wanted him to kiss her for weeks, and now it seemed she wasn't so keen. Why was that? But deep down inside she had a feeling she already knew.

Before she could explore her feelings, Tiffany appeared at the top of the stairs, looking all curvy and seductive in a clingy dress and stilettos. The woman's affronted expression was accompanied by a thunderous glare. 'Get your thieving hands off my man!'

Kenneth dropped Connie's hands and jumped away, trying to look innocent.

Lily-livered wimp.

Tiffany jabbed a long red nail at Connie. 'You're pathetic, you know that? You think you can shake that flabby arse of yours and he'll come running back?'

Flabby arse? How dare she!

'Well, over my dead body.'

'Fine, if you insist.' Connie had waited a long time for this. She adopted her boxing stance, squaring up to the woman. It wasn't like she'd started it – she was just defending herself.

Tiffany's alarmed expression at being confronted soon switched to outrage and she launched herself at Connie, arms flapping, screaming abuse. 'Why you...'

Tempting as it was to knock her flat on her own 'flabby' arse, Connie used her boxing training to duck once... twice... It was rather satisfying to see her nemesis flailing about like a drunken Bambi on ice, hitting nothing but air, and getting increasingly irate.

Kenneth stood at a safe distance, like the feeble coward he was, no doubt enjoying having his ego inflated by two women brawling over him.

After several failed attempts to down her opponent, Tiffany eventually ran out of steam and toppled off her stilettos.

Connie could have easily let the woman hit the floor with a gigantic thud, but instead she did the mature thing and caught her, receiving a face-full of hair extensions for her efforts.

As she spat lacquered hair from her mouth and disentangled herself, she inhaled a waft of Tiffany's strong perfume... musky almond with a hint of jasmine.

The world slowed. It took a moment for her brain to process the information, but when it did, she lowered Tiffany to the carpet, and then turned to face her ex-husband. 'You bought me the same perfume as your girlfriend's?'

He had the good grace to look sprung.

## Chapter Nineteen

*Sunday, 9th June – the day of the wedding*

Matt blinked up at the bright sunlight flooding the car park and breathed a sigh of relief. No one wanted a soggy wedding day. The sky was a pale blue, the wind had disappeared and the rain had dried up, so the Hardy family had been able to congregate outside the Smugglers Bar, at the side of the hotel, for their formal photos ahead of the wedding ceremony in the afternoon. But however sunny and bright the weather was outside, there was still a storm raging of a different kind – namely, the unexpected arrival of his dad yesterday. Like they'd needed any further drama.

'Can we have the two groomsmen either side of the groom, please,' shouted the photographer, who was rapidly losing patience. She'd been trying unsuccessfully to capture shots all morning, and so far she'd been thwarted at every turn.

'Have you told him to bugger off yet?' Leah looked like a cast member from the *Kingsman* films, in her fitted tuxedo and polished brogue shoes. Her hair was scraped into a tight ponytail, which bobbed about as she subjected their father to evil stares across the car park. Whereas his sister normally looked 'cute', today she looked primed for a pub brawl involving poisoned umbrellas and spiked bowler hats.

Matt sucked in his breath and rebuttoned his tuxedo jacket, which had popped open again. He was already hot, and it was only ten a.m. 'You know I haven't.'

Leah gave him one of her looks. 'He's not wanted here. Look at our poor mother, she's traumatised.'

Matt glanced over to where their mother was standing, with a glazed look on her drawn face. It was true. Despite her smart lilac outfit, and having her hair and make-up professionally done, she still looked like a woman who expected the world to implode at any moment.

In contrast, their dad was breezing about like the Godfather, bulging from the ill-fitting suit they'd managed to hire last minute from a shop in Launceston, and currently smoking a cigar.

It had taken all of Matt's energies to keep his dad away from the formal meal last night, taking him into town for a beer and a curry on the pretence of wanting a catch-up. His real goal had been to persuade his dad to rethink attending the wedding, but when it became clear that Pete Hardy wasn't to be dissuaded, Matt had accepted defeat, returned to the hotel and convinced his slightly drunk father to go bed, so as not to cause any further scandal.

This hadn't stopped his half-brother Chris from banging on Matt's bedroom door last night, accusing him of trying to sabotage his son's wedding. Which was a bit rich, in Matt's opinion, considering that Chris wasn't happy about the wedding in the first place. His half-brother wasn't above adopting double standards, it seemed.

'You were supposed to make him leave,' Leah said, still growling at him.

Matt wasn't sure how he was the bad guy in all this, but that seemed par for the course these days. He wasn't enjoying the situation any more than anyone else.

'Can you look at the camera, please?' the photographer yelled.

The three of them adopted fake smiles and posed for the shot. Leah's grin was akin to that of an angry wasp trapped inside a glass. Zac looked slightly dazed, and Matt's smile was about as genuine as the photographer's – who looked like she'd had less trouble photographing the local cattle festival.

'Zac doesn't want him to leave,' Matt replied through gritted teeth.

'Of course he does,' Leah hissed back, still holding onto her fake smile. 'He's just too polite to say so.'

'Like it or not, he's the kid's grandfather.'

'*Step*-grandfather,' Leah said, throwing him a steely glare.

'I am standing here,' Zac said, the only one still looking at the camera.

'Faces to me!' the photographer yelled. They all turned to the camera and resumed smiling, as their shot was taken. 'Can the grandparents join the group, please!'

Pete Hardy sauntered over and slung his arm around Leah's shoulder. 'How's it going, my girl?' he said, giving her a squeeze.

Leah ducked away from his embrace, choking from his cigar smoke, and repositioned herself on the other side of the group, next to Matt.

'Don't be like that, darling.' Pete gave a half-hearted shrug, before turning his attentions to his long-suffering wife. 'Come here, Susie, love.' He pulled her close and offered the photographer a huge smile, his cigar balancing between his teeth. 'It's good to be out in the fresh air, taking in the sights and being with my family. Look at that scenery,' he said, gesturing to the impressive landscape. 'You don't get views like that in prison.'

Matt groaned.

Leah swore.

Zac looked somewhat alarmed.

'I'm sure you don't,' Susan said faintly, trying her best to hold it together, no doubt for the sake of the family.

'Nice big smiles!' the photographer instructed. 'Say cheese!'

'Cheese!' yelled Pete, the only one who did.

The rest of them looked like they were attending a funeral rather than a wedding.

It was hard to imagine anything more excruciating than mediating the tense atmosphere between his family members…

until the door of the Smugglers Bar opened and the Hamilton clan emerged. Matt silently cursed. He wished he was someplace else. Anywhere. The Siberian desert would do. Anywhere but stuck in this damned tight suit, trying unsuccessfully to keep the peace. He didn't even have Beth as backup, as she was on maid-of-honour duties, assigned to looking after the bride this morning.

As Zac's family congregated on the gravel car park, nothing appeared amiss. Chris and Will were wearing their tuxedo suits, Gemma, Lily and Diane were dressed in colourful floaty wedding outfits, and Poppy was bouncing around in her sparkly pale gold bridesmaid dress. Only Bobby was absent from the group. If the man had any sense, he'd be in the bar, knocking back a stiff drink.

Matt's mind briefly drifted to thoughts of enjoying a relaxing pub lunch, maybe with Beth for company. That's assuming things were back to normal between them. It was hard to tell – he hadn't seen her yet today. Their relationship seemed to constantly swing between wanting and arguing, never fully one thing or the other, and never staying fixed long enough to determine if anything was actually happening between them. The arrival of his father yesterday, coupled with the news about Megan's first marriage, hadn't exactly helped. Their attempts to get together appeared to be thwarted at every turn. Maybe they were destined never to be a couple, a thought that depressed him even further.

His attention was dragged back to the present and the volcano he felt sure was about to erupt. The tense atmosphere became even more apparent when Will and Lily broke away from the group and pretended to engage in conversation with Poppy. Diane hung back by the bar door, as if waiting for her husband, which left Chris and Gemma – the Mr and Mrs Smith of the group – staring daggers at Pete. Their mean and moody stares switched to Matt and then back to Pete, making it clear he was also included in their wrath.

How was this his fault? But he knew there was no reasoning with his half-brother. Chris believed Matt was responsible for Pete Hardy showing up at the wedding, and no amount of persuading would convince him otherwise, so Matt wasn't about to waste his time trying.

'Can you all congregate together, please!' the photographer shouted, waving in an attempt to herd them into a group.

'Come on, Chris, don't be shy.' Pete beckoned his stepson over with an oblivious smile. 'You don't want to disappoint your mother, do you?'

Matt cringed. Of all the things his dad could have said.

If Chris was scowling before, he was now positively enraged. 'I'm not the one likely to disappoint her, am I?' he said, storming over.

Pete looked puzzled. 'Meaning?'

Susan reached out and touched her older son's arm. 'Not now, Chris.'

Chris reluctantly accepted his mother's request. 'I'm doing this for you, Mum,' he said, patting her hand. 'No other reason.'

'I know, love. And I appreciate it.' She wafted away a plume of cigar smoke that had drifted in her direction and smiled softly at him.

'I don't see what the problem is,' Pete said loudly. 'Anyone would think you lot weren't pleased to see me.' He took a drag on his cigar and looked around the group, most of whom averted their eyes. 'You're glad I'm here, aren't you, Zac?' He slapped Zac on the shoulder, filling the lad's face with exhaled smoke.

Zac nodded half-heartedly. 'Sure, Granddad.'

'See? All good. Now let's not keep the nice photographer waiting any longer. Smile for the camera everyone!'

To give her credit, the photographer took a shot, even though the group looked totally miserable… except for Poppy, who struck a pose and smiled at the camera, showing more maturity than her entire dysfunctional family put together.

A few further shots followed, with various people waving away cigar smoke, others glaring daggers at Pete, and some forcing manic smiles. If the photographer managed to secure one decent shot, Matt would be amazed. Eventually, she made an excuse about needing to fetch another camera lens from her car – although Matt suspected this was a ruse and the poor woman just needed a break. Who could blame her?

The sight of a police car pulling into the car park shouldn't have been a surprise. After all, this weekend had been one disaster after another. Why should things stop now? Nonetheless, the flashing blue lights sent a jolt of dread running through Matt's entire body. A feeling compounded when he saw the satisfied look on his half-brother's face. He couldn't imagine crime was a huge issue in this part of the country, which meant only one thing. It didn't take a genius to work out the police were here for his dad. Although why, Matt had no idea. His father had only been released late on Friday – he couldn't have had time to commit another offence, surely.

Two uniformed officers exited the car and wandered over, making a beeline for his dad and confirming Matt's fears. 'Pete Hardy?' one of them said, unearthing a pair of handcuffs.

Matt's dad stepped forwards. 'That's me. How can I help, officer? As you can see, I'm attending my grandson's wedding, I've not done anything wrong.'

'I'm afraid you've breached the conditions of your early release,' the second officer said, sounding bored. 'You were supposed to stay within ten miles of your registered home address.'

Matt's dad scoffed, as though his was merely a request and not a mandatory requirement. 'Surely you can't object to me attending my grandson's wedding? I'll be back home tomorrow.'

The officer shrugged and held out the handcuffs. 'We don't make the rules.'

When Matt saw Chris fold his arms in a self-satisfied manner, he turned to him. 'Did you report him?'

Chris's injured expression wasn't enough to cover his guilt. 'Why would you think that?'

Matt's blood boiled. 'You did, didn't you?'

Chris lifted his chin. 'He's not wanted here.'

'Whether that's true or not, you were out of line calling the cops on him. He's your dad, for crying out loud.'

Chris turned on him. '*Step*dad. And don't try laying the guilt on me. I'm not the one who was sent to jail, and I'm certainly not the one who's made our mum's life a misery for the last ten years. You want to be angry at someone, be mad at him, not me.'

It didn't matter whether Chris was right, or not. There were some things you didn't do, and shopping a family member to the cops was one of them. 'He's served his time, Chris. Deliberately doing something so spiteful and mean, and on your son's wedding day, too… well, that's just typical you, isn't it? You don't care who you hurt.'

'From the man who knows nothing about family.'

'I know about loyalty,' Matt snapped back. He was done letting his brother take the moral high ground. 'I'm not the one who's spent their entire life punishing our mother for having the audacity to have a second family.'

'A family that's caused her nothing but grief.'

'And you haven't?' Matt was now in his brother's face, fighting the urge to deck him.

They were interrupted by a tearful Susan. 'Boys, please. This is bad enough without you two fighting.'

Knowing his mother was upset was enough to quell Matt's anger. The brothers continued to glare at each other, but eventually backed down from the confrontation.

Matt turned to his mother and hugged her. 'Sorry, Mum. Are you okay?'

'Not really,' she whispered, clinging on to him.

Silence descended as Pete Hardy was handcuffed and taken away to the patrol car, complaining when he was forced to extinguish his cigar. It was an awkward moment, to say the least. A mixture of sadness, embarrassment and relief. No one had wanted Pete Hardy at the wedding, but this wasn't how Matt had hoped things would be resolved. And he certainly didn't want to see his dad back in prison. He just hoped the judge would be lenient and award a short sentence.

As the police car drove away, Matt experienced a sinking feeling in his gut. A feeling compounded when he realised he'd lose the deposit on his dad's suit hire. It was a minor inconvenience in the circumstances, but another annoyance to add to an already hideous weekend.

The awkward silence was broken when Bobby Taylor emerged from the hotel, looking grim. 'I'm sorry to say you were right,' he said, coming over to his son-in-law, before turning to look at Zac. 'I have some bad news.'

Zac looked alarmed. 'What is it?'

'Your dad was worried about you rushing into this wedding, so he asked me to use my contacts at the force to do a background check on Megan.'

Zac shot his father an angry look. 'Why would you do that?'

Chris looked unapologetic. 'We were concerned you were making a mistake.'

Zac shook his head. 'And you think that gives you the right to investigate my fiancée? There's nothing you can tell me about her that will make a difference. I love her. I know all there is to know about her, she's told me everything.'

Zac's grandfather cleared his throat. 'Has she told you she's already married?'

Zac stilled.

A collective gasp from the extended family was followed by another deathly lull.

A lull that was only broken when the photographer returned from her car and yelled, 'Okay, nice happy smiles, please! This is a wedding, after all!'

## Chapter Twenty

After the mayhem of make-up artists, hairdressers and manicurists filling the bridal suite with beauty paraphernalia and electrical gadgets that kept tripping Beth up, it was a welcome relief when the team finally finished applying various fixing sprays and perfumes, and packed up and left.

Opening the sash window, Beth took in the fresh Cornish air, enjoying the feeling of the billowing voile curtains tickling her skin. The weather had finally cleared and the views across Bodmin Moor were stunning. No longer a treacherous muddy bog to be feared and conquered, but a glowing lush landscape, green and sparkling in the morning sunlight.

The bathroom door opened and Megan appeared, wearing her bridal underwear – a see-through sheer corset that left nothing to the imagination. With her sun-kissed skin, her dark hair curled into seductive waves and her face immaculately made-up, she looked like a Victoria's Secret model.

'Do you want to get into your dress?' Beth checked the time on the bedside clock – they had ninety minutes before the ceremony.

'Not yet, I'm too hot,' Megan said, rummaging through the contents of the ornate dressing table. 'Where's my necklace? I thought I'd left it on the side.'

Beth went over and immediately located the jewellery. The bride was getting jittery. Understandable, under the circumstances. 'Sit down, I'll put it on for you.'

Megan perched on the stool in front of the mirror, skittish and nervous, unsure of what to do with her hands. It was odd to see her so rattled, she normally relished being the centre of attention.

'Keep still.' Beth fixed the necklace in place. 'There, perfect.' She rested her hands on Megan's shoulders. 'What do you need? Water? Valium? Gin?'

Megan gave a half-hearted smile. 'An annulment would be good.'

Beth sighed. 'Bit late for that, I'm afraid. Are you having second thoughts about the wedding?'

Megan shook her head, making her dainty silver drop earrings sway. 'Not really, I just wish I didn't have this lie hanging over me – it's taking the edge off the excitement. It's funny, I didn't think it would bother me. I was certain that keeping quiet was the right thing to do, but now I'm not so sure.'

'Do you want me to fetch Zac? Maybe if you confessed, it might ease the guilt and enable you to enjoy the day.'

'And spoil his wedding? I couldn't do that to him, he'd be devastated. This is my problem, and I need to take ownership of it.' Megan glanced up and their eyes met in the mirror. 'You look nice, by the way. The dress isn't what I expected, but I like it. It's very sexy.'

Beth ran her hand over the bronze dress with the cut-out back, suddenly self-conscious. 'Are you sure it's not too much?'

Megan laughed. 'Only you could worry about looking too good.' She stood up and turned to Beth. 'You look gorgeous. Especially, minus those hideous glasses. I can see your eyes for once.'

Beth gave a little shrug. 'I can't help being short-sighted.'

'You could wear contacts more often. How do they feel?'

'Fine at the moment, but I doubt they'll last all day.' Beth had tried numerous lenses over the years, but she'd always reverted back to wearing glasses. She liked the barrier, felt safer behind frames. 'Are you sure my hair wouldn't look better up?'

'I'm sure.' Megan brushed Beth's loose curls away from her shoulder. A few tendrils were pinned up at the side and decorated with gold flowers. 'You look perfect. Stop fretting and enjoy the moment.'

Loud banging on the bedroom door startled them both, followed by more banging… accompanied by the door handle rattling. 'Megan! Are you in there?'

It was Zac. He sounded distraught.

Beth went over and cracked open the door. 'Megan's not dressed,' she said, trying to obscure his view. 'It's bad luck for the groom to see the bride on her wedding day.'

'I don't care,' he said, pushing against the door and forcing Beth to take a step back. 'I need to see her.' He barged into the room, stopping with a jolt when he saw his fiancée. 'You're already married?'

Oh, hell.

If that wasn't shocking enough, Matt – wearing a smart tuxedo suit – was standing in the doorway behind Zac. The impact was nearly enough to distract Beth from the ensuing row. Aware that her jaw had dropped open, she closed her mouth and dragged her shocked gaze away from his tall figure, wide chest and neatly trimmed beard. 'Come in, so I can close the door,' she said, ushering him inside. The fewer people who witnessed this debacle, the better.

Megan ran towards Zac, seemingly unperturbed at being caught in her bridal underwear. 'I can explain,' she said, attempting to take his hands.

He was already backing away. 'So it's true?'

Megan's face crumpled at the rejection. 'I'm so sorry, Zac. How did you find out?'

He looked incredulous. 'How did I find out? I'll tell you how I found out. My granddad just announced it to the whole family. Apparently, my dad instructed him to run a background check on you.'

Megan's hands came up to her exposed neck. 'Why would he do that?'

'I don't know, Megan. Maybe he suspected something wasn't right about you. Turns out he was right.' He paced across to the window, as if unable to contain his agitation. 'My family have been against this marriage from the start. They told me I was a fool for getting married so young and I was rushing into things, but I refused to listen.'

Megan sagged against one of the chunky wooden bedposts. 'Your family don't approve of me? I never knew that, why didn't you tell me?'

'Because I was protecting you,' he said, turning to her. 'I didn't want you to know or be hurt. I defended every argument, I told them I trusted you and that I knew what I was doing. I told them they were wrong to have doubts about you.' He ran his hands into his hair, messing up his carefully styled quiff. 'More fool me, eh?'

Megan stumbled over to him. 'You're not a fool, Zac. And you can trust me—'

'You're already married!' he shouted.

'I can explain—'

'What's there to explain?' He held her at arm's length. 'You've admitted you're already married, which means you lied to me. Worse, you let me plan this fucking wedding and invite all our friends and family, only to humiliate me?'

Tears streamed down Megan's perfectly rouged cheeks. 'I didn't mean to.'

'Then what did you mean to do?' His anger was slightly derailed by deep heaving sobs. 'Because I'm struggling to understand how you could let this happen and not mention the minor detail of you already being married.' He turned away and sobbed harder.

Megan collapsed onto the bed, sobbing too.

Which left Beth and Matt standing by the door, looking awkwardly at each other, and wondering what the hell they should do.

Beth went over to Megan and climbed onto the four-poster bed to comfort her.

Matt walked around her and placed a hand on Zac's shoulder. 'Take a breath, mate. Try and stay calm.'

Zac shrugged him off. 'Why should I? I've just found out the woman I was supposed to marry is already married!' More sobs escaped.

Megan cried harder on the bed.

Matt and Beth exchanged another look.

Matt cleared his throat. 'I know it sucks, mate, but you need to let her explain. It's not what you think.'

A beat passed before Zac turned to face his uncle. 'You knew?'

Matt hesitated, before nodding. 'I found out yesterday.'

'And you didn't tell me? You're supposed to be on my side.'

'You're right, and I'm sorry, but once Beth explained the circumstances, I decided it would be better to let the wedding go ahead. Megan promised to tell you herself at a later date, and I felt that was better than ruining your special day.'

Zac let out an incredulous laugh. 'Oh, you mean after she'd committed bigamy? That's the right word, isn't it?' He turned to Beth. 'You're the lawyer, you tell me.'

Beth nodded. 'Technically, yes.'

'Well, just fucking great.' He pushed past Matt and moved to the other side of the room. 'Thanks, guys, way to go ruining my life.'

Matt followed him. 'Before you make any decisions about calling off the wedding, at least let Megan explain.'

'What's the point? She's not getting a divorce in the next hour, is she?' He rubbed his forehead. 'Shit! Is she still with this other guy?'

Megan lifted her head from the bed. 'Of course not.'

'But you're still married to him!'

Matt touched Zac's arm. 'Please, Zac. Let her explain.'

Zac pulled away. 'Fine. Explain. Tell me how come you're already married to someone else and conveniently forgot to mention it.'

Megan looked up at Beth. 'Can you give us a moment?'

'Of course, we'll wait outside.'

It was a struggle to get off the huge bed in her slippery dress and strappy heels. Matt had to help her, almost lifting her off it. The scent of his subtle aftershave, and the feeling of his warm body beneath his suit, would normally have been a welcome treat, but at that precise moment it was a distraction she could do without.

Beth opened the bedroom door, only to discover Zac's entire extended family congregated in the hallway.

Matt's brother marched towards her. 'What's going on in there?'

His wife, Gemma, was right behind him. 'Let me in, I want to see my son.'

Behind her, Matt's arm reached up and blocked the doorway. 'Not now, guys. Give them some space.'

'Move out of the way, Matt.' Chris pointed a finger at his brother. 'We need to sort this out.'

'No, you don't.' Matt pinned his brother with a steely glare. 'Let them sort it out themselves. Go to the bar, have a drink, take a walk. But you're not coming in.'

Chris looked enraged. 'Who do you think you are?'

'I'm Zac's best man. And until he tells me otherwise, you're not coming in. Now move away from the door, Chris.'

Matt's brother must have sensed he was serious, because he reluctantly backed away, allowing Matt to shut the bridal suite door and lock it.

He turned to Zac and Megan. 'Sorry guys, change of plan.' Taking hold of Beth's hand, he led her across the room and into the bathroom. 'Don't mind us. Talk all you need to, we won't disturb you.'

Beth allowed herself to be dragged into the small bathroom, which suddenly seemed a lot smaller with Matt inside. 'So, what happens now?'

Matt closed the door. 'We sit and wait.'

Beth glanced around. 'There's nowhere to sit.' Other than on the loo seat, but she wasn't that desperate to sit down. Which meant she was left standing in a cramped space, trying to focus on the marbled tiling and brushed chrome fixings, rather than on the man who was inches away from her, making her legs feel weak. Talk about torture.

Silence descended.

The effort not to look at Matt was enormous. It wasn't just his size, it was more his presence. His quiet strength, his imposing sense of calm and the way he looked surprisingly suave in his James Bond suit.

For some inexplicable reason, the *Casino Royale* shower scene came to mind, and she had to fight off the image of them getting wet and cosy, while he licked dead assailant's blood from her fingers.

If only she could create more space between them, but she had nowhere to go. She was stuck studying the way his wide chest slowly expanded with each breath, feeling the weight of his eyes that were watching her intently, while ignoring the heat between them that was making the bathroom mirror steam up.

She definitely needed a cold shower.

In an effort to focus her mind elsewhere, she strained to listen to the discussion taking place next door, but she couldn't hear anything above the whir of the extractor fan. 'I don't know who I feel more sorry for, Zac or Megan.'

Matt raised an eyebrow. 'Zac's the injured party.' There was no accusation in his words, he was merely pointing out the truth, and she couldn't argue otherwise.

'Megan didn't do this to deliberately to hurt him. She loves him, she's genuinely heartbroken.'

His eyes met hers. 'Keeping such a big secret was never going to end well.'

Beth sighed. 'You're right, and I'm not defending her, but my sister's an unrelenting optimist, to the point of delusion. She sails through life believing everything will turn out okay, and usually it does. I know this is going to sound weird, but this honestly wasn't a big deal to her. Getting hitched in Las Vegas was a silly prank, like acting out a scene from a play. It wasn't real, if that makes sense. She never loved Freddie Wood. He was just an inconsequential moment from her past life, like a load of other incidents involving unsuitable men and drunken misdemeanours. That's not to say Megan isn't a good person – she is, she's the best. She's funny and theatrical and passionate. Life is a series of adventures, a playground. In a way, I envy her. Most of us live life fearing the worst, mitigating against mistakes, and being cautious and worried about money or job security. It must be so freeing to act with such abandon.'

'Until someone gets hurt.'

Beth sighed. 'I guess there's always a price to pay, however you live your life.'

'Being cautious isn't a crime, as long as you don't let it stop you being happy.' His voice had softened, the resonance low and vibrating through her ribcage.

She risked looking up into his blue eyes, which had dilated to the point of being virtually black. 'When Megan told me Zac had proposed, I was worried for them. I'd never seen Megan serious about anyone before. She treated men like amusing playthings, flitting from one to another and never committing, but I soon realised things were different this time. I'm absolutely convinced she loves him more than anything else in the world. Losing Zac will devastate her.'

Matt reached up and traced a finger down her cheek, ending up settling on her neck. 'He'll be devastated, too.'

'I really hope they can work it out,' she said, ignoring the tremor in her knees. 'Thank you for trying to reason with him and getting him to talk to Megan. It was kind of you.'

His fingers slid into her hair, sending shivers racing up her spine. 'He needs to hear her side of things before making a decision.'

Beth swallowed. 'Do you think he'll forgive her?'

'Yes.'

'How can you be so sure?'

Matt's serious expression was filled with heat. 'He's crazy about her.'

The knee-shaking hiked up a notch. 'But she lied to him.'

'No one's perfect.' He leant closer and kissed the side of her neck.

She sucked in a breath.

'I like your hair down.' He kissed her again, his lips warm and soft, and the feel of his beard brushing over her skin was tantalisingly good.

Her knees weren't the only thing shaking – her thighs had joined in.

'And you look amazing in this dress.' His hand cupped the back of her neck and drew her closer. 'But I miss your glasses.'

'You do?'

'They never sit straight on your face,' he said, with a wry smile. He kissed one eyelid, then the other, his lips brushing against her skin. Any chance of controlling the shaking went flying out of the window... not that there was a window, but still.

His lips closed around hers, as one hand held her head and the other slid slowly around her waist, pulling her closer.

She'd gone from shaking to melting, her bones losing their density, her insides disintegrating like confetti in the breeze. Heat began to build, hands began to roam and the silence was broken by a soft moan that acted as encouragement to both sides. God, she liked kissing him. She couldn't get enough, he was intoxicating, addictive, an itch she couldn't scratch.

And then his sodding phone rang.

Talk about rotten timing.

The noise caused him to still. His lips were still pressed against hers, but he was no longer moving with such intensity and wanting. Reluctantly, his grip loosened and he pulled away. 'I'd better see who it is.'

'Sure… I mean, sure.' She'd lost the ability to form a coherent sentence.

Matt pulled out his phone from his suit pocket and checked the screen. 'It's the hotel,' he said with a frown. Beth watched him answer the call, nodding, and muttering the occasional, 'Right' into the phone, as his expression morphed into one of concern. This didn't bode well.

She extricated herself from his hold. Once again, it seemed they were destined never to be together – even though it probably wasn't the ideal moment to be getting frisky.

'Tell him to wait there, I'll be right down.' Matt ended the call and any brief hope of them resuming kissing. 'Freddie Wood is in reception, asking for Megan.'

Of all the things Beth expected him to say, that wasn't one of them.

Her insides did a double-flip – and not in a good way. 'For real?'

Matt nodded. 'What the hell are we going to do? If we barge next door and announce that Megan's husband is downstairs, all hell's going to break loose.'

'We can't let that happen.' Beth frantically tried to think. This was a disaster, what was the man thinking? 'It's probably better if I go downstairs and see what he wants. After all, I'm the one who contacted him. Can you stay up here and keep watch?'

'Fine, but if he's here to cause trouble then call me, okay? I'll be right down.'

'Don't worry, I will.' Beth unlocked the bathroom door. 'Should we warn them? We don't want to walk in on anything intimate.'

'More intimate than Megan in her underwear?'

'Fair point. Follow me.' Beth opened the door and averted her eyes as she crossed the bridal suite. Even then, she could see Megan and Zac on the bed, sitting crossed-legged, deep in conversation. 'Don't mind us, we're just… er… just getting a

261

glass of water,' she said, forgetting there was a jug of water on the dressing table. 'Sparkling. From the bar. Won't be long.' She felt like Hugh Grant in *Four Weddings and a Funeral* when he was trying to sneak out of the bridal suite without being seen by the bride and groom bonking like rabbits on the bed. 'Don't forget the key,' she hissed to Matt, as they shot out of the room into the safety of the hallway, which was still full of Zac's family.

'What's happening?' Chris demanded.

'Is the wedding cancelled?' chipped in Gemma.

'No news, guys.' Matt locked the door behind him and folded his arms, guarding the entrance like a really hot bouncer.

Beth ignored the barrage of overlapping questions being yelled at her, and ran down the hallway towards the stairs leading to the lobby. Hopefully, no one would follow her.

She spotted Freddie Wood immediately, recognising him from his Facebook profile picture. He was a handsome arty type, with long Harry Styles hair and an impressive set of angular cheekbones. She shot over to him.

'Come with me,' she whispered, hooking her arm though his and leading him into the quiet of the adjacent museum.

He looked alarmed, but to his credit, didn't challenge her and allowed himself to be taken into the dark space.

Once away from prying eyes, she let go of him. 'Sorry, I didn't want anyone to see you. I'm Beth, Megan's sister.'

Freddie's confused expression lifted. 'Ah, right, the woman who sent me a message about getting an annulment?'

'That's me.'

'No need.' He opened his arms, as if expecting a round of applause.

'What do you mean, no need? Of course there's a need, a great big fat need. Megan's getting married today. For real this time.'

'That's why I'm here.'

A horrible thought occurred. A man wouldn't travel all the way to Cornwall for no good reason. 'Look, if you're here to cause trouble, or stop the wedding—'

'Whoa, whoa, I'm not here to cause trouble.'

Beth frowned at him. 'Then why are you here?'

'To give you this.' He handed her a large envelope. 'Annulment papers.'

Beth sighed. 'They were supposed to be submitted thirty days ago. They're no use to us today.'

'They don't need submitting. The annulment was done eight years ago, the day after the wedding.'

Beth wondered if she'd misheard. 'Come again?'

'I realised what a stupid mistake we'd made, so I applied for an emergency annulment. The state of Nevada allows for a no-questions-asked annulment within twenty-four hours of the ceremony. I guess they're used to drunken tourists getting hitched and regretting it the next day.'

Beth couldn't believe what she was hearing. 'Please tell me you're not joking.'

'Check for yourself.' He watched her pull out the contents of the envelope. 'I messaged you, but when I didn't get a reply, I called a mutual friend. She told me about the wedding today. I figured you'd need these documents, so I thought I'd better come down.'

Beth skimmed over the annulment papers dated eight years earlier. 'Freddie Wood, you're an absolute star. You've just single-handedly saved the day.' Even if he had omitted to mention the annulment to the bride before now, which wasn't exactly helpful.

He grinned. 'No problem. Okay if I stay for the wedding? It'll be good to catch up with Megan.'

Beth placed a hand on his chest. 'Please don't take this the wrong way, but absolutely not. The groom only discovered your existence about twenty minutes ago.'

'Shit.'

'Exactly. So can you see why you can't stay?'

'I get it.' He shrugged. 'Oh, well, back to the train station.'

'Thanks again for this.' She turned and ran for the hotel, eager to get upstairs and break the good news. The wedding could go ahead.

She just hoped it wasn't too late.

## Chapter Twenty-One

The first Connie knew of her daughter's complicated marital status was when Kenneth started banging on her bedroom door and yelling at her, as though the situation was somehow her fault. Far from making her angry, Kenneth's heated claims that Megan had 'humiliated' the Lawrence family name simply made her laugh. The gall of the man. Who was he to talk about humiliation? His attitude really was beyond arrogance – the man was positively delusional.

That said, the news still shocked her. Megan was already married? It was too implausible to be true. Surely she'd know if her youngest daughter was already married? Megan would have told her... wouldn't she?

Needing a few moments to collect her thoughts, she shooed Kenneth away, slammed the door in his face – for no other reason than it felt good to do so – and quickly zipped up her emerald-green shift dress. Maybe wearing her wedding outfit was wishful thinking if Kenneth's ludicrous claims turned out to be true, but until she knew otherwise, she would assume the ceremony was going ahead as planned.

After buttoning up the jacket on her mother's pretty blue floral two-piece, complete with matching hat and handbag, the pair of them were ready to head off and find out what the hell was going on.

Any lingering doubts that Connie still had about the validity of Kenneth's allegations quickly disappeared when confronted with the scene in the bridal suite. Megan's face was tear-stained and Beth was in a heightened state of anxiety.

Her eldest daughter filled her in on the morning's events, detailing Megan's Las Vegas marriage, subsequent annulment, heated confrontation with Zac and emotional make-up session. It sounded exhausting.

Although Connie's first emotion was disappointment at being kept in the dark about the whole situation, motherly instinct quickly took over. Megan looked awful, soggy from crying, her flimsy dressing gown hanging from her slight frame, her diamanté tiara lopsided.

Connie immediately took control of the situation, and instructed Beth to fetch a pot of tea and a large bottle of gin from the bar. If Megan didn't need a stiffener, then Connie certainly did.

After positioning Doris in the chair by the window and handing her the bag of knitting to keep her occupied, she redirected her attentions towards her youngest daughter.

'First things first, we need to repair your make-up,' she said, manoeuvring Megan onto the stool in front of the dressing table. 'We can't have you walking down the aisle with panda eyes, can we?'

Megan sniffed. 'I'm so sorry, Mum. I've messed everything up.'

'Nonsense.' Connie handed her daughter a tissue. 'You're a Lawrence, this is par for the course – we wouldn't be us without a drama of some kind. And besides, you have some way to go before you surpass your father.'

Megan blew her nose. 'How can I face everyone after what I've done? Zac's family must hate me.'

'They'll get over it. Anyway, it's Zac you're marrying, not his family. Has he forgiven you?'

'Just about.'

'Well, that's all that matters. Lift your chin.' Connie used a cotton bud to wipe away smudged mascara from under Megan's eyes. 'Once the wedding gets under way, everything else will be forgotten – or it will be, once the alcohol starts flowing.'

Megan blinked up at her through watery eyes. 'I'm sorry I didn't tell you about Freddie.'

Doris looked up from her knitting. 'Who's Freddie?'

'No one, Mother. Carry on with your knitting.' It wasn't like her mother had the capacity to understand what was going on, and Connie didn't have the energy to explain.

'I guess I was embarrassed,' Megan said, looking glum. 'It was a foolish thing to do.'

'Who's Freddie?' repeated Doris.

Connie reapplied Megan's mascara. 'We all do silly things when we're younger. Your only real crime was letting it go on for so long and not telling Zac.'

Megan sniffed. 'I know.'

'Who's Freddie?' Doris demanded again.

Connie glanced over, deciding honesty was the best policy. It's not like her mother would remember. 'The man Megan married eight years ago in Las Vegas.'

Doris looked incredulous. 'Don't be daft. Megan's not married – she's marrying Zac.' She resumed knitting, tutting and shaking her head. 'And people say *I'm* losing my marbles.'

The bedroom door opened and Beth appeared, carrying a tray of drinks. Behind her was Lily Taylor, Megan's best friend and wedding dress designer, carrying a huge garment bag.

'I found Lily waiting in the hallway. I figured you'd be needing your dress soon, so I invited her in.' Beth placed the tray on the side table.

'I can wait outside, if you're not ready?' Lily hovered by the doorway, looking uncomfortable, as though she was intruding.

Megan waved her in. 'Come in, I need all the support I can get... How's Zac?'

'He's fine.' Lily laid the dress bag on the four-poster bed. 'He's playing pool in the barn with Matt and Will.'

Megan swivelled on the stool to face her friend. 'Is he really okay about getting married today?'

'They were all laughing and messing about, so I didn't get the impression he was having second thoughts.' Lily came over to Megan. 'He asked me to give you this. He meant to give it to you earlier, but things got a little sidetracked.'

Megan took the jewellery box from Lily and opened it to reveal a small silver ring embossed with blue sapphires. 'My something blue,' she said, welling up again.

Connie handed her a tissue. 'Don't cry, you'll smudge your make-up again. It looks a little small for your finger.'

'Oh, it's not for my finger.' Megan averted her eyes.

Connie looked at Beth and then Lily, who both surreptitiously looked away. 'Then where's it for?'

'Probably her nipple,' Doris said, without looking up from her knitting.

Connie's mouth dropped open.

'Excuse me, I need to use the bathroom.' Megan disappeared, taking her jewellery box with her.

Connie was left wondering how her eighty-four-year-old mother knew more about body piercings than she did.

A knock on the bedroom door shook Connie from her thoughts. 'I'll get it,' she said, glad of the distraction – something she quickly regretted when she discovered Kenneth standing on the other side. What did he want now?

'Where's Megan?' he snapped, aiming for a look of superiority.

'Using the bathroom.' She took in his attire of formal morning suit. 'Why are you wearing tails when the dress code is tux?'

'I already informed Megan I'd be wearing tails. It's the appropriate attire for a wedding. Alex is wearing tails, too.'

'No, he's not. We changed his order to a tuxedo when Beth asked us to, and I believe she asked you to do the same.' His suit wasn't even black, it was pale grey.

'She did, but I opted for tails.'

'Then you're going to look like a complete dick, aren't you, because all the other men are wearing tuxedos.'

He baulked at the rebuke. 'You can't speak to me like that.'

'I can speak to you any way I like. We're no longer a couple, Kenneth.' Something she'd decided on for certain last night, while lying in bed listening to her meditation app. It was time to cut her losses and start afresh. It felt both daunting and exciting, but no longer scared her.

'Because I happened to buy you the same perfume as Tiffany's? It's a little childish, don't you think? You're overreacting.'

Connie perused the man she'd shared her life with for nearly forty years. A man she loved but no longer knew, and a man she certainly no longer wanted. 'Buying me and your girlfriend the same perfume just confirmed a decision I'd pretty much already made, Kenneth. Our marriage is over.'

'You're being stubborn.' He puffed out his chest. 'Your feelings have been hurt and you feel the need to punish me. When you've calmed down, you'll see I'm right. I love you, Connie.'

She found it incredible that his constant use of the word 'you' implied that this was all her fault and nothing to do with his infidelity. 'I love you, too, Kenneth.' Which was true. He was the father of her children, the man she'd shared a home and family with. He'd always be the most important part of her past, but he was no longer a part of her future.

His self-satisfied smile indicated he'd failed to sense the 'but' coming…

'But I don't like you any more, and I certainly don't want to be married to you any more.'

He flinched. 'You need me.'

'Not any more. I have big plans.' Boy, did she.

'What plans?' He looked at her with disdain. 'You barely earn minimum wage as a doctor's receptionist.'

'True, but I'll be earning a lot more as a fitness coach.' It was the first time she'd said the words aloud, and it felt good. The idea had come to her gradually, a series of small revelations and realisations that had culminated in her devising a business plan.

'A what?'

'I'm setting myself up as a personal trainer and lifestyle coach for the over sixties. I've realised there are a lot of women like me – men, too – who find themselves a bit lost in their twilight years. People who've been widowed, or cast aside for younger versions, or for whatever reason have lost their self-esteem and need their confidence boosting.'

He looked at her like she was talking nonsense. 'And how are you going to do that?'

Connie shrugged. 'I'm still working out the details. Boxing will definitely feature, as will swimming. I've signed myself up for a counselling course and a fitness instructor course. By this time next year, I'll be running my own business.'

He shook his head. 'Running a business costs money. How are you going to afford it?'

'By fleecing you in the divorce,' she said, relishing the look of indignation on his face. 'You'd better prepare yourself for a fight, because I intend to play dirty.' She checked her watch. 'Now, what do you want? We're rather busy getting ready for a wedding.'

His shocked expression gave her a sliver of satisfaction. For once, she had the upper hand.

'No? Nothing to say? Fine, then bugger off and go find Tiffany, assuming she hasn't rejected you, too.' She paused before closing the door. 'By the way, just so you know, I'll be walking Megan down the aisle this afternoon.'

He stepped forwards. 'That's my job. I'm her father.'

She placed her hands on her hips. 'And I'm her mother.'

'It's my right. It's tradition.'

'A tradition you blew by insisting on wearing the wrong suit, Kenneth. A decision you made just to be bloody-minded. Megan has made her choice and I fully support her. Now move your foot.' She kicked his highly polished shoe. 'Poor Kenneth, demoted twice in one day, how will your ego survive?' She closed the door in his face, relishing an unexpected feeling of empowerment. She was finally taking charge of her own life. Boy, it felt good.

Megan had returned from the bathroom.

Connie went over and straightened her daughter's tiara. 'It's time we got you into your wedding dress. Lily, will you do the honours?'

'Of course.' Lily unzipped the dress bag.

Beth came over, looking concerned. 'Are you certain it's over between you and Dad?'

Connie removed Megan's strappy shoes from their box. 'Absolutely.'

'And you're really okay about it?' Beth sounded doubtful.

'I've never been more certain about anything in my life. Marriage is hard enough without compromising on love, too.' She bent down and placed the shoes in front of Megan, ready for her to step into them. 'The minimum anyone should expect in life is to be adored, and your father no longer adores me. And I certainly no longer adore him.'

Beth frowned. 'That's the key to a happy marriage? Adoration? Not love, or trust, or respect?'

Connie held Megan steady as her daughter shuffled into her shoes. 'The happiest relationships I know are when the two people adore each other. Simple as that.' She nodded to where Lily was removing the wedding dress from its bag. 'Does Will adore you, Lily?'

Lily blinked for a moment, and then nodded. 'He does, yes.'

'See?' Connie stood up and smiled at Megan. 'No need to ask if Zac adores you, my darling. It's evident for the whole world to see.'

Megan's expression turned dreamy. 'You're right. He does. Just as I adore him.'

Connie cupped her daughter's cheek. 'Which is why the wedding is back on and hasn't been cancelled. Anything less than adoration and it might have been the end of things. But you two are made for each other, and I predict a long and happy marriage. It's nothing less than you deserve, my darling.' Connie turned to her eldest daughter, noticing for the first time her missing glasses. She looked different, less serious. 'That just leaves you, my love. Can my clever, hard-working, loyal daughter ever allow herself to be adored, I wonder?'

Beth raised her eyebrows. 'I'm not the adorable type.'

Doris looked up from her knitting. 'That Matt chap might disagree.'

Connie frowned at her mother. 'What Matt chap?' And then a horrible thought occurred. 'Surely you don't mean Matt Hardy?' Oh, no, please say it wasn't Matt Hardy?

Doris smiled at Beth. 'I saw the way he looked at you yesterday when he rescued me.'

Connie was dumbfounded. 'You remember getting lost on the moors?'

Doris gave her daughter an admonishing look. 'I have dementia, not amnesia.'

'Right, yes. Sorry, Mum.' Connie's head was reeling. She rubbed her temples, wondering if it would be bad form to take a quick swig of gin.

Doris smiled at Beth. 'I'm not so far gone that I can't spot two people falling in love.'

Love? Connie swung round to face her daughter, who was blushing furiously. 'You're falling in love with Matt Hardy?'

'He has very nice arms,' Doris said, resuming her knitting. 'I've always liked a man with strong arms.'

Connie's mortification threatened to take her legs from under her. 'Beth, darling. I had no idea. If I'd known—'

'Really, Mum, it's fine.' Beth seemed as mortified as she was. Her hands came up in defence, as if to stop the onslaught she knew was coming. 'You were drunk, I get it. No harm done. Let's just forget it ever happened.'

'But there's no excuse. I'm so sorry—'

'It's no big deal, really.' Beth backed away, wobbling on her high heels, as they sunk into the plush carpet. 'We're not even dating.'

Connie paused. 'Why not?'

'Yeah, why not?' Megan echoed, heading over to Lily, who was holding the dress open, ready for her to step into. 'The man's crazy about you. Am I right, Grandma?'

Doris nodded. 'Smitten.'

Connie turned to Beth. 'And are you crazy about him, too?'

Beth looked flustered. 'I wouldn't say *crazy*, as such... attracted, sure. But crazy? I'm too practical to be crazy about anyone.' Her defensive words didn't match her flustered body language. She looked like she didn't know what to do with her hands, or where to look. One moment she was clutching the front of her bronze-coloured dress, the next she was fiddling with her loose curls. Her normally contained daughter, who was always so together and work-driven, was finally unravelling. And the cause, it seemed, was Matt Hardy.

Connie went over and took her daughter's hand. 'Darling, you're a Lawrence. Crazy is what we do best. If there's even a spark of interest between you, then you owe it to yourself to explore that. Let go. Let yourself be adored, be a little crazy. You more than deserve it. What's the worst that can happen?'

Beth rolled her eyes. 'Are you kidding me?'

'Okay, then what's the best that can happen?' She could see the cogs whirring in her daughter's mind, as Beth allowed herself to imagine a life filled with love and promise.

A faint blush crept into her daughter's cheeks. Beth had always been beautiful, but today she positively glowed. Doris was right, Beth was falling in love. She just didn't know it yet.

Connie tugged on Beth's hand, ensuring her daughter knew she was serious. 'You need to trust your instincts: stop finding reasons to say no and start finding reasons to say yes.'

Another eye-roll. Beth had never been good at revealing her feelings. She was an expert at covering up her anxiety or fear, as well as tempering any happiness with a healthy dousing of logic and rational thinking. But the time had come to let go of that restraint.

'I'll think about it,' Beth said, clearly embarrassed at being the centre of attention.

Connie drew her daughter closer. 'Don't think. Act. Throw caution to the wind, be reckless for once and see what happens. Please, Beth. You'll regret it if you don't.'

Beth shrugged herself free from her mother. 'Fine, I'll be reckless. Can we change the subject and focus on the bride now, please?'

Connie knew it wouldn't do to push things. Beth had to discover happiness in her own way and in her own time. She just hoped her daughter didn't deny herself the chance of love out of fear, or because she felt like she didn't deserve it. That would be such a waste. 'Whatever you say, darling.'

The focus shifted and they all turned in unison to look at Megan, who was now wearing her fitted slinky ivory silk dress, with the low-cut neckline and draping back.

Megan did a twirl. 'How do I look?'

How did she look?

She looked bloody amazing.

## Chapter Twenty-Two

Matt had never been consumed by so many conflicting emotions before. This weekend had wrung him dry. He'd experienced everything from anger, to panic, to fear, to joy. The sinking feeling of seeing his dad being carted off to prison had been the low point. Watching Zac and Megan finally exchanging vows at the makeshift floral altar bathed in Cornish sunshine had been the high point. Squashed in between had been fighting back tears during the exchange of rings, peals of laughter when Beth had caught the wedding bouquet and reacted as though someone had lobbed a hand grenade at her, and pure unadulterated dread when it had come to delivering his best man's speech. Mostly, though, he just felt exhausted. Bone-deep weariness that had zapped him of all remaining energy.

Slumped on a bar stool, he sipped his beer, his first today despite it being gone ten p.m. He'd been too preoccupied resolving family dramas to be able to relax any earlier. Fear of another argument, or an ex-husband turning up, had kept him sober. But with the evening reception in full swing and the guests enjoying themselves, the time had finally come to relinquish control and take a much-needed break.

The bar wasn't busy. A few of Zac's mates who preferred drinking to dancing were filling the tables, but no one else. Most of the guests were in the barn, enjoying the talents of The Smugglers. He could vaguely hear 'Come on Eileen' playing, complete with foot-stamping and off-key chorus when everyone joined in. It sounded like they were having fun.

A flash of bronze silk caught his eye and he glanced across the bar to see Beth arm-in-arm with her grandmother. Beth looked beautiful – tired, but beautiful. Her contact lenses had been replaced by her glasses and the curls in her hair had dropped. She'd never looked more gorgeous, and he was struck once again by a wave of longing. He'd given up fighting his attraction. He'd fallen for her. Hook, line, and sinker, as the Cornish would say. Completely, utterly and helplessly.

Admitting his feelings was the easy part. Convincing her to let go of her reservations about relationships was another test entirely, and one he had no idea how to overcome.

Beth led Doris across the room, smiling down at the older woman as they negotiated the array of tables and chairs in the bar. For all Beth's outward confidence, waspishness and pretence of being an unemotional badass, she was a complete softie at heart. Why else would she put up with such crap from her family? Anyone else might have walked away – the fact that Beth never did was testament to the depth of her love for them. She was loyal, kind-hearted and driven to solving everyone's problems. Was it any wonder he'd fallen for her?

'I've been looking for you.' His brother's voice snapped him out of his reverie. So much for enjoying a quiet beer.

Matt glanced up and suppressed a sigh. 'And now you've found me.'

'I'm not happy about the wedding,' Chris said, announcing this like it was breaking news and not a record stuck on repeat.

Unlike Matt, Chris looked unscathed by the day's events. His tuxedo was still pristine, his shirt uncreased and his expression as sour as it had been since Zac had announced his engagement back in March.

Matt took another swig of beer. He figured he was going to need it. 'You're too late. They're married. Get over it.'

'She's not right for him.' Chris banged his fist on the bar top. 'We had our doubts, and it turns out we were right.'

'Good for you.' Matt tried to search out Beth across the bar, needing a distraction from the grumblings of his brother.

Sadly, she'd disappeared into the lobby with her grandmother, no doubt taking Doris up to bed.

'I take no pleasure in being proved right.' Chris was tapping his foot in frustration.

'Yeah, you sound mortified.'

'The woman is already married.'

'*Was* married.' Matt swivelled on the bar stool to face Chris. 'Past tense. The marriage was annulled, remember?'

'Says who? Megan? A woman who's proved herself to be highly untrustworthy.'

His brother was questioning the validity of the annulment? Christ, did the guy never let up? 'The annulment papers were checked by Beth. She's a divorce lawyer – are you telling me she can't be trusted either?'

'She's Megan's sister, she would side with her.'

Matt wasn't going to sit there and allow Chris to bad-mouth Beth. 'Look, Chris, whatever you think about this marriage, it's not going to succeed or fail based on your opinion. The fate of this union lies with Zac and Megan. Nothing you can say or do will influence that, and if you keep interfering, the only thing you'll achieve is causing a deeper rift between you and Zac. A rift that's unlikely to heal, even if the marriage does fail, because nobody likes to be told they've messed up. Zac included. So take my advice, and stop trying to split them up and start trying to accept the situation instead.'

He held up his hand when Chris attempted to interrupt. 'Before you make a quip about me not being equipped to give relationship advice, I'd advise you to think twice. I haven't eaten all day, I'm starving hungry, I'm pissed off, and I'm fed up to my back teeth arguing with people. So unless you want a fat lip, go back to your wife and grumble at her, she's a much better listener than I am.'

Chris opened his mouth, as if to retaliate, but must have seen the warning twitch in Matt's clenched jaw and backed down. Sensible man.

'You're drunk,' his brother said, trying to maintain the moral high ground as he stormed off.

'Not yet, but I'm working on it!' Matt called after him, knocking back another swig of beer.

Chris turned back and glared at his brother. 'Careful, Matt, you don't want to turn into your father.'

Matt jumped off the stool and stormed over. 'I'd rather turn into my father, than turn into you, Chris. Because at least Dad supported Zac. He was excited about the wedding, he wanted to be here to celebrate what should have been a joyful and special family occasion—'

'Until he got arrested,' Chris quipped, but his bluster visibly deflated when Matt took a step closer.

'Whereas you didn't need to get arrested to ruin the day, did you? You've managed to do that just by being the sanctimonious prick you are. Congratulations, Chris. You must be so proud.' And with that, Matt turned and went back to the bar. He was done fighting. He didn't have the energy.

Thankfully, his brother had the sense to walk away. Good. Matt wasn't sure how much longer he could have curtailed his temper.

Slumping onto the bar stool, he took another large swig of beer.

Leah appeared, carrying a huge plate of buffet food, and slid onto the stool next to him. It seemed his torment wasn't over. 'How's it going?' she said, her cheeks pink from dancing. 'Having fun?'

'A blast,' he said, watching her devour a sausage roll.

His stomach growled in response.

'Chris being his usual joyful self?'

'As only Chris can.' Matt tried to ignore the waft of buttery pastry hitting his senses.

'Are you okay?' She took another bite of sausage roll, leaving crumbs around her mouth.

'Not really. You?'

'Peachy. Dad's back in prison. Mum's talking about divorce, and my half-brother's a jerk who treats us like lepers. What's not to enjoy?' She finished off the sausage roll and licked her fingers. 'Yummy. You want some?' She offered him the plate.

He shook his head, his stomach aching with envy. But after his curry blowout last night with his dad, he was having to abstain today. 'I'd better not.'

'Honestly, what is it with you and food. It's not like you need to lose weight. Stop starving yourself. It doesn't work and it makes you grumpy.'

She was probably right, but he wasn't in the right frame of mind to address his dietary issues. 'Mum wants a divorce?'

Leah nodded. 'And she's taking up boxing.'

Matt frowned. 'Are the two things related?'

'No idea.' His sister gave a shrug. 'Just so you know, I'm in favour of the divorce. I won't be trying to talk her out of it.' She held his gaze. 'Is that going to be a problem?'

Before he could answer, his attention was diverted to Beth returning to the bar, minus her grandmother. When she glanced over, she gave him a half-smile and his pathetic heart sped up, grateful for the minute crumb of attention she'd thrown his way.

He was such a sad sack.

'It's not a problem for me,' he said, with a sigh. 'Mum's probably better off without him. She deserves to be happy, and Dad hasn't made her happy for years.'

'Glad we're on the same page.' Leah picked up a vol-au-vent and licked out the mushroom filling. 'Talking of people being happy, what's happening with you and Beth?'

His eyes lowered to his beer. 'Nothing.'

'That's not the impression I get.'

'Meaning?'

Leah nibbled around the edge of the pastry case, like an animated rabbit might do in a kids cartoon. 'You could start a fire with all the sparks flying between you two. You should've seen her expression during your best man's speech. Positively dreamy.'

'Beth doesn't do dreamy.' He glanced over at her, wishing she'd come over, but knowing she wouldn't. He feared that ship had sailed.

Leah smiled. 'Then why did she look at you when she caught the wedding bouquet?'

'That doesn't mean anything.'

'And she sought you out again during the wedding vows.'

He frowned. 'Probably a coincidence. You're reading too much into it.'

Leah tutted. 'Quitter.'

He lifted his eyes. 'No, I'm a realist.'

Leah glared at him. 'Do you want to stay single all your life?'

'No, but—'

'Then grow some balls.' She shoved the remaining pastry in her mouth. 'You're not getting any younger,' she said, chewing a mouthful of vol-au-vent.

'Thanks.'

'Women like Beth do not grow on trees,' she said, stealing his beer and taking a sip. 'Trust me, I know.' She wiggled an eyebrow, wiping pastry crumbs from the front of her tux. 'Snooze and you lose, Bro.'

He had no idea whether his sister was giving sound advice or talking nonsense. But his mind drifted back to earlier in the day when he'd been stuck in the bathroom with Beth and they'd ended up kissing. His skin suddenly became hot, an instinctive reaction to the memory of her pressed against him. He'd never felt this way about a woman before. She pushed all his buttons, good and bad. His sister was right, what were the chances of finding another Beth? Non-existent.

His eyes searched her out. She was walking away from him, her long legs accentuated by high heels. Was he really ready to admit defeat? 'I'm not sure now is the right time, too much has happened this weekend. Maybe once this is all over, I'll contact her and see if she'd like to meet up for coffee.'

Leah kicked his foot. 'Seriously?'

He dragged his gaze away from Beth. 'What? I thought that's what you wanted?'

'To meet up for coffee? Could you be any less romantic?' She rolled her eyes. 'Matt, you're at a wedding. Weddings are romantic occasions that evoke sentimentality and inspire people to do crazy things, like kissing strangers. Emotions are heightened. The love of your life is here, waiting, eager for you to make a move. The champagne is flowing, the moment is ripe. For crying out loud, don't blow it. Don't give her time to cool off or return to being practical and sensible. Use the music and the ambience to win the girl.'

'Win the girl?'

'Win the girl.' Leah stood up and patted his arm. 'Now, I need more food.'

Matt was left pondering how on earth he was supposed to do that.

## Chapter Twenty-Three

Beth's feet were killing her. High heels weren't usually a problem, but then she was used to sitting behind a desk for most of the day. Tottering about in four-inch heels for the past twelve hours was taking its toll, and the balls of her feet were positively burning.

At least she could relax a bit now that the wedding had finally happened – albeit a rather unconventional one. The bride's mother had walked the bride down the aisle, given her daughter away and then ambushed her ex-husband's attempts to make a speech at the reception. Connie's speech had been funny, vaguely romantic – if you ignored the quip about women needing to rely on themselves rather than a man – and endearing. Beth had no idea what her father's speech would have been like by comparison, but his disgruntled expression left no one in any doubt regarding his feelings at being usurped. He'd sat there stony-faced, with Tiffany pouting like a guppy fish next to him. The pair of them looked about as happy as Zac's parents.

Thankfully, proceedings reverted to the conventional after that. Zac gave an emotional heartfelt groom's speech that left everyone in tears, and Matt's touching and amusing best man's speech made everyone smile. Including her. He'd been nervous, she could tell, but he'd overridden the tremor in his hands, kept his chin up and done his nephew proud. She'd been incredibly proud of him. The poor man hadn't had the easiest of weekends, what with his dad being arrested, discovering Megan was already married and being propositioned by the bride's mother.

But he'd kept going, overcome every problem thrown at him and ensured the day was a resounding success.

He'd also made quite an impression on her brother, who'd handed over his stash of weed to her this afternoon and asked her to flush it down the loo. He'd also vowed to quit drinking. The details of their encounter remained unclear – all Alex would say was that Matt was a 'top bloke' and he'd done him a 'solid one', whatever that meant. Maybe it was better to remain oblivious. Whatever had happened, she shared her brother's belief that Matt was indeed a 'top bloke'.

She glanced over at him, sitting alone at the bar, nursing a pint of beer. He looked weary and forlorn, lost in thought. He also looked famished.

Without stopping to rationalise her actions, she headed over and slid onto the bar stool next to him. 'I thought you might be hungry,' she said, placing a plate of food in front of him. 'I haven't seen you eat anything all day.'

His eyes met hers, hovered longingly for a second and then drifted down to the plate of food. The look on his face made her laugh.

'Please don't tell me you can't eat this because it's unhealthy.' She gave him an admonishing look. 'There's a time and place for dieting, and a time for refuelling.' She handed him a chicken sandwich, oozing with rich mayonnaise. 'You need carbs, you've been running on empty all day and I don't want you collapsing on me.'

He gazed at the sandwich. 'I shouldn't.'

'Yes, you should. You can go back to eating sensibly tomorrow – one night won't kill you. Besides, you need something to soak up the alcohol. You'll be no use to me drunk.'

'Use to you?' His eyes widened.

'I'm not venturing onto that dance floor alone.' She gestured for him to take the sandwich. 'Eat.'

He dutifully accepted the sandwich and took a bite. His face clouded over with pleasure and she felt a little flip in her belly.

She'd seen that look before – usually after they'd been kissing. It seemed food got his pheromones flowing just as much as smooching did. Interesting.

She ordered herself a glass of wine and gave him some space to enjoy his food, while surreptitiously watching him devour the plate of nibbles. He looked like a man starved of sustenance, and she imagined the satisfaction of sharing her passion for cooking with a man like Matt Hardy. Cooking was one of her favourite pastimes, and watching someone else enjoy her food would enhance the experience even further. She could imagine them messing around in the kitchen together, getting in each other's way, food forming an intrinsic part of their foreplay…

Whoa, where had that come from?

She turned away. Her imagination had given her a hot flush.

Still, was there any point fighting her attraction towards him? Only a fool would continue to deny her feelings. Everyone else seemed convinced they should be together – she was the only one resisting. But had she left it too late? She'd rejected the poor man so many times, maybe he'd got sick of being messed around. Perhaps he'd decided she was too much effort and had given up on the idea.

Sipping her wine, she risked a glance in his direction. He was picking at the crisps, staring at each one with loathing as if they'd been created by the devil himself. The sight made her smile. Poor man. He really did have an unhealthy aversion to food.

It was such a shame that a man who so clearly loved eating felt the need to restrict himself. She wished he felt more confident about his appearance. He was gorgeous. He didn't need to change a thing. If only he saw himself the way she did.

She waited until he'd finished eating. 'Things with your brother looked a little heated earlier. Is everything okay?'

Matt wiped his mouth with a napkin. 'Not really, but things with Chris are never good. I can't see us ever being close, so maybe it's time to stop wasting my time trying.' His eyes met hers and she wondered if he was still talking about the relationship with his brother.

'Family dynamics can be complicated,' she said, her gaze drawn to his mouth. 'I think sometimes we just have to accept that and not expect miracles. That's what I've had to do with my father. He's disappointed me, behaved appallingly, but like you said yesterday about your dad, it'll never stop me loving him.' She took another sip of wine, dragging her mind away from tantalising thoughts about the man next to her – whose warm thigh was pressed against hers. 'I feel better about things now I know my mum's stopped adoring him.'

Matt frowned. 'That's a strange turn of phrase.'

'It's the key to a happy relationship, apparently. Adoration. It's not enough to love someone, or simply like them. Happy ever afters only happen when two people adore each other.' She gave a little shrug. 'According to my mum, anyway.'

He seemed to mull this over. 'Maybe she's right. I think my mum's reached the same conclusion about my dad. She's talking about divorcing him.'

Beth placed a hand on his arm. 'I'm sorry to hear that.'

'It's probably for the best. Now I come to think of it, I'm not sure he adores her either. He relies on her, he needs her and depends on her, but I don't see adoration. I see a man who wants someone to make post-prison life easy, and Mum deserves better than that.' He looked down at her hand on his arm. 'She mentioned taking up boxing.'

'Oh, god. Has she been talking to my mum?'

He smiled. 'I suspect so.'

'Mum's setting up her own business. She plans to coach the over sixties into fitness and improve their self-esteem.'

'If anyone can do it, she can. Your mum's quite the force of nature.'

'As you know only too well.' She smiled so he'd know she was joking.

He smiled back. 'I do.'

Beth sighed. 'What a weekend, eh?'

He let out a laugh. 'No one's going to forget it any time soon.'

'True.' The heat from his arm began seeping through the sleeve of his jacket and she took a moment to savour the feeling.

She had a sudden urge to run her hands through his wavy hair and drag his mouth down to meet hers. She didn't, of course. Too many prying eyes. It was tempting, though.

Instead, she focused her gaze on his. 'Are you going to tell me what happened with my brother?'

He raised an eyebrow. 'I wasn't aware anything had happened with your brother. What is it you think happened?'

She held his gaze. 'I've no idea, he won't tell me.'

He gave a little shrug. 'Maybe there's nothing to tell.'

'Or maybe you're protecting him?'

'Why would I do that?' His hand rested over hers, big and warm and heavy. 'I have no loyalty towards your brother, I don't even know him.'

The sensation of his touch made her shiver. 'Whatever it was, it seems to have knocked some sense into him. He's talking about joining AA and enrolling in college to complete his accountancy training. I just hope it lasts.'

'If I did do anything... hypothetically speaking,' he said, the intensity in his eyes intoxicating. 'Then it wouldn't be about protecting him, it would be driven by a desire to protect you. You're my only concern. You're all that matters to me.' His thumb began to circle her wrist, making her breath hitch. 'I know you're uncertain about us, and you have trust issues, but I'm crazy about you.'

He was?

She leant closer. 'Matt, I—'

But she never got the chance to tell him she felt the same way, because her blessed father appeared. 'You need to talk some sense into your mother,' he barked, making her jump. 'She's being unreasonable! She wants me to hand over the house. As if I'm going to do that.'

Biting back her irritation at her father's terrible timing, she turned to him. 'Dad, how many times do I have to say this? I'm not getting involved in your divorce settlement.'

'But she's not thinking straight.'

'On the contrary, she's thinking straight for the first time in months.' She slid off the bar stool, dislodging Matt's hand. 'I'm sorry. Duty calls. We'll chat later, okay?' He looked disappointed. She wanted so much to stay and talk to him – they'd been on the verge of something – but once again family dramas had scuppered any glimpse of a happy ending. The story of her life.

Forcefully taking her father's arm, she led him away from Matt. This wasn't a conversation she wanted to have in a bar. When they were in the quiet of the reception area, she turned to her father. 'Where's Tiffany?'

'In the barn, dancing.'

'Right. So you're still together?' She folded her arms, so he'd know she was serious.

'I guess.'

She glared at him. 'What's that supposed to mean? Either you are, or you're not. Which is it?'

'It's complicated.'

'Explain it to me.'

He broke eye contact. 'I had hoped to get back with your mother.'

'Why? Because you genuinely love her? Or because you think financially it might be better to avoid a messy divorce?' Her father might be a hopeless romantic, but he liked money too much to ever behave totally irrationally. She wasn't naive, and neither was he.

After a drawn-out pause he said, 'I love her. We've been married for thirty-nine years. I don't want to throw that away.'

'But do you adore her?'

He frowned. 'I beg your pardon?'

'It's a simple enough question, Dad. Do you adore Mum?'

'Of course I do.' He checked over his shoulder, no doubt ensuring Tiffany hadn't snuck up on him.

'And what about Tiffany? Do you adore her?'

'Tiffany understands what we are.'

'And what's that?'

'We're having fun. She knows that.'

'Does she, Dad? It wasn't so long ago that you were telling everyone that Tiffany was the love of your life. Do you have any idea how much that hurt Mum? How much it hurt all of us to hear you say that?'

'I wasn't thinking straight. I was having a crisis of some sort, but I'm over that now. I know what I want.'

'And so does Mum, and it's not you.' She unfolded her arms and stepped forwards to kiss her father's cheek. 'Look, Dad, I love you, but your marriage to Mum is over. The best thing you can do is accept that and move on. Give her the house, she's more than earned it. Be compassionate, allow her the means to start afresh. It's the least she deserves.'

'I have my own security to consider.'

'You're loaded. You can buy another place outright, don't punish Mum. Like so many women, she's put family first all these years. She's run the home, brought up your kids and sacrificed a decent career so you could pursue yours. And her reward? Being left for a woman thirty years younger. If you really love her, as you say, you'll do the decent thing, Dad. Step up and be the good man I know you are deep down.' Or at least, she hoped he was.

He lifted his chin. 'I'll think about it.'

'Good, you do that. Now, go and find Tiffany. If you neglect the poor woman any more this weekend, you'll end up with no one, and how would that be?'

He shivered. 'Awful.'

'Exactly.' She patted her dad's arm, feeling more like the parent in their relationship than the child. Shouldn't she be the one seeking out romantic advice? Not that she needed it. She'd finally realised what she wanted – or rather who she wanted – and she was damned if she was going to let the opportunity slip away again.

She watched her father walk off, his cocky demeanour slightly dented. He'd foolishly thought he could run off with another woman, have his fun and then come crawling back when he'd had enough. More fool him, and good on her mum for sending him packing. It was sad to know her parents wouldn't be together, but hopefully things might be a little less intense now that her mum had found a new path in life.

Beth looked over and spotted Matt heading towards her.

She smiled with relief. Finally, they could be alone.

'How did it go with your dad?' he said, reaching her.

'About as well as the conversation you had with your brother.'

'That good?' He looked down at her, his expression soft yet intense. 'Who needs that kind of drama in their life, right?' His voice was tentative and he looked down at her, a questioning look on his face. 'If only love could be simple and uncomplicated.'

She looked up into his blue eyes, her blood beginning to fizz. 'If only, eh?'

'Imagine how much easier it would be if you had someone in your corner.' He closed the gap between them, his hands coming up to cup her face. 'Someone who you trusted completely, and who always had your back, and who you knew would never let you down.'

She'd stopped breathing. 'If only such a person existed.'

'And if they did exist, would you let them love you?' His face lowered to hers, his lips almost touching hers.

This was it, the time had finally come. She could feel his breath on her cheek and her belly began to flip in anticipation. 'I—'

The lobby suddenly exploded with laughter, and once again the moment was gone.

Beth and Matt stepped away from each other, as Megan and Zac appeared arm-in-arm, a crackling bundle of joy and energy.

'Here you are!' her sister said, rushing over and enveloping Beth in a hug. 'We've been looking for you.'

Zac came over and hugged Matt. 'We wanted to thank you for all you've done, it's been the best day ever.'

'We've loved every second of it.' Megan was slurring, no doubt from all the champagne. 'You're miracle workers, the pair of you.'

Zac switched to hugging Beth. 'You don't know what this day means to us.'

Megan threw herself at Matt. 'We love you both, you know that, right?'

'Yeah, we really love you,' Zac drunkenly concurred. His shirt was hanging open, his hair a mess, and he'd never looked happier.

Matt shook his head, smiling. 'I'm glad you've had a good time.'

'Have you enjoyed the day?' Megan leant against Matt's wide chest, the bottom of her dress grubby from dancing in the barn. 'Tell me you've had a good day?'

'I've had a good day.'

'It went like clockwork,' Megan said joyfully, seemingly having forgotten all the drama of earlier.

Matt's and Beth's eyes met. 'Couldn't have gone better,' he said, looking over the top of Megan's head and smiling. 'The dream wedding day.'

'I know, right! We're off to bed now.' Megan rose up on tiptoe to kiss Matt. 'Thank you again. And just so you know, my sister thinks you're hot.'

Beth reeled. 'Megan!'

'Well, you do!' Megan was still leaning into Matt for support. 'I'm just saying, that's quite a thing, because she doesn't normally do relationships. So you should feel flattered.' She patted his chest.

Matt grinned. 'I am.'

'Do you think she's hot?'

'Megan!' Beth went over and pulled her sister away. 'You're embarrassing the man.'

Matt looked at her. 'No, she's not.'

Beth stilled. 'She's not?'

'I do think you're hot.'

'See? I told you!' Megan stumbled and was caught by an equally tipsy Zac.

'Whoa, time I got you to bed, I think.' He helped his wife towards the stairs.

'Finally,' Megan said, kissing Zac. 'It's about time.'

Beth and Matt watched as the pair continued to kiss, stumbling up the stairs, fumbling and muttering slurred words of endearment. If they made it safely upstairs, it would be a miracle.

But Beth had other things on her mind and turned to Matt. 'You think I'm hot?'

He stepped towards her. 'You know I do.' His hands came up to cup her face again. 'Beth, I—'

'Here you are!' Susan Hardy appeared in the lobby with Connie and smiled at her son. 'I'm getting a divorce!'

'And I need to talk to you about your father.' Connie headed over.

Beth's heart sank. Would she ever get a moment alone with this man?

But Matt, it seemed, wasn't going down without a fight and held up his hand. 'Stop, both of you.'

Both women dutifully stopped in their tracks.

'Sorry to be blunt, but this is not a good time.' He turned to face his mother. 'Mum, I'm glad you've finally made a decision. Good for you. I'm happy to support you in any way I can, but not right at this moment.' His gaze switched to Connie. 'And with all due respect, Connie, you need to quit moaning to Beth about Kenneth. He might be your husband, but he's her father, and it's not fair to put her in the middle of your split.'

Silence descended.

Both women looked at Matt, and then turned to look at each other.

'I think we might be interrupting something,' Susan said, with a wry smile.

'I think so, too,' Connie agreed. 'Care to join me for a glass of bubbly in the bar, Susan? You can tell me all about your divorce.'

'Thank you, Connie. I'd like that. And feel free to tell me about yours.'

'I'd be delighted to.' Connie led Susan away. 'I warn you, it's messy.'

'Messy? My husband's a convicted criminal.'

'And mine's a cheating scumbag.'

Susan sighed. 'We have such a lot in common.'

'We're going to be so good for each other.' Connie glanced back and gave Beth a quick wink. 'Don't mind us, carry on as you were.'

Matt let out an exasperated sigh. 'I swear to god, if one more person interrupts us—'

Beth grabbed his hand and dragged him out of the lobby into the museum.

He didn't resist, allowing her to lead him further into the dark space, away from prying eyes.

'We should be safe in here,' she said, almost running in a bid to escape any further unwelcome intrusions. This conversation was happening, one way or another. When they reached the makeshift bar, with the upturned beer barrels and pirate statues, she turned to him. 'You were saying?'

He stopped and took a breath. 'Remind me, I've forgotten.'

Her stomach deflated a little. 'Are you kidding me?'

He grinned. 'Of course I am.'

She breathed a sigh of relief.

'Jesus, Beth, if you don't realise how I feel about you by now then I might as well give up.'

She took a step closer. 'Please don't.'

His face fell. 'Sorry.'

'No, I mean, please don't give up. I don't want you to give up.'

His eyes grew wide. 'You don't?'

She shook her head. 'I don't.'

He lifted his hand. 'Just so we're clear, I'm looking for a relationship. The whole shebang. Romance, trust, companionship, commitment. Nothing less.'

She tilted her head. 'Did you really just use the word shebang?'

He looked sheepish. 'I did.'

'My grandma uses that word.'

'Well, so do I. So, sue me.'

'No, thanks.' She stepped closer. 'I've made a promise never to get involved with legal matters concerning the people I love.'

He stilled. 'Love?'

'Worse. It appears I might... adore you.'

For a moment he didn't speak. Or he couldn't. She didn't know which.

He stepped closer, visibly swallowing. 'For the record, I think I might adore you, too.'

Closing the gap between them and kissing him senseless seemed like the right response. It was a forceful move, a bold act on her part, and one that took him by surprise.

He didn't object. In fact, he kissed her back. He kissed her with such intensity that they stumbled backwards and knocked over one of the pirate dummies... and then another one, sending Blackbeard's parrot flying... and then they crashed into a beer barrel... followed by another beer barrel... before getting entangled in the rope netting attached to the front of the bar. It was carnage.

And yet the kissing didn't stop – despite the hazards. Megan and Zac had nothing on them. They'd merely had stairs to deal with, whereas Beth and Matt faced an entire eighteenth-century obstacle course.

'Are we really doing this here?' she asked, breathless from kissing, trying to disentangle herself from the entwined rope.

He caught her when she tripped. 'You don't find this romantic?'

'Not really,' she said, laughing as his elbow smacked against the bar.

'Okay. Stop a moment.' He held her steady. 'We need to think about this.' He ran his hands through his hair. 'You're right, this isn't romantic. We need romantic.' He stepped away and dug out his phone, the screen lighting up his face as he scrolled through it. 'Give me one minute.'

A few seconds later music began to play. 'Up Where We Belong', the theme tune from *An Officer and a Gentleman*.

Beth started laughing. 'Seriously?'

He came towards her.

She stopped laughing when she realised what he was about to do. 'No way! Not a fireman's lift again! No!'

But instead of hoisting her up over his shoulder, he simply lifted her into his arms, Richard Gere style.

She slid her arms around his neck and leant into him, knowing she was in safe hands.

For once, she wasn't going to fight it. She was going to relinquish control and allow herself some fun. She'd closed herself off from relationships for such a long time, convinced they were more hassle than they were worth. They'd never been something she needed, but she now realised this was something she wanted, which was an entirely different thing.

It hadn't been a lightbulb moment with Matt. There'd been no epiphany, no explosive coming together. It had been a gradual process, a softening of her protective barriers. Her feelings for Matt had crept up on her. He'd infiltrated her thoughts, her dreams, her desires. It had taken her a while to believe that what she was feeling was real. And now she did.

Matt Hardy was the man for her.

And she was definitely the woman for him.

# Acknowledgements

Thank you so much for reading *Someone to Love*. I sincerely hope you enjoyed following the story of Beth and Matt as much as I enjoyed writing it. I once attended a wedding where the two families refused to agree on outfits for the men, so the groom's family were in tuxedos and the bride's family were in tails – just in case you thought the idea for this book was too far-fetched – apparently not!

The book is dedicated to my lovely dad, who passed away in October 2021. He was such a wonderful man and a huge supporter of my writing. He'd read every book I wrote and always leave me a glowing review – sometimes a little too glowing. I did try to explain that calling my writing a 'work of literary genius' was perhaps a little wishful thinking, but he was so proud of me that he wouldn't be dissuaded. I know I'm lucky to have had such an avid supporter in my corner. I'm going to miss him terribly.

As always, a huge thank you to my agent, Tina Betts, who has stuck by me through the years and always encourages me to keep writing. It's hugely appreciated. And a big thank you to my lovely editor, Emily Bedford, who always gives me such constructive and helpful feedback and makes editing a joyful part of the process. Thank you! And thank you to the rest of the Canelo team for supporting my books and helping to publicise them and make them the best they can be. It really is very much appreciated.

Finally, thank you to all the fabulous readers, bloggers and fellow authors for supporting my journey, sharing posts, posting reviews and generally being wonderful people. In particular, my wonderful friends at The Quince Players Amateur Dramatic Society, who are always the first to read my books, leave reviews and recommend them to their friends. It's incredibly humbling. Thank you!

If you'd like to follow me on social media or make contact then I'd love to hear from you:

Twitter: @tracyacorbett

Facebook: @tracyacorbettauthor

Instagram: tracyacorbett

Website: tracycorbettauthor.co.uk